Books by Marylyle Rogers

The Dragon's Fire
Hidden Hearts
Proud Hearts
Wary Hearts

PROUD HEARTS

MARYLYLE ROGERS

POCKET BOOKS

New York London Toronto Sydney Tokyo Singapore

An *Original* Publication of POCKET BOOKS

POCKET BOOKS, a division of Simon & Schuster Inc.
1230 Avenue of the Americas, New York, NY 10020

Jacket illustration by Sharon Spiak

Printed in the U.S.A.

Quality Printing and Binding by:
Berryville Graphics
P.O. Box 272
Berryville, VA 22611 U.S.A.

To my friend Patricia Atkinson—

*For that gift of sending encouragement
from the other side of the world
just when I need it most!*

Author's Note

In 1216–17 French Prince Louis led an invasion into England to secure the throne. His claim to the crown was shaky at best; yet, prompted by the invitation of a group of English barons who'd felt betrayed when King John rescinded the Magna Carta almost immediately after he'd put his seal to it, the prince made an attempt to take it by force.

On October 19, 1216, John died, leaving his nine-year-old son, Henry (III) the new king under William the Marshall's protection. The Marshall immediately began securing the loyalty of the once dissident barons to support the young king's cause against the invading French.

In this continuing struggle, he was—as King John had been—greatly aided by a comparatively unknown knight called William of Kensham or Cassingham. This William is a somewhat mysterious character, near lost in the shroud of time, who played an important part in the war. He was the bailiff of the Courts of the Seven Hundred of the Weald, and no lover of King John, yet he wanted even less to see a foreign prince take the crown.

Sir William demonstrated an uncommon skill as a guerrilla fighter and held the dense forest of the Weald impenetrable to the French who landed at the Cinque Ports but found it almost impossible to pass through the Weald to reach London. Using the Weald as his base, he made lightning strikes against the French, and soon the invading troops refused to venture out on the roads to the south and west. Louis could do nothing about the fast-riding, hard-hitting fighter and, although William was only a knight who led a group of common men—at the end a thousand strong —left him in full possession of the forest barrier.

The people of England, always preferring a bold leader of relatively

humble birth, acclaimed him their hero. To them he became Willikin—
Willikin of the Weald.

From the time of William the Conqueror's taking of the English
crown, the kings and barons of England—though most surely understood
English—spoke, in their view, the more noble Norman French. Those of
Saxon heritage who labored in their castles and towns spoke that language
along with their own. Not until John's great-grandson (Edward III) came
to the throne did an English king choose to use English rather than
Norman French. Yet all the while, the general populace of the land continued to speak English, and eventually English triumphed over French. It
is likely that the common people in the romote reaches of the Weald
seldom had contact with the ruling class and spoke little or no French.
(Those among the highborn who visited the Weald would surely understand both languages.)

Chapter

❧ 1 ❧

November of 1216

FOLLY, THIS WAS folly beyond measure! Another fat droplet fell from the crude cart's leather awning and splashed over one of the dark furs Cassandra Gavre clutched tightly to her throat. Her beautiful silk gown was in serious danger of being ruined. But then even on a day clear and bright, 'twould be eminently unsuitable for traveling, as she'd unsuccessfully tried to make her father understand. And disagreeing with her autocratic father's decision was a great feat of bravery for Cassie, whose painful shyness made so much as talking with any—save a few precious friends—near impossible.

From his viewpoint the only use for such expensive garments—indeed, for daughters—was to successfully win rich marriage settlements and cement important family alliances. This he had already done for her sister Jeanine, and almost once for her—a goal forestalled when her intended bridegroom, ten years her junior, had caught a fever and died the past spring, two years short of the age of twelve, when they'd have been wed. Cassie's father had been greatly distraught over the event—not for the loss of a young life, but for the lost alliance with an important family, and worse yet, for being left with an unwed daughter of twenty. Thus, when Guy de Faux, the boy's widowed father and a confidant of King Philip, offered to fulfill the marriage pact in the boy's stead, her parent had been more than thrilled to accept. Cassie had *not*.

For months now the unwanted betrothal had stretched across her future like the dark shadow of a ravenous monster. That she despised her prospective husband (who, it was said, had worn out three young wives already—with only one sickly son to show for his prodigious efforts) meant less than nothing. Indeed, her mother and brothers constantly admonished her to be thankful to her father for the fine match he'd arranged. Her sister's unhappiness in the "fine match" made for her was of no consequence and certainly no excuse for Cassie's folly in fleeing to escape the marriage contract. Even the unmistakable desperation behind an action so utterly out of character failed to shift her family's preoccupation with the important De Faux alliance.

'Twas her rash flight that had so infuriated her father that he'd ignored the obvious dangers, hauled her off on the next troop transport and brought her here to England, intent on seeing the marriage complete with all possible haste.

Beneath the weight of these bleak thoughts, Cassie shifted uncomfortably on the hard wooden seat, but instinctively held her protective covering ever closer. The weather mirrored her mood and robbed her of awareness, even less an appreciation, of the beauty in the autumn-bright leaves of the forest whose outer edge they skirted. Longing for her home in the sunny south of France, she had only disdain for this wet, chilly isle. Almost she could wish they'd soon arrive at the camp of fellow Frenchmen laying siege to Dover Castle. There the marriage would be performed, and though a dreaded deed, 'twould allow her to hasten away once more. Even the dismal certainty that her final destination would be Guy de Faux's forbidding fortress, rather than her family castle and the few people in the whole of Christendom with whom she was comfortable, failed to dampen her desire to be far, far from this cheerless land.

"Mon Dieu!"

Cassie's lavender eyes, alarm-darkened to amethyst, flew to the rude exclamation's source—her father's guard captain. Confusion dulled her normally sharp wits. Of a sudden the man lay soundless, motionless on the uneven, soggy grass of the meadow floor. From the left side of his chest an arrow seemed to sprout amidst a spring of red liquid welling up too fast to be diluted by the heavy rains. The reality of fearsome danger smote her with the force of a physical blow. She froze.

A storm of arrows fell as thick and fast as the drenching downpour. Yet only when the driver of her two-wheeled cart slid sideways from the vehicle did Cassie break free of her horror-induced daze to burrow under the furs. Beneath the luxurious covering the rounded lump she'd become found that a shield of anonymous darkness did nothing to muffle the desperate rallying cry which was her father's answer to a silent, deadly assault.

Willikin's band! Though she could see nothing, the clash of blade meeting blade and the howls of the wounded painted vivid pictures in her mind. *Oui*, their attacker must be the fearsome Willikin of the Weald. Even in France there'd been talk of the knight. In hushed voices it was said he led a sizable force of common men to hold the dense strip of forest in an inflexible grip, erupting from its shadows to attack with lightning force. Only the past night she'd overheard her father's guardsman apprehensively whispering the name of the seemingly invincible warrior deadly to all of French blood!

Holy Mary, Mother of God, save us, I implore you! Cassie gritted her teeth in momentary resentment. *'Twas not my wish to travel in a land of war!* Selfish, selfish, selfish. Even unseen in the gloom of concealing furs, her cheeks heated with a bright color ever too quick to rise. How dare she, an ungrateful daughter, beg boons of the mother of Christ? Cassie guiltily confessed her wrong, begging the Holy Mother's mercy, yet she lost no time in renewing her plea for divine aid in this hour of peril.

All too soon an ominous silence descended. Still Cassie waited. She hardly dared breathe until her cart's undirected donkey meandered to a halt. Then, nibbling at her full bottom lip and blinking rapidly against what was sure to be a fearsome sight, she peeked from beneath the ineffective defense of her pelt covering. Her gaze first met an expanse of plain brown homespun and a much-patched, protective leather jerkin, and next traveled up past the bloodstained sword held threateningly across a barrel chest to the grim face of a waiting man. Willikin?

An assuredly foolish and totally inexplicable disappointment nagged at the edge of her thoughts. Somehow she'd expected more of the famous warrior than this stocky figure of thinning hair and deeply lined face possessed.

In the next instant she realized she'd stared at him too long and must seem a witless moonling. Bright rose again washed her cheeks. Under the cold appraisal of gray eyes that plainly deemed her a pitiable figure unable to do else than cringe in fear, her spine straightened. Her own reaction surprised her, and she deemed the rare flash of courage a miracle of sorts. Fur wrapped about her like a royal cloak, she forced herself to meet his stare full on, comforting herself with the hope that he'd think her high color simply born of anger.

Only when the man shrugged and turned momentarily away was she free to glance over his shoulder and discover the majority of her party laid to waste. Cassie anxiously scanned the scene until she saw what she'd feared to find—her father among the dead. Even as she resolutely shifted her eyes to the brusque leader again studying her, she was horribly aware that the few of her one-time companions yet alive were the small figures fleeing in the far distance, leaving her truly alone and completely defenseless. As if in a physical emphasis, the fur wrapped about her shoulders abruptly slipped down her back to lay heaped on the seat behind.

"Who are you?" Harvey demanded of the utterly unexpected traveler plainly disconcerted by the errant fur's fall and unsure whether to wrestle it back into place or ignore it and retain her dignity. "Of more import, what are you doing here?" By the sapphire silk of her gown, fine features of her gently rounded face, and soft hands, her noble birth was as clear as the fact that she comprehended not one word of the questions he'd asked in English. Clicking his tongue in disgust, he turned to a young member of the band.

"Clyde." Harvey's order was gruff. "Take this sorry animal's reins and see that it and its load follows my lead." Although the young man could bridge the language barrier were he so commanded, Harvey decided that questions could wait to be asked by another more suited to the deed.

Unable to continue looking at those into whose hands she'd fallen, Cassie glared down at blue silk now abandoned to the rain's harm, just as she'd been forsaken. Deserted in a land where she couldn't understand the language its inhabitants spoke, Harvey's captive silently bemoaned the return of her natural cowardice. Where was the daring Lady Cassandra whom Cassie fantasized dwelling somewhere inside her plain and timid self? To be termed "Lady" was Cassie's right by birth. Yet never had she been comfortable with a title that seemed appropriate only for elegant, confident women like her mother—or the spirited woman trapped inside her ill-suited form. Where was Lady Cassandra? Hah! Where but crushed 'neath the weight of Cassie's pigeon-hearted nature.

Too depressingly certain of her own limitations, and filled with self-disgust, it required all the nerve Cassie could muster simply to brace herself against an instinctive desire to flinch away as a hulking youth of about her own age placed a dirty hand on the side of the cart. He vaulted into the seat next to her with a leer that sent shivers of panic down her spine.

You may be neither beautiful nor brave, but you are noble-born, Cassie firmly reprimanded herself. *Do nothing to shame your great family.* While the lesson long and relentlessly taught replayed over and over in her mind, she ignored her cart-companion's sidelong stare to wrap family pride—she'd little enough of her own—about herself like armor. She forced her depressingly unimposing figure to remain upright and, by virtue of a death-grip clamped on the plank seat beneath the sapphire silk covering her thighs, maintained her stiff posture as the crude vehicle jolted forward.

In an ominous silence broken only by the squeak of cartwheels and horse hooves over muddy ground, victorious horsemen led their cart-borne prize across an untrampled meadow where no attempt at a smooth path had been laid. That their journey cut a new route straight toward the ominous shadows of the Weald brought a tiny, unintended moan from Cassie. The Weald—that dark and frightening forest wherein who knew what end awaited.

Chapter

2

"You took a hostage? God's blood!" Will's voice changed from incredulity to controlled violence. "What earthly purpose will that serve?" His fingers raked impatiently through thick hair that seemed all the blacker for the dampness of the constant drizzle wending through branches twined overhead. With King John so recently dead, and the supporters of his heir still consolidating their position, a hostage would be more hindrance than aid. Thus, the men who served him by leading the various patrols daily throughout the Weald had orders to take none.

"We need gold to further our cause." Harvey gruffly offered the weak excuse he knew was too thin to justify his action.

"Aye," Will agreed, turning dark, piercing eyes on his longtime supporter. "But no matter how badly 'tis needed, it takes too long to demand and receive a ransom when all the while we've neither adequate housing for prisoners nor a surplus of men to spare as guards." He emphasized his words with a sharp glare through the first blue shadows of dusk at the ramshackle hovel holding their unwanted hostage. The daub and wattle of the structure was crumbling. 'Twas in a condition so poor it had long since been abandoned by men who now lived in the better maintained cottages a short distance to one side.

All that his leader said Harvey had known when he'd made the plainly unwise decision to bring the maid here. Moreover, the depth of Will's irritation with the deed was evident in the lack of even a faint glimmer of the mocking humor seldom absent from his face—as if he found the world and all within a huge jest. Feeling ever more worthy of blame, Harvey disrupted a bright pattern of fallen leaves with the toe of his boot. He studied their resulting arrangement of yellow, orange, and red with blind intensity.

"I got no hesitation in sending the French bastards who'd steal our land to the fiery ends they deserve. But . . . I found I couldn't outright kill a noblewoman," he sheepishly admitted.

"*Woman?*" Will was shocked. He stood rock-still for a long moment before whirling to storm across the muddied clearing between forest edge and dilapidated hut. Never would he believe the daft claim true until he saw its proof with his own eyes.

When the door flew wide, Cassie's heart pounded a desperate beat in her ears. Her startled gaze flew to meet the black glare of the huge man filling the doorframe, and then immediately dropped to her rain-spotted skirt. Although she had understood none of the words overheard, she'd recognized the anger in a voice like rough velvet. 'Twas an anger embodied by the towering figure standing on the small hut's far side—yet still too near.

It was true, then. Will's gaze swept over the silk-garbed figure so incongruous sitting atop a pile of half-molded straw. True but no less unbelievable. The sky's unending drizzle seeped through a haphazardly thatched roof, creating puddles on the dirt floor. The lady, though now but a captive in a hovel, delicately held her sapphire gown protected from their threat. Catching the flutter of thick lashes, Will realized she was surreptitiously peeking at him, and gave her a slow smile.

Realizing she'd been caught, heat flooded Cassie's cheeks and she clenched her eyes tightly against her foe's stunning smile. Reminding herself of the family pride she'd sworn to uphold, Cassie straightened her spine, lifted her chin and forced herself to meet his bold gaze, even though she couldn't prevent a wild blush.

Will recognized in his captive an unusually shy creature and yet one with courage enough to meet him eye to eye. Her posture was full of pride, yet the close-fitting wimple and veil she wore outlined a paradoxically vulnerable face bejeweled by apprehension-widened amethyst eyes of startling clarity.

Despite the outward smile, Will's foul mood deepened. As a part of the English nobility, and yet not, since the French invasion had begun he'd undertaken the task of holding the Weald impervious to the invaders. From the outset he'd been determined to hold the pivotal stretch of land under his control impenetrable to any who dared attempt entry or even drew near its natural barrier. Now he faced an unforeseen dilemma: he had given his oath to eliminate all French invaders, but far earlier had vowed as an honorable knight to deal gently with all females noble-born. His ill humor was not improved by an honest nature that disallowed putting blame on Harvey for bringing the woman here when, faced with a like problem, he would've found it impossible to treat her with less care. The worst knot in the whole tangle was the impossible question of what to do with her.

Dark eyes studied her so long and so well that Cassie's petal-soft cheeks deepened to an even rosier hue. In instinctive self-defense she tilted her chin ever higher and returned the pointed examination with an equally critical gaze. Taller than any man she knew, his hair was night-black, and his strong frame, dressed in plain mail over homespun, was so big he overwhelmed the room. In truth, he was a stunningly handsome figure— just what she'd subconsciously expected the famous English knight, Willikin of the Weald, to be. An invisible thunderbolt of comprehension struck. He, not the older man now peering over his broad shoulder, was Willikin!

"She don't speak English," Harvey whispered from behind, whispered as if the blushing maid's hearing the words would matter when, in the first instance, she couldn't understand their meaning, and in the second, was their prisoner.

"Damoiselle, who are you?" Will asked in French. Wry amusement for his man's whispered words tilted the tight curve of his lips.

To an overly sensitive Cassie the hint of mockery in his cold smile seemed proof that his appraisal had found her lacking. She came close to wilting 'neath the unnerving stare. By providing further confirmation of physical inadequacies taught to her by years of her older brothers' harsh teasing, his male response pricked an old wound anew. Her brothers still saw her as the fat baby and more than chubby child she'd been. Long past had she accepted their image of her—too short to counterbalance curves far too well-rounded and in no way a match for the willowy grace they'd never ceased to assure her was the embodiment of true womanly beauty. Worse yet, this handsome English knight's apparent distaste for her was the more difficult to bear when her reaction to him had been precisely the reverse.

"I am Cassandra Gavre." The desperation holding a perilously thin veneer of bravado about her loosed sharp words urged to her tongue by the far braver Lady inside. "And I presume you are Willikin—my father's murderer." Cassie was even more surprised by the audacious answer than he. Yet pride in her sudden boldness lent sufficient courage to repress the near-overmastering inclination to beg the powerful knight for mercy. All considered, she'd nothing more to lose and may as well refuse to humble herself to a man who appeared unshakably in control of himself, his world, and her!

Will's smile deepened slightly in acknowledgment of this plainly shy rabbit's suddenly valiant defiance—and a silk-soft rabbit she was, plump and tender prey for the wolf he, under different circumstances, could well be. Despite her undeniable apprehension, she'd remained steady before him as had few of the Frenchmen he'd dealt with face to face. They, in the main, had been little less than terrified of him—the notorious defender of the Weald. Aye, the timid rabbit had sharp if well-hidden teeth, and the gallant spirit that must be harder for one so shy to maintain earned from Will a measure of respect never lightly given.

"I am Sir William of Kensham," the man affirmed with a slow nod as he took two steps forward.

Gulping inaudibly, Cassie steeled herself against the desire to shrink from his formidable aura of command. How could she have thought she'd nothing to lose while she prized her life and valued the virtue no unwed maid dare surrender?

"Your father's death came not by my hand . . ." Will paused, his expression taking on the harsh impassivity of granite. "But all foreign invaders who dare trespass on the Weald's English soil are dispatched by my order."

Cassie's breath caught at his calm acceptance of responsibility, but it was the implied threat in his words that drove all color from her face. Wasn't she a "foreign invader" too? Instinctively knowing better than to admit her reaction was a terror of him, she kept fear from swamping fragile defenses by assuring herself that the fine tremor in hands tightly clutching smooth silk resulted from grief for her sire's loss.

As a child she'd seldom seen and barely known the distant figure who was her father, and when matured had found few reasons to love the inflexible man who directed her future without regard to her hopes, fears, or dreams. Yet still she did, truly did mourn the upheaval his passing would bring the family. Never mind that she'd had a whole night and near whole day to accept the unalterable fact of his demise and recognize her brother Henri's new position as Lord of Beauvoille. Her rising panic must be, *non*, was sorrow—mayhap distress for her uncertain future as well but *not*, definitely *not*, fear for the intimidating man towering before her. He was big—huge, in fact, tall and streamlined. An awed admiration slipped uninvited into her gaze. He terrifies you, an inner voice scoffed mercilessly. Not for his strength and power alone, but for the attraction he so easily wields over you.

The abrupt paling of her gently rounded face emphasized the bravely met fear darkening her amazing eyes to a wood violet's deep purple. Will unexpectedly found himself host to a desire to comfort, even protect her. From whom? Himself?

"Your countrymen could've saved their lives by staying where they belonged," Will muttered with a defensiveness he believed to the depths of his soul he'd no reason to feel. Vexed not only by his own unwarranted reaction to the maid's distress but by the folly of her dead father, he silently wondered what daft inspiration had prompted the man to bring his daughter to a place of war.

Cassie couldn't argue against a statement too obviously accurate and one with which she agreed. Saints' tears! She hadn't come by choice. Moreover, though men deemed a female's thoughts of little value, she'd always believed the invasion of England a useless endeavor sure to cost too many French lives. But then, the very few men she knew seemed to find bloodshed good sport.

"Come with me," Will ordered. Whatever else was true, she couldn't remain in this unworthy shelter. He turned to duck beneath the low doorframe.

What did he mean to do with her? Cassie nibbled her lower lip to berry brightness while all the whispered rumors of dastardly acts committed against the civilized French by the brutish English sped through her mind. Immobile, she watched until her captor paused to wait for her just outside. Plainly she'd no choice but to obey. She stood, relying on the questionable support of a false courage whose constant need had gone a fair way toward dangerously fraying already battered nerves.

The moment he turned to look her way, she dropped her gaze to the hut's floor, hoping to divert her misgivings. The view was revealed by weak light falling through the same holes in the roof that had allowed entry of enough rain to turn the dirt surface into a thick layer of mud pocked with pools of filthy water. She began moving forward, plotting her way around puddles that would do the least possible damage to dainty kidskin slippers. 'Twas a useless task doomed to failure, but enough to lessen grave fears that might elsewise see her become naught but a witling quaking 'neath the weight of a steady black gaze.

Watching the hesitant maid's careful progress, cynicism firmed Will's lips to a one-sided smile. He shared his noble uncle Garrick's jaundiced opinion of well-born females, the majority of whom—with the notable exception of Nessa, Garrick's lady-wife—were self-centered and too manipulative to consider else than their own betterment. An opinion not improved by his considerable experience with their number—women who found him more than worthy of a day's dalliance, but his heritage and prospects unworthy of a shared future. Thus from his viewpoint 'twas no surprise when, after her first glance through the open doorway, shock widened lavender eyes.

Dismayed, Cassie came to an abrupt halt. The ground beyond the threshold was a mire of muck which she could nowise traverse without destroying both slippers *and* the hem of her silk skirts. One part of her mind sensibly told her that compared to all that had happened, these were matters of minor import, particularly when rain had already damaged the gown, and the mud from the hut's floor caked her feet. Still, although she'd tightly held her composure throughout tense hours spent amidst the ghastly hovel's miserable conditions, this was the one drop of liquid too much which makes the bucket filled with thousands overflow.

Cassandra Gavre's horror at the sight of the small glade's trampled floor confirmed Will's annoyance with having any fine lady here. The Weald was no place for a female of her sort! Even less the place for *anyone* French!

"Ohhh!" Cassie's exclamation was a startled squeak. Intent on the view of mud-slimed grass interspersed with small rivulets and ponds of brown liquid, oblivious to the men standing there, she was unprepared when Will swept her up against his broad chest. Instinctively holding tight, her gaze flew to a face far too near—a dreadful mistake. At such close proximity his physical perfection was too potent. She must look away, truly must look away before he glanced down to see her shameful fascination. She must—but she couldn't! Bright pink heat washed up from her throat to glow inside the white frame of her wimple.

Will felt the gentle brush of lavender and sensed the involuntary admiration behind it. She was far, far from the first female to react to him in this way. 'Twas not uncommon even amongst those who considered themselves many rungs above him on the social ladder. He'd learned early how to control both his response and theirs. Thus as Will stood motionless he was shocked to reluctantly acknowledge his immediate and unappreciated response to the sweetly curved female. In one and the same moment he wanted to banish this enemy from his arms, from the Weald, and yet wanted to crush her temptingly soft form to the hard contours of his body.

Black, shoulder-length hair barely stirred at the infinitesimal shake of his head. He could not, would not permit any woman—this noble-born maiden, this unbargained for adversary least of all—to distract him from the overriding importance of strategies for war or even the matter of how to deal with an unwanted hostage. However, cold logic failed to chill the heat fired in him by the blushing damoiselle. He looked down, and eyes once cold now burned.

Already intensely conscious of their proximity, when he turned the full power of his gaze upon her, it seemed to Cassie as if golden flames were beckoning her into pools of black velvet where all too likely she would drown. More frightening yet was the certain fact that her alarm was matched, even eclipsed, by dangerous thrills. His slow, sensuous smile stole strength and rational thought from her.

"Our Willikin's fortune holds true!" a teasing voice proudly claimed. "That no Frenchman can stand against his might, already we knew. But here see the proof that French women are even more vulnerable to his lethal charms." A ripple of snickers greeted the words.

"Aye," another joined the raillery. "But we've always known he was a ladycharmer—did he wish to be. Famous—or is it infamous—for his conquests he is!" At the reference to their lord's well-known reputation, the snickers became roisterous laughter.

The bantering of these men who'd returned with him and lingered still in the clearing freed Will of his wrongful preoccupation with a foe. He looked to his men, none of them a part of the knighthood and none of them bound by its code. Plainly they saw nothing to hold him back from wreaking a vengeance upon this invader suitable to her gender. The mouth, which moments past had curved with a heat potent enough to melt feminine bones, firmed into a fierce frown meant to quell the escalation of bawdy comments, leers, and gestures whose meaning the female in his arms could hardly fail to interpret.

Indeed, although Cassie understood none of the foreign words, by their tone she recognized the coarse drollery for precisely what it was. Her detested blush deepened. Even the growing gloom of day's end was too flimsy a shield against curious eyes. Without thought she buried her face in the curve between her captor's throat and broad shoulder.

Will slowly, deliberately stared at first one man, then the next and next. Had Cassie the nerve to look up, she'd have seen eyes gone to black ice and surely cold enough to freeze any living thing. As if in proof, once laughing men went silent and slipped away.

When Will and his burden were alone, he swung around and strode toward a wood-framed building barely visible at the end of a narrow path on the glade's far side. By the standards of the Weald, his two-story house was very fine, but 'twas doubtless a hovel in comparison to her ancestral castle. He lived here rather than in a great fortress by choice, and never before had he been ashamed of his honorable home. More than once in the short time since they'd met, this unwanted hostage had, all-unknowingly, disrupted his tightly leashed responses, and now had even disturbed his satisfaction in the life he'd chosen. Will irritably kicked the door wide and fairly stomped through the lower floor's one large room.

Ever sensitive about her weight, Cassie was uncomfortably certain that being carried by the bold knight would confirm his poor opinion of her—until the sensation of his anger wrapping as closely about her as his arms overwhelmed her initial unease with fear.

She bit her lip, stifling a cry of panic. Did he mean to beat her? Or did he intend worse? His men's plainly crude jests had intensified her own fears, and she found no comfort in the fact he'd stopped their bantering. Not when the action seemed to have darkened his temper.

Suddenly aware of her compromising position—cradled in his arms, tightly clinging to broad shoulders, and her face nestled in the hollow below his chin—she promptly dropped her hands and stiffened against his hold.

Fearing for her virtue, how could she have allowed herself to go pliant in the grasp of a man so strong he carried her as if she were light as thistledown? Staring determinedly at the walls, the floor, or anywhere but up at *him*, Cassie barely saw the full-length stone fireplace. 'Twould have seemed unremarkable in any event, for she'd no basis by which to recognize how unusual was this luxury in such a dwelling.

Firm footfalls on wooden steps echoed in the empty house while the powerful figure steadily climbed a corner stairway to the upper level. Anxious to channel chaotic thoughts into more controlled paths, Cassie forced her attention to a careful scrutiny of the details of her surroundings. The hallway dividing this floor was flanked by two doors—meaning only two chambers occupied this level. Her captor threw open the door on the right and abruptly lowered his burden. Cassie immediately turned her back on the knight and, near frozen with apprehension of what might follow, blindly stared at the room as if 'twere of utmost import.

Further annoyed by the damsel's unjustified fear of he who had treated her better than any French interloper deserved, Will stepped back, unintentionally brushing the door shut.

Hearing the door close, Cassie thought herself alone. She let heavy lashes fall and loosed a long steadying breath. Having thus released a measure of tension, pale lavender eyes opened to study this new prison. Lit only by slants of dying daylight falling through shuttered windows on two adjoining walls, the chamber was in itself a distraction from weightier matters. It had not four corners, but three. Delicate brows momentarily furrowed. Then she realized the odd arrangement resulted from a hallway diagonally dividing the square of the upper level into two triangular rooms. In truth very strange.

The spartan room contained naught but a single crude chest, a simple three-legged stool, and a pallet of straw-stuffed homespun laid directly on the bare plank floor. It had limitations, yet a slight smile curled Cassie's mouth and she shrugged. Leastways the roof didn't leak and there was no mud.

Unable to see her expression from behind, Will took Cassie's slow, silent appraisal for disdain and shifted his weight to stand with feet firmly planted and hands clenched on hips. The thought of this uninvited guest finding his home, his unearned hospitality, lacking, made Will defensive —and vexed with himself for caring. By his present age of a score and sixteen he'd experience enough and more of ladies' preferences and desire for comfort above all else that he should find this newest example little surprise. And it surely shouldn't have the power to prick him. In the norm, nothing and no one could.

"No fine bower for a lady, yet a better cell than any foreign invader deserves."

Cassie whirled, startled to find the too attractive knight still near. Unlike the tiny hut, this room was fairly large, yet by his size alone he seemed to make even it shrink. Blinking rapidly against the intimidating sight, she apprehensively backed away, tripped over the mattress laying on the floor behind and tumbled backward onto its relative softness. That only her pride was bruised did nothing to lessen her crimson embarrassment.

The sight of the flustered damoiselle losing her tenuous grip on the refined decorum of a lady to lay in a welter of silk skirts drew from Will a grin of honest amusement. It flashed through his ill humor like lightning through the dark of a storm.

The fall had abruptly loosened Cassie's head cloth, releasing masses of ebony hair. Pushing tangled tresses from her eyes and struggling to sit up, she was mortified by the thought that she'd fallen at the devastating man's feet as if prostrate with admiration—a possibility uncomfortably close to reality, while the potency of his arrogant smile made it clear he'd adulation enough and needed no more.

Will was struck by an unexpected urge to reach out and discover if the dusky cloud of her hair were as soft as it appeared. Even more surprisingly, he wanted to apologize for the amusement she plainly believed was ridicule.

Attempting to conceal her fascination—a response he'd likely find distasteful from a female of her limited appeal, an enemy at that—Cassie sputtered a weak warning. "Stay away from me you . . . you . . . brigand!"

Will was certain he'd not mistaken the response behind a rapt lavender stare near constantly upon him. Yet the alarm blended with her embarrassment pricked his irritation anew. God's blood, what did she think he meant to do? Ravish her? In the immediate wake of his instinct to comfort the unsettling female, he found this expectation of a rape perversely amusing. A roar of deep laughter filled the room.

Cassie cringed from Willikin's unexpected answer to her warning. A cowardly reaction his earlier anger had failed to win. If he found her attempt at self-protection so amusing—weak though it was—likely he'd have no qualms about forcing her to his will—whatever direction it took. The sound of her own pounding heart almost drowned out the echo of his merriment.

Through eyes quickly losing their warmth, Will studied the prone woman whose fear, like the remorseless onset of night, had overwhelmed the daylight of other emotions. Aye, she actually did expect the worst of him—but what else, when he'd taken pride in the terrifying reputation he'd built amongst all people French? How could she know that, although he'd fought without mercy, never had he broken the code of a good knight, never had he purposely harmed a lady born, nor any other woman —an action he deemed the sign of a weak man? His men, not trained in the code, could be excused for expecting him to physically subdue and conquer a tender foe. But with the noble heritage that was plainly hers, she hadn't the same excuse, and he found the notion that this particular young creature believed him a knight of no honor untenable.

In the end her assumption returned a wry twist to Will's lips. 'Twas irrational to be disappointed that she believed no better of a man who'd proudly proclaimed himself her enemy.

"You've nothing to fear from me . . ." Even as he spoke, a new tactic in the uncharted war with a feminine opponent occurred to him. Mayhap encouraging unfounded fears would better succeed in holding her captive and yet keep her at arm's distance. "Nothing to fear—so long as you do nothing to rouse my wrath."

Even his one-sided smile was far too intriguing, and the sardonic glitter in a night-black gaze increased Cassie's apprehension, again deepening pale lavender eyes to amethyst.

When the heavy oak door had truly shut behind the departing man, she fumed at both her own inability to hide either alarm or fascination, and his knowing amusement. Comforting herself that such unruly reactions were merely the result of her fall's awkward position and subsequent disarray, she set about putting herself to rights. She longed for the travel trunks left in the cart. With them at hand she could've changed into garments more suited to these surroundings. Her practical nature shunted useless wishes aside. What needs must, must be. She'd make do with the goods available.

Cassie rose, smoothed her skirts, and ran her fingers through masses of dark silk strands. Believing herself alone for the night, rather than again donning her headdress, she divided and braided thick tresses until they laid over one shoulder in a single heavy plait. Holding the tip ends of twined locks in one hand, with her free hand she tugged a gold chain until it broke loose from her throat. For a moment she held it aloft to dispassionately study the necklace which had been a gift from Guy, her unwanted betrothed. 'Twas a rich trinket, but too flamboyant for her tastes and, as an emblem of ownership by a man she found the epitome of all things distasteful—obese, lecherous, and cruel—not overmuch liked. She'd no reason to feel guilty for reducing the precious ornament to the mundane chore of securing black strands. Lowering the shining chain, she began winding it repeatedly around the thick rope of her hair.

No man had seen Cassie's hair unbound since she'd left the far less than happy days of childhood behind. She'd grown up rich in all the physical comforts wealth and privilege provided, but a pauper in emotional support. Her distant parents had little concern for a mere girl-child's happiness, and had left her with no doubt but that she was a sad disappointment to them. From rising to day's end her life had been run by first her several nursemaids and then her elderly "companions." Bullying brothers and well-born boys sent to foster with her father had been nearly her only contact with the male of the species, and even they had never seen her knee-length ebony hair cascading free. No man had—until this knight called Willikin found such amusement in its disarray and hers! The vivid memory of his wordless mockery caused a deeper ache than any earlier rejection.

As she finished fashioning unwieldy links into a noose tight enough to restrain the weight of her hair, the door opened. She glanced up to find her captor again dominating the room. Had he not been truthful, then, when he'd said she'd no reason to fear him? She gasped, and in the next instant feared it had been loud enough to betray her alarm. Or, mocked the Lady Cassandra inside, was it simply her response to the wickedly handsome man's disturbing presence? The latter possibility, probability, increased her discomfort.

Noting the renewed anxiety widening purple eyes until they seemed to overwhelm her pale face, Will impatiently allowed the bundle of homespun held under one arm to drop to the mattress. Next he moved to settle a supper tray containing both food and a single tallow candle on the room's lone chest.

"Silk is useless in the Weald." His black gaze slid contemptuously over the fine gown now rain-bespattered. "Besides, there are none hereabouts for you to impress." To his annoyance, he suspected she'd look just as much a lady in homespun—a lady whom true knights were honor bound to provide for and protect.

Beneath the contempt she was certain he felt for a feminine form he found unappealing, Cassie bit her lip, but by effort of will held her eyes unwaveringly wide open to return his stare. What else could she do when there was no answer to his statement that he'd believe? Tell him she'd not worn silk by choice? Hah! Clearly a doomed ploy. He'd never believe her practical enough to prefer wearing a more durable gown in such surroundings.

"Thus," Will said, waving toward the crumpled brown cloth. "For you I borrowed this humble garb from Edna." He grimaced. She didn't know Edna and had surely no need to do so. Nay, that was untrue. In so small a military village—not really a village at all, as Edna was its only female inhabitant—there was little doubt but that she'd come to know the abrupt woman well. Particularly true as the aging Edna, for all she was short on words and frugal with smiles, had long insisted on devoting a substantial amount of time to caring for Will and his home. And this despite the fact that, although he'd men spread throughout the Weald, enough were based here—coming and going at irregular intervals—that Edna faced a burdensome task in keeping sufficient food ever waiting in a separate kitchen to meet their unscheduled needs. Will shrugged in an attempt to dislodge the unaccustomed haze the maid cast over his normally clear thoughts.

"However," he added gruffly, "you've no option but to wear your flimsy slippers and accept that they'll be ruined." In truth, they looked as if they were spoiled already.

Cassie was in no position to ask after her travel trunks, and knew it. Leastways, she comforted herself, it was this knowledge and not cowardice that prevented the question from finding voice. She must give thanks to the saints for their benevolence in providing even this little more than she'd expected. Eyes downcast, she nodded and turned to lift the heap of dull brown homespun. 'Twas a simple gown with raglan sleeves and neck slit laced by a thin leather cord.

Raised in the important fortress of Tarrant, Will had met many members of the too oft traitorous baronage and their families. He'd quickly learned that although they accepted his company for the power of his noble uncle, in their eyes his heritage and questionable future made him unworthy of more than a surface acquaintance. In the bitterness of scorned youth he'd set out to exact his own vengeance, and for more years than he wanted to recall had squandered time and energy taking their disloyal wives and daughters of easy virtue to his bed. Never by force nor against their will. Nay, they'd come seeking him with little effort on his part.

Perversely, once he'd found that by these amorous conquests he'd earned the noblemen's respect—each never believing his own womenfolk involved—the chase had lost its challenge. Leaving they and their like behind, he'd turned his attention to the deadly arts of war and accepted the challenge of life in this dense and distant forest where the very last thing he'd ever thought to be stranded with was a female of noble breeding. Nonetheless, she was here and here she would stay until they'd received ample payment for their trouble on her behalf.

"I give fair warning . . ." He paused with one foot in the hall and looked back over his shoulder. "Don't try to run from me." Dark mocking eyes studied her from head to toe. This timid rabbit, with her silks and distaste for mud, hardly looked capable of such brave deeds, but her courage had surprised him before. 'Twas always wiser to leave nothing to chance, and thus best she know the impossibility of successful escape.

"The Weald and all within are mine, and here you'd be found before you'd wandered far." The door went shut with an ominous lack of sound.

Chapter

❧ 3 ❧

RUN FROM HIM? Her attention on the unmoving planks of the door closed behind the mocking man, Cassie blinked at the thought. It had been unwise for him to speak of it. *Oui,* to escape an objectionable betrothal by proxy, in desperation she had obeyed the urging of her seldom loosed adventurous self and run from her father—but by horse, and only the short distance across familiar countryside to a neighboring abbey. And that folly had resulted in this ill-fated journey meant to end in an unwanted marriage. As were all well-bred females, she'd been raised to subservience, not rebellion.

The shy and lonely child she'd been had found few human friends—the sister soon married and sent away, a little brother who would grow into disdainful boyhood all too quickly, and but one of her myriad foster brothers. Far more reliable and comforting was her imaginary friend, the reverse side of herself—spirited Lady Cassandra. From childhood till now she'd created her own entertainment by envisioning the actions Lady Cassandra would take against realities that intimidated Cassie. Alone in a strange land, Cassie would never have found the bravery to do more than fantasize about a daring escape—had her captor not warned her against trying. His parting words were a flagrant challenge to the Lady Cassandra dwelling within, a challenge that lent a measure of bravery—likely fleeting—to Cassie's timid self. The sound of a door closing across the narrow corridor proved her foe had retired to his bed. Cassie braced her courage with a wild assertion that, all else aside, being lost in the forest offered a distinct advantage over remaining here in relative safety: she need never scrape together nerve enough to meet or talk with the alarming man again. She boldly told herself she had rather face ravenous wolves weaponless. And wished it were true.

Knowing hesitation would invite her natural reticence to hold her back, Cassie instantly directed her attention to the chamber's two windows.

Both were small and high up on their respective walls. Moving resolutely to the chest holding the evening meal Willikin had brought, she shifted the full platter to the floor and dragged the sturdy box to a point directly below the first window. Stepping atop, careful to be as quiet as possible, she slipped a thick rod from its horizontal position through rings driven into the wood casement on each side, unbarring thick oak shutters. She spread them wide, revealing a two-story drop to the wooden stairway leading up to the house's entry—a disheartening view. Yet, faint hope a hard knot in her chest, she lost no time in repeating the procedure with the second window.

Fiercely denying her growing trepidation, Cassie boldly peered into a world going colorless under night's inexorable descent. This portal looked over a roof slanting down near to the earth below. Plainly 'twas the covering of a lean-to stable built against the cottage's outside wall. The rain had abated at last and, although clouds remained and full nightfall neared, there was light enough to lay a dull sheen on wet thatching. A smile curved rose lips. Escape wouldn't be so difficult after all. She need only wait until her captor and his men sought their beds and succumbed to slumber's call. Then she would slide down the thatching to the ground. The thought gave her a confidence sorely needed to seriously contemplate the deed. Was it too simple to be safe? *Non*, the question was no more than the whine of her craven nature attempting to see the plan stillborn.

Stepping down from the chest, determination sparkling in her eyes, Cassie exchanged her silk gown for the homespun dress. A dress, she ruefully acknowledged, overlarge even on her. Cassie adjusted the voluminous cloth about her body and grimaced. Where silk caressed, homespun scratched. She cast a longing glance at the dress, lovely despite its rain spots, which must be left behind. Dare she wear it rather than this uncomfortable serf's garb?

Don't be a dolt! she warned herself. *You think to run, but how could you move undetected amidst a forest in silk? You'd stand out like peacock among hens.* Moreover, thought of the further and surely irreparable damage done to the expensive cloth were she to wear it while sliding down wet thatching was deterrent enough. The silk would be lost, but 'twas a small price for freedom from the fearsome English knight. Was she so certain, a mocking voice asked, that the detested betrothed to whom she ran posed a lesser threat? The disheartening thought near stole her nerve. Would that she could run from both—but 'twas impossible. No woman survived without a man to provide for and protect her. Purposefully freeing herself of foolish notions and useless regrets, Cassie reminded herself that to get away was the all-important first goal. Not until she'd accomplished that task dare she consider the difficulties waiting beyond.

To fasten the makeshift apparel's abundant material about her much narrower frame, she used the twined satin ribbons embroidered with gilt thread which had earlier belted her sapphire dress. The discordant sight of the rich belt against rough brown cloth earned a sad and fleeting smile.

Fearful lingering doubts might douse the weak flame of courage, Cassie resolutely turned her attention to the dark rye bread and cheese Willikin had brought. She settled on the floor beside the waiting tray. A bite from the slab of smooth cheese and the hasty nibbling of a chunk from the heavy loaf only served to increase a thirst seldom appeased in the last day and more. All unsuspecting, she lifted an earthen cup filled with a liquid whose color was lost amidst the shadows of the crude vessel and gulped a fair measure.

A fierce tremor shook her while lips pursed and eyes watered. He was an odious toad, a graceless lout! 'Twas not the fine wine to which she was accustomed. *Non!* 'Twas the strong and bitter ale with which fierce warriors and ill-bred knaves sotted themselves. How dare he ply her with such an unworthy potion? The next time she saw him, of a certain she would make him aware of precisely what was and what was not acceptable to a lady's palate. Blister his ears would she—hah, her timid self ridiculed, smothering the momentary flash of fire. That she would not. Not alone because she who seldom found courage to talk with any stranger would never have nerve enough to stand against the mighty warrior armed with naught but flimsy words—or, if it came to that, with even a sharp blade. More importantly, because she meant never to see him again.

Despite the inescapable admission of her cowardly self's predominance, she fumed at both the knight's audacity and her own impotence. Although she'd never be brave enough to follow through with it, she took pleasure in mentally composing a scathing denunciation of him, reworking it again and again until she deemed it worthy of some legendary beauty's rejection of an impertinent swain's wrongful advances. Without adequate appreciation, she took the last bite of a crisp, newly harvested apple and softly giggled. The thought of herself as a beauty was ridiculous, but not half so ridiculous as the notion that the incredibly handsome knight might ever make advances to her, wrongful or otherwise. Gentle laughter died and a mournful shadow crossed once gleaming eyes.

She resolutely glanced toward the window. Light had completely fled the view beyond. Lost first in anger and then in self-pity, she'd failed to earlier realize the room's only illumination now came from a single tallow candle nestled amongst the platter's mug and food offerings. Moreover, the house had gone utterly silent, and with her foe occupying the chamber on the corridor's far side, surely it was safe to go. She put the two remaining apples into the borrowed dress's capacious pockets, then moved to the chest once more.

Peering tentatively into the night gloom, she found a stillness uncanny to one used to the ever-shifting crowd of people and labors of castle life. After several futile attempts at hoisting herself up by the strength of her arms alone, she was discouraged. Getting down, she turned the chest on end, providing more elevation. This tactic brought her waist level to the lower edge of the window. Heart pounding and determination darkening her eyes, she bent her knees and jumped. Thus launched through the opening, her trip down the slippery thatching, headfirst and alarmed eyes wide, came to a distressingly quick end. Leastways she had a soft landing —in mud.

Less than thankful for that gift of fate, Cassie sputtered as she rose on her forearms—and froze. The stable inhabitant on the wall's other side banged about, noisily demonstrating his irritation at having his night's rest disturbed. Would his master come to investigate? Valiantly struggling first to her knees and then to her feet, Cassie dashed for the protecting gloom beyond the nearest towering tree.

Leaning against the sturdy trunk's far side, breath suspended, Cassie waited. Only after long, heart-stopping moments did the stallion quiet. When silence reigned again, she was freed from her fear-induced immobility to kneel and wipe large portions of mud from bare hands and clothed arms on the long, soaked grass at the tree's base. Feeling dirtier than ever before in her life, with an inventiveness she hadn't known she possessed, Cassie used the water stored in a fallen leaf's up-curled surface to wash the worst of the grime from her face.

Minimally refreshed, she was as prepared to meet the challenge ahead as she was likely to get—a disheartening thought. She had no idea what direction to take to reach any point, or even what point was her goal, yet now was no time to falter. Her one thought being to keep Willikin's cottage at her back and leastwise win free of him, she briskly set off.

On an open moor the moonless night would be dark, but in the midst of this dense forest it was completely featureless! Peering into the gloom ahead, she stumbled through rain-drenched undergrowth that clung to her feet and ankles like restraining hands. Moving from one trunk to the next, soon all sense of direction disappeared into a blackness suddenly filled with frightening noises and wavering shadows of threatening proportions.

Mayhap facing the English knight's remarkably restrained ire was not really so bad as meeting a wolf's sharp fangs? She shuddered at the prospect.

By the time the sky turned the dull gray of predawn, Cassie was forced to admit that she was utterly lost—if someone who was running away could be. Could a person be lost when that person knew neither where she'd been nor where she was going? After a sleepless night of aimless wandering, her mind was too muddled to reason an answer for the foolish question.

Unused to travels more arduous than a horse ride, an occasional jaunt in a wagon, or sedate walks through well-manicured gardens, Cassie was exhausted. Where her skin was exposed, it stung with small scratches yet felt stiff. She looked down and by the new day's first light saw that, despite her attempt to scrape off the worst of it, enough mud remained to coat her skin with a thin layer of dirt. Dirt—*oui*. Her eyes, too, felt as if in them resided a seashore full of sandy sleep-grit.

Sagging against the thin white trunk of a young birch, Cassie rubbed her eyes. She opened them, stared hard, and then rubbed harder. Would the vision disappear as she'd been told longed-for sights oft did when they appeared to people too weary? *Non*, it was still there. It was real—that humble hut in the center of a glade so small the branches of trees on either side joined above. Her initial relief was tempered by misgivings about the reception that she, a stranger, might receive. What if its inhabitants were more of Willikin's crude men? What might they do to her without his restraining presence?

While she hesitated in the shadows, two figures emerged from the simple structure—a gaunt man so stooped with years that, though plainly much taller, his head was near on a level with the short, white-haired woman at his side. The age of the two offered a measure of reassurance. Dare she approach them? There was no help for it, she must appeal to them for aid. Elsewise she'd either starve to death or fall prey to some wild creature in the forest.

In brown homespun Cassie blended with the autumn forest until the rustle of her feet crossing fallen leaves drew their attention. The elderly man squinted in her direction as she stepped from the wood's concealment while with difficulty the woman turned her way.

Cassie immediately launched into a fervent plea for help in escaping the Weald, escaping Willikin. From the confusion on their faces it was clear the couple failed to comprehend her French plea. Still, despite the threat of burning tears falling in defeat, she finished her plainly hopeless supplication.

Of a sudden the elderly woman brightened and turned to her husband. Among the words she spoke to the man, Cassie recognized "Weald" and "Willikin." In blind relief for a thing desperately sought and miraculously given, Cassie believed she'd been understood. Thus, when the now smiling woman motioned her inside the hut, Cassie followed without qualm. She was thankful, as she'd never expected to be, for her homespun peasant's garb. Surely its humble shield prevented these two from recognizing her noble birth and the French heritage which might well identify her as their foe and see her delivered back into the fearsome knight's hands. After all, the English serfs who served in castles spoke French. So, that her language was not theirs was, in itself, no betrayal of her nationality. The notion that soft though dirt-layered hands and fine features was betrayal enough simply didn't occur to her.

The tiny home's darkness was relieved only by the same fire in the center's rock-ring which produced billowing smoke enough to sting eyes and haze the view. Following wordless directions, Cassie took a seat on an upended firewood round at the firepit's edge and quietly watched as food and drink were assembled. She knew better than to insult her humble hosts by asking for water to cleanse hands and face in preparation for the simple meal. With a smile, she hoped was less strained than it felt, she ate the offered chunk of dark and heavy rye bread and washed it down with a draught of ale every bit as bitter as the brew Willikin had supplied the night past. To these plain folk she'd not complain of the crude drink's unworthiness. 'Twas clearly the best they had and hospitably, *non*, generously given. Despite her hunger, their obvious poverty was such that she felt guilty for taking even this small measure of their surely precious stores.

Once she had done, the man took a tall walking stave from its position beside the door. Plainly he was ready to comply with her plea, ready to aid her in attaining freedom from the Weald and its intimidating master. With well-hidden relief at the prospect of leaving the hut's smoky confines, Cassie rose but gave the woman a warm smile and heartfelt thanks whose tone if not words were sure to be understood.

The man slipped through the forest with more agility than his bent frame suggested was possible. Ignoring the blisters on tender feet, Cassie kept pace. In a time so short it proved she'd spent the majority of her night hours wandering in circles, he broke through the forest wall and into the same clearing she'd tried so hard to escape. Her stunned frustration deepened at the sight of a furious warrior dressed in mail and ahorse. The powerful knight was obviously preparing to set off in search of her. "Willikin."

The sound of his name being called from the forest shadows a short distance behind drew Will's immediate attention. His black gaze slid past Odo, a simple farmer who'd spent his life scratching a meager living from the Weald's sandy soil, to narrow on the sorry figure behind. In a face mysteriously dirt-layered, violet eyes widened while his errant captive backed away in dismay.

Sensible thought driven out by the frigid glare suddenly upon her, like a hawk sighting prey, Cassie whirled to dash headlong through dense underbrush.

Daft creature! Will inwardly denounced her action even as he urged his steed to trail her path at a slow, steady pace. Let her run and discover the futility of her flight. Again. Despite the brave face she'd turned to him at their first meeting, both the previous night and now this morn she seemed driven to run from him in terror. Torn between using her alarm to frighten her into submission under his restraints, and a useless urge to convince her she'd nothing to fear from him, he did neither. Rather he simply followed, allowing the maid to wear herself out, unable to blame him for her flight's certain result—the physical discomforts of sore muscles and scratched flesh. He had hoped her thirst would drive her to drink the potent brew left for her the night past. 'Twas a brew intended to see her safely lost to the conscious world for long hours. A plan plainly foiled by the taste which left her preferring thirst—unfortunate but not surprising.

Cassie desperately flew ever deeper into green shadows, heedless to the dragging hold of thorny bushes, dodging the fallen logs in her path, and quickly scrambling up every time partially hidden stumble holes brought her to her knees. The steady sound of hooves on her trail only increased her determination to win free. Despite breath grown ragged and a stabbing pain in her side, she persevered, until a deep rut joined forces against her with a branch that refused to give way when she pushed and was knocked flat on her back. Derriere bruised and twisted ankle throbbing, she hadn't the strength to rise. She lay in a limp heap on the ground when the mighty black stallion and his equally impressive rider arrived to loom above. The man was tall and big, his face deeply tanned and firm mouth faintly cruel. Cassie shivered involuntarily when his dark brows drew together as he studied her awkward pose.

Will gazed down at the prone figure tangled in overabundant cloth, scratched and layered with dirt. Self-contempt filled his faint smile. Despite her disarray and the apprehension visible in her soft features, she looked a lady born. That she'd fallen to such dire straits seemed an unspoken criticism of him for allowing this insult to her dignity.

Cassie thought the gold sparks flashing in paradoxically cold eyes had been struck off the flint of his disdain for her. Yet she was too exhausted to resist his will. She'd already done that and seen what little had been accomplished. Will bent from the huge destrier, extending his arm to her. His action was a silent demand that she give over and, yielding to his command, Cassie struggled to rise.

Wrapping one arm about the incredibly soft waist near buried beneath folds of homespun, Will lifted the defeated damsel to lay across the horse in front of him. He settled her more firmly in the circle of his arms, justifying his action with the need to prevent another escape.

Cradled close to his powerful form, soon the minor irritation of scratches and twisted ankle faded beneath the onslaught of new sensations —awareness of the steely strength in muscles that moved as he urged their steed to turn back toward its starting point, awareness of heat radiating from him to warm her chilled body. Breath grown embarrassingly short, she fell to temptation and looked up at the masculine beauty of the face resolutely averted. Although truly the shielded innocent of her upbringing, even she had seen enough of serfs' furtive embraces amidst a castle's shadowed corners to open the doors of curiosity. Now she wondered wildly what it would be like were he to turn her, clasp her tight against his massive chest, and put that hard, cruel mouth over hers. At the thought she went hot all over, and her lips opened on a silent gasp.

Will sensed the fear seeping from her body to be replaced by tension of a far different sort. Too, he felt the shy fascination in her stare, the faint hunger in the brush of her eyes across his mouth. Though refusing to look, he knew her soft lips had parted slightly as if in anticipation of a lover's kiss. His own firmed to a grim line. Exercising considerable control, Will fought to restrain his natural reaction to this mock embrace and her breathless but assuredly naive response. This curious little virgin was a hazard, more temptation than she could possibly realize. He could not, would not, let the noble maiden inadvertently entice him into foolish actions which could only insult her and stain his honor. While Will stared resolutely ahead, the stallion found his way home near undirected.

As they approached the back of his house, the sight of the bewildered farmer lingering still where they'd left him abruptly returned Will to awareness of his surroundings.

"Thank Odo for his care of you," Will ordered, with a smile for Odo that failed to soften the black granite of his eyes.

Despite the harsh expression of the man who'd never looked her way, Cassie found the undercurrent of huskiness in his deep voice strangely thrilling. Welcoming any distraction from the devastating enemy far too near, lavender eyes shifted to the stooped figure awaiting their return. The man had tried to help, and the only error was not his but hers in being unable to rightly state her plea. She did, in truth, owe her appreciation to the couple who'd lent aid and willingly shared their limited resources. Cassie complied with the knight's command—in a French that merely confused Odo.

Will gritted his teeth, irritated by this obstruction atop the physical frustrations built by their proximity on the return journey. Yet while teaching Cassie the English words to accomplish the task he'd demanded, he held his tone as steady as the shield of cool mockery he'd settled over his face.

Responding to Cassie's warm smile and honest tone, a pleased grin widened the creases on Odo's face as he touched his forelock, shyly looked away and disappeared into leafy green shadows.

Under the unexpected sincerity of the words she repeated, a brief and quickly repaired crack sundered Will's cynical mask. Cassie caught a glimpse of Will's reaction and was quietly pleased by her unexpected ability to disrupt his self-command. "The man and his wife generously lent their aid and were not to blame for misunderstanding the manner of help I sought." Her soft lips curled into a gently chiding smile. "For the attempt alone I owed them my gratitude."

Knowing full well the power of the weapon he effortlessly wielded, Will flashed her a slow smile of such strength, her eyes widened and breath stopped in her throat. Best she learn the danger in testing her wiles on him who was so much more experienced in the art. In accompaniment to the bone-melting smile, fires smoldered in dark eyes and burned as they swept over her.

Cassie's thick lashes fluttered in a wild response.

It was like hunting a tame doe, and Will was ashamed of himself. If even a simple smile produced this effect, the recipient was more innocent than any female in his previously rather varied experience. The prospect of what response a more concerted effort might produce was something he must not allow himself to ponder. Unlike the fine ladies and serfs he'd taken over the years of his maturity, she was not fair game for the hunt. Moreover, she was not so selfish as he'd assumed one of her station must be. Not only had she admitted, but paid a debt owed which had ended far astray from its intended goal. Few among the noble-born ladies he knew would have any care for the feelings of mere common folk. In truth, seldom even for the feelings of their peers.

Irritated with himself for finding good in any well-bred female, even worse, this particular *French* threat to his peace of mind, Will abruptly lowered Cassie to the ground. He'd enough enemies to fight, problems to solve without her added distraction.

Startled by his unexpected physical release while still caught in his sensual snare, Cassie forgot her injured ankle. She took a step back, wincing as she placed weight on the injured limb.

Will felt guilty on two counts. In the first for having allowed her to wildly run from him, nearly ensuring this injury, and in the second for letting his self-recriminations drive him to the thoughtless action which in turn had increased her pain. He dismounted, calling to one a mere shadow hovering in the background.

"Kenward, return Nightfall to his stable and join us inside." Without warning, Will lifted Cassie into his arms.

This constant losing touch with solid earth kept a maid giddy, leastwise 'twas Cassie's excuse for the increase in her pulse rate and urge to hold tight to strong shoulders.

Will carried her into the house. But liking the enticing feel of the soft damsel in his arms far too well, he lost no time lowering her into one of the two massive, cushion-padded chairs drawn close to the wall-length fireplace. He'd stated only the truth when he'd assured her she had nothing to fear from him. She was his hostage, and all personal desires, all temptations aside, he was honor-bound to preserve her health and, aye, her innocence, in exchange for the ransom he meant to exact. The faint dislike curling one corner of his mouth was belied by the smoldering fire glowing gold in his eyes. Naught but frustration and pain could follow any contact between them. Thus, he'd be best served by seeing they'd as little as possible. But first he must do his utmost to see that she remain here in his house for the sake of his plan—and her safety.

"You were blessed indeed to come first upon Odo and his wife. Though they failed to fulfill your intent, leastways they held you safe." His gaze narrowed in a long sweep down from her dusty braid to stained and tattered slippers. "You could as easily have been found by other men, whose natural instincts are restrained by neither age nor knightly training. Flee again and you may not be as fortunate."

"Your supporters are so uncivilized? So desperate?" She motioned toward herself with doubt that any man could be so desperate as to risk his lord's wrath for one as plain as she.

"My supporters *are* men most oft alone and hungry for a woman—any woman." He flatly stated it, intending her to realize her noble position in French society would be no impediment to their desires.

The fear he'd sought to rouse was the pigeon-hearted Cassie's immediate response, but the Lady Cassandra inside stiffened against the hurtful insult implied if unspoken in his statement. Although out of loneliness his men might be willing to lower their standards to claim her, he was not. Heavy lashes fell over eyes gone dark. What had she expected? A miracle? This man, this hero among the people of the land, must have his choice of female companions—beautiful, willing, and *English*.

"Pray heed my words," Will continued, with a cool determination to see his warning obeyed. Yet the distress in eyes quickly hidden won a smile of unintended gentleness and a reassurance. "So long as you remain in my home, you are safe. The men know you are mine, and will not tempt my displeasure."

As if saddled to a steed running uncontrolled, Cassie's emotions were on a gallop of wild ups and downs. Disoriented, she tilted her head to gaze at the source of such chaos. First he'd seemed to say his men would assault her without regard to their lord's wishes, and then that they wouldn't dare his displeasure. Too, hadn't he clearly said that while his men might find her adequate, he did not, only to now say that she was protected from them because she was his. In the whirl of thoughts and feelings jolted about too rapidly to be sensibly sorted through, apprehension strangely tangled with hopeful excitement.

"Yours?" The gasped word contained all the confusion she felt.

Will heard only alarm. This, from the French damsel he'd sworn had no reason to fear him yet whom he'd a persistent desire to truly possess, was the emotion he'd set out to rouse but now resented. A cold smile of self-derision settled on his lips as he amplified his statement. "My *hostage*."

Feeling thrown from a wild steed abruptly halted by the icy blast of his sarcasm, Cassie's gaze dropped to fingers twisting rough brown cloth, thankfully much sturdier than silk which by now would have fallen to shreds.

A timid tapping against the huge oak door shattered the room's tension and heralded the summoned Kenward's arrival.

"Come," Will ordered. The door opened just wide enough for a youngster of mayhap fifteen years to slip inside. As the boy waited to learn the purpose for which he'd been called, he curiously studied the odd sight of a pretty lady dressed in rags, a pretty lady who unaccountably seemed unable to meet his gaze.

"While I'm gone, which I am most days, Kenward will be ever near you." As Will made the statement, his stern glance passed from Cassie to the boy. "You will watch over our 'guest' diligently, yes?" Dark brows arched in such a way as to make the words more command than question.

Kenward nodded so vigorously, the raggedly cut ends of his light brown hair brushed narrow shoulders. And, taking a cue from his leader's French words, the youth answered in the same tongue. "That I will."

Cassie gasped upon hearing her native language spoken by the boy and, shyness overridden by quiet pleasure, glanced up into steady hazel eyes. After so recently falling to ill for being misunderstood, the welcome sound was comforting. She gave him a gentle smile of such sweetness his hazel eyes widened.

Another conquest easily made? Sweet Mary's tears, Will hoped not. He'd few options open for her guarding. French troops were on the move, and he couldn't spare men from battles looming near.

"Lest you think Kenward easily evaded or merely a boy of no possible threat," Will cautioned, turning an emotionless face to Cassie, "my young friend will demonstrate his skill with a dagger." True, he'd not underestimate her desperation again, but also he wanted Kenward to understand the importance of fulfilling his assigned task. Never shifting his penetrating gaze from the maid, he idly motioned toward the boy.

A flash of brightly honed metal caught Cassie's attention. Without a moment's hesitation, Kenward flicked his dagger from the sheath at his waist into the center of a knot in the timber frame on the sizable room's far side before turning to the newcomer with a proud grin.

Will was ashamed of himself for doubting Kenward's loyalty. In one sense the lad was his nephew, in another his foster son, and never would Kenward willingly fail him. He allowed the demonstration's wordless threat to sink in before disconcerting Cassie with a question on a far different topic. "Is the Gavre who is a member of the besieging force at Dover kin to you?"

Cassie was startled and showed it. How was it that he possessed such information about the makeup of his foes' army? Thrown off kilter by his unexpected knowledge, she failed to consider the possible consequences of her answer.

"My older brother, Henri." The thick rope of her single braid fell forward as her head tilted to one side in silent question.

With the reappearance of his mocking smile, Will merely nodded, turned his broad back on her and departed.

Plainly, Cassie realized, the bold warrior meant to ransom her. Ransom her without knowing that by sending word of her plight to Henri, he was telling a much more powerful man—the force's leader and her betrothed, Guy de Faux.

Willikin could reasonably expect her brother to pay for her release for family pride, if not love. But unbeknownst to her "host," the cruel De Faux would almost certainly view her capture a personal affront and never rest until his vengeance had been wreaked upon the perpetrator.

THE FURS CASSIE had hidden 'neath during her capture were again wrapped about her as she burrowed deeper into a wide, padded chair before the main hall's massive fireplace. Under autumn's brisk weather it was chilly even inside the house. Staring blindly into flames weaving a constantly shifting tapestry of yellow and orange, she listened intently to Kenward's patiently spoken English words.

"*Oui.*" Cassie lifted her nose from dark warmth to murmur in a mixture of carefully selected English words and French phrases, "I understand. You and your leader were raised in the same castle. . . ." Kenward, who sat with self-conscious dignity in a chair the twin of hers, reminded Cassie of her youngest brother, the only one too much her junior to remember her childhood self or to treat her as mere chattel. In answer to her plea of boredom, the only excuse she'd found which might not rouse suspicion, he'd spent hours patiently trying to teach her the land's native tongue.

"But whose castle?" She hid a teasing grin from the quiet boy with whom she felt more comfortable than with almost anyone she'd known before. "And why then are you both here in this uncivilized place?"

She maintained an expression of innocence, as if she believed the admonishing glance her questions earned was a response to her mixture of languages rather than to her choice of subject. Yet, although her questions were almost certainly awkwardly phrased in the unfamiliar language, he assuredly was vexed not by that fact, but by her curiosity on a subject he'd consistently refused to discuss—her captor's past.

The sparkle in amethyst eyes gave her true intent away; still Kenward slowly answered in the elementary English this shy lady-enemy might be expected to understand. Once he'd realized her nature even more reserved than his, he had discovered a growing liking for the maid. "Will has his reasons for preferring a simple life in the Weald and has made a great . . ." He gave up on his effort to explain complex issues in simple terms and lapsed into French. Intent on waylaying her invasion into particulars of a past which he'd been warned never to share, Kenward delivered yet another glowing account of what a great man Will was, of the loyalty and respect in which his people held him for his just leadership and honest dealings.

Cassie had heard it all before, more than once. Kenward obviously hero-worshiped the man she'd seldom seen since the day he'd assigned the boy to act as her guard. The name Willikin of the Weald struck terror in her countrymen, but wasn't that the ultimate praise to which a warrior could aspire? By virtue of Kenward's tales and her limited contact with the knight's people—most of whom, she'd learned, were spread throughout the Weald and always prepared to answer their lord's call—it was clear he inspired in his own countrymen not fear, but admiration and unquestioning support. Thus, despite or mayhap because of his absence, Cassie felt she'd come to know leastways some small portion of the man behind the reputation, though nothing of his mysterious past. In the privacy of her own healthy imagination she dreamed of knowing him even better—not as her plain self, but amidst the gentle haze of fantasy as the spirited Lady Cassandra who dwelled within.

Almost immediately after introducing her to Kenward, Will had departed. He'd not returned until long after nightfall, and she had retired to her simple pallet. Between that day and this she'd caught naught but rare and distant glimpses of the dark knight, and those won only by awakening early enough to hear him leading his steed from the stable beneath her window. Then, by clamoring atop the chest left conveniently below the portal and unbarring the shutters, she would peer into the half light preceding dawn for a brief view of the departing silhouettes of powerful man and mighty beast.

She knew that every night since her recapture a guard had been posted on the far side of the lean-to stable to prevent another window escape, just as Kenward napped on the floor outside her chamber door until his leader returned. However, believing Willikin disinterested in any action she took, short of a further attempt to flee, she'd no reason to fear any would note a secret watcher. Thus each time she heard the stallion stirring at his master's arrival, she hastened to the window without worry that a report of her deed might be given her captor.

A squeaking hinge interrupted Kenward's soliloquy. Cassie watched the stout woman who entered, carrying a bucket of frothy milk in one hand and a basket of eggs in the other.

"Edna," Cassie carefully began, pleased with her ability to find the proper English words. "Pray might I have a drink of milk?" Extending her hand, she pointed at the bucket as visual aid to soft and likely misordered words.

Edna's brows knit in a slight frown as she stared at the outstretched hand. She was no servant, and was tempted to tell the fine lady, who was plainly accustomed to being waited on, that here in the Weald did she want a thing, then best she fetch if for herself. But beneath her gruff exterior lay a gentle soul and generous nature. Thus, Edna merely shrugged and gave an abrupt nod.

"Aye." Edna had no fondness for excess words and never used more than strictly necessary.

Lacking the least notion of what constant insult her commands were, though phrased as gentle requests, Cassie was proud that she'd succeeded in making herself understood. She assumed the other woman's faint hostility born of the not uncommon resentment of all who served for all who were their masters. That the woman was a servant, Cassie never questioned. Every master, and surely Will was that, had servants. Moreover, while the fruit, cheese, salted meat, and bread of other meals were fetched by Kenward from the larder or cold house half buried in the glade outside, the woman came daily to prepare an evening meal. Though the knight had yet to appear for any, Cassie had shared each with Kenward. When they retired for the night, the remaining food was left to keep warm on the hall's banked fire. Its magical disappearance near every morn lent Cassie further proof that Will actually did return to his home most nights.

Heavy footfalls crossing a rush-strewn floor broke Cassie free from her preoccupation with the ongoing absence of her captor. Accepting the outstretched earthen cup, she steadily met the woman's iron-gray eyes and gave a warm smile and soft thanks.

As she sipped the cool white liquid Cassie remembered the irritation roused by Will's serving her bitter ale and the heated rebuke she'd devised, knowing she'd never have nerve to deliver it in truth.

A heavy metal sheet clunked against the trestle table standing before bake ovens built into the stone wall extending from the massive fireplace. Preparing to mix ingredients for a fresh batch of bread, Edna cast the female captive a considering stare and found the friendly smile still in place. They were strange creatures, Edna decided, these noble-bred ladies. In the distant past she'd once labored in a castle and learned not their language alone but that always did they expect others to do their toil. Yet this one, unlike most, offered sincere smiles and honest thanks for a thing done. Mayhap the younger woman simply knew no way to view the world save through the eyes of privilege? A new thought that, but one which took root and blossomed in a quicker mind than Edna's unwieldly body revealed. 'Twould be a limited view at best but doubtless ever warm and rosy. Must'a been a real shock to ha' found herself trapped amidst the Weald's rough life. A moment of pity stirred for the one caught like a fish out of water, and for the first time Edna returned the younger woman's smile.

Cassie saw the pity in Edna's slate-gray eyes. Although she appreciated the thaw in the brusque woman's manner, the thought of being reduced to the object of a servant's pity emphasized the depth of her plight. She gulped down the milk and rose, dropping the furs into the chair behind.

Her travel trunks had magically appeared in her chamber on the day of her return from the failed escape—the one gleam of pleasure amidst an otherwise bleak day of defeat. It had seemed a gift of sorts from her captor, a surprisingly thoughtful gesture of consolation for her loss at his hands, which enabled her to wear her own clothes. Giving way to an urge to look as well as she could, under the forlorn and quickly repressed hope that Will might return, she had dressed today in a well-fitted cream linen kirtle with a cranberry-red overgown. Though the top garment was sleeveless, 'twas wool and warm as she'd snugly laced the long armholes together. In the norm they hung open, merely loosely fastened from under each arm to the first swell of her hips.

"I'm tired, Kenward, and mean to rest in my chamber." She cast the brief and mumbled excuse over her shoulder as she hurried to the corner stairway.

Kenward exchanged a brief glance with Edna and both shook their heads, bewildered by the maid's odd foibles.

Abovestairs, Cassie found no distraction from troubled thoughts in her chamber's austere confines. Despite her initial certainty of Guy de Faux's unbending vengeance, time and worry shook her confidence. Would either Henri or Guy care enough for her to pay the ransom? Or would they seek to retrieve her by force? Might they both decide she was not worth the price in either coin or blood? *Non!* For the sake of their pride if naught else they would see her set loose. And failing that, once she'd learned the language well enough, she'd find her own path free.

The thought contained surprisingly little comfort. Once released from Will's captivity what was there for her—life with a brutal man she despised? Moreover, she'd never see her new friend Kenward again. *Far worse,* a quiet but persistent whisper insinuated itself into her thoughts, *never again will you see the bold defender of the Weald.*

But then, even here in his own home, she'd seen little enough of Will. 'Twas a fact that left her depressingly certain he couldn't abide the company of his unwanted, unattractive "guest." Where did he spend his days? Did he so hate all things French that he stayed away to avoid her? The possibility, *non*, likelihood, was distressing when with nothing to occupy her active mind in days past—save her worries and learning a new language, his language—she'd spent too much time dreaming of the absent knight. The image of the potent smile once turned on her had never faded, nor had the lingering memory of a dark velvet voice able to stroke as effectively as a caress. An irritated frown creased her smooth forehead. He seemed to have captured not her body alone, but her mind as well. And when she plainly held so little interest for him, it was shameful!

Vexed both with herself for giving in to hurtful ponderings and, illogically, with Will for being their source, the rebellious spirit inside overcame Cassie's natural reticence. She'd defy him in the only way open to her. She'd explore the private haven neither Kenward nor even Edna dared invade. Surely at mid-afternoon it was safe to cross the corridor on quiet feet from her chamber to Will's. Soundlessly cracking open her door, she peeked out, seeking proof Kenward hadn't followed to stand guard just outside as he did each night.

The hallway was empty. Before cowardly fears could erode this likely momentary bravado, Cassie stepped into the corridor and pulled her door softly closed behind. Taking two long steps straight forward, she stood directly in front of the door to Will's private haven. She cautiously pulled its leather thong. The slight clang made by the latch as the iron bolt slid free from its rings seemed unnaturally loud. She paused, breath suspended. From below came the unabated pounding of Edna kneading her bread dough. She was safe.

Cassie pressed her weight against sturdy oak planks and they slid across the floor with remarkable quietness. Lavender eyes blinked in surprise. Caught in amazement, she closed the door without consideration for possible noise and stared about a chamber that was luxurious compared to the austere room where she'd spent the past few nights. Intricately carved chests flanked a real bed—high above the cold floor and blessed with both a feather mattress and blue tapestried drapes to shut out drafts. Moreover, the wall-length fireplace below extended to this level. Although unlit, the hearth was laid with wood doubtless able to provide welcome warmth to the room's occupant when winter storms howled.

Stepping farther into the room, Cassie glanced to the side and gasped. A huge brass bathtub rested tucked away into the corner behind the open door. Its irresistible lure drew her closer. Cloth-padded for comfort, it was large enough to submerge even Will's massive body. The marvelous discovery thrilled Cassie as deeply as if 'twere Soloman's lost treasure. Since her unwilling return from the failed escape, Cassie had managed to perform her daily ablutions with the aid of a simple earthen basin and a pitcher of cold spring water. She'd welcomed even that inadequate and frigid refreshment to wash away the grime of her forest flight, but the prospect of an honest bath drove sensible caution into retreat as effectively as knight's steel against an unarmed foe. She rushed out into the narrow hallway.

"Kenward," she urgently called. "Fetch buckets and buckets of steaming water to the lord's chamber." With such pleasure so near, she'd grieve over the forfeit of each precious moment lost. Asides, she must have done while daylight remained. "Make haste!" Will had yet to return during daylight hours, yet even for the sake of a hot bath, she daren't take this risk after nightfall.

Footfalls rapidly ascending told Cassie of Kenward's upward dash, two steps at a time. When he appeared at the top, she motioned him to join her in the chamber. In direct opposition to his speed of moments past, he hung back. Unwilling to invade his leader's private quarters, he would do no more than peer reluctantly around the corner of the door to learn the source of Cassie's excitement. His eyes widened when at sight of the tub he realized what she meant to do. Had the French maid he'd thought shy gone witless?

"Nay," he vehemently shook his head, wide hazel eyes seemingly mesmerized by the shiny object in question. " 'Twould be unwise." That she meant to bathe in the lord's chamber, the lord's tub proved her either not near so timid as he'd thought or driven beyond rational thought by her captivity. "He might come home."

"Oh, Kenward." Cassie's voice softened into a gently wheedling tone. "You know as well as I that he never returns until we're all abed."

"Kenward's right, milady." Edna puffed laboriously after hauling her considerable girth up the stairway. She moved at a much slower pace but arrived in time to lend her weight to the worried lad's argument. " 'Tis Willikin's tub, and we don't none of us use what's his without his leave." Her words were stern and backed by distress at the mere thought of usurping a pleasure not theirs.

"In my home castle," Cassie desperately argued, "and surely any you know"—a pleading look of melting lavender drifted over Kenward—"to any guest who arrives, we never fail in first offering a bath for refreshment

from their journey's grime. 'Tis only right manners. Surely then . . ."
She stepped forward to clasp her hands about the youngster's forearm,
deeming her powers of persuasion more likely to succeed with him. "If, as
you say, your master was raised in a castle, he would extend the same
courtesy to me." That Will hadn't either the first night he'd brought her
to his home nor the morning he'd returned a mud-encrusted she to this
"prison," Cassie wisely chose not to mention.

The confusion on Kenward's face mirrored the expression on Edna's
and proved they both knew the custom well. In the end it was Edna who
made the decision.

"I'll set the caldron below to boil and he," she announced, motioning
toward the boy, "kin carry pails betwixt that chamber and this when 'tis
ready."

Kenward had seldom entered Will's chamber, and only when invited by
its owner. Now he lit the chamber's fire and struggled to drag the heavy
tub into the open space before it. As he made the first of many trips to
pour the steaming water filling wooden buckets into the brass receptacle,
he wished the fireplace in Will's chamber were equipped with a caldron
for heating bathwater. In the next instant he scoffed at the foolishness of
his own reasoning, when water would still have to be carried up from
below and, whether hot or cold, weighed the same.

Water fresh from the caldron was far too hot for bathing, but the first
would begin to cool before the last arrived, resulting in a bath of near the
perfect temperature. As Kenward continued with his repeated chore, Cassie rooted through chests on either side of the high bed and found two
cloth squares, a small one and one so huge 'twas obviously meant for use as
the towering knight's towel. She laid the smaller over the tub's edge and
spread the larger out to warm before the fire, yet close enough that she
could reach it when ready to rise from a liquid heaven. Also, she fetched
from her chamber a silver-backed brush and egg-shaped ball of sweet-
smelling soap brought from home. Thus prepared for the simple but
greatly anticipated luxury, once the tub was full and the door firmly
closed, she loosed braided hair, disrobed, and stepped into welcoming
water.

Putting the small cloth and her soap to good use, she washed face and
form, then raised a white lather amongst abundant ebony tresses. Forcing
herself to conclude practical tasks before sinking into the soothing warmth
of her bath, she rinsed soap bubbles from her hair and applied the brush
to lay long dark tendrils over the tub's edge. Free now to revel in this
unexpected good fortune, she leaned back, basking in comfort. She was

aware, in the near lost depths of hazy thoughts, of the fierce storm that had begun to roar outside the cheery room.

Below, Kenward silently aided Edna, first in tidying away the utensils employed in baking bread, and next in setting a recently snared rabbit to roast over low-burning coals. Each blamed a heated face and pounding heart on flames too near, striving to deny their actual source—guilt for taking part in a questionable deed by permitting it to happen.

Suddenly the door burst open and a weary Will entered. Tired from long days in the saddle and a skirmish harder fought than most, Will lent the room's occupants little more than a glance and no notice to the fact that one who should be there was not. He doffed his helm and unbuckled his sheathed blade, placing them on the peg beside the door before stripping off his mail hauberk and dropping it below to await the restoring attentions of his squire, Kenward. Longing to reach his chamber's promised rest, he strode toward the stairway. Soaked by the cold rain of an uncommonly heavy storm that had broken while he was still a distance from his home, Will wanted nothing so much as to be dry, warm, and left in solitude. In short, he wished for more than a few moments of peace and quiet. The attainment of which goal was hindered by an uncomfortable Kenward.

"Will—" Kenward's voice cracked on the single word. Maintaining courage enough to stop his idol when the man plainly wanted to be left alone was a difficult task to face. Yet he'd no choice. The evidence of a transgression was near and decidedly unavoidable, although he'd no notion how to tell Will what he must.

Holding his patience with difficulty, Will reluctantly turned, one foot on the bottom step. "What is it?" The question was harsher than intended, and Will silently berated himself for punishing an innocent boy for the difficulties of his day.

" 'Tis Cassie—" Again Kenward hesitated while Will's dark brows drew into a fierce scowl.

At the name Will realized that she was missing. "Where is she?" he demanded with a roughness now unmourned. Had she dared flee from him again? Had she charmed the vulnerable Kenward into allowing her escape?

In eyes gone as black and cold as obsidian, Kenward saw his leader's thoughts all too clearly. His answer was immediate and instinctive. "In your chamber."

"*My* chamber?" The news shocked Will as few things could, and his brows rose so high they near joined the dark lock of hair fallen forward on his brow. Not waiting for an explanation from the embarrassed boy, he turned and climbed the stairs with uncompromising intent.

Lazing in blissful ease, time slipped into the past unnoticed by Cassie. The cadence of rain pounding on the roof lent a hypnotic trance occasionally punctuated by the rumble of thunder. Thus, when the door quietly opened then shut with a thud, to Cassie, lost in the limited awareness of half sleep, it seemed but a further demonstration of the storm's fury and too unimportant to rouse her from the bath's pleasurable lethargy.

Broad shoulders resting on the closed door behind, Will took in the view. Her back to him, he saw only the ebony cascade of long, silky hair flowing like a dark river over the bright edge of his tub. 'Twas temptation enough. He'd dreamed about wrapping that lush cloud of black silk about his wrist and pillowing her on it while he laid her down. Aye, here was a temptation the likes of which he'd been fighting in his day fantasies and night visions since he'd first seen her. It must come to a halt!

"You've decided to claim my hospitality full well, I gather." That threat should send the timid rabbit scurrying from the wolf's path.

At the utterly unexpected sound of a mocking laugh too well-remembered, Cassie sat bolt upright. She looked over her shoulder to the advent she'd feared yet perversely anticipated. But not here! Not now! Black eyes, flashing gold, narrowed on the creamy satin of her bare back, a portion of her anatomy no male save husband should view.

Cassie abruptly sank below the rim of the tub. Rolling to her stomach, sending cooling water sloshing to the floor, she peeked over the edge at the man lounging against the door as if intending to stay. His wry smile proved he was enjoying her discomfort. As if 'twere a lifeline tossed to one drowning, she grasped the indignation floating in the sea of her embarrassment and reached over the edge to snatch up the huge, fire-warmed towel. She attempted to wrap herself modestly within its folds as she rose to step from the tub with the idea that to do so would reduce her vulnerability. It didn't.

Too aware of the blush emphasizing her exquisite complexion and glimpses of fire light gleaming on the water cascading down silken limbs, Will shouldered away from the door. Never in his life had he wasted time in dreams of a woman's company. So how was it that he found this particular female so enticing when others far more beautiful had failed to capture his interest for more than a few hours of pleasure? Or was that the secret of her allure? The fact that she—as his *French* hostage, his *noble-born* foe—was forbidden him?

The closing distance between them was so disturbing, Cassie could feel the too rapid beating of her heart and nervously backed away until her legs bumped against the edge of the large, draped bed.

With the potent, knowing smile he wielded so efficiently, Will taunted, "I give you my gratitude for delivering yourself all clean and sweet-smelling to my chamber—and near into my bed."

Pausing beside the abandoned tub, he stripped off the brown homespun of such a tunic as was ever worn 'neath mail, ruffling hair even darker for its rain-dampness. His eyes held hers in an unbreakable bond as he lifted the small cloth she'd used and left laying over the edge of the tub. Dipping it again into the bath, then wringing excess moisture out, he rinsed his own face, neck, and the broad planes of his bare chest.

Cassie was stunned by this first view of a nude male torso—magnificent and frightening with its impressive display of power in muscles that rippled under the wedge of dark hair running down to where chausses were tied at narrow hips. In wide violet eyes apprehension warred with helpless appreciation and lost. He was big and dark, all blatant masculinity, and frankly threatening.

Crooked smile deepening, Will watched the fascination mingled with fear in her widened eyes, the former inevitably overwhelming the latter. He dropped the cloth into the water and moved straight toward her with a new kind of slowness, a sensual grace that made Cassie's heart stop then skip wildly.

As he came inexorably nearer, Cassie was aware of every step he took. Trapped between the bed behind and the dangerous man towering a mere whisper away, her knees threatened to buckle and truly lay her in his bed. Her lashes fell, placing a pitifully weak shield between her and approaching peril.

Telling himself he meant only to frighten the maid into wiser behavior, Will reached out and steadily drew Cassie against his powerful form, easily quelling her token struggle. With the memory of her stunned reaction to a mere smile, he had wondered for days what response a little light seduction would win, and now meant to know the answer.

In defense Cassie laid her hands, palm flat, against his chest. Though intending to hold him back, the feel of iron thews under cool satin skin instantly proved the folly of her action. Her fingers instead closed into tight balls against the unbidden excitement discovered in this touch forbidden a virtuous maiden. Pulled nearer to the overwhelming man with a gentleness she feared more dangerous than force, unexpected pleasure trembled over her while his lips brushed hers once, twice, and once again.

Will continued to brush across soft lips until they went pliant beneath his. As he tasted their berry sweetness a tiny whimper came from her throat, and he deepened the kiss with a warm assault that quickly parted her lips, allowing him to search within.

Responding with a reckless passion she'd never known existed, Cassie sank headlong into a blaze of sensations and instinctively melded closer still to their source. As if seeking an anchor in the midst of the flood, she opened her hands and ran them up over muscled planes to twine her fingers into the cool black strands of his hair. She felt herself tilting, but the shifting of her world seemed merely an extension of the spinning vortex into which she'd been drawn.

Will laid the receptive beauty down across the dark fur covering his bed and hovered above, gazing into alluring violet mists. With devastating certainty he knew the inexperienced maid was his—yet a temptation to which he could nowise yield without costing them both their honor and his king the price of her ransom. But even with that daunting fact acknowledged, he near surrendered to her innocent wiles.

The intensity in eyes blacker than midnight pulled Cassie ever deeper into the depths of a liquid fire doubtless dangerous but beyond her experience or wish to escape. Rational thought lost in the deluge of new hungers and yearning toward an end unfamiliar, yet one to which she was certain he could lead her, she arched toward him and tightened her arms in an attempt to draw him down.

Only knowing he'd driven her beyond rational consideration of the price to be paid for the action she courted gave Will strength to refuse the imploring arms and trembling lips silently pleading for his return. He pulled back and, too aware of his unaccustomed vulnerability and the strain put upon good intentions by enticing glimpses of sweet flesh amidst the bath sheet's disarranged folds, set out to reinforce the wall betwixt himself and her.

"Are you so bored without all the French court's fine young swains to vie for your charms that you think to tempt me into playing the gallant for you?"

His words dropped like shards of ice into the waves of blazing sensations buffeting Cassie about like worthless driftwood. Struggling to the surface of desire's deep waters, she blinked rapidly against the dizzying sight of golden sparks glittering in the dark gaze above.

"Pray excuse me from that duty." Will rose and continued with words she was too disoriented to fully comprehend. "At present I'm far too weary to oblige." The huskiness of his voice alone would have revealed the untruth of his words to a more experienced partner. Aye, her naivety proved her guiltless—innocence further demonstrated by the fact that she failed to recognize the physical evidence of his lie. He was, at the moment, hardly incapable.

In the growing chill of his withdrawal, Cassie had an unpleasant return to rational thought when came recognition of the accusation in dark eyes studying her. Mortified by her own response, she curled into a tight ball as if to hide from his all-seeing gaze.

Will was irrationally vexed to see that by his disdainful action the maiden was now clearly shamed by their shared passion. With a rough tenderness more irritating still, he lifted and carried her across the corridor to her own chamber. He lowered her to the prickly pallet and tugged the huge bath sheet to more modestly cover her tempting curves. Since leaving childhood behind, his goals and emotions he'd held clear and steady in his mind, and he didn't like finding his normally unruffled responses constantly at odds. He was slowly being forced to recognize a purgatory all his own: although he wanted the French damoiselle, even were she English, he—a knight of the bend sinister—could never have her.

He paused at the door of her chamber, self-disgust hardening his handsome face into a mask of cool cynicism. "Damoiselle, you can avail yourself of the comforts of my bed anytime you choose to *truly* share its warmth with me." He'd no doubt the offer would keep her as far from him as her captivity allowed. "Elsewise, stay in your own chamber and out of my path!"

"Hah!" Cassie's reaction was so immediate her natural reticence had no chance to muffle the words. Horrified by her response to him, particularly when his actions had so clearly been intended as punishment and he'd shared none of the fiery enchantment in which he'd near drowned her, she made a fast retort. "The icy North Sea will boil first!"

On the one hand fervently hoping it would be so, and on the other utterly regretting the need for that truth, Will merely laughed with cold cynicism as he departed. Aye, he told himself again, that should keep the tempting innocent so ill-suited to his world far from his chamber, far from him—and protect his peace of mind.

Why then did the victory leave a hollow sense of loss?

Chapter

❧ 5 ❧

CASSIE HESITATED ON the stairway. Hoping to avoid a shaming confrontation with her devastating captor, she'd not left her chamber since he'd deposited her within the past eventide. That it had been a hope doomed to disappointment was clear now when, for the first time since she'd become captive in this house, its master sat at the table for the morning meal. An all too vivid memory of the previous night's events and her wild retort at its end washed bright rose embarrassment across her cheeks.

She badly wanted to slip away and hide again in the privacy of her chamber. Yet because such a cowardly action would be an obvious betrayal of how deeply she'd been shaken, and because it would negate the small spark of confidence earned by her rare flare of temper, she must play the Lady Cassandra of her fantasies and boldly join him. Striving to cool heated color and arrange her expression into lines of detachment, she paused for long moments.

"Come," Will called to the timid maid hovering like some shy forest creature suddenly scenting the danger of a predator and uncertain which way to flee. A one-sided smile deepened the crease in his cheek. The tender rabbit again, and he the wolf? The metaphor amused him, particularly after the events of only hours past when surely by his actions he'd proven himself harmless. Nay, harmless only did she stay out of his path as he'd warned. Most like that warning was the source of her present wariness.

"Hasten with your meal." The command, despite its underlaying thread of wry laughter, brooked no argument. "You've a task to perform once you've done."

Cassie was not brave enough to refuse. Will's silent amusement quelled any hope for her planned detachment, but still she was determined not to look as self-conscious as she was and bravely lifted her chin. Moreover, the last thing she meant to do was ask, as doubtless he expected, what task he intended she perform.

Beneath a dark, penetrating gaze she feared would delve deep into her soul and bare all the painful inadequacies desperately hidden within, she hastily took the only free chair at the table with an awkwardness that intensified her discomfort. Though some distance from Will, Cassie felt engulfed by his strong presence. Certain any bite she put into her mouth would choke her, she watched in dismay as Kenward rose to fetch a disgustingly full platter for her.

Desperate for distraction, she carefully examined each offering—fruit, cheese, and dark bread. Here lay the same choices as every morn and near every noon, with the occasional addition of a thick meat paste spread atop the bread or a slab of salt-preserved roast. Feeling the continuing weight of dark eyes and determined to turn aside the nervous tension it brought, her brows creased as she concentrated on the new realization of how limited was the diet of people less than nobility. *Non*, not all of lower station. Those serving in castles, leastwise those she knew, shared the remnants of their masters' rather more varied meals.

Every bit as aware of him as before, Cassie admitted the total failure of her attempted diversion and glared at the food untouched on her platter. She'd no appetite, but neither did she wish to lend her "host" further reason to find fault. Breaking a crust free, careful to prevent the escape of more than a minimum of crumbs, she nibbled at its rough texture.

Will studied his feminine table companion through dark eyes half hidden by lowered lids. The unusually quiet Kenward had been singing her praises since the end of their first day together. And Will had no justified reason to find fault—that was the source of his problem. Meticulous, genteel in all that she did, her every small action was further proof of her right place in the world and, he reminded himself yet again—as if he were like to forget—his humble abode was not it! Best he see her gone without delay. This undeniable need was amazingly distasteful, and when he spoke, made his tone rougher than intended.

"If you mean to consume no more than that"—he waved contemptuously at bread and cheese mangled but barely sampled—"then let's be about the business at hand—your apology to Edna."

Blinking in confusion, Cassie looked up. Apologize to Edna?

"You owe her, a free woman, respect." He shook his dark head slowly. She plainly had no notion of her transgression, and at the repeated fluttering of thick lashes—a sign of discomfort with which he'd become all too familiar—he wanted to soothe her unease. This exception to his famed ability to control his response to any female roused both a deep self-disgust and irritation that the one exception should be this French virgin. All humor died out of Will's once amused smile, leaving cool mockery in its wake. "Yet you've treated her as naught but a servant when she is capable of doing so much more than ever you could."

Startled by his sudden attack, Cassie's mouth fell open.

"What use are you?" Unexpected even to their speaker, the words had a honed dagger's sharp edge. "Do you cook, spin, work the garden, keep house—or merely order others to do your bidding?" Will was instantly irritated with himself for assailing the maid for being what a cosseted creature could not help but be. His broad chest expanded as he drew a deep breath and strived for a measure of cool objectivity.

Cassie was accustomed to having her brothers find her appearance wanting, to being a disappointment to her parents in near all matters, but never had anyone suggested her inadequate for failing to possess such menial accomplishments.

For the first time in a very long while Will failed to control the direction his tongue took. "Apparently you believe to be decorative is your sole purpose in life." As the words left his mouth Will recognized them as an instinctive defense against this maid who'd crossed the barrier shielding him from the opinions of all but a chosen few. At the same time, by taking out on her his long-buried disgust with such females, he was forced to acknowledge how deep was her incursion beyond a wall of cynicism built over a good many years. 'Twas a dangerous admission and one that hardened his determination to see her gone as hastily as possible.

The disdain in his words seemed proof that he found her unequal to such an endeavor. Cassie shrank back. This unanticipated assault on an area of tender sensitivities left her wishing she could sink to the floor and evaporate like rain against fire. Yestereve he'd seen her as no man ever had, and this succinct dismissal of her appearance was crushing.

He'd been alone in the Weald too long, Will told himself in an attempt to justify his inexcusable attack, nay, even more to explain his preoccupation with the maid. However, the honesty he'd been raised to hold above all else rejected his feeble attempt when only recently he'd returned from a victorious celebration at Castle Dungeld where willing female company had been plentiful.

Rising abruptly, Will bumped the table, and the untasted spring water in Cassie's cup sloshed over to dribble from table edge into her lap. She quickly stood, brushing droplets away before the sky-blue wool of her gown absorbed their moisture. When he motioned her toward the outgoing door, she went without argument. Although never her intent, she'd apparently insulted Edna. That Will meant her to pay penance for the deed was only just. How could she fight against him on this when she'd obeyed his command in thanking Odo? There was little difference between the two. Now, as then, she truly owed the required action and had no just cause to refuse.

Unnoticed by the two departing, a shamefaced Kenward remained alone at table. Doubtless 'twas his unthinking chatter with Will that had led the knight to believe this ill of the damsel Kenward sought as a friend. It was his fault she'd been blamed for actions that neither he nor, he was certain, Edna wished Cassie to suffer.

Pausing one step beyond the outgoing door, Cassie refused to look down at ground surely still layered with mud and dirty puddles. Although she'd no notion where Edna and her Harvey resided, she boldly set off toward the wretched clearing's center, anxious for Will to never again see her hesitate over details so trivial.

Surprised by her unflinching progress, still Will caught up with her in two strides and pointed out the humble cottage of their destination. Not waiting for him to act firstly, Cassie stepped to the door and firmly rapped on its weather-worn planks while mentally searching for appropriate English terms to accomplish the task he'd commanded.

Although Edna understood the language of their foes, Will had intended to teach his captive the English words for seeking forgiveness while they crossed to the cottage, but Cassie moved too quickly. Before he could begin, Edna opened the door. The woman's considerable girth filled the portal but fell back when in amazement she saw who her unexpected visitors were.

"I sorrow for my—" Cassie immediately began, stumbling over the few words in her limited English vocabulary, seeking just the right one. With a bright smile she produced the best she'd found. ". . . hurt of you."

Again Will was surprised. The words were not precise, but their meaning plain enough. "You know our language, then?" But how could she when, if she had, she might well have escaped him that first night? Likely 'twas her purpose now, and yet—

"Kenward's taught her," Edna announced, stepping forward and lifting her stern chin as proudly as if it were she who'd done the deed.

"I congratulate you." Will was impressed that Cassie had put forth the effort to learn even this small portion of her foe's foreign tongue, no matter the intended purpose. He gave her another of his rare, soul-melting smiles. "It takes a quick mind to learn another's language so rapidly."

The sincerity in quiet words and the warmth of a smile that glowed gold in dark eyes sent a wave of pleasure over Cassie. Yet knowing the purpose behind her feat was hardly pure, a guilty blush burned.

Will saw the rose tint in cheeks he knew were as soft as the rose petals they resembled. But as already this day he'd been overly rough on her, he chose to accept the blush as her response to the pleasure of his compliment.

Glancing up, he saw the benign smile Edna settled on the maid. Clearly Cassie had won even this suspicious woman's approval. What was it about the timid creature that so easily won all whose path she crossed? Was it that she, like a newborn creature of the wild, helpless in infancy, oft called forth even a hunter's protective instincts? His cynical side rose to ridicule the thought and warn that when full grown even a fluffy white rabbit might prove to possess the instincts and fangs of a rabid dog.

He was about to speak again when the faint pounding of approaching hooves sundered the glade's peace. Will whirled, dark eyes narrowing on the dense shadows formed by thick-grown trees. Men dispatched to ride patrol wouldn't return for hours and, for safety's sake, few others knew the location of his base.

Steel sang as Will pulled free the sword ever strapped to his waist. He thrust Cassie directly behind his broad back, putting his body between the women and the forest border from whence unheralded visitors would appear.

With Edna's massive form at the rear, Cassie apprehensively peeked around the formidable barrier of Will's battle-tense form in front. Three horses bearing two women with a young male escort broke through the woodland's autumn-toned wall. Her knight-protector's tension eased, but only to a lesser degree. That Will sheathed his sword as the group rode into the center of the clearing told her it was not they who were the threat. The older female, comfortably wide and surely approaching two-score years, immediately launched into a litany of English so rapid Cassie had no hope of following its meaning.

"Will, thank the Good Lord you're here!" As if she'd run the whole distance herself, Meg heaved a deep sigh but immediately continued. "There's been evil done at Forest Edge Farm, and I'd no choice but to bring Beata to you for protection." Though deeply upset, she instinctively spoke in the English tongue Will insisted be used in the Weald so the good Englishmen under his command and fighting the French would have no fear of betrayal.

Brows drawn, Will strode forward to lift his foster sister down even as, in distress, she began a tale muddled by equal parts of haste and distress.

"On our way here to visit Kenward, as always we do, Tom and I stopped at Beata's cottage. There weren't nothing left but a burnt shell."

In Meg's anguished face Will saw shadows of the horrified incomprehension induced by the discovery. Then quickly he glanced from Meg's misery to her delicate sister and found a sweet smile on a face unnaturally peaceful despite blackened eye and bruised jaw.

"We found her hiding in the forest." After pressing a much abused piece of cloth to eyes dribbling tears, Meg pulled herself together and continued the woeful account. "We looked for Beata's Johnny and found his dead body, a dagger wound in the heart, thrown atop the woodpile and certain sure meant to burn as well."

Will looked again from the sobbing Meg to Johnny's abnormally calm wife. Beata, sitting serenely atop her palfrey, seemed to comprehend no word spoken by her sister, to feel none of the pain her ravaged appearance revealed.

"She don't remember the attack, don't remember Johnny at all. Nothing reaches her except if one tries to free her of the cloak she was wearing when we found her, the cloak she's wearing still. Only does she talk like she were a child again at Castle Tarrant." This admission brought a renewed bout of tears, and Will wrapped his strong arms about the grieving woman, offering what limited comfort was his to give. Once Meg had herself again under control, he moved toward the smaller woman yet ahorse.

"Will?" Beata asked, anticipation in the soft voice of a child. "Are you going to the Chedsham Fair, too?"

Will grimly smiled into eyes unshadowed by the doubtless horrifying experience she'd endured. What wicked quirk of fate had allowed this evil to fall upon one least able to deal with its effects? Beata's spirit was as delicate as her slender form and even more unlikely to survive heedless violence alone. Was her need for the protection of others why she had somehow blocked the pathway of her memory at the day—near a score of years past—when not alone, but protected by Earl Garrick and accompanied by her brother, sister, and Will, she had first entered the Weald? They had been on their way to the Chedsham Fair. That Beata had retreated to those safe days made the secret ordeal she'd locked away in the dark caverns of her mind all the more poignantly real.

Strong hands curled into impotent fists, Will silently swore whoever had done this to Beata would pay with his life for the deed. He would see it so. He—not young Will of Tarrant, but the implacable knight who struck terror into the hearts of French invaders. He would see to it if it took his last breath!

"We had to bring her here, you ken?" Meg needlessly pleaded for understanding though she knew 'twas a thing their Will had never nor ever would fail to give those he loved. "Castle Tarrant is days distant and too far to take her as she is. Asides, Lady Nessa's health mightn't survive the blow."

"A right choice, Meg." Will clamped his anger under the iron restraints of his control and met hazel eyes with a steady reassurance in his black gaze that calmed her distress. "Though while I was at Castle Dungeld but a month and little more past, Garrick told me Nessa was recovering well from the sickness which claimed so many."

"Aye, praise God, that she is, but I don't like to risk her progress when there's no potion she can prepare to heal Beata's wounded spirit, and only time will heal the bruises. Moreover, I fear another hostile confrontation might wreak further damage upon Beata!"

Cassandra had taken only a step or two toward the newcomers. Still, she was near enough to hear the visitor's words and, although they tumbled out far too fast for her to understand more than a few, she picked up enough to know that the talk concerned both an attack and a death. Will's ever grimmer expression made it clear these events were serious indeed.

For all that, it represented no more than an impersonal subject to Cassie until, when Will lifted the smaller woman from her saddle, she noticed the cloak wrapped about the fragile figure. 'Twas a man's cloak, and one bearing the De Faux coat of arms! It could belong to any member of the De Faux contingent, she comforted herself. Except . . . 'twas fashioned from a very fine cloth which made it near certainly that of either Guy or one of his two adult nephews, Vauderie or Valnoir.

Kenward appeared with a welcoming whoop abruptly silenced by the quick action of the young man newly arrived. As the two fell into conversation, Cassie realized from their likeness in coloring and features that they must be brothers. Kenward went solemn in response to the quiet words of the older one, who appeared to be near her own age. While she watched, he suddenly turned and smiled tentatively at her. Embarrassed to be caught staring, she blushed and looked away until they slipped into the cottage where Kenward slept when not occupying the hallway outside her chamber door.

Cassie looked back to Will. As he cradled the battered visitor closer, his grim expression softened. On first sight she'd recognized this woman, despite the discoloration of her delicate face, as the epitome of the ethereal grace and beauty lauded by her brothers. Cassie trailed behind when Will turned to carry the beauty into his house. Eyes gone to lavender fog, she watched as he took his dainty burden not only into his house, but up to his chamber and, once there, surely his bed!

It hurt, the memory of how he had lifted her from that same bed only to deposit her plainly unwanted and hardly willow-wisp form in another chamber like so much refuse. She stared down at herself with distaste, uncomfortably conscious of how deeply she suffered by comparison with the fragile creature he carried with tender ease. No need to treat her with the gentleness given the other—a fact he clearly knew, for he had deposited her on the straw mattress in her cold chamber with little of the care he'd shown the new arrival—as if she were precious, a being beloved.

'Twould be just as well if Will cared for another, Cassie vehemently assured herself, trying to ignore the hollow emptiness left by the possibility, *non*, probability. Standing alone at the bottom of the stairway, she gazed disconsolately up into the gloom at the top, wishing the deep shadows would swoop down and swallow her up. Will loved the beauty! The hurt turned to a pain that filled the void in her heart.

They were enemies by birth and heritage, Cassie berated herself. A kiss or even more could never change that certain truth. She leaned back against the unyielding wall and struggled to scrape her defenses together. The presence of these newcomers merely meant he'd leave her in peace. Yet, rather than rendering solace, the thought deepened the ache.

An uncounted time later heavy footsteps from above broke her blind absorption with rushes strewn across the hard-packed floor.

"Kenward!" Will called from the top step for the lad's attention. "Take this to Harry."

Roused from her stupor, Cassie was surprised to discover two seated by the fire. She hadn't heard the brothers come in. Kenward jumped to his feet and hurried toward the stairway.

"What is it?" Kenward asked his grim leader as he brushed past a nerve-frozen Cassie with a quick smile.

"A sketch of the emblem on the cloak Beata wears." Will had no need to glance at the pattern. The image of a griffin with a snake in its toils was already emblazoned in his mind. He'd seen it before on one of the many standards raised by the invading French, and only wished he knew to precisely which foreign nobleman it and the rich cloak belonged.

"She won't take the fool thing off no matter what anyone says." Tom offered this bit of information. Unwilling to be left on the fringe of important events he, too, approached the knight descending another step to lay the scrap of parchment in Kenward's outstretched hand. Somehow his quiet little brother had won the right to remain in a famous warrior's military camp while he, near a knight, was left to while his days away on quiet Tarrant lands. It wasn't fair, and although he loved Kenward, love did not rule out envy.

Will nodded with wry recognition of the ever sociable older brother's need to be always at or near the center of any event and whose presence inevitably drove the younger into silent shadows. His attention then returned to Kenward as he continued his directions.

"Tell Harry to choose another to accompany him and next set out for Offcum to ask thereabouts if any recognize the emblem or know who its black-hearted owners are." With the words came his unspoken promise of an immediate first step taken in wreaking the vengeance he'd sworn to exact for the evil done. Black eyes were an impenetrable wall of ice.

Kenward glanced briefly at the drawing of a heraldic device he'd never before seen, then hastened from the house to fulfill his lord's command.

Though momentarily puzzled that they'd spoken French, apprehension for the purpose of the journey Will ordered drove all other thoughts from Cassie's mind. She feared he would discover the source of the cloak, the source of his love's harm, and learn it connected to her in even the unsought manner of a betrothal she abhorred.

The sight of his captive near clutching the wall for strength caught Will's attention. Instantly he wished he'd reminded the boys to speak the English he demanded be used in the Weald. Although Cassie had begun to learn his tongue, 'twould assuredly be difficult for her to follow a conversation. Had she understood enough of his earlier talk with Meg to know danger threatened? Of course she knew, even without understanding those words. She was here, and not as a welcome guest.

"Think you the drawing will lead us to Beata's attackers?" Tom's question called the man from matters of surely small import.

Will glanced toward the speaker and lifted his hands palm up in a peculiarly vulnerable gesture. "I don't know. 'Tis but one of many steps to be taken, and I *will* find the wretched toads responsible for this wickedness."

That and no more would he say. Tom was impetuous and too oft talked indiscreetly. Thus, his intention to send men to camp in the forest near the burned cottage he meant to hold secret even from this undeniable friend. Aye, he would dispatch men to the area about Beata's destroyed cottage on the chance her attackers might return. It was not uncommon for invaders long in a strange land to take pretty hostages to their camps as servants—of one sort or another. Beata had been fortunate in initially winning free, and Will wished he knew how she'd managed that doubtless difficult feat. Yet knowing her husband was dead, and anticipating an easy capture, might they not return to complete the deed?

Chapter

❦ 6 ❧

"SEEMS YOU LEARNED LITTLE from yesterday's exercise in seeking pardon." A voice deep as thunder in the distance broke the mid-morning silence of Cassie's chamber.

Whirling at the unexpected sound, the thread of amusement running through the words was lost on Cassie. Her startled reaction was dangerous for one precariously perched atop a chest ever waiting 'neath the window. A tide of rose swept from throat to cheeks. Although the sky was filled with sunlight weakened by the aging of a year huddling betwixt autumn and winter, she had heard the stallion stirring in the stable below and had hurried to catch a glimpse of his master—the man now standing uncomfortably near. She'd been caught and again, as too oft before, wanted to fade away like mists under the heat of day.

In the silhouette of the damsel's alluring curves, outlined by light falling from the open window, Will saw confirmation of a curious report. Unwilling to either add more problems without answer to his present burdens or face the possible forging of additional links in a chain of forbidden attraction, he'd chosen never to glance up during daily leave-takings. Yet, plainly she did watch his departures. For what purpose? Her obvious fascination with him—in honest interest or as prey are sometimes fear-charmed into immobility by their predators? Or did she seek such information for aid in planning escape now that she knew the language of the Weald? The fact that both possibilities were equally dangerous proved unequal to the chore of dampening his pleasure with the first.

His stunningly white smile was sardonic as he moved forward to sweep the maid safely from her unsteady perch. A fortunate action from Cassie's point of view as his smile's power had stolen strength from her limbs and she'd likely have fallen without his aid. Nonetheless, once her feet were on solid ground, she nervously pulled away. Why must she ever look a skittery fool when he was near? *Mayhap*, a silent voice mocked, *because in truth that's what you are.*

"Who now have I offended?" The question aimed as a sharp retort went far astray from its target and came out little better than a whimper. Leastways self-disgust over the missed goal lit amethyst flames in her eyes.

"I've no servants." Behind quiet words Will hid his amusement with the plainly irritated damoiselle. He had a talent, it seemed, for rousing a temper he'd wager seldom loosed. "By idling here you force Meg to work on your behalf." The powerful smile returned as he finished. "If you wish to eat, then best you do your part in preparing the meal."

Cassie blinked rapidly. Prepare a meal? How? Remembering too well his statement that she was incapable of proving herself useful, as mere decoration least of all, these were not questions she dared ask. Nor were they the reason she'd not left the chamber since fleeing there the day past.

Will watched the revealing flutter of dark lashes and wondered at the strange expression on the tender maid's sweetly rounded face as, giving him wide berth, she moved toward the doorway he'd left open.

Too aware of the big man following close behind, Cassie lifted the skirt of her favorite cranberry-red gown and descended the stairs with as much grace as she could manage. She entered the hall below and went straight to a matronly figure ladling butter over the spitted pheasant slowly roasting above a low-burning fire.

"Pray pardon, milady," she said in halting English. "I thought I was a prisoner confined to my chamber." It had seemed a proper assumption that she, a captive foe, would not be welcome to join the company of his guests. Moreover, that Kenward, rather than summoning her to Will's table, had delivered each meal since, seemed proof her supposition was correct. She cast Will a sidelong glance tinged with censure for his unjust accusation of slothfulness. 'Twas a convenient shield for her retreat's second purpose—staying far from his path.

When Cassie had failed to appear for recent meals, Will had sent food to her chamber as an honorable gesture of concern, but had grown impatient with her continuing expectation of such indulgences. Vexed, he'd gone to her intending to assure she knew better than to presume she'd receive the coddling a noble-born female might demand in her own home but not as a captive here in the Weald. Thus, he and his pretty hostage had once again misunderstood each other.

Despite the confusion in reasoning, Will found himself more entertained than irritated by the shy rabbit boldly standing against him with the intention of proving him wrong. There were few, even among his own men, who possessed courage enough to attempt such a deed.

"*All* of our visitors speak your language as well as do you." Like a peace offering he quietly gave the information, pointedly ignoring the surprised glance of the older woman who he'd cautioned never to speak the French of castle life here.

Having no notion of the brave nature in an action instinctively taken— elsewise likely she'd never have attempted it—with a solemn nod Cassie instantly returned her attention to the busy woman who'd set aside her ladle to watch the peculiar exchange.

"I would willingly aid your duties," Cassie said with an apologetic smile. "Yet although I've been taught to order food for an army or organize great feasts fit for a king, I've no notion how to prepare a single dish." Looking appropriately embarrassed by her lack, she continued, "Still, if you'll tell me what to do, I'd be pleased to help."

The older woman grinned. "Bless me. I'm not a lady born, only the cook in the fine castle of Tarrant. Yet your help with this stew I would appreciate." She bent to lift a small pile of leeks from a basket on the floor and lay them atop the wooden table bereft of cloth and bared for work. "Take the knife and one of these"—she selected a long stalk with succulent leaves, demonstrating as she spoke—"cut the green top thusly and thence the bottom."

Feeling the weight of a steady black gaze resting on her back, and discomfited by it, Cassie readily accepted the extended knife. She set to work, putting all her nervous energies into vigorously slicing the innocent tubers.

After pushing loaves of bread earlier readied into a bake oven built into one side of the fireplace wall, Meg noted both the state of the leeks and the state of the maid. She knew who was responsible for both, and cast Will a speaking glance.

Will watched the well-bred damsel gallantly strive to fill the role of a simple kitchen serf and felt guilty for forcing her to menial chores. He was irritated once by the mere possibility of a wrong in expecting anyone to earn their own way—even Nessa, a true lady, never thought herself above such tasks—and once again by Meg's reaction.

He briskly announced, "I've been summoned to attend a council of young Henry's war leaders and must be gone for the next several days." Though he'd not say it aloud, it was through contacts there that the ransom demand for his hostage would be sent.

"But, Will, we've only just arrived." Meg turned from her view of the soot-blackened fireplace's interior and the succulent aroma of her task to take two steps toward her foster brother, disappointment clouding her eyes.

Will, too, was unhappy with the abruptness of his announcement, and yet it was a fact unavoidable. "I am sorry, Meg, but always my first obligation is to my liege lord." He reached out to lightly wrap his fingers about her upper arms. "I can only pray you to remain until I return—by week's end if all goes well."

Meg tangled her hands in the length of cloth wrapped about her waist and nodded in woeful acknowledgment of his proper priorities. "For a fortnight leastways we'll be here."

After one lingering look at the ebony-haired damoiselle—justified as a rightful demonstration to Meg that he'd do as he chose—Will gently squeezed the woman in his hold and turned to stride from his home and the women in his charge. Specifically the one woman who threatened to disrupt his well-ordered life.

At the news of his absence a wave of loss swept over Cassie. 'Twas a reaction she refused to acknowledge, and blamed the dampness in her eyes on the tubers' pungent odor.

Not until long after the door had closed behind Will did Cassie realize a third woman had come to stand nearby. 'Twas the fragile creature Will had carried to his bed the past day. A woman he clearly did not expect to do her part in preparing the meal. Plainly, then, she meant something to him which a larger Cassie did not and never could. To forestall further tears, and deriding herself for allowing such useless self-pity, Cassie sliced the last of the leeks with an even fiercer fervor before dumping them into the waiting bucket of cold spring water.

A small hand tentatively touched her arm, as if fearing to be slapped away. Startled by the notion anyone could find her frightening when 'twas ever she who cringed 'neath the attention of others, Cassie looked down at delicate fingers so light they felt like the brush of thistledown. Thistles had thorns, too. Did she?

"I've never seen lavender eyes afore." As a quiet voice spoke these whimsical words, Cassie looked into the innocent expression of a child on the battered face of the very pretty woman wrapped still in the cloak of De Faux. "Purple is the color of royalty." Her logic was that of a child as well. "In truth, you must be a faerie queen."

"Beata," the older sister gently cautioned. "Don't be for putting yourself in the lady's way."

Cassie felt the frail figure standing near go tense with anxiety, and immediately met Meg's vaguely apologetic look with a quick, sharp shake of her head. Then she gave a warm smile to the one who looked nearer to faerie form than ever she would. How had this fey woman come to such a strange conclusion?

"Beata's not in my way," Cassie softly assured the worried sister. "And she's welcome to stay by my side as long as she likes." 'Twas a new experience for Cassie to be the person offering support to another more timid. Plainly the bruises on the other's face were not the only injuries she'd sustained.

While Meg gave Cassie a beaming smile of gratitude for her understanding, Beata happily settled on a small, three-legged stool she drew near to her new friend.

"I'm Cassie . . ." The speaker carefully laid her sharp knife aside and turned to meet an unblinking gaze more gold than brown.

"I know." Beata slowly nodded, sending a ripple through honey-brown hair streaked with blond. "You are Cassandra."

The words were said in such a flat, matter-of-fact tone that they startled their recipient, whose brows momentarily knit. "*Oui*, Cassandra I am. But everyone who knows me uses the name Cassie, and I hope you will, too." She had the odd feeling those strangely perceptive eyes could read her soul.

A slight frown creased Beata's smooth forehead, but she nodded her obedience to the other's wishes.

"Are you going to play me?" Tom's teasing voice taunted Cassie in hopes of rousing her competitive instincts. "Or do you fear I'll beat you yet again?" The verbal dare was tossed over the pitiful remains of the evening meal yet spread atop the table of gathered friends.

"Hah!" Cassie laughed, tilting her chin and tossing over one shoulder the thick ebony braid she'd recently discovered the comfort of leaving to fall free. "You won because you failed to teach me all the rules until 'twas too late. Had it not been for your brother's honesty, I'd never have known." She rewarded "honest" Kenward with a brilliant smile.

"So, are you game to try besting me now that you've no excuse for losing?" Tom grinned at the gentle young woman, all soft curves, honey-sweet smile, and eyes the lavender haze of dawn's promise. He thought Cassie the prettiest maid he'd ever seen, even clad in one of the two homespun dresses for which she'd bartered a velvet gown with his mother. And, although mayhap 'twas not a right thing to teach any lady to play dice, it had earned him her company.

"Oui." Cassie gave the older and far more outgoing brother the answer he sought—with a condition. "If first you help your mother and I clear the table." Cassie stood, sending Beata a warm, reassuring smile as she reached for the trencher they'd shared.

During the past several quiet days of Will's absence, Meg had repeated to Cassie the tale of how she'd set out to stay for a time in the Weald with her younger son, Kenward. Intending a short visit with her sister, they'd stopped at the cottage on the forest edge, but there had found Beata's husband murdered and the terrified younger sister physically hiding in the woods while mentally retreating to the safety of childhood. And though, according to Meg, Johnny was an immature man and Beata's "best" friend, whom she should never have wed, nonetheless, he had been as undeserving as Beata of such a dastardly deed.

Once Cassie realized what wickedness had been wreaked upon the fragile woman, she had put aside her own petty woes and jealousy to fully open her tender heart and truly welcome the company of one who seemed oddly drawn to her. Cassie wondered if the woman—though older in years, a child in mind—sensed within her a spirit in hiding, too.

With more domestic efficiency than previous acquaintances would have believed, Cassie helped Meg tidy away remnants of a meal far more varied than she'd once thought possible with such limited ingredients. Cassie had come to admire Meg, a woman warm and full of laughter, from whom she'd learned much about such mundane skills as the rudiments of cooking and the practical tasks involved in keeping a humble home tidy. Moreover, since she'd learned what a massive task faced Edna every morn—always keeping food ready and waiting for men who went out and returned at no regular intervals—Cassie had grown determined to ease the woman's way whenever the opportunity arose.

While reliable Kenward wiped down the table, Tom brought dice out from the small leather pouch dangling beside the dagger at his waist. Cassie took a seat at the table and made room for Beata to sit close.

Although Beata seldom spoke, beneath her placid expression muddled thoughts were at war. She woke near every night from horrid dreams whose events she couldn't recall once awakened—leastwise not beyond their numbing terror. Everything and everyone unfamiliar was a threat, save Cassie. Unexpected sounds and unknown faces set her heart to pounding so hard it seemed 'twould suffocate her. Only with her family or within the sphere of the faerie queen's surely magical protection was she safe until came the rescue promised by her shining knight. And he would come, he would because he'd given his oath. An unpleasant possibility struck a weakening blow at the too flimsy bulwark of her confidence. What if he couldn't find her? Had she been wrong in allowing Meg to take her from the forest where he'd told her to stay hidden? Unnoticed by her companions, a new distress began to build to terrifying heights.

"You toss first," Tom magnanimously offered Cassie from directly across the table, feeling he'd won already with the French damsel so near.

Cassie accepted the dice, balanced them atop her fingers as she'd been taught, then tossed them to the use-smoothed tabletop and squealed her glee over a surely victorious roll.

Ever frightened by sudden noises, Beata shrank back, pulling the protective shield of the dark cloak tighter around her apprehension-quivering form. Instantly Cassie turned to lay an arm around narrow shoulders and console the fear-filled woman-child. Cassie had days since come to recognize that such sweetness as Beata possessed could only summon love from a man, and thus understood—though still could not take pleasure in— Will's feeling for Beata. Truth be known, she too had a growing affection for the ethereal maid. Unfortunately, at the same time she had an ever deepening worry over the cloak Beata insisted on keeping wrapped about herself as if 'twere an invincible armor. Did it mean a De Faux had done this to her? And yet, if that were so, why would she hold a remnant of the foul deed near?

"I yield on this round." Tom ruefully laughed, staring at the result of his turn with the pieces of bone. "But I wager you can't best me twice."

That they wagered naught but the smooth pebbles fetched by Kenward from a nearby stream stole none of the challenge from the game. And of recent times Cassie had begun to enjoy the meeting of challenges.

"Twice or thrice—I accept the wager." Cassie scooped up the dice and again meticulously balanced them on the backs of outstretched fingers held steady.

In the combination of her squeal and Tom's groan as the dice skidded across table top to a halt, no one noticed the opening of the outer door. Black brows furrowed in thunderous accompaniment to the gold lightning flashing from Will's eyes. Dice! Had Tom lost all good sense? Plainly the young man had inveigled a lady-born into an unworthy game pursued only by lowbred males. Then Will saw the blatant admiration in Tom's gaze and gritted his teeth. It had been a grave error to leave Cassandra with two impressionable youths all too eager to please and as near alone as could be, what with only their indulgent mother to provide restraint. He could hardly blame the plainly smitten boys, yet although Kenward was a child still, Tom was nearer her age than was he. The unpleasant thought deepened Will's irritation.

A movement in the doorway and the familiar sensation of an anticipated presence summoned Cassie's attention. She turned and without hesitation her heart-shaped face lifted to send Will a blinding smile.

Cassie's welcome held such warmth it frightened him. Despite unsought daydreams and night visions, he couldn't have her for himself! No English lord would gift a knight of bastard line with his daughter, even less would the family of the French noble dead by his order. But despite such irreversible facts, he hadn't the will to break their visual bond.

The power in the depths of those black eyes was such that, even from across the room, Cassie felt as if she'd been swept into Will's embrace. Soft rose lips parted on a deep, silent sigh, and Will took an involuntary step forward.

So lost in each other were they that neither noticed the shadow crossing Tom's face in reaction to the warmth radiating between the maid and the great knight who was both his hero and mentor. However, the young man's mother saw his expression and silently determined to speak with him on the matter he'd no right to meddle in.

Will abruptly pulled back, shaking his head to free it of the subtle tendrils of attraction his tender foe wove so easily about him. "My ransom demand was dispatched yestermorn and likely reached your brother's hand this day." Will's harsh announcement reflected his determination to put an end to unrealistic dreams. Yet when the light instantly and completely went out of Cassie, 'twas as if a room's lone candle had been extinguished, and with the sudden descent of darkness, came a freezing chill.

Will's words threw a cold, black shadow across the cozy warmth of the chamber and seemed to mark the abrupt end of Cassie's bright days within. Automatically scooping up the dice, then realizing what she'd done, Cassie dropped them to the table as if they were poison and stiffly rose to her feet. "For that I am grateful. It'll be a relief to return to civilized society."

The sharp words wounded not only her audience, but Cassie, too, for they were a lie. Right or wrong, she'd enjoyed her time of learning, and praise for her efforts in Will's home, far more than all the years endured amidst the great family castle where she seemed destined to disappoint.

Holding herself proudly erect to hide the anguish inside, Cassie climbed the corner stairway to her chamber. All those left behind were hurt; but more, the woman-child shrank into a frightened bewilderment under this apparent defection while the knight damned the crack her words had opened in his formidable wall against emotions too painful to acknowledge.

The newly risen moon seemed to rest atop the towers of Dover Castle, and shone down with the white and frigid light of winter. In a large tent amidst the camp besiegers had laid out about the fortress's unyielding walls, a triad of sour-smelling tallow candles burned in a just reflection of their owner's mood.

"Where's your brother got off to, Valnoir?" The harsh words were as tightly restrained as the parchment crushed in the speaker's meaty hand.

"I am not my brother's keeper, Uncle." The sneer on the tall blond man's handsome face underlined his disdain for the subject of his words. Valnoir swaggered from the opened tent flap to face the heavy man seated at a low makeshift table in the abode's center, while another stood beside and slightly behind. "Surely you know after all these years that, despite our physical appearances, we've little in common and I've no care for what he chooses to do with his time."

Bald save for a ruff of graying ginger hair about the top of his ears and back of his neck, Guy De Faux's pale eyes narrowed on the new arrival. Though his nephews shared the same blood, 'twas Valnoir who possessed all the charm and had wits enough to use it to his own advantage. Vauderie's cold mien did more to repel than invite, and despite his emotionless facade, he cared too much about valueless people and worthless things to gain in prestige or power.

Returning his attention to far more important matters, Guy grunted an acknowledgment of his nephew's statement before slapping the much abused sheet to tabletop and roughly flattening its crumpled surface.

"Aye, I also ought to know him well enough to expect his absence when matters of import fall into our hands." The action of lifting his head to acknowledge his other standing companion smoothed out a few of his many chins. "Friend Henri has received news of his sister." The calmness of his tone would warn any who knew him well of the fury building beneath. "That wretched English bastard holds Cassandra in demand for ransom."

The last thing Valnoir wanted was to see Cassie returned, and with her, the threat to his future plans that she represented—slim though the possibility of her producing an heir for his uncle might be.

Guy knew how Valnoir's mind worked, if only because its pathways were oft so closely aligned with his own. Still, the amusement roused by his nephew's tension over Cassandra's danger to his hopes held more contempt than good humor. God's blood, now that her father was dead and her considerably less influential brother the only alliance to be won by the marriage, he'd happily set the damoiselle aside as more work than she was worth. There were other women, better opportunities to be had—but he *would not* stand for the English knight's manipulation of him, an insult deepened by his sending of the ransom demand to her brother rather than her far more important betrothed.

"And what do you intend to do?" Valnoir queried, face utterly emotionless.

"What you expect, my dear Valnoir." Guy's voice dripped acid. "I mean to see him pay dearly for his effrontery in seizing what belongs to me."

Chapter
⊷§ *7* §⊶

DESPITE THE BLAZING HEAT of the fire she labored over to tend roasting meat, Cassie felt as if the growing chill of autumn's slide into winter had spread its cold fog throughout the house. Though days had passed since the moment she'd uttered those unwarranted words, the relationship between herself and the others had become ever more strained. They'd been hurt by her apparent defection, her spurning of a friendship openly offered. She'd hurt herself as well and deeply regretted the ill-considered retort. That she'd spoken in self-defense mattered little when she'd achieved naught but the wounding of people undeserving. Meg had withdrawn into a disapproving quiet, while Tom's young and tender ego had plainly been bruised and the child Beata had become surely comprehended her faerie queen's apparent rejection as further abuse. Kenward alone seemed to understand and offered wordless smiles of encouragement whenever she glanced his way, smiles that increased her feeling of guilt over an unforgivable wrong. She desperately wanted to call back the words yet knew she could but repent and strive to atone for her misdeed.

Cassie loosed the spit industriously turned to see meat evenly done and carefully laid it aside on a waiting platter. Silent tears dripped down cheeks flushed by else than fire heat as she swung toward one laboring near.

"Meg, I didn't mean it." The words came out with a rush as if their speed might lend aid in bridging the distance reproach ever lengthened between them. "Truly, I didn't. You and Tom and Beata and Kenward"— she named each separately in acknowledgment of the apology owed all— "are more honorable, more 'civilized,' than any others I've ever known. You've been more friends to me than any save one, and your friendship is precious. Please forgive my hasty words. 'Twas pride which moved my tongue before good sense could halt its foolish claim." Cassie clenched her hands painfully together. "I don't know what wicked imp came over me! I swear, never afore in the whole of my life have I so oft lost control of my words as I have since arriving here!"

Meg thought it not so strange when one considered the drastic changes in Cassie's life that had followed her capture. In compassion Meg recognized the very real confusion laid upon the younger woman by the resulting emotional upheaval, and wordlessly held her arms open wide.

Cassie stepped within, finding relief and peace in their forgiving hold. She had spoken only the truth. Since entering the Weald's far different world, a good many discoveries had begun tilting her view of not only herself, but of all that touched her life. Beyond the unwelcome sharpness of her tongue, she'd discovered a new courage, a confidence in tasks never considered worthy before, a growing respect for the land which once she'd disdained as too damp and gloomy, and a growing fondness for this English forest—and its lord.

With Beata resting this afternoon in the bedchamber above to recover from yet another difficult night filled with frightening dreams, neither woman realized they'd an audience. Nor would they ever know that Will, with Meg's two sons, had arrived at an outer door cracked open to allow escape of what smoke evaded the chimney and laid a faint haze over the hall. At Will's silent command the small party backed quietly away.

Will was surprised by Cassie's apology and yet not. His mind lingered on the scene left behind while he absently led the brothers to the far side of his men's cottages where a space had been cleared to facilitate practice with various weapons. Cassie's claim of a suddenly unruly tongue he believed without question. After all, despite her natural reticence, she'd repeatedly flared at him. Only did he wonder what had prompted the change. At the same time, he rued the undeniable sincerity of her regret's further softening a heart he'd sought to turn to stone against the too likely unintended invasion of a hostage he must return to her own.

Tom's half-bantering, half-curious comment on his ferocious frown broke Will's preoccupation with the captive. Then when Kenward added a fervent plea that he demonstrate the right performance of a difficult maneuver in swordplay, with a wry smile Will fully turned his attention to the present and channeled his thoughts into more immediate matters.

In the room where two women were truly alone, Meg stepped away and looked into lavender eyes thickly fringed by tear-spiked lashes. "I'm glad you spoke of it now," Meg told Cassie. "In the morn, whilst Beata remains, Tom and I will set off for Castle Tarrant."

Cassie shook her head, distressed both by how narrowly she'd escaped a missed opportunity to set things aright and by the abruptly risen prospect of a new loneliness. "Must you go so soon?"

" 'Tis not soon, lass. Already we've stayed gone far longer than intended. Lady Nessa will begin to worry don't we quickly arrive. She's been ill, and the strain might see her sicken again."

"Sick?" Meg and her sons slipped in and out of French with little thought, and suddenly Cassie realized, to her own surprise, that she could easily follow the gist of their words no matter what language they used.

"Aye, she's too good, always insistent upon treating every person ailing on Tarrant lands—never mind 'tis her own health she risks. She was once near a nun, you ken? Nay, you don't, but she would'a been hadn't it been for our Ice Warrior, Will's uncle the earl."

"Will's uncle—an earl?" Cassie's brows lifted at this unexpected news. How could it be true? And why had Kenward refused to tell her earlier?

" 'S'truth." Were it possible, Meg would have unsaid the hasty revelation she'd promised never to share with any inside the Weald's boundaries and, despite an admitted love of gossip, never had until now. Once done, however, Meg thought to turn her error to good use. "Though not born of legitimate line, Will was raised in the castle as one of its own."

"But why then is he here in this . . ." Cassie waved in a gesture encompassing the whole of the wild forest and its rough company. True, Kenward had told her Will chose the Weald over castle life, and she'd found that surprising enough. But to hear now that he—a man noble-blooded, no matter the circumstances of his heritage—had turned his back on its prestige, power, and position, was nothing short of astounding.

Both the bemusement and admiration deeper than mere physical awareness revealed in lavender eyes brought a knowing grin to Meg's lips. " 'Tis what Will chooses. Earl Garrick and his son Galen would welcome him at Castle Tarrant, yet though he loves his family, Will never rested easy in their world. His father was a simple woodsman, but his mother the bastard daughter of the old earl. Will, I, and my siblings were all orphans. Lady Nessa it was who took us with our foster mother, Maud, to the castle. With great bravery she saw Will accepted by the noble grandsire he was named for but who had refused to acknowledge either his mother or him."

This intriguing new knowledge of Will's heritage increased Cassie's fascination with the man living by choice amongst peasants in a wilderness. In the first instant she'd thought it might be the shadow on his lineage that had driven him into retreat, but learning of his close relationship with an earl proved it untrue. Clearly, unlike her father and most men in the world from which she came, he was obsessed by neither wealth nor position.

Meg was pleased by Cassie's introspective expression, and certain she knew its source. 'Twas the same as what caused the normally laughing Will such repeated irritation. And a fine thing that. Will had been alone far too long. The fact Cassie was his hostage, Meg discounted with assurance that Will was more than equal to overcoming any impediment he chose.

"Best we turn in earnest to our preparations for the day's last meal," Meg said, hiding her satisfied smile behind a practical manner. "Want something special they will, once they know 'tis the last I'll make here for a time."

Oui, the diners at table tonight would expect "something special" from a fine cook. It seemed the sort of challenge Cassie was learning to enjoy. She'd an idea that quickly won Meg's support. Not surprising when 'twas a plan providing furtherance of Meg's own hopes. Cassie pushed up the narrow wrists of her raglan sleeves and set to work with a will.

"Meg," Will near groaned as he pushed away a trencher once heaping but now empty. "You outdid yourself tonight. The roast with its sauce was fine indeed. But, ever my favorite, the trout in verjuice and spices was splendid!" He turned a look of mock condemnation upon the matronly foster sister sitting across the pristine whiteness of the cloth-covered evening table from him. "But I am not such a poor tactician I don't see the path of your scheme nor am likely to overlook your intended target. You meant to be certain you'd be missed all the more." Golden sparks of laughter in the midst of black eyes warmed the admission that followed. "The deplorable part of it is that I cannot regret your success with so delicious a weapon."

"Miss me?" Meg asked with a surprise betrayed by the repeated appearance of mischievous dimples in the plump cheeks she sought to hold smooth. "For loss of your favorite dish?" Matronly in form and years she might be, yet never had she lost a child's joy in pranks. "There is no need. 'Twere I who prepared the underappreciated roast. The cook responsible for your trout will remain whilst I depart."

Will's startled gaze instantly shifted to Beata, who sat close to her older sister's side. He'd not thought her yet capable of such chores.

"Not me, silly," Beata giggled, returned to better spirits by the renewed friendship with her faerie queen. " 'Twas Cassie who toiled the whole afternoon to see your trout just so."

Ever too aware of the dark knight now at her side, when curious black eyes fell on her, Cassie found herself unable to sustain their penetrating power. Wildly fluttering lashes descended while bright color swept upward.

The brothers waited in curious silence for near the first time during the whole of this lingering meal as, in his thoughts, Will returned to the day he'd insisted Cassie aid Meg in meal preparations. His memory faithfully reminded him of her claim to be untrained in such homey arts.

"Once again you've proven an uncommonly quick mind—first learning our language with amazing speed, and now learning the ways of cookery so swiftly and so well." Cassie was full of surprises—each more uniquely formed to destroy his preconceived notions of what she was or should be, and each destined to make more difficult the day he must return the damsel to her brother's care.

That Will's gentle gaze rested like a caress atop the damsel's ebony hair, restrained in a single shiny plait, lent a satisfied grin to Meg's lips. Its meaning was plain enough.

Blush deepening under Will's compliment, Cassie hastened to see credit turned to where it rightfully belonged. "Nay, 'tis Meg who possesses the knowledge." Cassie admitted her lack freely. "Merely did I put it to use." No point pretending elsewise, although the possibility of earning this man's approval was a tantalizing incentive to pursue further culinary talents. In truth, she'd give over near any price to hear him admit she was not so utterly useless as once he'd claimed.

The glow from many candles amassed on a single brass platter at table center reflected a white light on the dark head Will slowly shook in wordless refusal to accept her modest disclaimer. "You did a fine job of putting Meg's facts to worthy purpose. The result was delicious, and I thank you for the effort."

The brilliant smile Cassie glimpsed from 'neath yet lowered lashes was reward enough.

That she'd gone to such lengths, obviously to please him, knocked Will off stride. Why, when he was striving to put distance between them, must she seek to please and thus disarm her captor? Did she think to work her wiles on him and win her release? A wry curve added a cynical twist to the smile still upon Cassie. He was not, he assured himself, so easily charmed, and she would lose. She must, or they both would lose far more than either dare risk.

Cassie was relieved when Will rose to adjourn with the boys to seats before the fire. The house's lord took one of the padded chairs, and the brothers each occupied a three-legged stool. Beata immediately slipped away to curl at Will's feet while the other two women tidied away the remnants of the meal. Sensing dark and thoughtful glances too often turned upon her, Cassie scrubbed the table with unnecessary vigor. After all had been put to order, she and Meg moved into the fire's ring of light as well.

On the floor at the group's outer edge Cassie settled half in the flames' flickering gleams and half in shadow. She drew her knees up under voluminous homespun skirts, wrapped her arms about them and rested her gently rounded chin atop. Talk was desultory and general although the brothers continued their unceasing efforts to pry from Will as much information on recent forays as they could win from the reluctant warrior. Cassie thought the knight's reticence odd. Her father, brothers, and the male visitors in their castle had always taken great pleasure in bragging of victories doubtless inflated by the ego behind their words.

"Why can't I stay behind and join the fight?" Tom tenaciously repeated a plea made all too oft in recent days.

Will shook his head. "You've an obligation to see your mother safely home to Tarrant." Will's forced and one-sided smile hardened like brittle ice. There was danger enough to people he loved without adding this young man to their number. A young man, moreover, known for impetuous behavior and, in a place of war, likely dangerous actions.

"But *why* not?" Tom argued, certain his age was the deciding factor even if Will would never admit it true. "Kenward lives here and he's younger than me."

"Your little brother," Will pointed out, "is allowed never to leave this village nor, though ostensibly my squire, does he ride with me into a fight. I doubt you'd be satisfied to stay safely behind. Thus, I choose to hold the door closed against your arguments." A gently teasing smile accompanied his decision, but the dark eyes above held an implacable warning even headstrong Tom knew better than to defy, and the conversation continued with no more talk of who would go and who would stay.

Yet, by her own experience in having her company too oft rejected by arrogant older brothers, Cassie sensed the hurt behind Tom's view of the injustice in allowing a younger brother to stay while "closing the door" on the older. When he glanced her way, she gave him a particularly sweet smile.

Tom impulsively jumped to his feet. "Walk with me?" he asked, and offered his hand to aid her rising.

Shocked by this suggestion of a deed Tom surely couldn't believe a captive would be permitted to blithely undertake, Cassie looked to Will, expecting to be forbidden.

In eyes deepened to amethyst Will saw hope at odds with the futility of expected opposition. Vexed by the uncomfortable position into which he'd been thrust, he turned his attention from Cassie to the young man who'd issued the unwise invitation.

As was too often the case, Tom hadn't stopped to think before requesting Cassie's company. But the moment the damsel's gaze shifted to her captor, he recognized the ill-considered nature of his action. Still, the likelihood of another refusal so close on the heels of the last lifted Tom's chin to a belligerent tilt. "You mean to deny me even this simple joy when 'tis an opportunity which by your first exclusion I'll lose all too quickly?"

Will knew that for he, an older and stronger man, to crush young Tom's hopes twice in so short a time would be to risk crushing his spirit. Yet with regard to the first, Will stood firm in his resolve not to have Tom remain in the Weald, and in the second, thought it foolish to allow such easy movement of a captive earlier proven anxious to escape. Even more, though unwilling to admit it, he'd an aversion for the thought of Cassie strolling with a plainly smitten boy near her own age.

In the lengthening silence during which both Cassie and Tom waited with growing anxiety, Will admitted to himself that there could be little real danger in granting Tom's request. Leastways Tom knew a guard was posted in forest shadows every night—although the young man did not know the practice dated from the night of Cassie's attempted flight. Thus, were Tom foolish enough to allow Cassie to steal away, the other would prevent her success. Asides, Will had learned respect enough for Cassie's mind to believe it unlikely that she'd take the risk while others were about and she unprepared.

"Nay." Will's voice dropped into a deceptively mild tone. "I've no objection to you leading *my* captive on a brief walk, and only do I insist you not leave the glade's open ground."

Tom was more than pleased, and this minor victory pacified his ruffled pride. Unwilling to waste a moment for fear Will would change his mind, he reached down, pulled an unprepared damsel to her feet, and hustled her toward their goal. He paused next to cloaks hung from pegs on one side of the door, lifted his own and asked, "Which is yours?"

Dazed by the unanticipated permission and Tom's swift reaction, Cassie looked blankly at the row of mostly empty pegs and shook her head. "None here. I've never needed one afore."

"No matter." Tom was quick to answer. "Kenward's should fit, and he won't soon need it." The grin Tom cast his brother melted into a soft smile as he turned to meet lavender eyes before opening the door and proffering an arm to formally escort his companion into the dark beyond.

Cassie lightly laid fingers trembling with excitement for this surprising outing atop the upheld forearm. Dare she hope she'd won a measure of trust from Will? Nay, it could not be, not so long as she was his captive, and yet . . .

Although in the first days of her captivity she'd told herself she would flee did the opportunity arise, with her apology to Edna had come acknowledgment of the undeniable fact that she never wished to leave the Weald. How could she run from Will when to never see him again had become the very last thing she wanted? The focus of her anxieties had been pulled inside out. Where once she'd feared Will's hold, now she dreaded the day he would send her away. That distressing realization was instantly overwhelmed by a near paralyzing terror—Guy would never let the matter end with her recovery by ransom! Though she assuredly meant little to her betrothed, her capture was too certainly a blow to his pride of possession, and to avenge such a blow he would doubtless devote all of his considerable resources.

Lost in disturbing thoughts, she hardly noticed as Tom led her through the open door until the chill reality of a late autumn night rudely jerked her free.

" 'Tis truly a fine night, don't you think?" Tom's stilted words were as awkward as he felt. Now near alone with the French beauty, he was nervous and anxious to ease his tension by striking up a conversation no matter its content.

From her blind contemplation of light slivers glittering through cracks about cottage doorways on the glade's far side, without forethought Cassie glanced toward the speaker. Her faint frown plainly questioned his good sense. Had it been stolen by the same aching winter cold seeping through Kenward's cloak, her gown, even her flesh, to burrow down to her very bones?

"I mean," Tom lamely clarified, "surely on a November night any glimpse of the moon makes it so." Through the tendrils of fog drifting overhead he gestured uncomfortably at the glow that must be that silvery orb.

Cassie knew she'd unintentionally affronted him and, on top of comments made when Will interrupted their last game of dice—for which she'd yet to apologize to him—'twas shameful. "Any night, or day, when

I'm allowed to walk freely beyond the walls of Will's home is fine indeed. And I am grateful to you for making it possible."

A momentary rift in the haze allowed moonlight to settle full upon the warm smile Cassie gave Tom. 'Twas thanks enough for a demand he happily forgot possessed any other purpose. So lost in admiring her gentle beauty was Tom that he gave no thought to a path treacherous in the dark of night and led Cassie across a rut so deep they both stumbled.

Cassie gasped and Tom instantly wrapped an arm about her shoulders to hold her safely upright. By the time they'd recovered steady footing, embarrassment blush-darkened the faces of both.

Tom dropped his arm and stepped away as if burned. "Cassie, pray pardon my blundering steps. I should've given more attention to watching where we went."

"Nay," Cassie instantly argued, more concerned by Tom's flustered reaction than her own. "I, too, should know enough to watch where I step. My first sight of this glade should've taught me the value of going with care." Her exaggerated grimace was meant to cool the heat of his self-consciousness.

"Aye, children like as you both should know better, but seldom do." The nightguard who stepped from forest shadows to confront the pair had observed them since the moment they'd left the house's bright warmth.

Forgetting her recent unsteady footing, Cassie whirled. The taunt's source was a male not much older than either she or Tom, and seemed familiar, although she wasn't sure why.

"There's no more than a few months betwixt us in age, Clyde." Tom's eyes narrowed while the new heat of anger eclipsed the warmth of embarrassment. He and Clyde were clearly destined to be ever irritated by the other's mere existence on the same earth.

" 'S'truth," Clyde agreed, casting Tom a contemptuous smile. "Although your inability to protect a lady, as demonstrated by actions just past, gives leave to question your maturity. 'Tis why I, the *man* posted as guard for the night, must see the task done aright."

As Clyde stepped forward, Tom moved back, pulling Cassie with him. Stumbling at his side, Cassie was amazed by how little care her erstwhile escort gave to avoiding the rut that had precipitated this scene. She peered down into shadows about their feet and found that by some miracle of fate they'd sidestepped the danger.

"We thank you for your concern." The coldness of Tom's voice made it plain gratitude was the last emotion he felt for the other. "But I assure you there's no cause for your solicitude."

"Mayhap, mayhap not," Clyde answered with a false grin which grated on Tom even more than the earlier sneer. "Nonetheless, as not only am I the posted guard but have experience in the duty, Lady Cassandra will be safer with me, and I claim the right to stand as her protector."

Cassie's eyes widened. Of course he was familiar, because 'twas he who'd driven her cart into the Weald from the scene of her father's death. As the realization came to her, action erupted.

Clyde took another step toward Cassie, and Tom's unsheathed blade flashed into the open space between them. Instantly Clyde's sword appeared with clear intent to meet and match any aggression.

Shocked by the unexpected eruption of hostility, Cassie instinctively fell another pace back, heart pounding.

"You wouldn't dare strike a knight!" Tom fair sputtered with angry disbelief, and glared at the malevolently glittering weapon raised against him.

"But you *are not* a knight—not yet." Clyde's response came through gritted teeth and was equally harsh. "Not a knight, and no more noble-blooded or worthy to be one than me. Moreover, 'tis I who am part of this garrison's guard, I whose official duty it is to see her protected. So, go home to your safe castle and play at games of war while I fight one."

Rage for Clyde's verbal attack on an area already bruised overwhelmed Tom's never strong self-restraint, and he tensed to leap at his opponent.

"This 'duty' you both claim belongs to neither of you." The ice-sharp thrust of a deeper voice provided as effective a barrier to the attack as the towering figure who stepped between the two protagonists. "Both the responsibility and damoiselle are mine."

So intent was Cassie on the fearful prospect of imminent violence that Will's sudden appearance caught her by surprise. Yet as the two younger men subsided into glowers of lingering animosity, her first response was quiet pleasure in Will's second claiming of her as his own, but her next was shame for the complete lack of courage revealed by her failure to make any attempt to calm the conflict. Once again brave Lady Cassandra had remained hidden inside. In weak self-defense she comforted herself that her faltering dismay had merely resulted from the speed with which danger had burst into being and passed. 'Twas an inadequate excuse which left her feeling only more the most timid of cowards—far from the image she wanted the powerful knight to have of her.

"Of greater concern is the clear error in your thinking." Will drove relentlessly to the core of the matter. "The task in question is not one of her protection, but rather one of guard against her possible escape."

Not until the door closed on the couple whose departure he'd permitted had Will remembered which of his followers held the night's rotating chore of perimeter guard. Then, too familiar with the long-term enmity laying between that young man and Tom, he'd followed with the stealth of an experienced knight, hoping this scene could be avoided and his interference unnecessary. Only one good had come from the incident. Leastwise, now he knew the source of the rancor between the two younger men—Clyde resented Tom's opportunity to become knight, while Tom was indignant over Clyde's accepted participation in the Weald's defense.

During the confrontation's first moments Will had thought the sight of two young bucks vying for Cassie's attention amusing. But amusement had quickly faded under the certain truth that here was yet a further demonstration that the Weald with its men of war was no proper place for the divisive complications brought by the presence of a lady-born.

Struggling across emotional ground turned treacherous by the simple walk detoured down a path fraught with unforeseen difficulties, Will's extended arm seemed to Cassie a welcome guide to safer plains. She gratefully laid her fingertips atop the iron-strong forearm and, pushing still tangled feelings aside, moved forward at his side with as much pride as she could muster.

Cassie blinked against a much brighter light as they stepped from the dark outside into Will's house. Will took Kenward's cloak from Cassie's shoulders and tossed the garment unceremoniously at its owner in an unspoken order that he depart to join Tom and the other men sharing one of the cottages on the glade's far side. Cassie instantly wondered if his abruptness was born of irritation with her for being catalyst of the scene just past. If so, 'twas unfair and she'd a momentary impulse to tell him so. All too soon a far stronger urge to hide swept the first away. From the near empty hall she realized Meg must already have led Beata to Will's chamber above. Beneath the intense weight of a black gaze, she felt awkward and anxious to escape to her own.

"Stay, Cassie," Will quietly said.

The gentleness in his request, like a stroke of dark velvet, soothed her anxiety and tempted amethyst eyes his way.

"Talk with me awhile," Will coaxed, purposefully wielding the additional incentive of his slow, devastating smile as he settled again in one of the chairs before the undiminished warmth of still leaping flames. It was wrong to give into the desire for time alone in her company, more dangerous than her countrymen's keenly honed weapons. While the wound from a French sword would pain only once, he feared her able to render an ache to linger a lifetime. Despite danger acknowledged, the will to hold her distant slipped from him unmourned. She was too sweet a temptation to resist. Just this once, for a short while and with a physical distance between them, he would seek consolation for the certain loneliness of a future without her presence. 'Twas merely the innocent consolation provided by the same warm comfort she generously shared with Beata, indeed, with near all who crossed her path.

Cassie hovered uncertainly, lavender eyes gazing into the soul-melting power of the golden fires in black. She felt as if he'd snared her spirit, was drawing it ever closer and her restraints fell to ashes. Whatever purpose lay behind his request, 'twas a risk—but after her recent display of cowardice, also an opportunity to prove she'd some measure of bravery. Moreover, 'twas full of thrilling possibilities and one she'd willingly accept to store the memory against the day he returned her to face an unwanted future.

Will held his hand out, and she instinctively laid smaller fingers inside. With an even more potent smile he tugged her gently down into the chair he pulled close to his own. Moments of silence lengthened while Will intently studied the faint wild blush on her modestly averted face.

Under a growing awareness of him so near she need only take a deep breath to brush against his broad shoulder, Cassie was anxious to turn his attention from herself and the events of the past hour. She rushed into speech on a subject that had occupied her mind for much of the day.

"Why do you live in the Weald when, by virtue of your heritage, you could have more?" The moment the words left her mouth, Cassie again silently chided the tongue turned imprudent by the Weald.

Will was startled by her knowledge, but only momentarily. He'd no question but that the source was Meg, his talkative foster sister. Yet how complete was Cassie's understanding of his noble connection? Did she mistakenly believe him heir to something greater, see him as a possible mate able to guarantee her a lifetime of position and privilege? Was such an inaccurate assumption the true reason for her mealtime attempt to please him?

His impassive face revealed nothing of the cynical thoughts inside as he gave an evasive answer intended to provide time to decide what and if to share further. "I've no desire to linger amidst a society wherein a king forsakes his solemn promise and men their oaths of fealty."

Despite her tongue's recent repeated defections, Cassie was normally circumspect, and quietly pondered his statement, searching through the facts behind England's present political wrangling as she knew them. He referred, of course, to King John, who had put his seal to the Great Charter one day and denied it the next. That was plain. Then, too, he must refer to the barons who had sworn fealty to their king but, upon being betrayed by John's reversal of the charter, had broken their oaths and offered the English crown to the French king and his son.

Will watched Cassie weighing his words and coming to the right conclusions. Then, with intent to see her robbed of any foolish delusions about his expectations—not that it could matter, given the many invisible walls betwixt them—he continued. "Apparently, I've more of my woodsman father in me than noble grandsire." He wanted to be certain she knew the truth of his tainted heritage, knew how unjustified would be any thoughts of he as provider for one accustomed to more than was here. To reinforce this purpose he added, "I prefer a simpler existence." He cast the damsel a sidelong and considering glance. "How anyone might deem living a quiet life in a simple house and eating plain fare more satisfying is doubtless difficult for one of your upbringing to understand."

"Non," Cassie answered, surprised at how easily she revealed to him thoughts and emotions earlier only half formed in her own mind. "During my days here, I've learned to appreciate uncomplicated ways. There's much to be admired in their lack of petty rivalries." She blushed. Considering the scene they'd so recently left and which she'd meant to avoid discussing, these were ill-chosen words.

Will missed her blundered reference to rivalries, so interested was he in the soft but immediate answer which proved her already aware of his illegitimate lineage. By his knowledge of Meg's fondness for gossip it was no real surprise, leastwise not by comparison with Cassie's unexpected agreement with his philosophy. Likely she claimed it only as a form of apology for the implied condemnation in her fiery retort days past of a return to civilized society. She couldn't possibly understand the true nature of the Weald's harsh life and all it entailed. Yet not wishing to belittle her attempt to make amends, he merely nodded.

" 'Tis a simple life, but once the conflict is done, one with which I'll be content." Even as he made the assertion, the quiet self-mockery in his soul taunted: *Content? Alone in the forest—without Cassie?* He immediately clamped down on the assuredly irrational thought. No woman had ever meant that much to him, and he must see that no woman ever would. Their temporary company was easy enough for him to come by, and he needed no more. Still, when he glanced down at his tender hostage, a mental battle broke out between what he might want and the realities of what could be.

Looking up, Cassie fell into mesmerizing black depths where brewed a storm and golden bolts of lightning flashed. Despite the self-contempt fiercely throwing warning daggers sharp-to-point within, Will gently smoothed back the few tendrils escaping a braid's tight confines to frame Cassie's heart-shaped face. Then, without fore-intent, his hand cradled the back of her head while he lowered his mouth to sweet lips he'd never stopped longing for since his first taste of them.

Cassie threw all caution aside to welcome "her" knight's caresses—and leastways in her dreams he *was* hers.

Even as Will deepened the kiss, he acknowledged 'twas wrong. But the fact that he couldn't possess her only seemed to increase a desperate need. In the same moment his strong-held sense of honor demanded he accept his place in the world and forced him to hear the voice of conscience reminding him that by birth he'd been forbidden the claiming of any noblewoman, least of all this soft and tender foe.

Striving for control, he pulled back with every intention of halting dangerous temptations here; and yet, yielding to the worst kind of folly, he gazed down. At sight of the sweet damoiselle with her dark head tilted back, eyes deepened to a purple drowsy with new desires, and lips a deep rose color—moist and softly swollen—he wanted her more, far more, than was safe. His chest rose and fell in deep, uneven breaths, and despite the self-given oath to stay distant, he couldn't stop—not yet.

Having already defeated her natural shyness to discover a new courage in the promised pleasures beckoning her deeper into the circle of his arms, Cassie was determined Will not rob her of a single precious memory. Only did she wish she knew more of the means to tempt a man, but settled for returning the same caresses with which he'd set tendrils of delight burning in her. Lifting her mouth to his, she brushed its soft curves across his firm lips in an attempt to lure him to failure in his intent to put her aside.

Powerful arms swept the tender damsel from her seat to lay across hard thighs, and as Will took control of the kiss, it became long and slow and hard. Cassie's world shifted amidst a dizzying whirlwind of fiery sensations. She wrapped her arms about its steady center, instinctively savoring the strength of Will's broad back.

Under the willingly given pleasure of her response, Will crushed lush curves closer, but apparently no closer than she wanted to be, for she struggled to be nearer still. His mouth left hers to trail fire across her cheeks, and Cassie let her head fall back, laying vulnerable the white arch of her throat. His lips instantly followed its path. Cassie was dazed by the wild sparks erupting wherever he kissed. Lost in his firestorm, she trembled beneath its welcome power while together they spun ever higher into a searing maelstrom.

Will began heedlessly loosening the laces holding the temptress' homespun gown tight about her neck. Once tugged wide enough, his mouth dipped from throat to the quivering tops of breasts he ached to see, yearned to touch. While his lips nuzzled lower, his hands slid up, and he damned the overabundant cloth betwixt they and lush mounds. He continued impatiently tugging restraining cords, anxious to free her bounty to the ravishment of lips hovering a whisper above.

Cassie's hands had lifted to the dark head tormentingly near, and her fingers twined tight into cool strands to urge the source of such hot pleasures nearer. Overcome by the shocking sensation of a melting fire rushing through her veins and the tantalizing approach of an intimate caress unknown and distressingly withheld, a small, sweet moan came from her tight throat.

Will knew that the wildly exciting sound had never been heard by another man, and he'd an impossible wish to ensure that no other ever would. Successful at last with his task delayed by haste-twisted fingers, he spread the once impeding neckline wide and lowered his hungry mouth. He intended to coax from his wonderfully wanton "shy rabbit" another such revealing sound—but 'twas a sharp, piercing scream from another throat that he heard. It broke them apart as effectively as a dousing of icy water fresh from the North Sea.

Cassie stared up at the dark, concerned face lifted attentively to the level above. Clearly Beata had awakened with yet another of her not infrequent night terrors, as attested to by the muffled crooning of Meg comforting her anguished sister.

The mood had shattered like a flimsy raft tossed by cruel waves against a rocky shore. In the splintered debris of her abandoned responses, Cassie recognized the hopelessness of its restoration while Will so plainly hurt for another woman.

Will initially resisted Cassie's attempt to pull free. But as the cries turned to whimpers above, he acknowledged the abrupt descent of cold reality lowered by Cassie's rejection. How could he have forgotten all reason and duty? He had wrongfully initiated the embrace, and it could be prolonged only by a dishonorable force more unpardonable still, thus he accepted the error in his urge to wrap her ever tighter in his arms and instead relaxed his hold.

Cassie unsteadily rose, slipped from the warmth of their shared embrace and up to her own cold chamber while secret tears for a lost dream seeped down pale cheeks, purposefully directed toward her cheerless destination.

IN THE EASTERN SKY'S DAWNING, red shifted to orange then blended with yellow, reflecting the last bright shades of the autumn forest surrounding the small glade. 'Twas a sight far too cheerful for the sadness of farewell in Cassie's heart. During the short time she'd spent with Meg and her sons within the confines of the English knight's den, they'd become dear to her. Truth be known they'd become more dear than the vast majority of her own family who, in the manner of most noble homes, she saw little of and who had small care for her.

"I'd stay were I allowed, Cassie." Tom cast a glance at Will, but when the man sent a frown his way, quickly looked back to her. Under a suddenly returned memory of the strained circumstances surrounding their previous night's parting, he qualified his claim. "We'd *all* stay longer if we could."

Tom's earnest words and pained grimace earned a faint smile from the one to whom he spoke. "I know," Cassie whispered, throat too tight for louder words.

"Tom speaks true," Meg affirmed. "I'd willingly linger weeks more were Yuletide not so fast approaching. In a castle, preparations are many and long in the doing." Meg paused, abruptly aware she spoke to one as familiar with castle life as she. With a half-apologetic shrug she explained the particular need for her presence. "I must be there to see foods and feast preparations done rightly. Our countess's friend Merta supervises kitchen tasks when I am not there, but though she has a good heart, she's far too impatient to take time for important details."

"Like measuring proper amounts of correct spices for mulled wine." Tom's sotto voce comment brought a hoot of laughter from Kenward.

Meg sent her son an admonishing glance for his reference to an infamous debacle wherein the castle's high table had been served a vile potion whose bitter taste earned a round of gasps, pursed lips, and tight clenched eyes.

"Asides, she's aging and the strain of sole responsibility for such festivities might prove too much." Meg pointedly turned her shoulder on the young man unable to control his broad grin. "So, give us a hug." She held her arms out to the sweet French damoiselle clearly dreading their departure and looking as forlorn as if she were being abandoned.

Cassie walked into them as unhesitatingly as she had the day past. Tightly closed lashes attempting to hold welling tears at bay, she fiercely hugged the older woman before stepping back. "Never fear," she mumbled in words strained by the unabated lump in her throat. "I'll give Beata the care of a sister."

Will's home was a safe retreat Beata hadn't left since the day of her arrival, not even this morn for the sake of a few more moments with her sister, the last for some time to come. Cassie knew herself unequal to calmly watching these new friends she'd likely never see again disappear into the shadows of the Weald, and rushed to join Beata in the house's private haven for unhappiness.

A chill breeze rustled fallen leaves about the feet of those who remained in the glade. Shriveled and stripped of once bright color, they were a reminder of time passing and things to be done before it was gone. Will gave Meg a hug that would threaten to crush a less sturdy form, then, while Kenward stepped into his mother's fond embrace, he offered his arm to the young man standing proudly upright at her side.

Tom grasped the extended arm below the elbow and joined their forearms together in affirmation of firm family bonds. Although he wished Will's avuncular ways were not his bar to the excitement and glory of battle, Tom's admiration and love for the exceptional man was strong. Since their father's death, ten years and more past, Will had stood as mentor to he and his little brother.

Accompanied by several of Will's men who would see them safe to the Weald's border, the departing pair soon disappeared into woodland shadows. At almost the same instant on the glade's opposite side, two men rode from the gloom to dismount before their leader.

Dark brows lowered over eyes gone to obsidian while Will waited for news they'd not have returned without.

"As you directed, we journeyed to Offcum and showed the sketch to all thereabouts." Harry, a hulking giant of a man grimly delivered the opening statement.

"And learned more than we'd hoped." The second speaker, half the other's bulk but possessed of twice his nervous energy, was far too impatient to wait on Harry's formal report yet quickly subsided under the older man's glare.

"Duncan's right." The irritable admission was accompanied by a deeply drawn breath bespeaking a long-suffering and undeserved forbearance with his excitable cohort. "We learned not only the source of Beata's attack, but that the band's leader, Guy de Faux, had come searching for his betrothed—"

"Cassandra Gavre!" Again Duncan interrupted, too agitated to restrain his tongue.

Will's chin jerked up against words that felt like an unexpected physical blow. Betrothed! Moreover, her intended groom was near. Yet, even during quiet time spent together before the past night's fire, she'd held the potentially crucial information from him—plainly by choice. He felt betrayed. Despite his repeated self-proclaimed assurances that no woman could succeed in games of trickery with him, he'd actually begun to believe that Cassie, alone among the well-born women he'd known, understood his pleasure in a simple life. He had thought they shared a common view. Now, knowing her pledged to a great French lord (a deadly blight upon any mad dream that she could ever be his), it seemed certain she'd schemed to control his treatment of her—and near attained a humiliating success few had achieved and none without a price paid for the deed. Pain flared, burning serious inroads into the fortress of pride holding him impervious to the opinions of others and threatening to unleash a dangerous temper seldom freed.

The two messengers fell back from the golden fires of anger glittering in dark eyes, near the only sign of life in the cold of Will's ice-carved face. He stomped past them toward his house and the betrayer inside.

"You bitch!" The words reverberated with the same force as the door which crashed against the wall behind and bounded a ways back.

Curled like a babe into the consoling warmth for her melancholy mood provided by a padded chair drawn near the blazing fire, Cassie sat bolt upright. With wide, uncomprehending eyes she stared at the furious man filling the doorframe. What had she done? She rose and instinctively held her hands out toward him, palms up in silent supplication for an explanation of his ire.

"Oh, aye, you share my love for the simple life . . ." Will's smile held the bitter acid of self-mockery. "You lie with a traitor's sweetness even as doubtless you long for the finery and comfort your wealthy betrothed will one day provide." He kicked the door shut but kept clenched fists tight to his hips, as if by so doing he restrained the physical retribution his anger demanded. "You sought to lull me into coddling you, stealing by trickery what little I have while deceiving me on the true nature of your relationship with the invaders who seek to steal my land." His fingers uncurled and he shoved them roughly through black strands as if to punish himself for the folly in yielding to her ploy. "God's blood! Betrothed to their leader! What a fool you've played me for."

He knew about Guy and was furious! That certain fact smothered Cassie's hazy dreams—dreams born of the remembered warmth of his smile, the fire of his kisses, and nourished by the heat of roaring flames—dreams in which she and the handsome knight lived happily ever after in the peaceful green depths of the wildwood. Slowly shaking her head in horrified denial, Cassie backed to the foot of the stairway, then turned to flee upward.

His accusations echoed in her mind over and over, faster and faster, louder and louder. Their painful roaring initially prevented her from comprehending the tiny sobs of terror coming from the throat of the fragile woman huddled in a corner near the bottom step.

Having descended the stairway just as Will arrived, Beata had heard only the fury, sensed only the violence behind the confrontation. Thus mentally driven into a dark, horrifying corner of hidden memories too awful to face, she'd fallen cringing against the wall, head buried 'neath shielding arms.

Moving to follow the fleeing damoiselle, Will heard the sounds of Beata's terror all too well and couldn't ignore her distress, certainly not when his actions were its cause.

"Beata, love, you've no reason to fear," Will soothed, kneeling at her side. Forcing control over his spiraling anger and sending a last glance to the figure disappearing around the corner at the top step, he gently lifted Beata and then carried her to one of the padded chairs.

Although Cassie had barely heard Beata's sobs, to her ears Will's comforting words for the maid came as clearly as had his earlier accusations against her. Beata had no reason to fear him. To him Beata was "love." She'd known it true before, had accepted it as fact, but it hurt far worse to hear it from his own lips and to hear it when so very recently he'd used a far different term for her. Quietly closing her chamber door, she leaned back to use its solid planks' strength to survive the anguish within.

After first assuring Beata that she was now and could, if she chose, be ever safe here with him in the Weald, Will coaxed a tremulous smile from the maid before moving away to climb the stairs and stand just outside a door firmly shut against him. Although doubtless he could force his way inside, he hesitated to either deepen the rift between he and Cassie or to further frighten Beata. Hot anger dampened by his foster sister's fear, rationality enough had returned to Will that he knew the error in not calmly making known to Cassie his discovery of her wrong. But what further was there to be said now? He'd caught her in the midst of a scheme, and she surely recognized it hopeless to continue. The matter was done.

On waking, Cassie had thought it impossible for the day to descend lower than where it began with a depressing farewell to friends she'd likely never in her life see again. Unfortunately, she ruefully acknowledged, she should of recent times have learned the wisdom of never assuming the impossibility of anything.

Wrapped in bed furs and disconsolately sitting cross-legged on her lumpy mattress, she noticed a pale yellow straw bravely poking through rough ticking—as if striving to escape its constraints. Without a moment's consideration she pulled it out. There, the straw was free. But what now was she to do with it? As she held the brittle strand between the fingertips of one hand, an unpleasant thought occurred to her. She and this flimsy piece of rubbish were much the same. Not only was her value in the world as questionable, but even were she to be successfully freed from captivity, what was there for her? What purpose had she? Her assigned destination in the fortress of De Faux was no more welcoming than the floor's scattered layer of rushes where, if loosed, this lone straw would be lost. Just as it would be at the mercy of carelessly crushing feet, she would be at the mercy of her always heartless and too oft purposefully cruel betrothed. As if a life hung on the task's success, she began desperately trying to jab the straw back into the mattress.

"Cassie . . ." The call was so soft that its distracted subject at first didn't hear. "Cassie . . ."

Cassie looked up to find a nervous Beata hovering in the narrow opening of her doorway, tugging a never-loosed cloak even tighter about her frail form. Instinctively Cassie gave a reassuring smile.

"I knocked but you didn't answer, so I peeked in to be certain you're well." Gaining bravery from the smile despite its failure to erase the unhappiness shadowing violet eyes, Beata came forward. "You are well, aren't you?"

Cassie, caught in her own distress, failed to recognize the desperation in Beata's voice. Yet, desperate Beata was. The scene below had increased her certainty that there was but one solution to the endless fear of the formless terror looming always near. She needed help to win that security, and 'twas help only Cassandra could provide.

"Don't I look well?" Cassie's gaze dropped from too perceptive eyes and realized the straw's yellow nub was still visible amidst the ticking's muddy hue. She resolutely tucked the errant object back into safety amidst its fellows before again looking up to the quiet woman who had yet to respond.

"Your eyes are sad." With no thought to subterfuge, Beata's answer was literal and direct.

Heavy lashes dropped over the eyes in question. Cassie told herself she should have known better than to ask such a question of this one who, though robbed of her memory, seemed blessed with the power to see beyond masks donned to conceal feelings.

"I'm sad your sister and nephew have gone." She spoke the truth, if only a part, and hoped it enough to evade the crystal-clear vision of this woman-child.

Beata nodded and wisps of honey-streaked hair brushed her pale cheeks. "Their leave-taking makes me unhappy, too. But a faerie queen shouldn't ever be sad."

"Proof, I fear, that I am not the faerie queen you've named me," Cassie answered with a crooked smile.

"Oh, no, you are her, though I don't understand why you wish to be called Cassie rather than Queen Cassandra."

Cassie found the other's unfaltering confidence amazing in itself. Queen Cassandra? How could she be a queen when she wasn't even comfortable being termed "Lady," and that was a title rightfully hers.

"You are Cassandra, are you not?" Beata asked. Mayhap her friend had somehow forgot her past, just as she knew she'd difficulty remembering far too many things. If so, she must help Cassie. She reached out to touch a long ebony braid with awe as she murmured, "Hair like the night and eyes amethyst like pools the same, she parts the mists of time and distance by the magic in her name, Cassandra."

Of a sudden, from the corridors of not so very distant childhood memories, Cassie recognized this as a line from the rhyme one of her nurses, more kindly than most, had quoted more than once. 'Twas the tale of the faerie queen entrusted with guarding the Amethyst Pools in the center of Elfland. Even as a toddling the notion of herself in so illustrious a position had seemed impossible, and for her the rhyme held no significance. Yet here was answer to the long-standing question of how Beata had mistaken

her for an ethereal being to which this fey creature with her instinctive
understanding of human heart had surely more similarity.

Growing impatient, as seldom she did, Beata dropped to her knees
beside the straw pallet and urgently clasped the other woman's hands.
"You are Cassandra, aren't you? I've got to know because I have a plea you
must grant. Will you help me?"

Cassie nodded to the first question but was lost to understand the
nature of the second. "I would do anything I could for you, Beata, but I've
few resources."

Beata beamed and turned a deaf ear to the qualifier. A faerie queen had
no limitations. She could cast a spell under which all things were possible.

"Help my 'shining knight' find me," she urgently pleaded. "He saved
me from a dreadful evil and promised to return—but he'll never find me
here, not without the aid of your magic."

Cassie was certain Beata's words were as close as she had yet come to
talking about the events that had stolen reality from her. Cassie hesitantly
probed the opening. "What 'dreadful evil'?"

"I don't know . . ." Beata's delicate brow furrowed and she slowly
shook her head to ward off the ominous shadows threatening to swoop
down and consume her. "I can't remember." Golden eyes lifted to meet
Cassie's concerned gaze full on as she proudly defended herself against
any possibility that she'd done less than she ought. "I've tried and tried
but I can't—save for the awful dreams I have but can't truly recall when I
wake."

With gentle persistence Cassie continued. "But what then of your
'shining knight'?" Cassie watched as distress smoothed from a face near
healed. If only Beata's memory were as easily mended.

"He's golden and wonderful and carried me to safety. He promised I'd
be safe so long as I wore his cloak, and he promised to come back for me."
Her face crumpled again, and her hand on Cassie's arm gripped with a
strength unintended. "You must help me—please."

Cassie was perversely thankful she'd no power to grant Beata's plea, for
she feared she knew precisely of whom Beata spoke, had suspected the
truth for some time. Despite an honest wish to help this new friend, she
would pray the subject of her plea, a friend of long-standing, would never
appear in this place. Considering Will's oath to see those responsible for
Beata's assault pay with their lives, to do so would almost surely mean her
"shining knight's" death.

Once her plea was made, with apparently no lingering fear but that her
faerie queen would grant it, Beata slipped away as quietly as she'd come.

Cassie remained in her chamber, ever more dejected by this reinforced prospect of danger. Despite an odd banging about in hallway and over steps, she refused to bow to curiosity and peek out. She'd answered only Kenward's knock on her door when he brought meals for which she'd no appetite.

As the sky darkened to night, her attention returned to Will's accusations, and the self-pity of her first response gave way before the innate honesty of her soul. His anger was a just anger. She *had* kept the truth from him, but not to play him for a fool! He deserved an explanation, and by the time the quiet of a village settled for the night arrived, Cassie had surrendered to the demands of her conscience. She wondered if Will were preparing for the dark hours' rest in the hall below. Could she go to him now? Should she? She would.

Anxious to appear at her best, leastways to bolster what sparse confidence and pride she could scrounge together, Cassie rose and exchanged simple homespun for the cream kirtle and cranberry-red overgown that complimented her coloring. She ran a brush through loose ebony locks and drew several deep, steadying breaths. Before her craven nature could rise up to prevent the deed, she quietly opened the door. She heard Kenward wishing his leader good night, then the outgoing door close as he departed.

Belowstairs Will poured a last pitcher of still boiling water into the brass tub and gazed blindly into its rising steam. He was tired of bathing in the chill brook and more than ready to ease both tired muscles and strained temper in the bath's warmth. This he'd promised himself as just reward for reaching the end of a difficult day wherein he'd fulfilled his duties while Cassandra remained secluded in her chamber. During the afternoon Kenward had helped carry the tub down to the hall, and as soon as the day's last meal was cleared away, had begun heating water.

Will stepped back, stripped off his forest-green tunic and turned to toss it across a chair pushed aside from the hearth to make room for the tub. Dark eyes widened at the sight of the tender damoiselle hesitating a mere step beyond its tall back, lavender gaze stroking his bare chest. Their unquestionable admiration offered more provocation than he could easily bear. He snapped at her.

"What trick do you mean to perform for me tonight?"

Gulping, Cassie shut her eyes tight against the frighteningly beautiful sight of powerful muscles at rest. Though she'd seen him thus before, the view had lost none of its ability to halt the breath in her throat. He was surely the epitome of masculine perfection from broad shoulders to narrow hips.

"I came to offer yet another apology," she weakly answered, vexed by the ragged edge of too soft words. " 'Tis the task for which I seem most useful, leastways the one I'm most oft called to perform. You never asked me if I were betrothed." She flared with sudden and regretfully momentary courage. Subsiding beneath the cold glitter chilling black eyes, she defensively added, "You only asked if I were kin to the Gavre taking part in the siege of Dover Castle."

She met his still freezing gaze directly and joined her hands tightly together while attempting to channel her efforts back toward the purpose for which she'd come—to apologize, to explain, but *not* to quarrel.

"I failed to tell you about Guy not to fool you, but in a feeble attempt to fool myself." She took a step forward and curled apprehension-stiff fingers tightly about the chair's high back. "Don't you see, I want nothing —have never wanted aught to do with the wretched man. In truth, 'tis my distaste of him which brought me to your land."

This claim won Will's attention. He'd wondered from the first what had possessed her sire to bring the damsel to a place of war, and beneath his impassive facade, he listened intently as she continued.

"To avoid the alliance, I fled to an abbey, thinking to seek shelter with the sisters there. They returned me to my father without question. He brought me here to see the marriage performed forthwith and I under my new husband's iron hand."

Cassie feared she saw disbelief hovering in dark eyes, and desperately sought to make him understand. "Guy is a wealthy and powerful man. Anxious to form an alliance with him, 'twas first arranged that I wed his son, a decade younger than me. But the boy caught a fever and died last spring. My sire, determined not to lose the bond, then welcomed the substitution of the father for the son as my bridegroom."

The depth of disgust in her voice seemed proof of the sincerity in her claimed misliking for the man. Yet Will was wary of being duped again, and by the same woman. Dark brows drew into a fierce frown as he considered the many possible schemes that might lie behind her words.

"You had the right of it when you questioned my value in this world," Cassie stated with more bitterness than she realized. "I've always known my only purpose is to be bargained for items of more worth. So, you see . . . ." She shrugged with feigned unconcern. "I am not expected even to be decorative. 'Tis unnecessary. As you must surely know, females are of value only for bartering, and whether tots in the cradle or toothless hags, it makes little difference so long as the dowry and family connections are sufficiently attractive. As a pawn to secure fine alliances and great wealth, what I want or do not want means less than nothing." The palm of one hand rubbed across the other as if brushing off inconsequential remains of the flour, once important but now superfluous, that adhered to sticky hands during the baking of bread.

These were facts Will knew all too well. They were why, even were they not foes, she could never be his. Not only had he no wealth or influence to barter, he'd no pure claim to an illustrious lineage that might compensate for other lacks.

"I did not speak of Guy earlier because I dread belonging to the hateful man. Likely he is responsible for the wrong done Beata, and he has laid three wives in the grave already. I've no wish to be the fourth, and I beg you not to put me within his hold." Her breath came in pleading gasps that lifted full breasts until they were enticingly outlined against the fine wool of her red overgown.

The response the sight drew from Will was all too physical, and he wondered if 'twas done apurpose to weaken him to her cause. Here she stood, pleading for his aid. Now, when it was too late. *If* this were the truth, why hadn't she told him in the first instance, told him when there was hope he could do as she asked? But was it the truth she spoke or did she merely lie again to excuse her culpability and to fool him once more into lending her what few comforts he could provide? Whichever made no difference now.

"Your confession comes too late." Will grated out his response. "I cannot, even did I wish it"—his cutting tone left little possibility that he did—"change what's done. I told you the very day a ransom demand was sent, a sennight and more past. Once delivered to your brother, you must know of a certainty, would immediately share it with De Faux." By that fact alone Will thought 'twas plain she'd enacted this whole scene solely for some subtle scheme of her own.

Cassie's shoulders slumped in despair. He spoke of facts she could hardly deny nor could she expect him to perform some miracle to cancel. Yet the harshness of his response was devastating proof he'd no care for her. Before tears pricking uncomfortably at her eyelids could break free, she abruptly turned to climb the stairs.

As Cassandra turned her vulnerable back to him, Will regretted slapping away the extended hand of peace. Even were his worst suspicions true, he'd been as needlessly cruel as he had in his earlier accusations. What wicked demon had come to possess him of recent days? For a good

many years he'd subdued unruly emotions by maintaining about himself
an impenetrable wall of laughter and charm until any who knew him
would say he'd a warm nature to temper his fierce military prowess. Now,
twice in one day his temper had escaped its bonds to attack one unequal
to its assault. Without knowing of a certainty what he meant to do, Will
quickly followed Cassie's path. At the top of the stairs he put his arm
about her shoulders, trying to turn her to face him.

It felt like a blow, this pitying gesture. Cassie jerked free of his hold.
Wounded pride roused, she glared at him from eyes burning with restrained tears.

"Do you seek to use me? Use me as you sought last night? Use me as
Beata was used, as you mean to see Guy use me?"

Will was stunned by her rejection to his well-intended attempt at rec-
onciliation. Use her? Is that what she thought of the embrace they'd
shared the past night? Use her? He'd not coerced her. She'd come into his
arms willingly. Nay, more than willingly. Far worse, she had enticed him!

"Merely have I answered the blatant invitation in your unwavering gaze
of days past. Only do I call your unspoken promises forfeit!" His pride
launched the counterattack, cold humor a gold glitter in his eyes. "I've no
need to compel you."

Cassie's mouth fell open in denial, giving him the perfect opportunity
for the proof he meant to exact. He swept her into his arms, taking her
soft lips with his—yet not with the painful force she'd have expected. Had
there been force, she might have been able to resist. But *non*, his mouth
stroked hers until she followed its teasing withdrawal, aching for a more
fulfilling contact. When he settled his lips over hers to drink of the berry
sweetness within, the fiery whirlwind that seemed his to command returned and swept her into the vortex where reality was lost.

World shrinking to one of the senses, she wrapped her arms about his
bare shoulders, savoring the feel of muscles rippling beneath rich satin
skin, the wiry padding of black curls across the chest she mindlessly
pressed against. Her fingers tangled into his cool hair just as he wound his
into her dusky locks, urging her head back, arching her throat for kisses
that burned down to the dip at its base. While one arm locked her ever
tighter to his powerful body, the other hand began a tempting tour from
waist to under her arm and forward to cup one lush breast. When a
thumb stroked its peak, a heartfelt moan accompanied the fierce quiver
that rose from her depths.

Suddenly Cassie found herself upheld only by the cold planks of the
door behind while the man who'd reduced her to a boneless mass stood a

step away, a sardonic smile on his lips and gold glittering from half-shielded eyes.

"No force needed. You'd come and give to me all that your eyes have promised with little enough urging from me." Will turned his back on her and steadily descended the stairs, pride salvaged.

His pride was saved, but Cassie's was badly lacerated. By letting him melt the ice of her anger so easily, she had utterly betrayed her wicked fascination with him. He, by walking away without a second glance, had just as plainly demonstrated that he felt no more than a passing physical interest in her.

Cassie nearly fell through the door of her chamber and stumbled to lay facedown on the prickly straw mattress, a just residing place for her wounded self-image. Useless he'd called her and useless she was. He found her not even attractive enough to use her for the purpose he'd roused her to fulfill. Tears too long restrained now refused to flow easily, and her pain found release only in dry sobs.

Standing directly below Cassie's bed, Will heard the wrenching sobs. They doused the fire of his temper to cold ashes of regret. He had never in his life set out to hurt a woman—until tonight. Why? Why had he done it when she was the last woman in the world he wanted to see in pain? Ignoring the fast cooling water in the tub, ignoring his bare torso, Will strode to the door, snatched his dark cloak from its peg on the wall and walked into the chill air of a late November night.

Chapter
~§ 9 §~

I N THE GLOOM of early morn Cassie paused at the top of the stairs to survey the hall below, herself unseen. Narrow back to her, Kenward bent over the fire, urging renewed life to banked but red-glowing coals. He was the only person in the large room, and Cassie found in that fact a confusing mixture of relief and disappointment.

She'd slept poorly and risen early. Still, plainly Will had already departed for the day's business. After the humiliating scene the night past, she should be relieved. She was relieved. Yet . . .

Vexed by unsettled emotions, she hastened down the steps with enough noise to demand Kenward's attention.

"Good morrow, milady."

Cassie found the boy's grin depressingly cheery and had difficulty restraining a frown as she nodded a wordless greeting.

While the damsel made her way to the table, Kenward poured a mug of frothy milk and set it at her place before turning to polish a crisp apple. When the fruit had achieved a ruddy glow, he gave it to her as well.

His attempt to silently serve without the possible irritation of words left Cassie ashamed for taking her ill temper out on him. She gently caught his arm as he made to turn away.

"Kenward, pray pardon my gloom. You are a friend, and I have too few to risk losing any." Kenward found the smile she gave reparation enough for her small wrong.

" 'S'truth, we *are* friends, and the bonds of my friendships are not so fragile that, like thistledown, they blow away in the gentlest breeze."

Kenward made the statement with the self-conscious pride of one struggling toward adulthood, and Cassie's ever tender heart melted beneath the spoken pact. She saw that he'd given not only his friendship, but his loyalty—a gift of great price and one few had extended to her. Tears annoyingly near the surface since entering the Weald rose dangerously.

Although here they were as oft born of temper as sorrow, they were unwelcome, and she hurried to waylay their path with plans for mundane tasks.

" 'Tis time for making rye bread." She'd been in this house observing both Edna and Meg long enough to learn the schedule, and had aided the latter more than once. "By midday I mean to have a batch ready for the baking. Thus, I charge you with laying a fire in the ovens sufficient to raise the temperature to a level what will see loaves evenly browned." This was the opportunity she'd been waiting for, the one that gave her the chance to lighten Edna's burden by sharing the weight—if only this little.

Kenward was a wee bit worried. Did Cassie know the mysteries of bread baking well enough to embark on such a task by herself? Still, he wouldn't argue with her after the scene just past, and promptly turned to his assigned chore. The oven's iron door opened waist high. He placed a bundle of faggots inside the oval-shaped recess and set them alight with a burning twig from the fireplace's open flames.

Gulping down the last of the cool white liquid in her cup, Cassie rose. She held the apple in one hand while struggling to lift the deceptively thin iron sheet on which loaves were formed then slipped into the oven. Only with the apple put aside and Kenward's help did she succeed in hoisting the heavy utensil from its vertical storage position into place across one side of the tabletop.

Next Cassie began searching out needed ingredients. She pulled forth a big sack of rye flour, a smaller one of salt, checked the tub of lard, and touched the basket of fresh eggs which must have arrived with the morning milk and been left on the tabletop. Slowly turning about, she ticked the items gathered off on her fingers once again. A slight frown creased her forehead. More was needed—but what?

The outer door swung noisily open. With her back to it, Cassie froze. Had Will come home? Memory of the last words they'd exchanged and the scene that had preceded them flooded back. Into its wake flowed shame for her wanton response to his insincere seduction. She couldn't turn; she wouldn't turn.

"Don't need me at all." The gruffness of the words did nothing to hide the unique combination of hurt and affront behind them. Edna had thought, as Meg was gone, she'd be needed again. But 'twas clearly untrue.

It wasn't Will. Cassie whirled about. Of course it wasn't Will. She hurried toward the massive woman already rolling out the door. "Edna—"

The one addressed paused, blocking the open doorway with her width, but still she stared toward the empty glade beyond.

"I had hoped to be your assistant and ease the pressure of your many tasks, but find I haven't the skills to succeed and am that glad to see you." She snapped her fingers.

Edna looked suspiciously back over a beefy shoulder.

Cassie had stopped a few paces behind the other woman but took a step forward as she earnestly explained. "I watched Meg make rye bread, even helped her a little, and thought I could do it myself." The weak light of a cloudy day falling through the opening above Edna's bulk rippled over ebony hair in its single fat plait when Cassie gave her head a forlorn shake. "But I can't even remember all the proper ingredients, much less the right measures to be used. Won't you teach me how to lend aid in this small way—and any others you'll allow me a part in?" She held out her hands palms up to the older woman. "Please?"

Turning, head tilted consideringly to one side, Edna pondered the request. Her decision came with an abrupt nod and a sudden forward motion that had Cassie scampering aside to open the path for her return.

Edna took stock of the ingredients the French damoiselle had gathered. A hearty laugh shook her considerable girth, but the face she turned to Cassie held more honest amusement than scorn.

"What you got here won't be nothing without warm ale berm and a wee measure of sugar to see it rise."

She went to a series of shelves backed into the corner between fireplace and wall. From one of the highest shelves she took a small material-wrapped package, and from one lower a large crockery jug. These she set atop the table, the sugar loaf with care and the heavy jug with force enough to rock the sturdy structure. Last, from beneath the far end she lifted a huge cloth-covered bowl.

Cassie stood at Edna's side, carefully watching as a fair measure of ale berm, an egg white with only a touch of yolk, a chunk of sugar, and spoonful of salt came together in the bowl. Once they'd been well blended, Edna handed Cassie the large wooden spoon.

"Stir whilst I pour the rightful amount of flour."

Cassie nodded and set to slowly stirring the brown liquid which lightened but a little as into it like a smooth river rye flour flowed. When the stirring became all but impossible, Edna took the spoon away, tossed more flour on the iron sheet, and upended the bowl so that the sticky dough landed on the sheet with a plop that sent puffs of flour dancing in every direction.

"Now do thusly," Edna advised, scooping up a handful of flour and sprinkling it over the lump before punching it with a strength Cassie couldn't hope to imitate.

A willing pupil, Cassie did as commanded in so far as she was able. It was amazingly hard work, but a fine sense of accomplishment filled her when, some time later, Edna told her she'd succeeded in seeing the dough become the proper consistency—smooth yet flexible.

The door opened. Arms bared by sleeves rolled up still buried in dough, and expecting the return of Kenward—who'd been sent to fetch more wood for the fireplace—Cassie glanced toward the open portal with a proud grin on her flour-smudged face. The grin faded as a haunting shadow darkened her eyes to deep violet.

Black brows lifted in surprise, Will took in the sight. Near dwarfed by the huge figure of Edna standing behind, Cassie looked like nothing so much as a wee urchin caught wrongfully amidst the childish joys of making mud cakes. He said as much.

"Why do toddlings find such delight in substances the consistency of mud?" Dark head tilted to one side, a teasing smile lit his strong face while a tide of rose washed her softly rounded cheeks. "Leastwise your creations will have an honest purpose."

Face burning, Cassie stood dumbstruck by the broad smile he'd gifted her with—as if the past day and night's exchanges hadn't happened. Edna reached around to brush Cassie's hands from dough she then scooped into the bowl and set to rise on a warm corner of the table.

"Bread." Cassie weakly offered the unnecessary one word explanation. A deep lavender gaze dropped as she applied an excessive depth of attention to rubbing flour from hands, arms, and face with the cloth laid aside for that purpose.

"A worthy accomplishment." Will's compliment was sincere and intended to reassure Cassie that he didn't find her so useless as once he'd claimed. Obviously, from her words the past night, she'd taken them all too seriously.

Cassie's blush deepened. Did his comment mean he knew that, at least in part, she'd toiled to placate him? *Non.* He couldn't when she hadn't fully realized it herself—until this moment. More importantly, by his teasing manner did he mean to tell her the accusations of the previous day and the past night's scene were to be forgot—as if they'd never been? Hope at the notion that, even if he couldn't—or wouldn't—grant her plea to not be returned to Guy, he wanted to erase hurtful accusations, and relief at the prospect of blocking the shame of her wanton response, were counterbalanced by a painful ache at the idea that he wished to forget the few moments of intimacy they'd shared.

To distract the embarrassed maid, Will cast about for another topic. A quick survey of the hall showed a strange lack. Although Beata's presence during daylight hours was never conspicuous, she was always there and close to Cassie—but not now.

"Where's Beata?" His short question began with simple curiosity but ended on a deep note of concern.

Cassie gasped, stricken with guilt for her selfishness in not earlier wondering the same. To the flour-strewn tabletop she dropped the nervously twisted cloth and hastened up the stairs. Will followed close behind.

Beata's petite figure looked lost amongst the rumpled covers of Will's huge bed. She was feverish and mumbling incoherent words. Will thrust aside the bed's interfering drapes and bent close in an attempt to decipher the sounds while Cassie rushed to fetch a clean cloth soaked in cool water and wipe a burning brow.

"Did she cry out in the night?" Will asked, tone harsh with worry and self-disgust. To avoid hearing the condemning sobs he'd roused from Cassandra, he'd chosen to spend the night outside the walls of his house, beyond hearing distance of Beata's night terrors. Thus, he feared that by his wrongful actions against Cassie he'd not only insulted her, but failed Beata, the sister of his heart if not of his blood.

"*Non.*" Cassie immediately answered the man too concerned even to glance up from the shadows of the blue-draped bed where he hovered over a restlessly thrashing woman. "Leastwise I think not." Cassie bit her lip hard. Had her own sounds of anguish deafened her to another's? Pray God, 'twasn't so.

After their brief exchange the two worked in silence to ease the unconscious woman's fever and make her more comfortable.

That afternoon Cassie insisted on staying at Beata's side with Will. She deemed it a penance far too small for her wrong to the ailing womanchild. She had failed Beata, failed even to realize she was missing. A shameful fact.

Throughout that night and all the next day, while Will had perforce to ride patrol in the Weald, Cassie sat tirelessly with Beata in the knight's darkened but luxurious chamber. Thus, it was Cassie who heard the whispers of a woman living anew the time of horror and pain blanked from her conscious mind. It was Cassie who heard the name that confirmed a fact suspected and struck fear anew into her own heart. "Vauderie." The single

word came out with a deep sigh just as the fever seemed to break and
Beata slid into a deep slumber.

Straightening from where she'd thrown herself across the wide bed to
restrain a thrashing Beata, Cassie stiffly stepped down from the platform
and settled into a padded chair long since pulled near. She buried her face
in her hands, raking fingers through strands of black loosened the night
past and never re-bound. Vauderie? Yet, it wasn't, *couldn't* be Vauderie
who was responsible for the wicked deed! Valnoir very possibly. Guy without a moment's hesitation. But *not* serious, patient Vauderie.

Still, amidst one of Beata's night terrors the sound of his name on her
lips was damning, and something Cassie dare not allow Will to hear. To
any man who loved this fragile creature, 'twould surely be all the proof
necessary to convict and condemn Vauderie to pay the ultimate price. By
her promise to Meg, caring for Beata was Cassie's responsibility, one made
the more important now, and something she must do alone. She allowed
her head to drop back against cushioned slats and let eyelids fall while she
offered up heartfelt prayers for Beata's quick recovery—from both the
fever and from the pain that had driven her to retreat into childhood.

During the day's fruitless patrol Will had difficulty restraining an impatience for its conclusion. When the end finally came, he returned to find
both women sleeping undisturbed. He stood in the doorway of a chamber
—his, though one he'd seldom entered in the past many days—and
watched the steady rise and fall of Cassie's breathing. At the same gradual
pace a sense of peace crept in to soothe the dark impatience of his soul
and spread the bright light of warm peace in its place. How could he bear
to send this rare source of such contentment away? The possibility of her
being anywhere but within arm's reach, or leastwise waiting in his home,
brought the dull ache of a loneliness he'd long feared certain to follow.
The only option open to him, as a man of honor, was to savor—at a safe
distance—what few days she might linger in his captivity.

Slowly the feeling of another's presence, of being watched, crept into
Cassie's sleep, scattering insubstantial wisps of dreams into the secret
corners of her unconscious mind. The weight of thick, dark lashes lifted a
fraction. Hazy lavender eyes, though soft and unfocused, instantly settled
on the man who would dominate any room.

Will gave her a smile so gentle she felt herself melting beneath its
warmth as he quietly moved to within a pace of where she half sat, half lay
across a chair sized for his large frame. Too newly roused to be fully awake,
she gazed up at him with a welcome that boded of more than mere
friendship. Will nearly sank to his knees and swept the doubtless uninten-

tionally enticing damoiselle into his arms. Only the faint stirring sounds of
Beata turning in her sleep restrained the impulse which, did he allow
himself the questionable right to enjoy her company, must never be permitted.

Instead, Will spoke quietly, "Edna has a tasty meal awaiting." His arm
was formally proffered as if to escort a fine lady to a king's feast. "Come
and dine."

Cassie sat upright but firmly shook her head. "I can't leave her." Now
wakeful enough herself to remember why it was so important she not leave
an ailing Beata alone in Will's company, Cassie gestured toward the frail
woman gone motionless again.

"You've been in this chamber near a whole night and day." Will
frowned. "You must come down. Don't fret, Edna will sit with Beata
while we eat."

Lavender eyes narrowed on the still offered arm. Surely, so long as 'twas
not Will who remained with Beata, she could safely be gone for leastways
a short time. She laid small fingers atop the waiting forearm and rose to
her feet. Of a certainty Edna would call them should any need arise.

"I'll go with you . . . ." She paused, bolstering her courage to fearlessly
look straight into the bottomless depths of his black gaze as she offered a
pact. "So long as you allow me to sleep here this night and every night
until Beata is recovered."

Will stood unmoving under the challenge, studying the sweet beauty
whose softly rounded and all too feminine curves plainly covered a strong
will and fine courage which had begun to appear ever more frequently.
Despite widely divergent suspicions and hopes regarding her earlier actions, he could find naught but good in her insistence on attending the
ailing woman who so plainly worshiped her. Aye, no matter possible con-
flicts between loyalty to family and honest dealings with him—her foe—
Cassandra was a true lady, yet not one so self-centered as to place her own
welfare above another's. A true lady, he silently repeated a fact earlier
admitted, but one unlike the many he'd known before.

Cassie could feel his warm approval, and a guilty red tide burned her
cheeks. *Don't be a dolt!* she told herself. *Even without Beata's mention of
Vauderie, I'd want to stay by her side. I need feel no shame that two goals
are met by the same action.*

Will thought Cassie's blush a charming demonstration of her still oft
timid nature and was amused by the shy smile she gave him as she made
an understandable request.

"Pray allow me to tarry a moment in my own chamber." Cassie was certain she must look a wretched sight with unruly mane all atangle and clothes creased by more than a day and night's wear. Though privately she admitted her lacks, she'd wanted never to appear before Will less than the most attractive she could be.

While one hand still rested atop his arm, her other self-consciously brushed back a glory of flowing locks. Abruptly aware that her motion had brought attention to the very problem she wanted to hide, the rose in her cheeks deepened. Weakly she excused the action. "My hair is in need of a good brushing." That was true but too disgustingly vain. She rushed to add, "And I'd much appreciate even a hasty wash."

Gold glints of humor sparkled in dark eyes as Will gave the damoiselle plainly distressed by her sleep-disheveled appearance a knowing smile. From his point of view, did she but know it, she'd no need for the endless primping indulged in by most. With her mussed cloak of heavy black satin, slumber-hazed lavender eyes, and emotion-tinted cheeks, she looked as if awakened moments past from a night in her lover's arms—a sight impossible to improve upon. But he nodded, waving her toward the chamber door. "I'll see that Edna joins Beata here whilst I wait for you below."

That evening and every evening for the next fortnight, Will made a special effort to be in his own house when the day's last meal was laid, living for the hours spent over the table and before the fire with soft, sweet Cassandra. Though young Kenward was ever present to act as an odd sort of chaperon, seldom was he noticed in the aura of awareness stretching between the other two like an intangible cord binding them together. They spoke of many things. Yet in all their talk, there were subjects never discussed, avoided as if each were afraid to risk sundering the fragile harmony.

Beata was slowly recovering from her mysterious ailment, but though she oft came to the great hall during the day seeking the reassuring nearness of her "faerie queen," each night she was abed before Will returned. And as the woman-child's delirium passed, so too did Cassie's fear of misunderstood revelations.

On the fourteenth night Will sat beside Cassandra in one of the lower chamber's matching padded chairs and complimented her on yet another fine meal. Since the day of Meg's departure, Cassie had taken on ever more of the household's chores—with Edna's blessings and occasional support. So much had passed between them that they could sit, as now, in companionable silence. And so much faith had Will in his own control that he'd allowed Kenward to join his men in an evening of ale and dice, leaving he and Cassie alone. While his feet stretched out toward the leaping flames of the fire providing the room's only light, dark eyes rested on the pure profile of the too tempting figure so near. Black tendrils had escaped the coiled confines of braids wound atop her head to lay like a caress against fire-rosed cheeks. Her white teeth gently nibbled a full lower lip to berry brightness, proof she felt the power of his gaze.

Indeed, Cassie could feel the thrilling weight of his attention. She reveled in it yet bit her lip to restrain the smile certain to reveal too fully her pleasure in his company. She feared that were he to know how thoroughly she'd surrendered to the power of his allure, he might again be driven into the impenetrable distance of spirit she'd learned he could easily adopt beneath his jesting manner. 'Twas something he'd done whenever they'd seemed to be slipping across the invisible line he'd plainly drawn betwixt them.

During quiet evenings gone by, they'd talked mainly of abstract philosophies or mundane daily events, but never again of his noble past and seldom of hers. Too, by unspoken agreement, they avoided recent events and political problems of the present. Tonight, however, she had begun to tell him more of her cold family and, as she'd once claimed in the heat of anger, their uncaring expectations for her.

"I am but a pawn on my family's chess board—the lowliest piece, and worth only what their bartering of me secures in lands or position." With a sidelong glance, eyes deepened to violet delved directly into the dark shadows of Will's steady gaze.

Will nodded slowly. Although neither had mentioned her powerful betrothed since he'd accused her of playing him for a fool by not revealing her relationship with Guy de Faux, he read aright this roundabout way of reasserting her claim that she'd had no part in the choice of a mate neither sought nor wanted. He had never ceased to wonder, if she'd spoken true, leastways of her distaste for Guy. If in that she'd been honest with him, then he owed her no less.

Nudging a log fallen from fire center to hearth edge, Will focused his attention on the resulting storm of sparks as he began to talk on a decision long since made and one that might provide some relief to her anxieties.

"You've no reason to fear the man's claim on you."

In irrational and fleeting hope that by these words he stated an intent to claim her for himself, Cassie's eyes flew to his profile, but found in it a dark and uninviting chill.

"The man will not live to do the deed." His words were as cold as his expression.

Cassie had heard him swear such vengeance before and had believed it then as now—just as she knew to the depths of her being that a reverse and far more frightening prospect was equally true. She also stared into the consuming flames dancing in a violent battle against soot-blackened walls, and felt as hopelessly flung against a destiny not hers to hinder.

"Without doubt Guy means to demand the same of you—not because he cares for me, but because he assuredly views your actions as a personal insult which demands his retribution be wreaked upon you."

Will heard the honest apprehension in Cassie's voice—but for him or for Guy? Whichever, the result would be the same.

"I've made an oath to see the man dead. He and all those involved in Beata's attack." The gaze he turned to Cassie was a black wall of determination lit by no flicker of gold. "And even be it at the cost of my own life, it will be so."

In an effort to hide the terror roused by his dangerous resolve which must be all too obvious on her face, Cassie let her head droop until her chin near rested on her chest.

Indeed, despite the lowered ebony head, Will saw the sudden difference in rosy cheeks abruptly stripped of color. Plainly his attempt to ease her anxieties had gone far astray, and now he must find some topic of interest enough to woo her thoughts from the gloom into which he'd apparently dropped them. The only subject that came to mind was the one that he'd long refused for any to discuss; one he knew from Kenward was of great curiosity to her.

"Earlier I told you of my uncle, Earl Garrick; his lovely wife, Lady Nessa; and their whole brood—whom I love. Doubtless my affection for them made my decision to live apart the more difficult to comprehend."

Cassie kept her face down, striving to keep all expression from her face. She feared the wrong reaction might halt his opening of this long forbidden subject, and most fearful 'twould happen did she reveal her delight in his sharing with her of matters it seemed certain he'd discussed with few others.

She'd not realized how easily Will could read her interest in brows slightly raised and a lower lip firmly held between teeth. However, her attention, far from causing him to stop, urged him on to speak further—a luxury he seldom permitted himself. All too soon she would be gone, he rationalized his action. Moreover, she was unlikely to share it with others hereabouts, and beyond the Weald's boundaries 'twould be a matter of minor import.

"But how could one such as you, born and bred to an unchallenged position in the world, understand the difficulties I faced in winning a position in any society?" He smiled, but the curl of bitter humor was unmistakable. "My heritage is not pure. I fit into neither the patrician world of my noble grandfather nor the earthy world of my woodsman father." At the frown of disapproval quickly gathering on her face, Will realized he'd left the door to misunderstanding open and hastily came to his family's defense. " 'Twas not the well-born portion of my mother's family who rejected or were ever uncomfortable with my existence. They love and accept me wholeheartedly."

Expression clearing, Cassie dared to nod and look up. How could they not? He was more a man of honor and bravery than any lord she knew, far more than her own brothers.

Will's grim smile deepened in acknowledgment of her wordless defense of him. " 'Tis their peers who have difficulty seeing past the stain of my illegitimate lineage." His mask of cynical amusement firmly in place, Will shrugged, but looked away from too-seeing lavender eyes to again stare blindly, unblinkingly, into weaving fire tongues of orange and yellow. "The problem is as much theirs as mine. Still, I do not choose to foist my unwanted company upon them."

But surely, since the war between her country and his began, Cassie thought, the English lords must have found a deep appreciation and admiration for this man who had done so much to stave off their enemies. Then she remembered that a goodly number of those same barons had invited her French prince to take the English crown and were the very people Willikin had on occasion fought against—at least before King John's death. Uncertain how to sort out the facts, Cassie was afraid to speak and waited for him to continue, but when he did, he'd turned the tale in a new direction.

"Far harder for me to understand was the rejection of the common folk of my father's heritage." By the crease between her brows he saw that Cassie shared his initial surprise at their attitude, and explained. "Although I had thought they'd have no reason to disdain my bastardy and be willing to accept me amongst their number, because of my blood ties to those who are their masters, they're ever uncomfortable with me."

"But how did you come to be here in the forest?" Cassie's curiosity overwhelmed her determination to hold silent, and she shifted closer to better hear his quietly spoken words.

" 'Tis here that I am accepted for who and what I am—a simple knight and no more. The people of the Weald know I was raised and trained to knighthood in Castle Tarrant, know that there I've humble friends such as

Meg and Tom, but they know nothing of my blood tie with its earl. I have always and will always strive to see that fact remains a hidden truth. Thanks to Meg, you know more than you were meant." The golden glint of humor had returned to his eyes as he shrugged in mock defeat. "But how can I condemn her for the deed when 'tis I who now have told you even more?" His face went solemn and a dark gaze held violet eyes as he quietly said, "I can only pray you will preserve my privacy in this matter for so long as you remain within our borders."

Despite the ache in his offhand reminder of the limits to her stay, in response to this gift of a rarely shared knowledge Cassie instantly nodded her agreement with his request. "No sooner asked than given."

The grin accompanying her statement held a sincerity Will had no wish to disbelieve.

"But you've yet to explain the 'how' of your coming to the Weald." Wanting to win from the knight another smile and a better understanding of him, Cassie repeated the earlier question which he had yet to truly answer.

Amused by her tenacity, Will complied, although the answering smile on his face soon surrendered 'neath the descent of somber lines. "I had traveled through the remote reaches of the Weald with my uncle more than a few times as a youngster. Thus, when as a young adult I set out in search of my place in the world only to be frustrated at every turning, I fled here into its most secluded shadows, thinking to retreat into isolation. I intended to become a hermit amongst the forest's dense cover but found it not so uninhabited as I'd thought. Rather 'tis claimed by an independent group of honest folk who refuse to lend more than perfunctory notice to the rank of any man unless it be earned and given by the will of the people."

Even while struggling to comprehend this foreign concept, in it Cassie recognized the greater need for his privacy and more fully understood Will's determination to hold his noble ties in secret. "But you hold a royal claim to the land?"

"Aye. Once the people chose to lend me first their welcome, then their acceptance, and finally the right to be their leader, I began to use the inheritance my noble grandfather bequeathed me to purchase and maintain my position as Bailiff over the Courts of the Seven Hundred of the Weald." Dark eyes narrowed on the damsel, clearly confused, as he added, "But although I have a royally granted claim to the Weald, 'tis only by the will of its people that I am their leader."

Cassie heard in his voice the unmistakable ring of pride for his position and was struck by the sudden realization that its worth was far greater than that of any position won merely by accident of birth or marriage bargain. Will had earned his place in the world, and held it now through fair dealings with his people. Her admiration for the man he was beneath his handsome exterior increased fourfold.

A form of panic struck Will as the soft caress in her gaze stroked over him as surely as a physical touch. Why had he allowed Kenward to be elsewhere this night? By what folly had he fooled himself that there was no danger? But then, this was not his first mistake. He'd erred initially in thinking Kenward's near invisible company adequate protection. Oh, aye, they'd not touched in body since the night before Beata fell ill, but in the last two weeks they'd touched even more intimately with heart and soul. And his, he knew with a pang of searing truth, would never again be without the imprint of hers—a tie far more binding than mere physical lust.

A scream shattered the stillness between them, sundered their dangerous visual bond as easily as a fire-warmed knife slices through butter fresh from the cold house. Two pairs of eyes lifted to the ceiling above.

Will felt as if bitter reality had reared up like a ferocious dragon, blasting truth out with the flames of its breath, to instantly reduce his witless romantic dreams to ashes. In the end Cassie must return to the noble life awaiting her in France, while he must ever fight his doomed feelings for *Lady* Cassandra. Never could the flimsy fact of a simple English knight's love change her position in the world, the one she was born to inhabit. Even with Guy de Faux dead, she could never be his!

Although since the night of her attempted apology Will had treated her only with honor and gallantry, Cassie felt bruised when Will stood and left her side without a single word or lowering his eyes from the ceiling. In the next instant shame flooded over her for begrudging Will's attention to the vulnerable woman whose friendship she prized. How dare she blame him when she'd known near from the first of his love for Beata. Nay, all the blame was hers. With Beata never present during her hours with Will, Cassie had all too willingly and wrongfully repressed her knowledge of where Will's affections lay.

Feeling the hopelessness of her love for the proud man, Cassie rose and climbed the stairs. Beyond her control to prevent it, her glance slipped into the firelit room where Will gently held a sobbing woman in his arms while he stroked golden brown hair and, in the low velvet voice Cassie remembered too well, whispered unintelligible words of comfort into Beata's ear. The sight lent a pain so piercing that even the goal of preventing Will from hearing Vauderie's name on Beata's lips could not force Cassie to join them.

Instead, Cassie turned to quietly enter a cold chamber full of shadows —a just receptacle for her guilt and anguish.

Chapter

❦ 10 ❧

THE MORN WAS OVERCAST and from its outset struggled 'neath the cold of
a lingering frost. Yet the lord's bedchamber remained warm by virtue of
the fire Kenward kept stoked while Cassie maintained an unfaltering
watch over the woman lost in a sleep of emotional exhaustion.

'Twas as murky dawn began sifting through the gloom of cloudy day
that Cassie had first peeked inside to discover a slumbering Beata alone in
the large blue-draped bed. The imprint on the pillow beside the fragile
woman made it plain Will had spent some portion of the night there,
although, by the rumpled state of the covers, 'twas equally clear he'd not
slept beneath them.

Shamed still by her failure, a fortnight past, to recognize it as a problem
when last the other woman remained abed so late in the day, Cassie had
crept within to settle once more into a chair drawn near the high bed.
Here, these several hours later, she remained on vigil. Having no notion
how to combat such ailments as suffered by this frail woman, Cassie felt
helpless and retreated to the one support all were taught to rely upon.
Bowing her head over palm-joined hands, she prayed, beseeching a divine
healing—some spiritual tisane to restore Beata's physical health and return both memory and strength enough to deal with the events of the
recent past.

A muffled roar from below abruptly breached the stillness and severed
the thread of Cassie's repeated supplications. Instinctively she rose, then
paused, head tilted to catch the words. It was useless. She moved to crack
open the door. The voice belonged to Will and, by the tautness in his
tone, he was plainly exercising the full strength of his chilling control to
restrain a powerful fury.

"Again, I ask for what purpose were you skulking about a burnt-out
cottage not yours? Did you think to steal what remained—either material
or human?" Will's words were as layered in frost as an implement formed

of iron and left outside of a winter's night. "Only the most witless brigand or thieving Frenchman would commit so foolish an act in, even near, the Weald."

Although the man had yet to speak a single word and wore a plain cloak lacking an insignia of any kind, Will had no doubt but that the man was French. For that fact alone, in the normal way, this foreign intruder would already lie dead. He had survived this long only to tell his purpose in appearing at Beata's home and provide answers to questions about the wicked deed perpetrated there. The other's impassive mien increased Will's dangerous irritation. This, atop the vexing folly of his own men, was near enough to burst through the ice jam restraining the boiling river of Will's ire. He'd have sharp words for the men who had brought this new captive to him here rather than seeing the man bound, gagged, and left in the damp and dismal confines of the dilapidated hut more suited to housing such vermin. But 'twas a sharp dagger such as had been planted in Johnny's heart that Will intended to see sprouting from this man's chest. Will was impatient to have done with the deed he'd given his oath to execute upon all response for Beata's woe—but 'twas an impatience that he must restrain until he'd exacted from his foe every detail of truths he meant to know.

From where she stood, Cassie had heard but didn't understand the one-sided conversation. She carefully moved to the top of the stairs, realizing of a sudden what was odd about the words. They'd been said in French, and for some time she'd been talking, thinking, even dreaming in English. The unexpected use of her native tongue was an ominous fact. Laying one hand against the wall to brace her unsteady descent, she quietly moved down the stairway, unnoticed by the two unyielding, powerful men facing each other before the wide fireplace, intent on the implicit perils of their conflict.

"I'd come searching for a possession gone astray in the area." Soft French words were delivered in an utterly flat voice while Cassie slipped nearer, hardly stirring the floor rushes with her light tread and slightly upheld skirts.

Will was far from mollified by the excuse of a man who made no attempt to hide his nationality, although he must know to whom he spoke.

"What had you lost?" Despite the mirthless smile Cassie could now see on Will's face, his words had gone from frost to a pure crystal ice too treacherous to stand upon, as if daring the other man to attempt a verbal evasion of the issue.

Why hide a truth that could surely mean little to this infamous knight?

The newcomer tilted a blond head and dispassionately answered. "My favorite cloak."

A De Faux! At the casual statement which Will heard as a confession, wrath overwhelmed rational thought and his arm flew up. Honed metal reflected the hearth's violent, ruddy hues even as a blur of sapphire-blue wool flashed between the two men.

Caught in the startled visitor's arms, her vulnerable back becoming Vauderie's shield against Will's anger, Cassie looked up to breathlessly ask, "How came Beata to have your cloak, Vauderie?"

Vauderie's gaze, locked on Will's gleaming blade, had not shifted despite the new arrival. His face was as chilled as Will's own until he glanced down into eyes darkened by violet concern. It softened into the gentle lines of a relieved smile. His missing friend was safe, albeit in the hands of the infamous Willikin of the Weald. Leastways she was alive. After members of her escort had arrived at the encampment about Dover with news of her father's murder and her disappearance, he had worried she might not have survived.

Although Will had no inkling of how this captive fit into the De Faux family—certain only that the man was not the aging leader, Guy—he could hardly fail to recognize that these two knew each other. How well?

"Beata's here then—and safe?" No hint of ice remained in either Vauderie's expression or tone.

Steadily meeting a gaze the same bright blue as a summer sky, Cassie strived to ignore the deadly dagger upraised in Will's hand. One part of her feared for Vauderie's safety, while another, smaller portion noted this second strong man's tenderness for Beata.

"Aye." Her answer was prompt, and firelight danced amongst the dark curls framing her tension-pale face as she nodded. "She's here and will not let loose of your cloak for any price."

"Wise maid." Vauderie smiled, a deed Cassie knew was rare, though it had the power to make an already handsome face near as stunning as Will's.

This exchange between the pair plainly well-acquainted did nothing to improve Will's mood. Just see what a change her arrival had wrought in the blond knight and how trustingly she rested in his hold. He lowered his weapon but backed to the outgoing door from where he gave a loud command.

"Harvey, Clyde, come!" He glanced again to the two still standing with arms about one another. Gold flames flashed at odds with the icy black depths in his eyes. "And bring an abundance of stout ropes!" He wanted nothing more than to dispatch the blackguard doubtless guilty of heinous crimes against Beata to the surely fiery end awaiting him in the afterlife. Yet he found himself unable to deliver the lethal blow before Cassie's unflinching eyes, least of all upon one she deemed, at the least, a friend. It was a discovery able only to increase his ill temper.

Cassie had little choice but to stand back and watch while with stout ropes Will's men restrained Vauderie tightly enough that any struggle against his bonds was certain to render painful wounds. As her friend was hauled off to the same hut where she'd spent her first night of captivity, Cassie comforted herself that leastwise she had saved him from Will's deadly fury—but what of later? Had Will not told her from the first that all French invaders were put to death at his command? And had she not heard from the implacable knight's own lips, more than once, of the oath he'd sworn to bring an end to those he deemed responsible for his beloved Beata's assault?

Once the disruptive stranger was gone and they were alone in the house, as if despite divided views their thoughts were still attuned, Will spoke to Cassie.

"Surely you see that your Vauderie was one of the evil toads who attacked Beata—the woman you claim to love as a sister." He paused while she recognized from his statement that he had news of the attack previously unshared. "Oh, aye, I know your betrothed was involved, but from people who would never lie to me I know also that he was not alone."

Will had sworn to see her betrothed pay the ultimate price for his wicked deed. And, though he'd not consciously admit it true, in his never before experienced jealousy he would not grieve an opportunity to see the handsome younger De Faux removed from Cassie's future as well.

"Non." Cassie smiled with sham sweetness and unthinkingly reverted to her native French to give her simple reasoning. "Guy or Valnoir, but never Vauderie."

"Why not Vauderie?" Will snapped out the question. Vexed by both the loyalty she gave the other man and the ease with which she'd reverted to the language of her noble upbringing, Will's words carried the sting of a whiplash. "He admits 'tis his cloak she wears."

Cassie felt the bite of his contempt for Vauderie and knew that, leastwise for the moment, it extended to her. "Vauderie is as unlike his uncle Guy or brother Valnoir as ever a man could be. He despises pointless violence and, 'neath the emotionless facade he presents to the world, he has a sensitive heart and a nature too caring to win approval or even acceptance from either his brother or uncle." Her voice unknowingly softened as she added, "He's a friend of many years, and I know him too well to believe he could ever brutalize a woman—any woman, but last of all one thrust back into terrified childhood."

Cassie sensed a growing pain under the fierce knight's increasingly darker temper. Likely he felt as if his beloved Beata's wounds were reopening in him. Despite a forlorn wish that he might feel as deeply for her, Cassie's compassionate heart went out to the hurting man. Wanting to step forward and wrap comforting arms around him, but afraid of rejection—or worse, acceptance of her as an unsatisfactory substitute—she forced herself to turn and climb the stairs without looking back.

Will watched the retreating figure, thick black braid swaying with the graceful undulation of enticingly rounded hips. He should be pleased with the wedge the other man's arrival had driven betwixt them. After all, he'd spent most of the past night's dark hours seeking some plan to achieve and maintain just such a safe distance. He should be—but decidedly was not! How was it, he wondered sourly, that Cassie knew this Vauderie so well she could claim him a "friend of many years"? Had she sought to reject the uncle for spouse because she loved his young and handsome nephew?

Cassie peeked into the lord's chamber and found Beata sleeping undisturbed by the crucial scene enacted below, a scene revolving about her "shining knight." Aye, her champion had come, but all too likely would reach his mortal end without the woman-child ever knowing the price he'd paid for his attempt to fulfill the promise. Cassie quietly withdrew, reminding herself 'twas best Beata never know of Vauderie's coming, as, were she to learn of his attempt, it might well drive her emotions permanently into realms where no other could follow. Undoubtedly that result was the very last Will sought, yet 'twas a probability he was certain to disbelieve an honest threat.

Entering her own chamber, Cassie settled on her rough pallet, unnoticing of either its lumps or the chill of the room. From Will's inadvertent threat upon what she feared was Beata's only hope for recovery, she resolutely turned her thoughts to the friend in trouble and locked in a wretched hut. Sooner or later Will was sure to demand Vauderie pay the fatal price for a wrong he had not committed. On his own he had no chance to evade that certain end. She alone in this place was his ally. They had been friends since he and his arrogant brother were sent to foster with her father when she was little more than a toddling. She must come to his aid, not solely for sake of the rare gift of his friendship, but also for the kindness shown Beata in a rescue the woman-child spoke of with gratitude and trust. Set him free she must, and before 'twas too late. To Cassie's mind the deed was her duty, a matter of honor. Unconcerned by the courage surely required or the price to be paid for success, she was determined to save Vauderie's life. Her only regret was the action's violation of the small measure of hard-won trust Will had given her.

Lavender eyes shifted to a shuttered window. An upended chest waited below as accomplice in stolen glimpses of a departing knight. Her one attempt at escape through that unintended portal had resulted in Kenward sleeping in the hall just outside her door and a guard posted always to watch the glade during dark hours. These facts, which once she'd likely have found overwhelming, were merely obstacles to be overcome. Clearly she couldn't wait and accomplish her task amidst the shielding shadows of night.

Cassie rose to restlessly pace from one window to the next, then to the door and back again to the first window in a triangular path oddly inverted within the larger triangle of the room. From below came the familiar sound of a steed's stirring response at his master's arrival. It broke her blind absorption with the regular pattern of her steps, and she instinctively followed an established habit. Climbing atop the chest and easing the shutters open just wide enough to peek outside, she watched as Will lead Nightfall from the stable. He mounted and rode out to join a group of men awaiting him on the glade's far side. It seemed plain to her that they intended to set off on their long delayed daily patrol. As Will departed with most if not all of his men, surely that meant the village would be near deserted. Kenward doubtless waited in the hall to serve as her guard-companion, but he would settle there and climb the stairs only to keep Beata's fire stoked. About these meager facts Cassie plotted her course.

Cassie stepped down from the sturdy chest to hunt out her fine woolen cloak, thankful it had never become her practice to leave the garment hanging on pegs beside the outgoing door below. Tying decorative cords of twisted threads about her throat, she rued a captive's understandable lack of dagger. Not that she'd any more wish to harm another now than before, but a sharp blade would certainly lend speed to the loosening of Vauderie's bonds. What needs must, must be. She repeated her favorite old saying in acceptance of the precious minutes sure to be wasted while striving to work tight knots free.

Once again climbing atop the upended chest and, as quietly as possible, spreading shutters open wide, she bent at the knees to launch herself through the opening. She was thankful that leastways this time there was no rain—thankful until she landed on ground not merely lacking the softness of mud, but hardened by frost.

Yet she'd no time to lose on thoughts of bright bruises likely to appear in the near future. With an absent grimace of discomfort she rose and hastened into the gloom of forest edge. She skirted around open ground, grateful that even without leaves the multitude of trees provided dark shadows enough to hide amongst. After stress-lengthened moments spent moving stealthily from one towering sentinel to the next, at last she paused shielded behind the trunk of the massive oak nearest a sorry hovel looking even nearer to collapse than the day she'd left its unhappy confines. She drew a deep breath for courage. Then, before a moment's hesitation could steal it from her, she dashed from shadows into the clearing about her goal.

The hut's poorly attached door squeaked open. Thank goodness there'd been no one lingering in the glade. She'd been fortunate. In the next instant it hit Cassie just how strangely fortunate she'd been—how was it that no man of Will's was posted to guard a prisoner of such import? Her heart kicked up a wild pounding. There hadn't been, she reassured herself while quickly slipping inside, and that was all that mattered.

The squeaking door had apparently not been so noisy as she'd feared, for Vauderie slumbered undisturbed. Leaning back against the rickety door's questionable support from the inside, she studied Vauderie, who despite his bonds, seemed almost to be lounging at ease in his own home —curled on the piled straw where once she'd resided, and napping in what must surely be an uncomfortable position.

Anxious to see him immediately freed and safely gone, Cassie knelt in the moldering straw at his side and lightly touched his arm. He jerked awake and twisted to look up into her familiar face. Thinking no greater danger could come upon him here, Vauderie had permitted himself the first deep rest in many a week.

"Quiet." Cassie whispered her caution even as she pulled a gag free from his mouth. As she toiled, bewilderment clouded her gaze. Silently she wondered why Vauderie had been gagged when there were no French warriors about to come to his rescue.

After working dry lips to free them from the discomfort of knotted cloth, he murmured the wry explanation likely to solve her puzzlement. "Methinks our 'host' fears Beata might hear my voice and be troubled."

Mists of confusion scattering, clear lavender eyes met sky blue as Cassie nodded her agreement with his assumption.

"How did you get in here?" Vauderie whispered, glancing about the dingy hovel as if expecting to find some secret entry.

"Through the door." Cassie couldn't resist the obvious answer he was certain to hear as an inappropriately timed jest.

Mildly surprised at the playfulness of a damoiselle he'd found ever solemn, Vauderie lifted an inquiring brow. "Found the secret comforts of folly here in the forest, sweetness?" Any possible jab in teasing words was deflected by the affection brightening his blue eyes.

"Truly," Cassie assured him even as her brows drew into a frown while she bent to concentrate on the problem of the knots binding hands behind her friend's back. "I climbed out my window and walked through this door. Wasn't even a guard posted."

"No guard?" Vauderie's amusement was gone. He'd heard too much of the fierce Willikin of the Weald to trust a move so seemingly witless. Had the knight hoped he would try to win free, justifying—even to Cassie— the killing of an escaping captive?

"No guard," Cassie repeated in a firm undertone, refusing to consider probable motives behind this lack as the ropes wound about Vauderie's wrists loosened enough for him to wiggle his hands free. The absence of a guard was a fact that would work in their favor, must work in their favor or all was lost. He sat up and began dealing with the ropes about his ankles far more efficiently than she'd dealt with those on his wrists while Cassie, anxious for Vauderie to understand the full depth of his danger, rushed to explain.

"Will believes you claimed his foster sister by force." Cassie sat back on her heels, clasping her hands tightly together. "Claimed and brutalized Beata until, to escape the horror of it, she became a child again."

Vauderie shook his head fiercely, but Cassie laid fingertips against his mouth to stop the words he plainly meant to speak, and likely so vehemently they'd give no regard to the need for quiet. "You were not responsible. I know 'tis so, but he won't believe it. She has the cloak you admitted was yours. To Will 'tis proof enough for all he believes."

Vauderie tilted his head back and away from the obstruction of her fingers. "I thank you for your trust despite the damning cloak."

Cassie's warm smile was sincere while she shrugged as if 'twere a matter so obvious as to need no saying. Yet she saw that Vauderie had failed to recognize the full significance of her words. He had failed to realize Beata was not only Will's foster sister, but his beloved, for the bond of fostering was no bar to more intimate bonds. A moment later her winsome face was utterly solemn. "You must leave immediately."

Vauderie had dared venture near the dangerous Weald for Beata's sake, and he'd not intended to leave without her. But by Cassie's explanation of the English knight's misbelief, he recognized a new peril—a hazard greater even than those already associated with the fearsome Willikin. To forgo an opportunity to escape his bonds would be foolish in the extreme, and a fool Vauderie was not.

Aware of the frown her words had laid on his brow, Cassie urgently pleaded, "Go before any come to prevent it."

"I'll go," Vauderie agreed, although to himself he reaffirmed his oath to soon return for the fragile woman he'd promised to rescue. First he must free himself of the English knight's restraints and deadly threat. With renewed dedication to this cause, he rose to his feet, oblivious to the stinging discomfort of rope burns about wrists and ankles.

"We'll both leave this very instant." Vauderie took Cassie's hands, pulled her up and started toward the door.

Cassie didn't move, forcing Vauderie to pause and glance back into her serious expression. Keeping her silence, she gave her head a brief, sharp shake which shifted an ebony braid to catch errant gleams of cold light falling through gaps in the thatching above. She'd no desire to join her unwanted betrothed, and far less did she desire to leave Will—even if he did love another.

By virtue of more than a decade of friendship between himself and this young woman, ever as ill at ease amongst most others as was he, Vauderie recognized Cassie's reluctance to return to his uncle Guy's hold. He'd not seen the damsel since her father had put his seal upon the marital pact, but on first learning of the arrangement he'd been saddened by the unpleasant prospect of Cassie doomed to a lifetime with the man. The dismal reality behind such a future was something he knew all too well. Yet was staying in the forest with a fierce captor a better option? Of a sudden he realized she called the fierce knight Will and apparently lived in his house. 'Twas a shock, but 'twas her life and, unlike her family and his uncle, he'd not force his choice upon her.

Vauderie wrapped Cassie in a tight embrace, murmuring in her ear, "Good fortune be with you, sweeting."

Cassie had caught a glimpse of her friend's understanding in the softening of his blue eyes. The gallant smile that curled her lips was pressed against his broad shoulder while a tear caught and glistened under another stray gleam of daylight.

Vauderie whispered into her ear a final word of caution. "You may need it to remain in the company of that dangerous man." Hands curled about her shoulders, he leaned back and gazed into eyes gone to violet, seeking final confirmation of her choice to remain within the enemy's hold. Cassie steadily met his inquiring scrutiny with tilted chin and a smile of calm determination on her lips.

"Neither of you are going anywhere." The words were as dark as night and equally as forbidding.

The pair broke apart as cleanly as if the unsheathed blade of Will's sword, held threateningly across his broad chest, had sliced between them.

They were right in thinking no guard had been posted. No guard had waited in full view because no guard was needed while he watched the hut from the same forest shadows Cassie had used to work her way here. He'd watched her slide down the lean-to roof and not been surprised—still it hurt that she'd chosen to flee with this man rather than stay in the Weald with him. Fool! he berated himself. Utter witless fool! How else but that a hostage seek freedom from her father's killer? How else but that she wish to escape with a man beloved—a fact proclaimed by their interrupted embrace.

"Will, I meant to stay." Cassie moved toward the furious man but halted, feeling frozen in place by the black ice of his gaze.

Meant to stay? Hah! She merely thought to yet again play him for a fool, with sweet lies wooing his mercy for both herself and her "friend." When would she learn? Nay, when would he learn? It was ever he who yielded to her honeyed persuasions, although in his right mind he knew how unlikely they were to be sincere.

He had made a great production of departing on a normal day's patrol, hoping to set the stage for an escape whereby he would have her Vauderie alone in the forest. Aye, alone without Cassie to interfere as he extracted the answers he sought or to watch him exact the price he'd sworn the invader would pay. 'Twas necessary, for even under the force of his anger, he found himself unable to wreak his vengeance upon Vauderie while she watched. Now she had forestalled that plan and proven him a greater fool by her single action. From between gritted teeth he bit out an order all the harsher for its total lack of emotion.

"Back to the house!"

Violet eyes wide with fear for Vauderie, Cassie glanced between the two men glaring at each other with such enmity it was near tangible. She wordlessly refused to go and leave Vauderie to meet Will's deadly temper alone.

Unlike his captives, Will was all too aware of men waiting without and doubtless striving to hear every word. Cassie's action was more than a simple blow to his pride. By allowing her such latitude that she'd been able to attempt this release, he was surely weakened in the eyes of his followers.

"Both of you—to the house now!" The gold blaze of fury near overwhelming the black in Will's eyes brooked no further refusals.

Vauderie turned and put his arm about Cassie's shoulders, urging her to a motion her legs seemed unable to take of their own accord. They moved through the stillness of a glade filled with accusing eyes. Cassie kept her attention upon the uneven ground, glancing up only once, to find on Clyde's face a bewildered expression both hurt and condemning. Her gaze immediately dropped to her feet and remained on the bleak view of ground frozen into perilous ridges and ice-crusted puddles.

Halfway across the glade Will issued a harsh command that in an hour's time two men again bring stout ropes to his house.

Chilled to the core by the gauntlet of accusation she'd passed through, Cassie thought it would be a relief to enter the house promising leastways the fireplace's heat. It wasn't. No sooner had they moved through the door than it was slammed so angrily behind them that the walls shook. Turning to stand with backs toward the fire, she and Vauderie faced the dark man whose incredible anger was emphasized by the flames' ruddy glow.

Silence lengthened while Will struggled to rein in his temper, a battle not aided by the sight of Cassie so close to the French knight 'twas as if she were drawing strength from the man.

Unnoticed by the three absorbed in their wordless conflict, Beata glided down the stairs and moved quietly forward to wrap her arms about Vauderie.

Will was stunned, and Cassie less so only for knowing the other woman's fascination with her "shining knight." Even Vauderie was surprised, yet he instantly sheltered the maid in his embrace.

"I did not, would not hurt this fragile butterfly," Vauderie quietly told Will, blue eyes meeting black over the sheen of the sleep-mussed, tawny curls cradled against his chest. "Surely her response to me proves it true."

Caught utterly unprepared by this strange event, Will gave his head a sharp shake and frowned. What on earth did Beata's action mean? She'd blanked all memory of the dastardly deed from her mind, so how could she know this man? Yet she had his cloak. Nay, she treasured it.

Vauderie tucked the velvet cloak at issue closer about Beata's slender shoulders as he made an equally strange offer. "Although I'm not to blame, I'll pay the price for my companions' wicked deeds. Gladly will I wed the woman they wronged."

Cassie gasped. She should have warned Vauderie of Will's love for the woman, but had he escaped, 'twould have been unnecessary. Will heard Cassie's involuntary response and thought it even greater proof of her love for the man who sought to wed another.

"You came back for me." Oblivious to the currents flowing around her, Beata looked adoringly up into Vauderie's gentle smile. "You promised and you did."

Both startled by the man's unexpected marriage offer and sensitive to the hurt that the prospect of such a union appeared to plainly threaten Cassie, to Will Beata's seemingly nonsensical words were just one more piece added to the puzzle of the whole. Will was caught between finding them confirmation of his worst expectations—that the attackers not only intended but had threatened to return and take her into virtual slavery—and believing Vauderie cleared of wrong by Beata's lack of fear. Yet whichever was true made no difference considering her mental retreat to childhood.

"Marriage may be the just price for the wrong done, but not with—" Will halted abruptly and his lips firmed into a hard, cold line. He couldn't speak of Beata's condition while she stood before him, aglow with innocent happiness.

Vauderie softly responded to the clear source of Will's objection. "It was a child I took from the cottage and into the woodland's shield. A child playing dress-up in a woman's form. I couldn't then nor would I now despoil her returned innocence or abuse the trust she's given me. On that matter you've my oath as an honorable knight. Nonetheless, I am willing, nay, anxious to give her the shield of my name." The English knight's glittering eyes earned a one-sided and cynical smile from the Frenchman, who explained his reasoning. "I am as determined to assure her safety as are you. With your fierce reputation, you can protect her from all men English while I, by my name and position, can shield her from those of French heritage."

Will knew better than to make important decisions while temper clouded his judgment. "We'll talk of it on the morrow." By his honorable offer, Vauderie had stolen Will's justification for seeing him dead, and yet how could— A firm knock on the door interrupted his disgustingly tangled thoughts.

Certain the sound heralded the two men summoned to again see Vauderie restrained, Cassie quickly stepped to Beata's side. She shep-

herded the too delicate damsel upstairs, preventing her from being subjected to the likely devastating sight of her "shining knight" helplessly
bound and hauled back to a dismal imprisonment.

Beata went willingly enough under the guidance of a woman she
trusted. In the chamber above, once she'd been settled before the fire
which her friend prodded to renewed life, Beata took Cassie's hand in
both of hers and brushed a grateful kiss across its back.

"Thank you, Queen Cassandra. Thank you for guiding my champion
back to me."

Cassie's mouth opened to deny any part in a deed sure to reach a finish
far from the happy ending of a faerie tale. In the next instant she knew
'twould be cruel to steal this moment of happiness from one who of recent
times had been gifted with few. Nay, let Beata savor this magical elixir as
long as possible against the day it would evaporate—even within the
tender hold of cupped hands.

Chapter
❧ 11 ❧

"BUT WHERE'S VAUDERIE?" Confusion clouded Beata's eyes. She stood beside a table laid out for the day's first meal but where sat only Will, Cassie, and Kenward. "We can't begin without him." A slight frown creased her forehead and she took a step back as if the mere thought offended her.

In the maid's troubled expression Will saw a problem he should have foreseen. From her view all matters were simple. Vauderie was the friend who'd come for her, and Vauderie should be here. He wasn't. A vague but threatening storm had begun to build behind her precarious serenity.

"Not yet," he soothed, restraining his vexation over a need he had far rather avoid. "But soon he will be, so settle beside Cassie while Kenward goes to hasten his arrival." The glare he sent the boy stifled a surprised gasp and sped young feet on their unexpected errand.

Startled lavender eyes peeked surreptitiously at the glowering knight. That Will would allow the man he didn't know but clearly despised to join a meal at his table was incredible. Proof, she decided, of his love for Beata —his concern for her happiness. She, too, wanted Beata's happiness, but even her affection for the fragile creature couldn't ease the ache in knowing of Will's love for another.

On the previous day Will had posted guards at outgoing door and stable side by the time Cassie had descended from seeing Beata to the chamber above. She'd been consigned to the care of a Kenward cautioned to renewed vigilance before Will departed as if unable to bear her company a moment longer. When Will failed to return at any point during the evening, she had recognized his intent to spend the night with his captive in the sorry hut. All these were precautions he'd taken to prevent any further escape attempt. Yet for Beata's sake he would permit his enemy to dine with him.

"Beata . . ." Will's call was a gentle rumble. "You ate naught but tiny nibbles the whole of your day abed."

Pleased by Vauderie's imminent arrival, Beata grinned at him like a guilty child.

"Eat now." Dark brows lowered as he issued the order with mock sternness, then ruined the effect by adding, "Please?"

Her lingering withdrawal into childhood's safe haven had Will more worried than he'd like to say—and feeling more helpless than he had since his own childhood days as an orphan welcome nowhere. Though not an overly pious man, Will shared the strong faith Nessa had taught the orphans in her care, and more than once already had he turned to God with earnest prayers for remedy to Beata's illness.

Beata's smile widened but, determined to wait until Vauderie was at her side, still she didn't obey. Her attention shifted to Cassie before she said anything at all.

"I told you my shining knight was wonderful. And he is, isn't he?" Beata's golden gaze glowed as she looked trustingly at Cassie—both a friend and the faerie queen who'd granted her plea.

A shadow crossed Cassie's face. She feared that when Beata turned from Will to speak adoringly of another man, the action must hurt him as deeply as his care for Beata hurt her. Still, she smiled warmly at the smaller woman and nodded.

Will saw Cassie's distress; and when eyes darkened to purple lifted to meet his gaze, he felt their impact. Plainly it stung Cassie to hear the other woman's admiration for the French knight so clearly revealed.

Amidst the silence of the table's company the sound of a door swinging open was unnaturally loud, and Will turned toward the pair stepping from the cold gray light outside into the mellow glow of the fire-warmed room. Lifted to the stranger, Kenward's open face was lit by laughter for some unheard comment from the other. Will hadn't thought Kenward's acceptance so easily won, and an unwelcoming scowl descended. The boy's apparent defection was but a foretaste of displeasures to come when both women smiled brilliantly at this man freed of his bonds.

Vauderie was as tidied as a quick wash from a bucket of icy spring water allowed. It appeared to have stood him in good stead. A day's growth of pale beard and the gleam of water on blond, finger-combed hair merely added a golden sheen to his appearance. A "shining knight"? Will's mood was not improved. Indeed, it threatened a return to the previous day's low ebb.

"Did you summon me to hear the decision you promised?" Vauderie halted two paces from the edge of a table where his unwilling host sat, a wicked glitter in cold black eyes.

"No." The one cold word was the best Will could manage in that first moment. Seldom in all these many years had he been so constantly plagued by ill humor, and it *must* change. After an instant's battle he clamped down a famous iron control and replaced his frown with a mocking smile. "You were 'summoned' to share our meal."

Vauderie was astounded. A fairly polite request to join their meal was the very last thing he'd thought to receive from this man who, for the wrong done to Beata, had plainly rather gift him with a fatal blade in the heart. Nonetheless, Vauderie returned the mocking smile full well while, with a gracious bow, he accepted the invitation and took the vacant seat at Beata's side. Gazing into the openly adoring face upturned to him, his smile gentled into a tender warmth.

Sensing none of the uncomfortable currents swirling about the table's company, Beata fairly beamed with delight—and each of her table companions deemed her contentment worth its unusual cost.

Vauderie was a warrior with experience enough to know when the time was right for confrontation, for pressing an advantage and when 'twas wrong. Now was purely the wrong time to push his suit with the English knight. He'd made the offer, proving his willingness to pay honor's price for a wrong not his. Thus, were his opponent a knight of honor, no longer had the Englishman justification for claiming his life. Moreover, if this Willikin of the Weald had rather they spend days, weeks, even months as things lay at this moment, he'd wait. In truth, he'd little choice.

"Have you seen one of our number hereabouts?" The question was a snarl as bitterly cold as the winter day that had laid a dense fog atop the thatched roofs of Offcum's clustered cottages and coated the ground with a thick layer of frost.

This tiny hamlet was edged on one side by broad, open meadows and tentatively cultivated fields, yet seemed to cringe close against the Weald's looming protection on the other. Guy de Faux glared into the forest's secretive shadows with disgust—disgust for the nephew whose inconsiderate disappearance had brought them here. Vauderie had come and gone without explanation more than once in the past few weeks, but this time he'd been gone for more than a fortnight. Guy meant to know if the fool had provided the wretched English knight with further means to insult him.

When no answer was forthcoming from the solemn villager standing before him in mute defiance, Guy spurred his steed and motioned his small contingent to follow in a slow circuit of the forger's fire struggling to survive in the tiny hamlet's center. Despite his deceptively unwieldy size, he leaned down to snatch up a burning branch. Those riding behind did the same. Holding his makeshift firebrand like an ominous club, he led the way back to tower over the peasant, annoying in his rebellious silence.

"Answer my question, you miserable oaf, or we'll see how quickly even ice-covered thatch can turn to ashes." The threatening flames at his command swooped to within a handsbreadth of the cottage roof.

Stalwart and proud of being both a free man and, as the village's iron worker, its strongest man, Denart refused to easily quail beneath these unwelcome intruders' enormous leader, a man all the more imposing for being mail-garbed and helm-protected. While dead leaves scuttled across cold ground, his steady gaze shifted to a younger man whose fine cloak bore the same insignia as that on the leader's. This second man waited with a condescending sneer and was apparently too certain of his invulnerability to don the helm resting before him on the saddle.

"Ask him—" Denart nodded his shaggy head at the arrogant, fair-haired stranger. " 'Twere he what were taken into the Weald by our lord's men." Under the sudden flare of the leader's eyes, he shuffled uncomfortably and defensively added more. "Leastwise 'tis what I heard."

"If the deed be no more than hearsay, how then do you know this was the man?" Guy was inflexible in his determination to force the giving of every known detail behind the event.

"First he were here and then he went off to Forest Edge Farm what was burned." Denart shrugged idly, but the look he cast the subject of this speech held a dislike so pointed it pierced his too thin veil of the subservience demanded of common men. "There's some as say that, if he thinks his cloak lost there, he must'a been the one what done the wicked deed."

An abrupt commotion at the low doorway behind the speaker's back summoned the attention of unwanted visitors. A woman, plainly the iron-worker's wife, pulled a briefly glimpsed girl-child of wispy dark hair and huge brown eyes away from the open portal.

While the blond knight had met the child's unblinking gaze for a long moment, Guy wasted no time on the unimportant interruption and immediately continued his interrogation. The man's last comment had hinted at the information he'd come seeking. "Why was he here?"

"Ask him." Denart rashly repeated his earlier defiant reply. At mid-morn on a day when most men were about tasks elsewhere, he'd none to support him. Therefore, 'twas foolish to challenge this foreigner—but then stubborn Denart had never been noted for sensible restraint.

" 'Tis you I've asked." Guy's eyes narrowed to perilously sharp daggers. "And best you be quick with your answer or your home and all within will be no more."

The villager responded to the threat yet refused to fall craven, and steadily met the Frenchman's dangerous glare as he answered. "Said he was looking for his cloak." A contemptuous smile tilted his lips. " 'Twas a daft purpose to send a foreigner alone into his enemy's lands. Be the cloak of more value than his life?"

Turning his attention from the irritating villager, Guy glanced to the blond companion at his side. The look they exchanged made it clear that the perpetrator's folly was to them a fact well known.

"Moreover . . ." The exercising of good sense enough to restrain an impulsive tongue was for Denart too difficult to achieve. " 'Tis witless for any of you to ride so close to the Weald from whence, you know for certain sure, 'death rides the wind and strikes from the shadows.' " Denart quoted a popular ballad composed to honor their Willikin and sung not only here amongst the knight's own, but across the land.

Guy had no appreciation for the peasant's proud reference to a foe accomplished at making fools of all men French. "Think you that your precious Willikin can save you from us?" Guy's laugh was as cold and vile as the weather. "Then let us see how quickly he can douse the fire of *my* wrath!" Guy's dark cloak fluttered in the chill breeze as his arm rose and dropped in a signal his companions immediately obeyed.

The company ahorse swarmed through the tiny cluster of fragile buildings, applying firebrands to every vulnerable surface from thatched roofs to wooden doors. Denart retreated into his tiny cottage and barred the door. He was certain the Frenchmen, plainly unaccustomed to the constant damp of English weather, would be defeated without need of the men and weapons he lacked.

Once it became apparent that winter-wet thatch would smoke but not burn, a weather-foiled Guy's rage exploded. His method of attack he would change to see the whole village pay, and pay dearly, for this defiance, and the heedless Denart would be the first to die!

After guiding his destrier into a position some little distance from the weathered planks of the man's cottage door, Guy spurred the steed forward. Just short of the impediment, he reined in and the mighty animal reared back to beat against the flimsy obstruction with his hooves. What

didn't fragment into splinters was smashed from the hinges and fell useless to the dirt floor within.

Viciously pleased by his own ingenuity, sword drawn, Guy ducked low
enough to ride directly into the small cottage. Towering above the man
who'd dared oppose him, without pity for the wife or children fearfully
cringing in the shadows behind, Guy drove the deadly blade down again
and again until an unrecognizable Denart lay in an awkward mass on the
floor. As Guy rode from the cottage, he set alight the neat stacks of
relatively dry straw pallets between the fallen man's family and the door,
the only escape. Amidst screams of terror and cries of pain he led his
followers in heartlessly slaying every living thing to be found within the
village's borders. That those who died were mostly unarmed women and
children meant nothing to him. They were English and Willikin's people.
Thus, they were foes and deserved to die.

Accompanied by the desolate moans of the dying, laughing perpetrators
turned to depart, only to find themselves subjected to a sudden hail of
arrows launched from woodland shadows. Laughter abruptly turned to
shouts of panic and angry curses as steeds were urged into a disorganized
retreat. Several Frenchmen fell to the winter-crushed grasses of the field
while from the arrow firmly embedded in their leader's back a trail of
blood flowed.

It took hours of hard riding to reach the encampment besiegers had laid
about the high, gray walls of an unyielding Dover Castle. By the time they
arrived, Guy de Faux was ahorse by sheer effort of will alone.

"Come, Uncle, let us help you down." Valnoir spoke firmly to the
mountainous man whose eyes were glazed over with pain and seemed only
partially conscious. Possibly close to death?

Guy immediately proved his nephew's unspoken hope in error. "Then
see me down. And get this thing from my back. But, nephew, don't allow
your anticipation to rise too high. I am still among the living and intend to
so remain." His voice held a vigor to back his words. "Therefore, your
dreams of supplanting me must needs tarry unfulfilled for yet a while."

Valnoir's mouth clamped into an unattractive line. What his uncle
intended might not be so easily attained. Whether or no a man's life
continued or reached death's end was not a question left to humankind for
answer, and many a battle wound had putrefied and robbed men far more
robust of life. Only the passing of days could provide true answer. With
this comforting thought, he and another struggled under the older man's
more than substantial weight until, staggering beneath the load, they
hauled him into the dark interior of the large tent whose flap was held

open by Henri Gavre. Henri had remained in camp to act as commander in Guy's absence.

Once his uncle lay facedown on a pallet near the cold central firepit, Valnoir lit several oil lamps and put flame to awaiting kindling. The one trained for such tasks hastily entered and began the work of removing the arrow. Guy gritted his teeth but no sound escaped his throat. When the arrow was gone from the immense white expanse of his back and Henri Gavre had departed, Guy returned his attention to the purpose behind their visit to the village.

"So, the infamous Willikin has our Vauderie? Why should I be surprised when my nephew so oft and so clearly shows his preference for company less exalted than ours?" The sneer on his lips settled into a spiteful smile. "Nonetheless, I see a way his wrong can be turned to our advantage."

Although Valnoir had dutifully remained at his uncle's side, his thoughts wandered. Now these curious words called him from pleasant visions of all that would be his when—and if—despite his moments-older twin and the old man's propensity for remarriage, his uncle's possessions became his.

"Cassie would be a tender morsel . . ." Still on his stomach while an unimportant third dressed his wound, Guy twisted his head far enough to the side that he could see Valnoir's reactions. "But she is of little account when balanced against the greater prize of seeing an end to that bastard knight of the Weald who did this to me and much worse to others of our number."

An appraising gleam filled Valnoir's eyes, and Guy's answering chuckle held little honest amusement. "Aye, nephew, I know your wish to be rid of her threat to your aspirations. And, if you rightly execute your end of the plan so recently come to me, I'll see you eventually receive what you seek —the inheritance of my title and lands."

Chapter
❦ 12 ❧

Vauderie had reason to regret his unspoken pledge of patience in awaiting Willikin's decision as day after day passed with no further mention of the marriage bond he'd offered. The time passed monotonously—nights spent with Will in the depressingly inadequate hut, and days in the house. 'Twas surprising how often Will spent some portion of the day there, too. Whenever the fierce knight had perforce to be about his duties elsewhere, Kenward was near, although Vauderie's captor must surely know he could easily overcome the youthful guard did he wish to do so.

At table one morn near ten days after his capture, Vauderie gazed down into Beata's gentle face. Her every smile provided more than adequate reason for him to remain, and remain he meant to do until able to fulfill his oath to take the lovely woman-child away with him.

"Would you consent to a game of chess with me today?" Vauderie formally requested of the petite damsel.

Regret cast brown shadows across golden eyes as Beata slowly shook her head. "I promised Cassie I'd lend her aid in bread-baking chores."

During the days since he'd arrived, Beata had begun a slow shift into reality, and pleased by this further sign of the fragile woman's return from her mental retreat, Vauderie could do naught but applaud her acceptance of responsibility. Yet he was easily as disappointed by her prior commitment as she. Without her company, the prospect of the day ahead stretched endless and depressingly quiet for an active man too long restrained in one place.

Watching the blond knight and his foster sister, Will silently acknowledged how, under Vauderie's tender attentions, Beata had seemed to blossom from the tight bud of renewed childhood into a maid on the edge of womanhood. Too clearly Vauderie was the cure for her ailments which Will had beseeched divine powers to provide. Yet 'twas a mystery how

Beata had so instinctively recognized Vauderie but still held her memory closed to the time of evil responsible for bringing him into her life.

While December days advanced and winter settled its icy grip over the land, French invaders had settled down to besiege various fortresses rather than venture near the Weald, leaving Will with little more to do than ride monotonous patrols. Not until Christmastide and Twelfth Night had come and gone would he, with his followers, begin planning for the battles sure to arrive with the warmer days of spring. Thus freed, Will spent more time near Kensham than usual, and to him it was plain that even in the relative comfort of his house the drag of sedentary hours had begun to weigh heavily upon Vauderie. Will recognized the problem as, in a like position, he'd no doubt he would feel the same. In truth, the strain of waiting for an inexplicably delayed response to his ransom demand had built a similar restlessness in him.

With a sympathy for his French foe he'd once have deemed impossible, Will rose and extended an offer. "Would you care to spend the day riding the land with me?" Startled by his own action, he quickly qualified it with safeguards enough to prove—to himself not least of all—that he'd not gone completely witless. "Unarmed and surrounded by my followers though you'll be."

Vauderie fairly leaped to his feet, renewed light dancing in his eyes. "Shackle my hands and feet, toss me across the back of an aging nag like a sack of grist for the mill, and still I'd welcome the opportunity."

This jesting comment from a man Will had thought ever serious, won from him a startled burst of laughter soon joined by Vauderie's own merriment.

Gleaming azure eyes shifted to a longtime friend. Cassie, initially worried by Will's offer was calmed by the sound of the men's shared laughter. She had wondered if he merely intended taking Vauderie beyond the view of either her or Beata to see him fall mortally injured under a none too accidental "accident." Slightly inclining her glossy head in approval, she wordlessly comforted herself that, all else aside, Will would do nothing to risk hurting Beata and thereby sending her back into the dark shadows of her mind.

Vauderie's bright grin greeted the French damsel's blessing on a choice already made. Although since the moment the English knight had burst upon them in the hovel, they'd yet to speak privately, he saw how changed Cassie was from the timid maid he'd come to know during his years of fostering in her family castle. Not once in past days had he seen her previously ever-present blush, and she'd actually been proud to announce

Edna's intent to "allow" her to take responsibility for the menial task of
bread baking. Shaking his head with mock wonder, he turned to join his
unexpectedly generous captor.

Will struggled to squash the sharp pangs of an ever-growing jealousy.
This forest jaunt would leastways take the Frenchman from Cassie's near
vicinity. In the painful truth he'd been taught to value over all, he acknowledged this end was more than partial motivation of his offer.

The boy and two women were left at table to watch the men disappear
and listen to the continuing echo of their shared laughter. Within Cassie
a prickling of anxiety remained. Why had neither Henri nor Guy responded to the ransom demand in all this time? Caring less for her than
for revenge upon the bold knight they assuredly believed had insulted
their honor by his capture of the woman who was a personal possession,
had they found a way to intercept and fall upon their unwary foe? Each
time Will left to ride the land, the fear grew stronger that Guy, Henri, or
even Valnoir would fall upon him and see him dead. This day a new qualm
was added. Would not Vauderie, now riding with an acknowledged enemy, be a willing participant in such a deadly deed?

Cassie abruptly realized that the two knights were more alike than
readily evident. Both had become the stronger for surviving rejections
during childhood and youth. Yet though hesitant to give trust, neither
took the pain of past frustrations out on those weaker or dependent upon
them. Moreover, they each had a strong sense not only of honor, but of
justice. Surely, Cassie told herself, this meant Vauderie was unlikely to
repay Will's kindness with violence.

Beata saw lavender eyes narrow on the now closed outer door. Even she
had recognized Will's invitation for the uncharacteristic boon it was, and
Cassie's reaction aroused in her a vague fear for Vauderie's safety.

"Where are they going?" she plaintively asked.

"Not to worry," Cassie gently reassured Beata, hoping her voice betrayed none of her own lingering anxieties. "They are simply off on a ride,
and as it's Will's habit to take foodstuffs from Edna's cook house out with
him on patrol, they're near certain to be gone the whole day. But on
returning, our brave knights will doubtless be hungry, so once we've done
with the bread, best we see to it that by nightfall a good meal is waiting."
The wink Cassie sent her worried friend won a girlish giggle. Whereas
Cassie had felt like Beata's mother when first the injured damsel arrived,
with the other's steady improvement their relationship had shifted until
now her role was more one of older sister.

Kenward hoisted and laid the heavy metal sheet required atop the cleared table. Of recent times Beata had begun helping Cassie with daily household chores as smoothly as if it had been done always. Once the task at hand was under way, 'twas soon plain that, whatever else she'd forgot, Beata remembered well the actions required. She made no attempt to take the reins from Cassie but performed every task requested with an efficiency the other envied.

Black tree trunks, thick-grown here amidst the forest, were half shrouded in dense fog and, to Vauderie, had the ominous appearance of an enemy force surrounding intruding horsemen on all sides. A heavy mist completely hid the bare branches overhead and prevented more than a dull gray daylight from touching the soaked layer of fallen leaves and winter-crushed undergrowth below their destriers' hooves.

Will led the way. Vauderie, mounted on his own massive steed, rode at his side while guardsmen of the Weald followed at a respectful distance, allowing any words spoken between the two in front to remain private.

"Then you've known Cassie near since she was babe?" Will confirmed, casting a sidelong glance at the Frenchman.

"Since she was a toddling ever hiding behind her nurse's skirts." During the early days of his captivity Vauderie had thought that as the infamous knight possessed a surface charm as potent as Valnoir's, he must therefore also share the same self-centered, ambitious greed. But after watching Will for more than a week—solicitous of Beata and gallant to Cassie while dealing with his followers in both justice and honesty, Vauderie had revised his first opinion.

"Timid then, too?" Will questioned, striving to keep his tone so light it revealed naught but curiosity or the polite interest of one searching for common topic between two who shared little else.

"Shy always," Vauderie confirmed. He was perceptive enough to hear the thread of deep interest in the other's question and was relieved. Suspicions roused by Cassie's preference for remaining in the Weald had been confirmed by seeing her gaze ever resting upon Will with an emotion impossible to hide from a friend of so many years. Watching a dark profile determinedly averted, Vauderie added, "Until now."

Will's face was an expressionless mask but his black brows arched in silent query as he looked to the other knight.

Vauderie shrugged slightly as he answered. "In a group of more than two, even if well-known to her, I've seldom seen lavender eyes lift from the floor or heard Cassie speak in more than a whisper. Must be some magic to this place." He waved his hand around the fog-draped forest.

"Some lingering trace of Merlin's sorcery?" He grinned at the man startled by his foolery. Yet he wondered if that same magic were working on
him. In the norm, he was comfortable enough to share such bantering
words only with trusted friends.

After a moment's surprise, Will laughed and shook his head at the daft
suggestion, although he had earlier recognized the changes slowly being
wrought in Cassie.

" 'S'truth, Cassie is different now than she was the day she arrived."
Will believed the importance of acknowledging truth and immediately
added, "However, the place is not responsible. 'Tis more likely the result
of events that have occurred herein." Will wanted to think that, despite
Cassie's becoming fatherless and captive, some small good had come to
her by his hand. At the same time, he conceded 'twas too likely a desperately grasped self-deception.

Anxious to move away from the uncomfortable subject, Will rephrased
his original question. "But there must be more reason behind how two of
such different ages grew so close." By such probing he hoped to discover
how deep went the bond between his French captives. Did Cassie have
reason to anticipate a relationship warmer than that of mere acquaintances?

"The explanation of how we became friends despite the decade separating us in age has more to do with our natures."

Will frowned. Their natures? Vauderie hardly seemed to share Cassie's
timorous nature.

"You are right." Vauderie gave a short bark of laughter when he realized
how Will had misunderstood his poorly expressed meaning. "Our natures
are little alike, yet we each are oddities amongst family members ever
striving for more power and greater wealth." Warmth left the
Frenchman's face and blue eyes shifted to an unseeing preoccupation with
vague shapes barely visible in the fog. "Long years past, Cassie and I
decided we were like daisies striving to survive amidst a field of wheat."
Again Vauderie glanced to the side and found Will's dark brows raised.
"You are surprised that I, a warrior, would compare myself to a flower?
Why not? Make no mistake, I'm very good with sword and lance, but I
had rather live in peace—something neither my uncle nor brother understand. Yet 'tis a goal Cassie shares."

A goal Cassie shared? In these words Will found a similarity between
they three for he, too, shared their goal. He longed for the day when his
Weald would be safe against foreign invaders, enabling him to settle into
the peaceful administration and farming of its expanse. Was this why,

before Vauderie's arrival, the evening hours he and Cassie had spent together had passed in such pleasurable companionship? The warm thought was immediately overshadowed by the cold of another—she also shared the same goal with Vauderie. 'Twas useless in any event for he, a common knight, could never have the noble lady.

Vauderie saw Will's introspective expression and decided the time was ripe to approach a subject that must be addressed although too likely it would spark the other's anger.

"I've told you before but must repeat it again: I saw Beata brutalized, but I had no part in the doing."

Despite eyes as hard as obsidian and face seemingly carved of granite, Will made no attempt to stop the flow of Vauderie's words.

"The only comfort I can give is the assurance that never was she raped. My uncle is seldom physically capable of such a violation." Vauderie met Will's black glare directly and disgust coated his voice. "But he takes his pleasure—or frustration, I know not which—in other ways."

To Will the loathing plain on Vauderie's downturned lips revealed De Faux's habit of beating innocent females unable to rouse him. Will's blood went cold at the thought of how near Cassie had come to being entrapped by unbreakable bonds with one so brutal. Her father must surely have been aware what type of man it was who sought to wed his daughter, just as Will knew others of a similar ilk. How could any father wittingly put his child in such jeopardy? Had wealth and position meant more than flesh and blood? Instantly came the memory of Cassie emotionlessly telling him 'twas so. Only moments past he'd wished for an opportunity to see some small good come to Cassie from her crossing of his path. Such an opportunity was his by a deed promised long ago. Silently he again reaffirmed his oath to see Guy de Faux dead and Cassie forever delivered from the man's threat.

Once begun, unaware of Will's inward turmoil, Vauderie continued. "My brother Valnoir views all women as his inferiors, existing only to serve a man's needs. He has no compunctions against such assaults upon those not shielded by noble blood. Indeed, at Forest Edge Farm he tried. Fortunately, sotted on the ale of his victim's dead husband, he fell senseless across her bruised body long before the deed was complete."

"How then did Beata win free?" Will saw the horrifying scene all too clearly and was further amazed that his fragile foster sister had escaped at all.

"While both my uncle and brother slept in a drunken stupor, I bundled Beata into my cloak and secreted her off into the forest. I spent the night's

darkest hours with her there, casting about for an alternate plan . . . ."
Vauderie's voice trailed away and he stared into a forest view as hazed as
his desperate search had been that night. "In the end I'd no choice but to
leave her and accompany my companions on their retreat. By that action I
could at least be certain they were away as far and as soon as possible.
Before leaving her I promised I would return, and within a day's span I
did, only to find her gone. I greatly feared for her safety and returned to
hunt for her at every opportunity until your minions found me. And even
that I do not regret, for it brought me here and allowed me to fulfill my
oath."

Although shielded from human eyes by unabated fog, when the sun was
half done with its descent from noon zenith to sunset, risen bread dough
had been divided into flat, round loaves ready for the baking. Disdaining
feminine aid, Kenward struggled to slide the metal sheet and its burden
into the sooty firewall's oven.

Trying not to appear as full of hopeful anticipation as he was, Kenward
made a diffident request. "If you've no further need of my help, might I
join the men in bow practice?"

Cassie gave a sweet smile to the boy who'd labored long hours without
complaint and nodded permission. She and Beata could do without him,
and she had just as soon he were not present to see her set about the
special dish with which she planned to end the night's repast. Asides,
since the morn when Vauderie first joined their meals, she'd been allowed,
during daylight hours, to fetch needed items from the cold house halfway
between Will's home and the open glade. Doubtless Will rightly assumed
she'd not flee without her friend and thus deemed it safe. On these quiet
winter days there were ever too many men about for her to slip unnoticed
anywhere, even did she wish it, and she emphatically did not.

Meal preparations continued smoothly with two pairs of hands working
steadily. When Cassie looked up and absently glanced through the slightly
opened shutter of one of the windows flanking the outgoing door, she
discovered dusk descending all too rapidly. She'd nearly lost her last opportunity to retrieve butter and cheese for the meal awaiting the men's return. Wiping her hands on a length of coarse cloth wrapped about her
waist, she hurried to the door.

"Where are you going?" Beata questioned, still troubled by any prospect of being left alone.

"Only to the cold house, and I'll return in a trice." With a warm smile,
Cassie called the words back over her shoulder as she stepped into the

gloom of lingering fog. Peering through damp tendrils of mist, carefully watching uneven ground, she hastened toward a small stone structure half buried in the earth for the purpose of retaining cold no matter the temperature of day. She descended several steps to reach its door.

It was chilly outside but far colder within, and Cassie shivered. The room was lined with shelves. From one near the bottom she lifted a thick round of cheese, tucked it awkwardly under her arm, and then reached to a shelf one down from the top for the crock of butter she'd churned the day past.

"I've come to rescue you."

The sudden voice at her back caused Cassie to near drop the heavy crock still balanced on one outstretched hand. Clumsily shoving it back on the shelf and clasping the slipping cheese round in both hands, she whirled to find Clyde blocking the doorway.

"What?" She shook her head as if there were some hope the action would knock daft words into sensible order.

"Like a knight from a minstrel's song, I've come to rescue the captive 'lady fair,'" Clyde repeated, proudly squaring his husky shoulders as if to demonstrate himself adequate despite his lack of knightly training.

Cassie bit her lip. Here was an utterly unexpected complication. Someone sought to perform a heroic feat for her, considered her a "lady fair." Never mind that she didn't want to be rescued. Yet how could she tell Clyde 'twas so when he meant only to do a shining deed for her sake, although one at odds with his loyalty to his lord—another requirement of knightly honor. Were she to baldly deny his offer, he'd almost certainly think her response a denigration of his abilities for not being the knight he obviously longed to be. She had belatedly recognized his aspirations from the conflict between he and Tom. 'Twas something she'd failed to consider at the time, what with the shock of Will's unexpected arrival.

"I thank you kindly, gentle sir." Cassie slipped the round of cheese onto a partially empty shelf waist high and lifted the corner of her simple homespun gown to curtsy. "You do me great honor by your willingness to perform this deed on my behalf—forgoing your lord's approval, your parents' love, and even your own honor."

Heard stated so plainly, Clyde suddenly realized the offered action required more than he dared give. His gaze dropped to shifting feet.

"Such is what you propose—is it not?" A thick black braid tumbled over Cassie's shoulder as she tilted her head inquiringly.

"I—I—I am sorry," Clyde stammered. "But I cannot after all." His cheeks attained a ruddy glow to rival any blush that had ever crept across Cassie's face.

Had he looked up he'd have found an expression of fervent relief. "I had thought you too honorable to do your lord this wrong, and am pleased to hear it true. And . . ." She shrugged and sent him a sheepish grin. " In truth, I must confess I've no wish to be freed."

The erstwhile rescuer looked at Cassie in surprise. Was her admission honestly said? Had he almost put everything of value to him at risk for a deed unwanted? Thank the saints she'd kept him from the disservice to his lord that would surely have prevented him from ever attaining the position he longed to occupy. It came to him with frightening clarity that, by speaking of his offer, she still could rob him of his goal. The blood drained from his face, leaving it a sickly white.

Seeing his discomfort, Cassie hastened to reassure him. "I've no doubt, Clyde, but that by your loyalty and honorable service you'll one day win your spurs and become the bright and shining knight you wish to be."

"Cassie, I swear on the honor I mean never to stain, that you've my aid wherever and whenever you ask it." He seized her hand and laid a fervent kiss atop its smooth back. 'Twas the least, the very least, he could do to repay her gentle understanding.

Hand still clasped in both of his, Cassie once more curtsied and rewarded Clyde for a promise never given her before with a smile so brilliant it seemed to him the sun had risen again.

Unseen in low hanging haze to one side of descending steps, Will heard every word spoken below. On their return he and Vauderie had found Beata alone. Fearing—with more than tender masculine pride—that Cassie might take advantage of a trust given to again flee from him, he had hurried to this destination named by Beata. Cassie's urging of his supporter to remain true to his lord rather than defect to her French fellows was remarkable, but 'twas her claimed preference for remaining in the Weald that warmed him. Yet, a chilling fact mocked his pleasure in her words—even did they desire the same end, she could never be rightfully his.

"Will!" At the sight of the tall black shadow of formidable dimensions standing rock solid amidst shifting clouds of gray fog, Cassie paused midstep.

Forcing depressing thoughts behind a mask he'd learned to adopt with relative ease, Will flashed a white smile at both the damsel and the escort who looked far more fearful than she. "Beata told me you were here, and I came to lend my aid, but see you've already the services of a worthy gallant."

Clyde mumbled an incoherent explanation, bright color again flooding his face.

"However, Clyde"—Will looked at the younger man with a mock sternness belied by gleams of amusement in dark eyes—"I remind you that, as your lord, my claim to the right of lending the lady honorable service supersedes yours." He would not punish the supporter who'd recanted his wrongful offer before harm was done.

As the mighty knight bent and took the heavy butter crock from Clyde's tension-stiff fingers, the younger man chewed nervously on his lip. Once his hands were free, he rubbed damp palms against his thighs and silently prayed for some reason to get himself as far from this uncomfortable scene as possible.

"I will see my lady back to the house, Clyde." Will restrained the honest grin threatening to break free as he gave the younger man an excuse it was clear he desperately sought. "While you return to the duties I am certain await your coming."

Losing not a single moment, Clyde hastily disappeared into thickening fog and twilight's deepening gloom.

Unequal to quelling the pleasure in even an offhand claim of her as his, Cassie's cheeks, too, were tinted with a rosy blush which she prayed the fog would hide. That she climbed the remaining steps with—she was certain—a depressing lack of grace, seemed proven when Will shifted the butter crock under one arm and wrapped the other about her shoulders.

Will justified his action as an honorable knight's duty to guide a lady safe across treacherously uneven ground barely visible in mists grown so thick they could see neither tree nor building on any side. That he'd drawn her body's tempting curves far nearer than needful for the task was a fact too dangerous to admit. Thus, 'twas one he refused to dwell upon. He had longed for even a few innocent moments alone with her, and this short walk permitted a privacy they'd not shared for days.

The feel of Will's big and powerful body did strange things to Cassie's senses and, unwilling to jeopardize so welcome a bond for the sake of useless pride, she nestled closer until her cheek laid lightly against his broad chest. She could hear the beat of his heart beneath her ear. It was pounding hard and fast, in rhythm with her own. Surely 'twas proof he was no less affected by her nearness than she by his.

Mayhap she could take advantage of this small weakness—likely the only one the mighty warrior had, apart from Beata. He loved Beata, but he must realize Beata loved Vauderie. Might Will accept her in consolation? She had once left his arms for fear of being only this to him, but now she was willing to seek whatever he would share before the opportunity was forever lost. Her timid side cautioned that he was far more likely to reject her inferior charms. Yet, her growing bravery argued, he might not. After all, he had kissed her and more on several occasions. 'Twas a challenge, and now when the goal was so desperately sought and likely soon beyond her reach, would she fall faint-hearted? Nay, she would not!

His warm maleness wound about her, beckoning her nearer still. Like a sinuous kitten she rubbed her cheek against the strong wall of wool-covered flesh beneath and smiled as muscles flexed in revealing answer to her caress. That involuntary response summoned wildly exciting memories— the feel of firm bronze skin and abrasive hair. The memories aroused shocking sensations. She glanced up through a drifting haze to discover golden sparks in dark eyes, and by them knew that he, too, was remembering the feel of flesh against flesh.

Will thought Cassie unaware of the temptation she offered, but his blood warmed under her innocent provocation. His jaw went tight, and as they moved ever farther into the dense fog, their pace slowed with every step until, halfway across the open space betwixt departure point and destination, they halted. Here thick mists enclosed them so completely that did they stand even a step apart, they'd more easily sense than see one another. Moreover, the soft haze seemed to sunder their ties with the realities of time and place—a loss neither regretted.

Determined to claim whatever fate offered, despite the impediment of the awkward round of cheese become so heavy as to near demand two hands to carry, Cassie turned toward Will. Eyes deepening to violet, she mindlessly leaned forward, seeking his warmth and strength.

Taking terrible pleasure in her eyes' unshielded revelation of a growing hunger, Will cursed himself for a weak-minded fool even as his hands slipped beneath the weight of her glossy braid to gently cup the back of her neck and lift her face. His mouth gradually descended to move gently, enticingly, across hers, and violet eyes closed as the liquid heat of his touch lit a slow steaming fire in her veins.

This melding of mouths drained the last of Cassie's strength and she trembled. Though he would inevitably turn away from her, she meant to accept—even shamelessly seek—all that he would give. Without thought, Cassie's lips parted beneath the warm assault, inviting that further sweet invasion he'd demonstrated before.

A low growl broke from Will's throat as he accepted her offer and deepened their kiss to a devastating intimacy. Heat-thick blood had slowed Cassie's pulse to a dragging and uncertain rhythm, but now it blazed and sang. Soon the distance enforced between them by the burdens they carried was unbearable. Will pulled back. Feeling bereft, Cassie moaned in protest of the unwelcome loss while he bent and roughly deposited his butter crock on mist-damp earth, then balanced her cheese round atop. Cassie gladly yielded to strong arms which returned to pull her pliant body tight to the whole long length of his form. As he buried his face in the tender curve between her shoulder and throat, she willingly submitted to urgent hands sweeping from nape to the base of her spine, where they molded her hips against the hard muscles of his thighs.

Exalting in his strength, she arched instinctively as shudders of wild excitement trembled through her. In his embrace she'd found her place in the world, the one place where she belonged as she'd never belonged anywhere in the whole of her life. It became ever more difficult to breathe properly—a minor loss overbalanced by the excitement of being within the embrace of her beloved. She nuzzled her face against a portion of sun-bronzed skin exposed by a gap down the front of his tunic provided by laces loosened at his throat. Striving to lay her lips against his, she rose on tiptoe, nipping at his chin and tasting his cheek. All the while her hands moved restlessly over muscular biceps, broad shoulders, and strong neck.

Will gazed down into the bemused desire on the winsome virgin's face. She was more beautiful in her passion than any female he'd ever known, and his craving for more of her was far too dangerous. It was time to draw back—while he could. Instead, he surrendered to enticements too intense and claimed her mouth again. It was wilder, hotter, and more unbelievably sweet.

To position her more intimately against the hardening contours of his body, Will curved his hands over her perfectly rounded derriere. Lifting her up, he rubbed her against his throbbing need, groaning under an almost painful pleasure. With any other woman, under any other circumstances, he would have lowered her to the ground and by their joining have driven them both down into the blazing depths of passion's satisfaction.

When, as a low moan of desire escaped her tight throat, Cassie unexpectedly returned his hungry demands, writhing against him in helpless response, he lost his balance and had perforce to take several quick steps to regain it. He kept Cassie close and safely upright, but with returned balance came cold reality and the realization of how near he'd come to surrendering to animal need, disregarding his duty and honor, and despoiling a *noble-born lady.*

Once Cassie stood steady, Will abruptly released her. He bent to lift their forgotten burdens while struggling to tame his raging pulse and temper his desperate hunger. This time he tucked the cheese under one arm and the butter crock under the other, as if they provided weapons against her allure. He nodded for Cassie to precede him to a house hopefully not far ahead and yet far enough to lend time for him to fully recover his control.

Cassie stood unresponsive to his silent command. Though devastated by his rejection, she refused to accept total defeat on her most important challenge. This battle she had lost, but she was determined to win the war. He undeniably wanted her, and eventually she would overcome his resistance. Yet by knowing its source, she would better her chances of prevailing.

"Why, Will?" Hurt replaced passion in her gaze while, head tilting to one side, her thick ebony braid fell forward and settled heavily between her breasts. Unbeknownst to her, the errant plait drew attention to the tempting bounty of flesh Will ached to uncover, to touch, to taste.

Deep in frustration, he was irritated the more by the damsel's question of an action taken in protection of her—aye, he'd fallen so low that he had to protect her from himself. The need to focus the full measure of his willpower on that task drove beyond his reach both the ability to exercise his natural tact and his easy mask of charm. Thus, the words of his response were deep and more harshly spoken than he'd normally allow.

"You are my lady-foe and hostage. Never will I risk my honor by being guilty of the same violation your countrymen attempted to wreak upon Beata."

" 'Twould not be a violation, Will." Cassie's confession of her own desire was soft but more bravely made than the girl she'd been on first entering the Weald would have believed possible—even of the imaginary Lady Cassandra dwelling inside.

"Sully I even a willing virgin of noble blood, my honor is forfeit." His flat statement brooked no argument. Cassie's admission merely placed a greater strain on his already tenuous control, and in desperation he verbally lowered an additional barrier. "More, and worse by far, would be taking the chastity of a foe's daughter or sister, the claiming of a hostage I mean to accept ransom for holding—unspoiled."

Will turned and began stalking away. Even if only to avoid being left alone in the foggy night, Cassie was forced to hurry and keep pace with him while her thoughts spun in a haze as thick as the mists hovering all about. Given quiet time, she would sort them through. But a niggling and seldom silent voice at the center warned that by retreating from the fray now she would loose a prize never again within her grasp. How could she abandon all hope of securing the few memories that would have to last her a lifetime?

Chapter
13

"VAUDERIE, I'M TRULY SORRY I hadn't time to play chess with you earlier." Beata took a step closer to the broad back of the man she wanted always to please, but by the half-shuttered blue gaze resting cold on weaving flames, it seemed clear she'd disappointed. She must have done some wrong, and only the game denied could be its source.

Will had left them to go in search of Cassie, and Beata had been delighted. 'Twas the first time she had been alone with Vauderie since the morn she'd awakened in his arms amidst a nest of ferns in the shadows 'neath a massive oak. When he'd pulled away and made to leave her, cautioning her to stay quietly hidden until he returned, she had been frightened. He had wrapped his cloak more closely about her with assurances that so long as she wore the rich garment, she'd not be harmed. She wore it still and couldn't bear the thought of having disappointed her "shining knight" returned at last.

The soft, choked voice pulled Vauderie's irritable thoughts free from the enemy he'd discovered too likable. No honorable Frenchman would "like" the notorious Willikin of the Weald—mayhap respect his military prowess, but never like this deadly foe. He instantly turned toward the damsel and found silver tears welling in golden eyes gone near to pure velvet brown.

" 'Tis a fine thing you'd other responsibilities, sweeting." With a reassuring smile, Vauderie gently stroked long silken strands of hair allowed to flow free down her back, as was the habit of children such as she had become when he'd rescued her. "It led to the kind of outing I've spent days longing for." The tentative hope in the tender damsel's expression added warmth to his face. She wasn't to blame for his muddled reactions, and he must not allow her to suffer for them. The slight shake he gave his head sent a lock of blond hair down to lay across his forehead.

Beata instantly took the one short step forward necessary to bring her body a breath from Vauderie's and reached up to brush tawny strands from his brow with a whisper-soft touch.

Vauderie instinctively turned his head away just far enough to evade Beata's touch. Since his arrival she had daily moved further from an unnatural childhood, and of recent had begun exploring normal instincts undulled—intense gaze constantly upon him, she always stood too close, and touched him whenever the excuse arose. These were temptations difficult to withstand, but to fail in doing so would be to break an oath given and besmirch his proudly held honor.

Beata fell a step back from the man who'd rejected her touch. If her refusal of the chess game were not the cause of Vauderie's disappointment, 'twas plainly something else. Only one other possibility presented itself. She had made progress enough in recent days to know her inability to remember any event betwixt childhood and Vauderie's rescue was abnormal, and now assumed 'twas this lack that disappointed him. For the better part of a fortnight she'd been silently striving to wrest free the memories hidden in the dark and secret caverns of her mind despite an ominous certainty that 'twas also the origin of terrifying dreams that she sensed were the key to release the whole.

But what fact beyond her recall could be so serious 'twould see Vauderie ever drawing away? Had she done some wicked deed he found repellant? Or did she belong elsewhere—was she a nun like as Lady Nessa had near become? Or—

"Have I a husband I've forgot? Is that why you rebuff my every attempt to approach you?" The possibility hurt, but by the widening of azure eyes she thought 'twas clearly so.

Although Vauderie had observed Beata's growing bewilderment, he was shocked by the conclusion she'd reached—one accurate and yet not. Expression gone solemn, he told her the truth.

"You once were wed—but are not now." Unsure how much more to reveal, and mayhap yielding to a coward's way, he decided the best course was to wait until she remembered of her own. Hopeful of diverting her attention, he quickly continued. "I, too, have been wed."

His ploy was a success. Beata went utterly motionless, though with her head tilted questioningly to the side, shining hair flowed over one shoulder. "What happened to your wife?"

"The marriage betwixt Matilda and I, as is to be expected, was arranged between our families for the purpose of confirming a valuable alliance."

That this was the way with the marriages of all people well-bred Beata knew. Did he tell her this as warning that a peasant, even one free-born such as she, could never be a suitable match for the nobleman he was?

Vauderie thought the worry knitting delicate brows a result of her discomfort with the idea of another woman in his life. A slight smile curved his firm mouth as he explained.

"We were wed shortly after my fifteenth birthday—she was near two decades older than I. Matilda had been wed before, and by the fact she'd borne no children during earlier years as wife, 'twas assumed by my uncle that she was barren. This was a fact not shared with me. I barely knew the wife with whom I'd nothing in common, but what was expected of me I'd early learned and believed 'twas my duty to produce heirs. Thus, together we proved that barren she was not."

Hearing this confession, it occurred to Beata that perhaps 'twas not her marital state that placed an immovable wall between them, but his!

"You have a wife and child?" Beata bit her lip to restrain the moan of distress threatening to escape her throat.

"Nay, sweeting." Vauderie hastened to correct the wrongful impression he'd given. "Both she and the babe died with the birthing."

The faint hint of pain putting clouds in the sky blue of his eyes left Beata ashamed both for thoughtlessly begrudging these unknown others life and for unintentionally bringing pain to her beloved with her probing. This she had done to him when he had only ever brought good to her. Vauderie was her shining knight, her rescuer, and she sensed only he could see her well again. Once more Beata moved forward and brushed her hand across his tense face, seeking to smooth away its lines of hurt.

Thoughts of anything save the delicate being so temptingly near vanished as Vauderie's lashes fell. He felt her light touch move to gently scrape across the day's growth of beard on his cheek. This was dangerous and too alluring from one surely not ready to handle the actions she invited. He laid his hand atop hers, intending to lift her fingers from their tender adventures, but he erred in opening his eyes at the same instant and tumbled into a brown velvet gaze wherein lingered an age-old knowledge never forgot. Heedless to wiser caution, rather than removing her hand, he turned his head to nuzzle his lips into her palm and felt her fingers curl with pleasure.

Beata trustingly leaned full against him, wound her free arm about his wide shoulder and stroked up to tangle fingers into the shining hair at his nape. Burying her face against his chest, she rubbed her mouth over the limited expanse of smooth skin and powerful muscle revealed by gaps between laced edges of his tunic.

Blood thundered through Vauderie's veins as the soft curves of her slim body melted against his much harder form. He'd gone hungry for her too long, and the tantalizing feel of her lips on his flesh was too much for him to withstand. He released her hand to wrap his arms tightly about her, molding her closer still while his mouth dove down to claim teasing lips with a fiery retribution.

Beata welcomed the kiss which almost immediately became an intimate mating of tongues as well as lips. Whatever else was true of her past, she was suddenly certain never before had she felt anything like this fierce hunger, this sweet assault.

As deep into passion's well as the pair were, the instant the outer door creaked open they broke apart. While Beata stared up at him in wonder, Vauderie's face flushed with guilt. He'd sworn not to take advantage of the woman-child, yet here he was caught. Squaring his shoulders with rigid pride, Vauderie turned prepared to meet Will's wrath, determined to restate and demand answer to his offer of marriage.

"I—I'm sorry," stuttered Kenward, his embarrassed gaze fair digging holes in the floor. "I—I only come to take the loaves from the ovens afore they're burnt."

Like a longed for rainfall on a hot summer's day, relief flowed over Vauderie, although likely 'twas only a temporary reprieve. Doubtless the boy would speak to his lord of what he'd seen.

Anxious leastwise to lessen Beata's embarrassment, Vauderie sought to refocus Kenward's attention on other matters. "You've been practicing your talents with the bow—yes?" On returning from the day's ride, he'd seen the boy lined with others involved in the same pursuit and knew it was so.

Kenward nodded, peeking at a man surprisingly well-informed. Having early discovered the wry humor ever lurking beneath a cold facade, he'd come to enjoy this second French captive's companionship near as much as Cassie's. Yet he was far too well trained to turn a blind eye upon the other's possibly suspicious knowledge.

Vauderie saw the concerned gleam in Kenward's narrowed gaze. He almost laughed, but restrained a merriment that might hurt the boy's tender young pride, and explained, "I saw you with the others as Will and I returned from our day's ride."

All fears allayed, Kenward gave the man a sheepish grin.

"But," Vauderie added, "as you've already been working hard while I have done precious little in these past many days, allow me to do this chore for you." Not waiting for Kenward's response, Vauderie suited actions to words. With a physical strength more than equal to the task, he soon had the heavy metal sheet and its load of delicious-smelling bread laying safe on the table.

While Vauderie stepped away, through the door left open Will guided a pale Cassie. Will absently laid both butter crock and cheese round on the table, too preoccupied with his own thoughts to note Kenward's gaze curiously examining the streaks of damp earth on items fetched from a dry cold house.

What had happened to his normal even temperament, Will demanded of himself, even charm of manner? Were any of the many English lords he knew asked their opinion, he'd no doubt they'd say Sir William of Kensham was a famous ladycharmer, a lover of legendary prowess and control who had *no* interest in inexperienced women. Yet now he had not merely yielded to the French virgin's naive wiles, but had sought to arouse the innocent and forbidden damoiselle in ways no man of honor would dare. For a good many years he had prided himself on the ability to take or leave a feminine companion as he chose, and never had he permitted one of their number to disrupt his life or interfere with his cool and rational decisions.

Self-disgust burned the brighter for the further admission that since Cassie's arrival this one woman had consistently distracted him from important concerns while an increasing frustration turned his temperament to a dark and unpredictable thing that made him a stranger to himself. These facts drove away thoughts of such lesser concerns as the subject of Clyde's offer and Cassie's rejection or the solemn matters Vauderie had spoken of during their ride.

He moved to drop into a padded chair awaiting before the fire. As if the weight of many problems were too great to be borne, his dark head fell against the high back. From this viewpoint he sought in the flames' ever-shifting patterns impossible answers to important questions.

Without need for spoken words, Cassie and Beata set to work in easy cooperation to see fresh-baked loaves properly stored. Once the iron sheet was cleared, Vauderie hoisted the heavy utensil back into its upright storage position, leaving Kenward to lay the table with first a white cloth and then trenchers formed by split halves of day-old bread. Once the table was ready, Beata placed a slab of slow-roasted venison on each trencher and Cassie ladled a thick broth over the top. Kenward poured draughts of bitter ale into the men's crockery goblets while Vauderie poured sweet cider into the female's and the two women cut slices from the round of cheese.

Kenward alone appeared comfortable this evening. Even Beata seemed, for the first time since Vauderie's arrival, to have difficulty meeting the uncommonly quiet man's blue gaze. Meal ready at last, Cassie gingerly approached the glowering knight glaring into the fire.

"Will," Cassie hesitantly began when she stood less than an arm's length from him. "The meal awaits your coming." Dark eyes lifted, and Cassie, discovering anew the power in even so brief a visual contact, was all too aware of her part in tempting an honorable knight into actions he plainly regretted. She nervously looked down while rushing to finish telling what she'd come to say. "And I've a surprise to end your repast." Yielding to craven urges such as she had thought uprooted days past, Cassie immediately turned toward the table, hoping her surprise would be the pleasant one Edna claimed.

While the group took their seats in an uncomfortable silence, Cassie peeked sidelong at the devastating man whose innate attractions settled around her again and more firmly claimed an unsought heart. Aside from the difficult barriers he raised betwixt them, there were other troublesome matters and potential misunderstandings stirred into a muddled stew by events in cold house and glade. Will had asked for no explanation when she and Clyde came from the cold house, despite the hard glare he'd given them both. Did he harbor a wrong notion of the purpose behind the privacy she'd shared with his young supporter? Did he think, as once he'd accused, that she so desperately missed the fine gallants of the French court—none of whom she had ever met—that she sought to work her wiles on his men, even lure them to set her free? This theory was so mistaken 'twas almost amusing, considering her refusal of a like offer for the sake of staying with Will as long as possible. Yet it held no humor for Cassie.

The gentle touch of lavender eyes eased through Will's self-absorption but he refused their call. He dare not look upon the once timid rabbit daily becoming more of an alluring temptress, a matchless treasure which honor demanded he return—never to a cruel man's arms, but to the brother from whom he'd sought ransom. The fiery memory of an insatiable desire so recently lit anew but doomed to blaze unfulfilled was so real it felt like a mocking presence. He had been a fool, an incredible fool, to allow this eve's sampling of sweet delights which could render only greater pain when came the inescapable moment when he must surrender her to the world where she belonged. 'Twas an action he feared certain to rip the heart from his chest.

While the heavy frown settling on Will's face did nothing to alleviate

Cassie's anxieties, it also worried Kenward. The boy watched his lord with growing concern. Had Will news of the war he couldn't share at table with the two French foes and a foster sister too involved? Did things go badly for their cause? Serious by nature, Kenward's nameless worries grew until he did more nibbling of his lip than of food on the trencher below.

In the meal's lengthening silence Vauderie saw the troubled expressions of the three and welcomed the puzzle of their cause as distraction from his own problem, seated so very near. Vauderie had sworn not to take advantage of Beata's trust, but he hadn't counted on being called to resist the enticements of her innate sensuality. She, unlike the women of his world, looked at him with an adoration owing nothing to calculations of his potential value as a source of position, wealth, and power. However, that adoration had its foundation on the unsteady sand of a rescue unnecessary had he and his companions never crossed her path. 'S'truth, Beata must recover her memory, but he feared when that happened she would view him only as one of her husband's heartless murderers. 'Twas a problem with no answer, yet still Vauderie would wed her were he allowed.

When the remains of the tense meal had been cleared from the table, Will turned to Cassie with inquiringly lifted brows.

"Where is this promised surprise?" 'Twas unfair, he had realized, to take out the ill temper roused by his own wrongful deeds on a damsel not to blame for possessing the form and character he desired so strongly it led him to folly. 'Twas hardly her fault she was French and noble-born while he was naught but an English knight of illegitimate line, and he was ashamed of his curt actions.

Ever more nervous about the moody man's reception of her long-planned surprise, Cassie stumbled as she rose to her feet but quickly recovered her poise. A grinning Beata joined her at the fireplace to pull down the long-handled pan ever suspended above flames and smeared a layer of grease over its shallow interior. Meanwhile, Cassie fetched two covered earthenware bowls. First lifting away their lids, she took a piece of thinly sliced apple from the larger. This she dipped into the smaller one's batter of flour, salt, egg, and ale before placing it in the pan to fry.

"Fritters!" Will exclaimed with delight, and Cassie's attention immediately shifted to the man whose devastating smile curled her toes.

Cheeks rose-tinted with pleasure and ebony curls ever escaping her braid's restraints to riot around her pale ivory face, Cassie cheerfully turned back to her chore. Plainly her surprise was more than welcome. Edna had told her true—not that Cassie had truly doubted it so, only had she fallen prey to a natural bent toward worrying increased by a great wish to please "her knight."

The wolf in Will watched this tender prey, and felt the predator he was pulled ever deeper into the bog of despair created by her further demonstration that she was the only woman he wanted, not for her delectable body alone but, too, for her generous understanding and soothing spirit.

When the whole large bowl of apple slices had been fried and laid atop a long wooden platter, Cassie sifted a light drift of precious sugar across them before laying the flavorsome dish on the table before Will's appreciative gaze.

"You are remarkable, Cassie." Will's compliment was quiet and deeply textured. "I thank you wholeheartedly, for I know full well what labor is demanded to prepare such a treat."

A very becoming blush cast its crimson hue across Cassie's cheeks once more, but this time she had no desire to look away from the gold sparks in dark eyes. Those sparks kindled fires of awareness within her, and beneath their heat she renewed her determination to win what few precious hours could ever be theirs.

The fritters were special made for Will, but there were far more than he could consume alone, and he generously divided the bounty amongst those gathered about his table. In a quiet now born not of tension but of an honest enjoyment, near all had been consumed before an unwelcome knock at the door broke the mood.

"Come," a surprised Will called, frown returning. There wasn't a man amongst his garrison who would dare interrupt at this time of night for less than an urgent matter.

The door swung open and Harvey hesitated on the threshold, uncomfortable about coming uninvited to his leader's home at any time, and worse at this ill-advised hour.

"What matter of great moment brings you?" Will's question emphasized his expectation of a grave purpose for this elsewise unjustified visit.

"I've only now returned from a patrol which brought a meeting with the French bastards—" Abruptly recollecting the presence of a well-born lady, he flushed, yet continued with naught but a grimace of apology. "Afore we got to them, they fell upon the poor village of Offcum like a plague of vile rats and slimy vipers."

Will slowly rose, leaving a half-eaten fritter on the table forlorn. "Fell upon Offcum?" He approached the messenger with such threatening intensity, Harvey had difficulty restraining an urge to turn and flee, even though he knew the dangerous fury in a piercing gaze of black ice was not meant for him.

"Aye, it's been burned fair to the ground and all as was there—mostly woman with their young—been brutally slain." Harvey's broad face closed into lines as bitter as the wretched facts he delivered.

"Did you learn who was responsible for the deed? Did you see the perpetrators?" Will's emotionless queries held a chill at odds with the gold flames in his eyes.

"We arrived at the edge of the forest as their attack came to an end, and saw the faces of none save those who fell to our bowmen's arrows." Harvey paused and cast a glowering look toward Vauderie. "But the leaders wore cloaks with the same insignia as what's on his."

Beneath the table's white cloth Beata's hands twisted together with anxiety. There was no insignia on the cloak Vauderie wore, but rather on the one he'd given her. What did it mean? He was French. Of a certainty she knew that and knew, too, that the French were foes to all of English blood—such as she. But Vauderie was not her foe. Vauderie had rescued her, so why did Harvey look at her beloved with such malice? She instinctively leaned nearer her "shining knight," this time not to seek his protection but rather to lend him hers, as inadequate as it might be.

Vauderie deemed Beata at a loss to understand any of this and likely sought his warmth as comfort for her confusion. He wrapped his arm reassuringly about her yet felt like a hypocrite for his gentle giving of something unnecessary had he never entered her life in the first instance.

Harvey's words had painted somber visions in Will's mind. Lost in their bleak contemplation, he was unaware of similar dismal tensions raised in those still at table and sent his man off to seek his own meal and bed. When Will did turn, he spoke absently.

"The day has been overlong, and surely we are all in need of rest. Thus, I suggest we retire to our beds." When he'd troubles enough to sort through, the prospect of another uncomfortable night in the dreadful hovel was more than Will would voluntarily face. He devised an alternate plan.

"Tonight, Vauderie, we'll sleep here in my hall and allow Kenward to return to his own bed." Will spoke as much to break the room's unnatural stillness as to tell of a decision his to make and needful of no response.

Vauderie nodded. He'd no choice but to obey his captor's command, a fine excuse for welcoming the notion of a night spent near a fire rather than in the damp and chill of the cheerless hovel.

Desperately uncomfortable amidst the shifting emotions of his present

companions, Kenward was relieved to depart from the table and slip off to
the cottage on the glade's far side which he shared with uncomplicated
men. The two women quietly and efficiently toiled together in clearing
the remains of their meal and tidying the area before escaping to their
own chambers and their own worries.

Although the two men left alone below had found little difficulty con-
versing during their ride, in the strain resulting from the revelations of so
short a time past, each felt constrained by their clear positions as foes.
Talk was thin at best while they prepared for their night's ease by laying
out pallets ever leaning upright against the back wall.

Will could hardly discuss with Vauderie the details of his various forays
against the French, nor had they common acquaintances. Nonetheless
they each felt an added discomfort in silence and struggled first with an
awkward comparison of the relative merits of various weapons used in the
hunt for wild boar and deer and then with talk on the fine points of a good
destrier. By the time these topics were exhausted, the two men were
relieved to stretch out with eyes closed.

Amidst the gloom of the night's darkest hours, the fire Will had banked
before laying down fell to a dull glow, but still faint orange gleams flickered across the heavily beamed ceiling and out over prone forms. Having
attained the measure of ease won by fighting men accustomed to harsh
nights in the wild now gifted with a rare warm comfort, when came a
terrified cry, it shattered the hall's peace and instantly jerked both men to
their feet. Linked to its source by cords of the heart, Vauderie whirled to
rush to Beata's comfort, but Will threw out an arm barring his way.

"Such near nightly terrors are a product of the vicious attack in which
you had a part, even if only spectator. Your appearance now would likely
do more harm than good. So, 'tis I who go to her."

Vauderie saw the gold glitter in Will's eyes daring him to deny the
claimed right. Gritting his teeth, he watched the dark man rapidly ascend
the stairway and fumed until his frustration boiled over into resolute refusal. No! He would not wait here helplessly. It was *not* his attack that had
caused these painful dreams. He had saved her once and would not be
prevented from going to her aid again. Firmly climbing the steps,
Vauderie followed the sound of anguished sobs to a door slightly ajar.

Will cradled Beata across his lap like a baby, softly stroking her long
soft hair while murmuring the meaningless nonsense parents use to soothe
a frightened child.

Vauderie was startled by the explosion of jealousy that surged through
him at sight of Beata in another man's arms, even a foster brother's. The

fragile damsel was his. It was his right to care for her. With the side of a clenched fist, he shoved the door wide and stepped into the chamber.

Beata's tear-drenched eyes flew to the broad figure filling the doorframe, golden hair and sun-bronzed skin catching and reflecting flame light. "Vauderie . . ." The single word ached with longing, and her arms instinctively reached out as she leaned toward her shining knight.

The sound of his name on soft lips drove the harsh determination from Vauderie's face and replaced it with a gentle smile all of tenderness. He stepped forward and swept Beata from Will's hold into his own embrace.

A blond head rested atop Beata's tawny curls while her arms tightly wrapped about the Frenchman's shoulders. In the sight Will recognized the impossibility of forbidding the hurting woman the comfort she sought. He stood and stalked out, aware that neither of the two left behind knew or cared.

A fierce frown laid a crease between Will's lowered brows. Beata wanted Vauderie, but how could he give his foster sister to a French foe? Yet it seemed only Vauderie had hope of bringing her back from the past into which she had fled. Only Vauderie could make her happy.

Abruptly an unbidden parallel occurred to him. Only with the French Vauderie would Beata be happy, just as only with the French Cassandra could happiness ever be his. 'Twas a fact he'd acknowledged before, yet under the weight of this disheartening truth reality bared its vicious fangs. What had happiness to do with marriage—or to do with the life partner chosen for those well-born? And both Vauderie and Cassie were that. Doubtless the two of them were better matched with one another—as he feared Cassie, despite their passionate embrace, hoped she and the French knight would one day come to be. His frown deepened into a glare near powerful enough to burn holes in the wooden floor he heavily trod.

From a slightly opened door, unnoticed in the dark corridor, Cassie watched a pained Will pass. Had Beata's turning to Vauderie with her fears hurt Will so badly? How could it be elsewise when one's beloved turned to another? 'Twas the same lesson in pain she relearned each time Will left her side and rushed to answer Beata's cries. Still she wanted to call out to him, to give him the consolation she'd earlier sworn to provide. 'Twas only her certainty that he'd never knowingly allow another to see the expression of anguish on his face that held her back.

Prying into matters of the heart which he'd as soon not reveal was decidedly not the right opening for the seduction she intended. There

would be another time, there must be another time and, pray God, soon—
before the unavoidable confrontation came, before she was returned
where she'd no wish to go, without the memories she wanted desperately
to carry with her.

Chapter

❦ 14 ❧

WITH CHRISTMAS EVE but two days hence Cassie sat at a table cleared of the morning meal's remnants and stared blindly down at fingers slowly tracing the line where two planks joined. With their limited stores 'twould take careful planning to devise meals worthy of the traditional Christmas and Twelfth Night feasts. But, surely, even here in the wilds amidst days of conflict, 'twas only right holy days be observed.

While Kenward poked at the flagging fire with a sturdy stick stripped of bark, Cassie pondered the chores ahead. She could manage the mince pie with but a few minor changes in the recipe. It might not taste precisely the same, yet 'twould suffice. Asides, there were other traditions whose doing required less creative actions and one for which they'd plentiful resources at hand.

"Do you know where awaits this year's yule log?" Her question broke the companionable silence left between her and the boy after Beata had excused herself to spend a private time abovestairs.

Kenward paused in his self-appointed task of idly sweeping cinders escaped from hearth back into the flames' renewed hunger. Having been given no earlier hint of what subject held Cassie's attention so firmly she'd given naught but distracted nods to his previous attempts at conversation, he was unprepared for this odd query.

During the past few days life had settled into a deceptively quiet pattern wherein Vauderie oft, as now, rode with Will through a snow-laden forest while Cassie and Beata carried forth the work required in seeing the house tidied and meals prepared. Kenward lent whatever aid they asked, although his nominal assignment was to act as their guard. He was better content with this responsibility since Will had agreed to his participation each afternoon in a much anticipated knightly practice. Yet he was not unaware of the formless sense of an impending danger hovering over the Weald, one more focused than those long posed by continuing warfare.

"At Castle Tarrant always did we go out in a joyous party to find the tree cut down at the close of holidays one year before and left to age." His expression went dreamy as he gazed into the hearth's smoky depths. "We'd drag the yule log back to our hall and on Christmas Eve set it alight with a branch from the previous year's." The memory put a forlorn hollowness in his tone. Though thrilled to be Will's squire, he'd missed such merry customs since moving into this military hamlet.

Cassie knew well this tradition observed on the estates of all nobles; and surely, she thought, amongst families less exalted, too. Holding her patience, she sought specific answer to her question. "But what of here?"

"With only Will and I here . . ." Kenward shrugged his response.

Cassie was surprised. "Don't Will's supporters resent their loss of the season's celebrations?" Had any lord she knew failed to supply their tenants with the advantages of these boisterous revelries—the more precious for their scarcity amongst the endless drudgery of the people's lives— 'twould cause more of an uproar than even did ever-increasing taxes.

"Here in the Weald 'tis different." Kenward struggled to explain. "These are men of war, few families, and fewer common rituals apply."

"More reason, I'd think, that his people should be provided an opportunity to enjoy what rare occasions for merriment are afforded them." Casting the boy an absent smile, she resumed her contemplation of the tabletop.

While Cassie's timid spirit constantly fretted over her decision to seize sweet memories from Will, her resolve had never wavered. Unfortunately, however, no opportunity to pursue her goal had presented itself. Indeed, Will seemed consciously striving to ensure they were never alone. 'Twas a depressing fact. Joined with the unforgotten look of condemnation Harvey had cast Vauderie, and her growing worries over the impending clash betwixt Will and Guy, additional layers were built in the accumulated tensions of Kensham's inhabitants. The small village had been buried for days under dense fog and falling snow. Uneasy in their relative idleness and too sensitive to their lord's dark mood, all within its boundaries seemed on the verge of a dangerous eruption of one sort or another, further convincing Cassie of the importance in taking action to ease the strain. Toward that goal she began laying her plans.

"This year"—Cassie looked directly into Kenward's anxious face— "they'll have every tradition upheld that I can arrange." Hopefully Will, as host to two captives and his beloved Beata, would not forbid such a celebration, particularly as Cassie would gladly shoulder the burden to oversee its various events. Moreover, she was willing, wherever possible, to perform the tasks required. "We may lack the choicest ingredients for our feasts, but of a certainty in the midst of the forest we've an ample supply of trees to provide a yule log."

"But—" Made uncomfortable by the prospect of arguing with Cassie, Kenward's Adam's apple rapidly bobbed up and down as he swallowed hard. "No tree was felled for that purpose last year." He felt compelled to point out this obvious flaw in her plan.

As Cassie rose to her feet, determined amethyst eyes remained steady on the boy who seemed bent on hindering her way. "Somewhere in this vast forest there must lay a naturally fallen tree, well-seasoned and able to serve our purpose."

Kenward had once found the damsel more timid than he, but within her now he recognized a courage quiet yet growing in strength, and made no attempt to restrain a wide grin. If she could accomplish so radical a metamorphosis, mayhap there was hope for him.

" 'S'truth," he readily agreed, anxious to prove himself still her willing assistant. "Might take us a while, but with perseverance we'll succeed."

"What goal demands such perseverance?" The deep question broke the visual bond between maid and boy.

Cassie's gaze immediately shifted to the dark man whose broad silhouette filled the open door. Saints, he was tall! The physical impact of his presence near drove all pretension to right wits from her grasp, but she valiantly collected scattered senses and directly met his unsettling black gaze. Given a choice in the matter, she'd have sought more time in which to devise the best method both to lay her request before Will and build the courage to do so. But—she silently repeated yet again—what needs must, must be. She drew a deep breath and took several steps toward him, praying the brave smile forced to stiff lips would hide the heart-thumping agitation behind.

"We mean to search the forest hereabouts for a fallen tree worthy of becoming our yule log."

Will's brows dropped into a frown that the two watching took to be the first sign of rejection. Instantly deciding that, having now begun, she had as well lay out the whole of her design, Cassie continued speaking before Will could respond.

"Moreover, I mean to seek Edna and Beata's help in preparing fine feasts for everyone in Kensham on both Christmas Eve and Twelfth Night."

"Is that all?" Caught between amusement with the winsome damsel's grandiose plan and amazement for her courage in presenting it to him so abruptly, the mocking question was accompanied by golden glints of silent laughter in his gaze.

"Nay," she promptly answered. "I intend, also, to open your home each of the season's twelve nights and welcome your people to share their lord's bounty in ale, festive games, and merry company."

This further audacity truly startled Will, but the determined line firming berry-sweet lips tickled him as well.

"I, too, pray you'll permit these celebrations." A near forgot Kenward added his earnest plea as he moved forward to stand at Cassie's side. "I miss the castle and my family during these holidays, and sharing the same traditions—despite the distance betwixt us—would lessen my loneliness." Uneasy about the childish feelings he'd revealed, the boy shifted his weight from one foot to the other but directly met the knight's attention, of a sudden full upon him.

This was a brave admission from the boy striving to prove himself a man; and Will wanted to grant leastways the pair's initial request. Yet there were restricting facts he couldn't change.

"Truly, I am sorry. I've no time to lend your quest, as a messenger has come, summoning me to a meeting far too important to miss—'tis why our ride ended so early. A return before late this night is impossible." He held his expression impassive as he added a final objection. "The men I leave behind have duties enough and more to demand all their attention and can neither accompany you in the search nor give the time to haul so great a weight here."

Cassie saw the barrier—unmistakable and immovable—that he'd raised against her courageous proposal. When her shoulders slumped, the blow he'd delivered to her growing confidence smote Will's conscience. But his deep regret for the deed's result made it no less unavoidable. He could not refuse the call of his lord—no matter the poor timing or frustration of preferred actions denied.

"I could accompany them in the search, Will." Vauderie stood barely noticed behind the English knight's wide back. "Once 'tis located, we can return to wait on your arrival and another day's freeing of men enough to drag it to your hearth."

In answer to the dark, startled glance thrown over a broad shoulder, Vauderie shrugged and stated an obvious fact. "By virtue of our daily rides, I am familiar with the forest immediately surrounding your home— as, no doubt, is Kenward."

Will was unconvinced of the wisdom in a scheme that would send two hostages out with naught but a young boy to provide guard against escape.

"Please, Will, please." Beata softly made her supplication from shadows at stairway top, hands clasped together and eyes gleaming in hopeful anticipation.

Faced by this combined appeal, Will felt well and truly trapped, yet still hesitated. He was far too skilled a tactician to risk so much merely for the fleeting enjoyment of others.

Vauderie saw the predicament the entreaties of so many had thrust Will into and sympathized. Without forethought, Vauderie stepped around to face the other man and sought to ease his plight.

"No matter the differences in our heritage, Will, we *are* brother knights, and by that truth we share the same code. On my honor and by the Holy Cross I swear that as surely as we four go out, we four will return."

During their daily rides and quiet talks on all manner of subjects—save the present conflict—Will had come to know and understand Vauderie better than near any man not of his family. They were enemies by virtue of their rightful allegiance to liege lords at war, but Will had no hesitation in believing Vauderie too honorable to break a sworn oath.

"On the health of your honor then rests the deed." Black gaze steadily holding blue, the agreement was sealed as each knight held and shook the forearm of the other. While Vauderie solemnly nodded, an excited Beata flew down the steps to tightly wrap her hands about his free arm.

"I've my cloak," Beata joyously laughed up into Vauderie's gentle smile. "And you have yours, so let's set off on our quest."

Firelight gleamed on Vauderie's bright hair as he shook his head in mock sorrow. "I fear I'd soon fall faint to my hunger, leaving you three to drag my weak yet not inconsiderable form over the whole of the return journey."

"You are hungry?" Beata's golden eyes went wide with concern. "Forgive me my selfish demands."

"Nay, sweeting." Vauderie laid his much larger hand atop the two smaller ones still clasped about his arm. " 'Twas naught but a poor jest. I've been without food for far longer periods of time and remained healthy enough to stand strong in battle."

"But you are hungry?" Beata smiled, refusing to leave the subject of his possible discomfort behind.

Vauderie shrugged with an apologetic grimace. "I fear at my size 'tis seldom elsewise—a failing Will surely knows as well." He arched an inquiring brow at the other man of like size.

Will laughed freely in response to this further example of the dry wit his male captive had revealed ever more frequently during recent days—another example of natures more alike than readily apparent.

"Aye. I, too, confess a near constant hollowness within."

"Come and sit." Relieved by this shift to a mood of easy friendship, Cassie rejoined the conversation. "Though we've no freshly roasted meat, just after you left this morn I set a stew to cook in the caldron. It should be edible by now."

She hustled to the hearth and peered into a huge iron pot standing on four long, sturdy legs above glowing coals and low-burning flames. The bubbling mixture—including salt-meat, leaks, mushrooms, and herbs harvested from the kitchen garden and dried by Edna—was proven ready for the table by its pungent aroma. Two powerful men took their seats as Kenward hastened to fetch and fill their mugs with ale while Beata split loaves of rye bread for Cassie to ladle stew atop.

Once all five were served and eating, Will gave suggestions on the most likely areas to find a log worthy of its purpose to the party soon setting forth. He did not insult their good sense with a reminder that the one chosen must be well-seasoned yet not so aged 'twould burn with such speed as to be gone before Twelfth Night arrived. They assuredly knew that such a disaster, by tradition, would leave ill fortune in its wake to haunt the home until appeased with a proper doing the following year.

Sitting quietly at the devastating English knight's side, Cassie was fully conscious of the oddity in finding such camaraderie amongst diners at table where sat captor and captives, but she was pleased. She meant to disallow any intrusion on the here and now by the ever looming threat in Guy's likely violent response to the ransom demand. Were she to fail in winning precious memories of time spent within Will's embrace, leaving her with only such distant meetings as this, then she would grasp them with both hands to prevent the prospect of an unhappy future from robbing her of even these small joys.

Pray God, the fact that Beata had suffered no further nightmares since Vauderie began sleeping in the same house had proven to Will that the other man was not her wicked assault's perpetrator. Asides, Beata seemed near hourly to move more firmly into reality, even though she'd yet to remember the events that had caused her retreat. Mayhap with her unique perceptiveness Beata sensed there were facts she had rather not know.

Preoccupied with these many thorny matters, Cassie missed the peculiarity in the departures of a famous warrior and his captive French knight. After laughingly bidding each other safe journey, the former set off with his warriors in one direction while the latter, with only a boy and two women for company, went out in another.

Snow no longer drifted down from above, but laid heavy on the ground while seemingly endless banks of fog hovered above. Moreover, the day was bitter cold. Yet this warmth of friendship shared was far more welcome to Cassie than would ever again be the sunlight of her French home. Those intent on the festive quest's goal found many a fallen log amidst the dense forest's snow and tangled undergrowth, but each ended in regretful dismissal. Either 'twas so aged it fair disintegrated at a gentle kick and was surely unable even to survive the trip to the castle, let alone burn for twelve nights, or 'twas so freshly toppled 'twould likely refuse to burn at all.

"I found it!" Kenward's shout was muffled by the distance between himself and the rest of the party.

Cassie grinned. Her young friend, despite long hours of wandering over rough and twisting paths, had energy enough to rush ahead in earnest pursuit of their goal. The afternoon was fast fading toward dusk. Soon they must turn back to the house, so best this be as fine a specimen as Kenward plainly believed.

"Truly! Come see!" Kenward's excited voice lent renewed vigor to his companions' steps but 'twas the quieter gasp of pain that followed that urged them to leap across a small stream and rush at a flat-out run to his side.

In a stark pattern atop the ground's pristine white coating Kenward lay parallel to the thick trunk of a fallen oak. Cassie instantly dropped to her knees beside the boy writhing in pain but biting his lips to stifle cries. Feeling helpless with little training to ease such distress, she simply brushed tangled hair from his eyes and murmured meaningless words of comfort.

Vauderie it was who, with one look at the leg bent at an odd angle, recognized the problem of a broken limb. Possessing the experience of a warrior oft times required to administer medicinal aid to those under his command, he immediately set about the necessary tasks. Carefully loosening the cross garters holding chausses tight to an injured leg, then rolling back the surrounding cloth, he was relieved by the finding of unbroken skin and signs of a clean break more likely to mend without permanent damage. Mercifully, the boy passed out under his swift execution of the vital resetting.

At sight of the boy in agony, the fleeting memory of a similar experience flashed through Beata's mind; but, under her concern for Kenward, she pushed the nebulous image aside. "What can I do?"

The soft question drew Vauderie's attention. A haunted look of recognition added new depth to honey-hued eyes. Caught in the uncomfortable position of wanting for her the full health of a memory restored, and yet fearful of what changes in their relationship it might bring, he hastily found for her a task able to divert dark thoughts.

Vauderie removed the cloak he wore and, borrowing the unconscious boy's sharp dagger, split the fine wool. Driving the blade safely point down into earth buried 'neath a layer of snow, he took each side of the cloth in a strong hand and ripped a strip free.

"Take and dip this into the stream, then bring it back to lay over Kenward's brow." That the water-chilled cloth's purpose could as well be achieved with a layer of hard-packed snow he consciously chose to ignore.

As Beata gladly accepted the proffered strip, he glanced up to see Cassie silently finishing a helpful chore.

While Vauderie worked over the boy, Cassie had recovered from her momentary absence of common sense and remembered seeing enough of set bones to know what more was needful. Jumping to her feet, she'd wasted no time in searching out slender but sturdy branches straight enough to serve as splints. These she now delivered into Vauderie's outstretched hands.

Making use of cross garters earlier removed, Vauderie affixed one of the two stripped branches supplied by Cassie on either side of the injured leg.

Dusk's murky mantle drifted down through an ever-thickening fog. Even the dark fingers of barren tree limbs spread overhead had been obscured by deepening shadows when the cool cloth applied to Kenward's forehead revived him to wakefulness—and pain. Despite discomfort-pinched face, he gave the three who gently tended him a valiant grin.

"Your leg is broke." Vauderie smiled and almost apologetically added an explanation of the unavoidable action whose agony had robbed the lad of his senses. "I had to see it set elsewise no hope would there be of it healing straight and strong. Then, to assure you'd not slip too far from us, 'twas important you be summoned from an unnatural sleep."

A now solemn Kenward nodded. "I'm thankful you were here and willing to tend my injury." By this expression of gratitude he also gave his oblique appreciation for the French knight's honor. 'Twas surely that which prevented a captive from using the fortuitously incapacitating injury of a lone guard, inadequate as already he was, to make a successful escape. "Without your aid, I'd have been left to drag myself back to Kensham."

Cassie cringed at the thought. Alone in the dark of rapidly descending night and with wolves ever about, 'twas unlikely Kenward would have survived to see the dawn. She, too, recognized the honor upheld in Vauderie's treatment of the wounded boy and gave her friend a blinding smile.

Vauderie acknowledged their approval with a self-deprecating shrug and immediately turned the focus of their talk away from himself. "You may wish we'd left you asleep, Kenward, for I've no method to alleviate the distress sure to assail you on our return journey."

He couldn't carry the boy without rendering excruciating pain, nor could Kenward hop all the way to Kensham upheld on one side. There was but one choice left. Vauderie laid the mutilated remains of his cloak on the ground beside the boy and set about building a stretcher—cumbersome for him to lift on one end and drag the other behind, and able to provide only a lamentably bumpy and hurtful ride for Kenward.

Will stood alone before the massive fireplace in his hall. The sole light in the night-dark house came from coals near gone cold—as cold and dark as his heart.

During his meeting with young Henry's war leaders, he'd heard rumors of a prince to be recalled by the French king. If proven true, although hopefully it would mean good news for the struggle as a whole, 'twould add greatly to his responsibilities during the two months following Twelfth Night. This possibility was burdensome enough without proof of his poor judgment—a wrong choice which hurt more than he wanted to admit.

As expected, he'd returned late. Once in his home he'd been forced to face a dreaded but seemingly obvious reality. He'd been a fool to either trust his knightly foe or believe Cassie truly preferred to remain in the Weald. A firestorm of cinders arose from roughly kicked coals, and their light flickered over the harsh expression of the man whose temper burned as bright.

Before full daybreak he would set out and find the boy the French pair were certain to have tied and left at nature's mercy. He'd no doubt but what Beata would go wherever Vauderie directed. Find the wicked pair who had succeeded in lulling him into granting boons undeserved he would, find them and see them pay for their wrong. In self-disgust he slapped the palms of his hands against the mantel. How could he make them pay when never would he harm a single strand of Cassie's ebony tresses. Vauderie, now—Vauderie was a villainous Frenchman like as any other, a foe whose just punishment was the same end as required of all invaders—death. Yet the knowledge of Vauderie's treachery hurt the worse for the liking Will had allowed to grow for the man.

"Damn you, Vauderie! Damn you to hell!" The snarl accompanied another vicious kick at smoldering logs.

"We've been gone overlong, Will, but I don't think I deserve such punishment for a deed not of my choosing."

Spinning about, Will found the tall blond man standing square in the open door, hands on hips and head tilted quizzically.

Vauderie stepped to the side and waved at the small group a few paces beyond the threshold. "When one is forced to drag an injured boy and go slow for the sake of lessening his discomfort, it takes an inordinate length of time to retrace even the short distance we'd journeyed."

Will shook his dark head to free himself of both stunned surprise and an overwhelming sense of relief that Cassie had returned and would remain for a little while more. Striding forward, he gazed down into the sheepish smile on Kenward's strained face.

"What happened?" he sympathetically asked the boy.

"I found the perfect yule log—by falling over it." Kenward's rueful explanation won smiles from his erstwhile rescuers and lord alike. "Leastways we'll have no trouble once more finding and fetching it—my mode of travel must'a left a path so wide any moonling could follow it."

"'S'truth." Will nodded. "But the 'we' you speak of will *not* include you, for when others go to drag it home, you'll wait here."

Between the two men, Kenward was gently carried inside and lowered onto a straw pallet hastily positioned near the hearth soon host to a roaring fire. The hour was late, and after the group had shared a quick repast of cold salt-meat, cheese, apples, and a few shelled nuts, the weary women gladly climbed to their chambers and slid into welcoming beds. In the stillness of the dim-lit hall below, Kenward gratefully drifted into dreams more pleasant than his uncomfortable reality, while the two knights lay wakeful in silent pondering of the day's events.

"Vauderie . . ." Will's quiet word drifted through the dark above the pallets where they lay. "I misjudged you, and for that I owe you an apology."

"Nay, were I in your place, doubtless I'd have made the same assumption. In truth, 'tis I who owe a debt to you for lending me your trust in the first instance. I pray you've confidence now that I am a man of honor and would never betray an oath."

"I'll never doubt it again." Will spoke with a firm conviction which was of greater value than any apology. "And only do I hope you know the same is true of me."

"Aye." Vauderie was quick to offer a like trust, but could not stop there when this was the best opening he'd had or was like to get for addressing an ever more pressing issue. "Yet I am compelled to seek more from you."

Will tensed. What more could he give? Surely by his statement of honor, Vauderie knew he could release neither of his French hostages—not without besmirching his integrity and defying the king to whom he'd sworn fealty.

" 'Tis a request I've made before and one you've yet to answer." Vauderie's tone was deep with urgency. "Again I ask you to grant my petition to claim Beata for wife."

"But—" Will began the same argument he'd used before. Vauderie interrupted.

"Though Beata once had the mind of a child, she daily improves, and I swear she has the body and instincts of the grown woman she is. 'S'truth, I gave you my oath to not physically claim her, but by her actions she makes holding to my word ever more difficult. I beg that you release me from the promise and give her into my care by virtue of a church-blessed union."

Will had seen the many small lures Beata cast out to Vauderie. He sympathized, knowing how difficult it had become holding to his own honorable duty when, even without the same deliberate provocations from Cassie, he'd difficulty keeping tight restraints upon a growing need to claim—and keep—her. Yet though Vauderie was noble-born, Beata was not. Then there was the consideration of how Cassie felt about Vauderie extending to Beata the place in his life she too likely hoped to fill. Where once he'd thought to rid Cassie's path of the blond and handsome knight, he'd long since realized the painful truth that he had rather see her happy in the other man's hold than unhappily wed to a possibly brutal stranger chosen by her uncaring family. For Cassie's sake as much as any other, he questioned the suitability of Vauderie's request.

"While my blood tie to the baronage is only of an inferior illegitimate source, Beata has none at all. Moreover, what of Cassie?"

Although Vauderie knew of Will's blemished heritage, as did likely most French nobles, neither it nor Beata's background was of any import to him. While he shrugged this impediment aside, Will's last question perplexed him.

"Cassie?" What had Cassie to do with his desire to wed Beata? Of a sudden it occurred to him that Will must think the relationship between he and the French damsel was more than it was. "As I told you earlier, Cassie and I are friends of long standing—but no more than that. Nor could we ever be when she is betrothed to my uncle." Will's misunderstanding was almost amusing, considering the feelings Cassie plainly harbored for the English knight.

Will heard surprise in the other's voice and knew that, for Vauderie at least, 'twas true. But for Cassie? On the other side of the matter, he had seen Beata blossom under Vauderie's attention and felt in all justice he could not rightfully deny the man its fruits.

"On the morrow or the day following I'll go out to make arrangements for the visit of a priest, and our Twelfth Night feast will have an additional cause for celebration."

Chapter
🙚 *15* 🙘

" 'TWILL BE EPIPHANY yet, for the sake of the great good you do for we of the Weald, I'll commission another to perform the rites and come myself." The abbot's broad smile was sincere and near as wide as his hefty frame. Along with those born to the harsh life of this dense forest, Abbot Jerome had learned a respect for Willikin's military skills and an admiration for his evenhanded dealings with men of all stations. "Although," the abbot gently teased, "I had rather it were your wedding I presided over, Will."

Will's soft laughter filled the tiny chamber, bare save for a narrow cot, simple table, and corner prie dieu barely visible in the weak light of a lone and malodorous tallow taper.

"Should that day ever arrive, I swear I'll send for you." As Will counted the abbot a friend, he'd ask no other. Moreover, he felt safe in the giving of a promise he was certain would never demand fulfillment—not when the only woman with whom he could envision sharing his life was both well-born and French. Two immovable barriers. Her betrothal to another man was of no import. He meant to free Cassie of the despised Guy de Faux for her sweet sake alone. 'Twas a fiery determination stoked to greater heat by the knowledge that Cassie's betrothed and Beata's abuser, whom he'd given a solemn oath to see dead, were one and the same. Together the two fierce goals had tempered the steel of his intent into a sharp, double-edged sword.

Abbot Jerome saw the abrupt descent of an icy mask erase all the warm laughter of moments past from his guest's face. He regretted having said anything to upset Will, but only God could know what might rouse a man's inner demons. With a rueful grimace he reminded himself that nowise dare he allow the other's mood to deflect him from a needful task.

"As I grant you this boon"—while he folded his hands atop the worthy shelf of his belly, even his smile held a plea—"I beg you will grant me one in return."

After the momentary betrayal of an inner turmoil and despite the abbot's surprising words, Will schooled his features back into impassive lines. Never afore had the devout man asked aught of him, and no matter what its content never could he refuse so rare a request. Although the abbot's uncharacteristic unease puzzled him, Will nodded without hesitation.

"Wait, Will," cautioned the abbot uncomfortable with the awkward appeal he must make. "Wait until you know the facts of the dilemma I've no source save God to solve."

Not even this unusual admonition from a man seldom uncertain weakened Will's decision, though it succeeded in deepening his curiosity. What earthly event could cause this man of God such difficulty? The humble Abbey of St. David lay well within the Weald's boundaries, and as such was protected from marauding French soldiers profane enough to risk the sin of blasphemy by defiling hallowed ground. Thus its pious inhabitants had no reason to fear attack. Moreover, their temporal needs were adequately met by the harvest of their own toil. Judging from the abbot's healthy size, they were blessed with more success than most who scrabbled to survive on what could be grown amidst the Weald's unforgiving soil. What further need, then, had they of him?

"I prayed long and fervently before coming to believe *you* are His answer." Abbot Jerome stared earnestly at the bare dirt floor as if hoping the words of an appropriate explanation might be written there.

To say Will was amazed by this news would be to say the icy North Sea was naught but a wee bit chilly.

"You know all which occurs on your lands." Watery blue eyes met a patiently waiting black gaze. "Therefore, doubtless you know of the devastation wreaked upon Offcum."

It was not a question, but still Will nodded when the priest paused while mentally seeking the best path to approach the knight, as if an unmindful step might throw him into a treacherous bog.

"And you know we are a colony of men where no female may enter." The abbot shifted uneasily from foot to foot.

Again Will nodded, interest increased by an unaccustomed color rising in the abbot's cheeks.

"Imagine our dismay one morn on finding a small girl-child deposited at our gates." The abbot had no reason for shame when 'twas the choice of none within that their abbey now harbored a forbidden female. Unfortunately, that certain fact did nothing to cool the heat of his face.

Will immediately recognized how disconcerting to the abbot was this unwelcome guest, and dark brows arched while, with difficulty, he restrained an inappropriate urge to grin.

"Never afore have we been faced with such a problem." The flustered abbot began to dither. "Oh, now and again, a man of the soil delivers a son to be raised in our ways, or an orphan boy is given into our care—meant also to become one of our number." Realizing he'd begun to ramble, the abbot paused and clenched his teeth for a moment to regain control of good reason before emphatically shaking the fringe of gray hair ringing his head. "But never, never has anyone left a female at our door." Amazement twined with indignation in his voice. "Though undeniably one of God's children, she cannot remain here." Hands lifted palm up swept out in a wide arch encompassing the whole of the abbey's walled grounds and then back to the center in a gesture of supplication.

Agreeing with Abbot Jerome's initial caution that 'twas wisest to first obtain all relevant information, Will returned to the subject with which the other had begun. "What has this child to do with Offcum?" he asked, yet had little doubt of the answer. 'Twas too close a parallel to his own past and the fire from which his mother had saved him before being consumed by its flames herself.

"Says her parents died in the fire from whose burning clutches she was rescued and carried safe away by the only family to escape. They cared enough to save her, yet as already they have twelve children to feed, they abandoned her at our gates. Their destination is unknown to her, except that 'tis not Offcum, for the village is no more." The pain in pale blue eyes made it clear that although the small orphan posed a complex predicament for the abbot, he shared her sorrow in the many losses of a village heartlessly destroyed by uncaring foes.

In part the Weald was special to Will, an orphan himself, for the practice whereby its independent denizens took care of their own. Despite the hard life faced by all, when parents were taken—whether by ailment or accident—most always another family took in the children left behind. Yet he understood the impossible plight of a family of such size robbed by consuming flames of what little they possessed. Naught but severely limited choices had they. Raised to rely on the church as their only hope during the bleak span of mortal life, how else but that they should leave this added burden to its mercy?

"What would you have me do?" Will's question was not an idle one.

" 'Tis undeniable that a small girl should never be amongst a religious community of men. However, a military encampment is no more proper place for her."

"Even in our relative solitude we hear many things . . ." Abbot Jerome pursed his lips in gentle reproof while weak candle flame glowed like a halo on the hair encircling his shaven head. "Aye, many things—such as the female hostage who shares your home. And you've just requested my assistance in a matter involving the foster sister who lives with you, too. Surely, as a gift to God for all He has done for you, if naught else, you can put the young foundling into the women's care until a family be found to take her in?"

Will's eyes narrowed. Did the abbot's words mean he knew more of this knight's past than had willingly been revealed to any dwelling in the forest? Did the abbot know, Will wondered, that he was where and what he was because someone had taken pity on him and extended to him the same understanding he was being asked to give this girl? No matter, he could no more turn aside this orphaned child than he could forget his own childhood.

"I yield." Although Will's smile was tight 'twas not angry. "But as I've much to be done before daylight is gone, I ask that you send for the child now and see us soon on our way."

No need to mention the sole task urgently beckoning him was the desire to arrive home in time to join in the festive gatherings and amusements Cassie had arranged to fill each night of the twelve Christmas days. Thanks to her efforts, he and his men had been eased into merrier spirits than enjoyed for many a month.

With all the haste his portly form could manage, the abbot rushed to the door opening into a narrow corridor. Once thrown wide, revealed was a bench against the opposite wall, and seated upon its wide, crude plank a small figure with thin arms, like brittle branches, tightly crossed about her middle, and legs dangling above the floor. Of perhaps six or seven years, she was all dark tangled hair, singed at the ends, and eyes huge brown pools of apprehension despite the upward tilt of a pointed chin.

Staring into those unblinking eyes, Will saw reflections of himself at the same age—defiant and yet terrified. He strode forward and dropped to one knee beside the little maid.

"So, you are the unanticipated offering left at abbey gates?" he gently teased, hoping to lessen her fears.

Wisps of dark hair brushed pale cheeks as she solemnly nodded.

"And you are alone in the world?" Will's voice dropped to a purring depth which was comfort in itself.

Again the girl nodded, but now crystal tears silently coursed down from between lashes tightly closed and her once proudly lifted chin dropped almost to her chest.

"I am Will, and in my house a fine lady awaits to welcome your company." He only hoped it was true. By virtue of Cassie's response to Beata and winning of Meg, Edna, Kenward—in truth all of his supporters—he was near certain she would. "You'll remain safe with us until a family is found in need of a girl just like you." Will added the qualifier too glumly aware both Beata and Cassie would one day be gone, likely one day soon. "But first I must know who travels in my company. Will you tell me your name?" He put one finger beneath her chin and softly urged it upward.

Brown eyes still drowning in tears opened to meet his gaze as she gulped and whispered, "Sarah."

"Then, Sarah, come with me." He rose and held his hand out to her while casting the abbot a quick glance which warned the man not to speak of his full identity to the frightened child for fear of deepening her alarm.

Having earlier seen the famous knight, the great protector of the Weald as he rode through her village, Sarah already knew precisely who he was. She unhesitatingly slid forward on the broad bench until her feet touched the hard-packed dirt floor, and put her fingers in his.

"I pray you will grant me pardon for neglecting to provide you a palfrey for our journey." His formal apology, as if she were a lady born, won a shy smile, although her gaze remained on the floor. He realized 'twas unlikely Sarah knew how to ride, but continued his gallant ruse. "Mayhap you will consent to sitting with me atop Nightfall, my destrier?" He gave her one of his most potent smiles.

Brown eyes shielded by half-lowered lashes peeked up. Despite her youth, Sarah was not immune to his smile, and anticipation pushed apprehension aside as they departed the abbey proper. By the time she'd been lifted to the huge stallion's back, tears were gone and she was chattering to the handsome knight as if they were friends of old.

Standing aside the dusty track leading out through the two abbey gates spread wide, Abbot Jerome bade the odd-matched pair farewell with a heartiness not unmixed with a fine measure of relief.

Returning the abbot's glowing smile with a wry one of his own, Will reminded the other of his original purpose. "I'll send one of my men to fetch you in time to assure your safe arrival on the appointed day."

Even in the limited daylight of a foggy late afternoon, the abbot's pate gleamed as he nodded emphatic cooperation. Will held the fragile child safe in his arms and turned Nightfall down the homeward path.

"Enough, you win." Cassie ducked a hand threatening to become too adventurous in its quest for her identity. This game of blind man's buff was, indeed, dangerous when only one woman played amidst a much larger group of men. Beata preferred to enjoy quiet time in her soon-to-be husband's company, and the pair had withdrawn into the quiet shadows in a corner of the hall.

Cassie's laughter trilled against the wall as the hood once a grain sack dropped over her head and, to prevent possibly revealing peeks, was affixed about her neck by a loosely tied cord. Next she was twirled and twirled and twirled. More oft, she suspected, than customary. At last they were done and she was abruptly released. Senses spinning, she staggered and almost fell to the rush-bestrewn floor, near incapable of so simple a task as remaining upright. She stumbled into a solid wall and held tight—not, in truth, to learn the wall's identity (the game's goal), but purely to keep from falling into an ignoble heap.

Slowly recovering her sense of balance, she lightly ran the palms of her hands across her captive's shoulders—enabling her to measure both height and width, but in so doing her fingers caught and tangled in a handful of thick, coarse hair.

"Ow!" The one so abused gave a mock protest.

"Clyde, it's you." Cassie recognized the voice and had no doubt her guess, backed by earlier detected physical facts, was true.

"How is it you always find me?" Clyde moaned, caring not at all that none in their audience believed 'twas an accident. Having her so near was worth the teasing he'd assuredly be subjected to for days to come.

As Cassie pulled the hood free, the thick, ebony braid once neatly piled atop her head tumbled down to trail over a shoulder covered in soft rose velvet. For this season's each eventide of entertainment she dressed in one of the fine gowns seldom worn since near the first day of her arrival. In deference to the battle plan she'd laid out for this night, she'd chosen one whose color not only flattered her fair complexion, but laced down the front and required no under camise.

"I can't imagine, Clyde." Lavender eyes were innocently wide and her tone too guileless to be sincere. "But I appreciate my good fortune."

Pleased she hadn't shown him for a fool out of hand, yet embarrassed by his discovered ruse, Clyde hastily stepped away.

"And now 'tis your turn to again have a go with the hood." Anxious to lessen his discomfort, with a laugh Cassie daintily dangled the object's rough cloth before the young man's sheepish smile. "Meantime I retire from our play to resume my heavy duties." Shoulders slumped in mock weariness, she slowly retreated a few paces as if carrying a great weight upon her back.

As Cassie moved aside from the clustered men, 'twas not Clyde alone who protested. In the past few days this amazing French captive had toiled to assure their enjoyment of the season, and they'd come to appreciate her willingness to be friend of men not only her social inferiors, but assuredly the foes of her countrymen. Moreover, her quick laughter and equally quick compassion had earned both their respect and their affection.

The noise of the boisterous game had hidden the sound of an opening entry door. From this vantage point in a hall well lit by resin-dipped torches suspended in metal rings at regular intervals down two parallel walls, Will saw the response of his men to Cassie's giving spirit. He was proud, and yet perversely begrudged its sharing with other men when he feared 'twould soon be lost to he and they all.

The news that had delayed Will's journey to the abbey increased his dread of a day too quickly approaching. Along with another message sent from Lord Marshall, commander of his child-king's armies, had come confirmation that the French prince had indeed been summoned home for a consultation with his royal father. This meant both that, shortly after mid-January, the French prince would be forced to attempt either passing through or circumventing the Weald. Likely it also meant that Guy de Faux and brother Henri would be driven to take action on Cassie's ransom. Elsewise they would miss their best opportunity to see her returned to their land. Although he longed for the opportunity to dispose of the vile Guy, the deed would assuredly be followed by the necessity of surrendering his captive.

The thought of releasing her was devastating, and a prospect Will had purposefully chosen to block, leastways for the length of the holiday season. Still, too aware of the necessity for maintaining a realistic view of the whole, and ever-mindful of his honor-bound duty, he had turned away whenever she was too near. To temper the aching temptations of her inexperienced and tentative wiles, he'd taken pains to be certain they were within a pace of each other as seldom as possible—only to find that if he weren't by her side, another would be. He knew the irrationality in his jealousy of a soon-to-be-wed Vauderie and even the near-beardless whelp

Clyde. But he couldn't stem the flow. The forceful thud with which Will sent the massive door closed earned everyone's attention.

When lavender eyes settled on the new arrival they instantly deepened to amethysts sparkling with welcome. That he met her gaze full well was a boon unexpected after days during which he'd consistently refused to give the attention she had ever more boldly sought, a strategy begun after she'd seen what victory Beata had won with similar weapons. Bound to him by the power of his soul-melting gaze, she reassured herself, this boded well for her hopeful campaign. Only as the dark knight stepped farther into the hall did Cassie notice the small girl apprehensively peering from shadows created by the calf-length black cloak flowing down from wide shoulders.

Studying Cassie's face intently for any hint of her true response, Will found only a growing smile of warm acceptance as she hurried forward to greet both him and his companion.

"I am so glad you've safely returned. 'Tis gift enough of itself, but I see you've brought me another—an exquisite faerie doll."

Peeking at Cassie, Sarah giggled.

"Ohhh! She's real!" Cassie promptly dropped to her knees beside the child. "I'm glad you've come to play with us."

Sarah looked dubiously at the men who'd returned to their game, Clyde wildly lunging after the others while raucous laughter echoed against the stone wall of a fireplace wherein burned a cheery blaze.

" 'Tis Christmastide, you ken?" Cassie asked, head tilted to one side. "A time for merry games, fine feasts, and friends. I hope you'll be our friend, too." All too aware that only a sad loss would have brought the wee maid here, Cassie offered her hand to a child seemingly as timid as she had once been—but proudly was no more.

Sarah bravely stepped from behind the protection of Will's back to lay her fingers in the waiting palm.

"Saints! Your hand is cold. Come, let's get you to the fire and see you warmed." Cassie led her new friend in a circuitous route about boisterous men.

As by this wide path they approached a long fireplace, Sarah took stock of its array of conveniences—amazing to a child born into the simple life of a humble cottage served by naught but a central hearth. Here were assorted spits capable of holding a variety of meats, and room enough for several caldrons, although now only a single great pot slowly bubbled at the end where flames restrained in fury were carefully tended by a very large woman. The maid's curious brown glance ventured out from the fireplace itself. She discovered a downcast boy about twice her age laying atop a wide expanse of soft pelts and plainly mourning the injured leg preventing him from joining in the men's spirited game.

While Will watched the damoiselle and small maid move away, a softness such as few had seen entered his dark gaze. In Cassie all the golden strands of traits he had admired in the different women of his experience, and more—far more—were entwined to form a matchless treasure. The desperation of knowing 'twas one that could never be truly his and of how short was his time with her, reinforced the importance of not losing a single moment. Surely, he told himself, here in this sizable company, he could safely savor the sweet joys of Cassie's company. He turned a deaf ear to the whispered warning of his good sense that this was a dangerous delusion.

"Will . . ." Beata breathlessly approached, her unspoken question far too obvious to require words. Will had been busy with mysterious duties in recent days, too busy to go and arrange for the priest he'd promised would come. Clutching Vauderie's arm with anxious hope, she prayed Will had done the deed during his solitary absence this afternoon.

Amusement lit golden sparks in dark eyes as Will glanced from Vauderie's loving indulgence to her hopeful expression. "Did I not get for you that cloak lined with white rabbit fur, even though 'twas the midst of summer?"

Beata grinned and nodded. A more unlikely demand had there seldom been, when during the warmest season few rabbits had white fur. Still, Will had provided what she begged to have.

"And was it not I who rescued for you that wretched cat that climbed a tree with ease but couldn't get back down?" His lips turned down in mock aggrievement. "Even did I withstand the beast's repayment for my good deed—lacerations that took weeks to heal."

Beata nodded again, laughing freely at this reminder of the heroic deed a teenage Will had done for the child she'd been. Certain to what end he was leading them, she released Vauderie and flung her arms about Will in an exuberant hug.

Once Beata had settled back into Vauderie's waiting arms, leaning in full trust against the blond knight, Will spoke again. "I'm hurt, truly hurt . . ." His words were mournful. "How could you think I would fail in providing answer for so simple a request as a priest?"

It was Vauderie who responded, voice tinged with admiration. "You found a priest willing to come here on Epiphany?"

Light from resin-dipped torches burning on either side of the door gleamed on black hair as Will nodded with a wry grin. "Aye, and not merely any simple priest, but an abbot."

Both knights laughed in easy camaraderie as they, with Beata, moved toward where Kenward, Cassie, and her young charge comfortably sat atop one of the several bed furs spread before the hearth—ostensibly to provide a resting place for the many enjoying an evening's entertainments. As they approached, Will drank in the sight of the seductively rounded damsel who grew increasingly lovely in his eyes. The ebony wisps of silky hair ever escaping her thick braid formed a lustrous frame for an alabaster face and cheeks warmed to a rosy hue complemented by the deeper shade of her velvet gown.

A festive spirit filled the hall, whose rafters rang with merry laughter as Will delighted Cassie even more by dropping down to sit at her side rather than seeking the large padded chair properly his. Sarah lay half curled in her lap, eyelids drooping already, while Kenward reclined on her other side, so intent on the game's every movement he hardly noticed the new arrivals. Vauderie took a chair and Beata settled at his feet. Cassie, with her beloved so near, amidst close friends and the men of the Weald's good cheer, experienced a contentment never before known. If only, she sadly wished, this could continue.

"What are you thinking?" The rough texture of Will's voice summoned Cassie from hopeless longings, and its dark edge seemed proof he shared the same desperate awareness of their ever-dwindling time together. She willingly turned to him, silently reaffirming a bold determination that this night would see wistful dreams fulfilled. Warm memories she meant to claim, warm memories enough to hoard away and hold against all the cold days in her future.

Of a sudden she realized she'd gazed wordlessly into dark eyes long enough that the golden fires burning within threatened to sear her with their heat. In answer, her slow smile enticed him nearer.

Irresistibly drawn, Will leaned forward. He could near taste the berry sweetness of soft lips. Cassie's heart kicked up a wild pounding as his approach enclosed her in the heady power of his closeness.

"Ow!"

Will jerked back, feeling an unaccustomed heat warming his face as he glanced down at the small girl he'd forgotten existed. With Sarah's tumbled tresses falling away from the joining of neck and shoulder, a livid red patch of skin lay revealed. 'Twas a doubtless painful burn he'd bumped. Assuredly the monks of the abbey had seen it treated, and more efficiently than he or his could, but he wished they'd warned him of the injury, the better to avoid inadvertently rendered pain.

"I'm sorry, Sarah. Never would I willingly add to your discomfort, 'tis only that I did not know you'd been hurt." Will's dark eyes were filled with a wealth of regret which won a shy smile from the little maid who, like all in the Weald, already thought Willikin incapable of wrong.

Acknowledging the impossibility of maintaining any semblance of normal conversation with the woman he wanted too badly, Will turned to speak with Vauderie.

Sarah's gaze followed the shift in Will's attention. Instantly petrified, she went stiff. Cassie was unprepared when the child abruptly pushed as far back in her hold as possible. She lost her grip on rigid limbs. The resulting flutter of rushes and thud of a young body flailing against the floor recalled a black gaze. Will saw the terror in the eyes of a child staring at Vauderie as if he were Lucifer himself.

"Sarah . . ." Will calmly began. "This is Vauderie, our friend and yours."

"No!" Sarah scrambled to her feet and scooted around to hide behind Cassie's back. "He were one of the beasts what done wickedness at my home."

Will's brows dropped into a deep frown. Vauderie couldn't possibly have had a part in that deed, as he had already made the knight his captive.

"Nay, little Sarah," Vauderie denied before the others found words to respond. "'Twas not I, but very possibly my twin brother, Valnoir. In appearance he is as like me as two beings can be. Yet I swear to you, beneath our outward forms, he and I share nothing, and never, never would I harm a child."

Under Cassie's gentle coaxing and Will's reassurances, slowly Sarah returned to shielding arms, but huge brown eyes continued watching the blond man with suspicion.

To ease the awkward silence that followed, Will began a desultory discussion of past holidays. Vauderie, Cassie, and even Kenward contributed, but a distracted Beata sat motionless. Puzzlement furrowed her brow and through her mind wafted shadowy images and disconnected thoughts frustratingly just beyond her reach.

Cassie welcomed Will's diversion from a difficult moment in a night of festivity. When blind man's buff had sufficiently worn even the most energetic guardsman down to more placid pursuits, the whole group settled, like the house's inhabitants, upon pelts before the fire to listen while tales were repeated. Some stories came from remembered minstrels' songs, while others were given life in the oft vivid imaginations of their tellers.

In the end even this entertainment began to slacken, as did the energy of both participants and audience. Cassie glanced down to find a circle of dark lashes laying heavy on childish cheeks. Sarah and her apprehensions had succumbed to the lateness of the hour. This poor child's need of a bed represented a difficulty to the fateful campaign Cassie intended to commence this night. Nibbling on her lower lip, she sought an alternative. It came to her with more ease than expected—surely a good omen.

"Sarah was as cold as the winter wind when she arrived. She cannot spend the night alone with men before the fire in the hall. Yet for her to sleep in the chill of my chamber would be, I fear, risking illness. Thus, Beata, I pray you will permit her to sleep on the floor before the fire in your chamber—this night leastways?"

Beata's eyes softened to honey as she instantly agreed, glad of some diversion for troubled thoughts. "Tonight and every night—until the wedding." Her cheeks warmed, but with anticipation rather than embarrassment.

Cassie had shown such easy compassion for Sarah that Will was surprised she would now send the girl with Beata. But likely 'twas true the chamber wherein she slept was too cold for the child. Too cold for Cassie, as well? Unbidden came the tantalizing thought of sharing his warmth with her.

"I deem it best that I retire now." Beata rose, lifting the child thankfully deep asleep. She was anxious to slip away from the site where uncomfortable mental images had assailed her.

"Aye, best you get all the rest you can now." Will teased his foster sister as she set out to carry the small burden abovestairs. "Soon it may be the last item on your chosen list of pursuits for dark hours."

Cassie was relieved as she watched the now seriously blushing Beata escape the laughing knight's jest. One barrier to her goal had been successfully removed, and it gave her confidence to move forward. In the norm, she'd have retired when Beata did, but tonight she lingered beside the two powerful knights while slowly the gathered guardsmen drifted off to their cottages in search of a much shortened night's rest.

When only he, Vauderie, Cassie, and a sleeping Kenward remained in a hall gone quiet, Will turned to the lone woman with guarded eyes. He thought it best to warn her of possibly painful events to come while within what limited privacy he dared allow.

"Abbot Jerome will arrive on Twelfth Night to see Vauderie and Beata

wed." The words were unadorned and emotionless, but he watched
Cassie's face closely for any betraying glimpse of honest distress afore the
certain descent of a welcome enforced by her compassionate nature.

"I'm so pleased!" Clasping her hands together in excitement, Cassie's
instant response held a sincerity that could not be doubted. She had
worried Will delayed the needful action to postpone seeing his Beata
wedded to another. Mayhap 'twas so, but he had done as promised, and
surely this meant he'd accepted Beata lost to him.

Cassie's reaction gave Will some small reason to believe she truly
viewed the French knight as friend and no more. With night-black eyes
curiously upon her, Cassie felt compelled to make her first move in the
chess game wherein she meant to capture her king.

"Will," Cassie quietly began. "Doubtless I should've asked your aid
earlier, but there've been so many chores in preparation for the season's
entertainments that my trivial troubles were forgot." She paused, knowing
the request about to be voiced was embarrassingly weak. But after hours of
planning, she'd found a dearth of believable deceptions. "The shutters of
the stable-side window in my chamber refuse to close completely. 'Tis why
my chamber is colder than usual." Subjected to his full attention, Cassie
was proud of her ability to meet the power of the dark gaze despite the
heat of her cheeks. "Pray lend me your aid in its repair so that I may sleep
warmer this night."

Enjoying her company, Will had been loath to earlier question the
lingering of Cassie by his side, and deeply surprised by the strange timing
of this request, he failed to see the amused recognition of a deception in
widened azure eyes.

So, Vauderie concluded, Cassie had taken lessons from his Beata's bold
actions, meant even to move beyond at the pace of a giant's leap. He
restrained the mirth threatening to break free. 'S'truth, Cassie was greatly
changed from the timid creature he'd known for so long. Must be love
that lent courage of such strength she meant to abandon a lifetime's
training in the importance of treasuring her purity.

This unexpected development caught Will in a tangled maze of emotions, but he was not so far gone that he failed to see through her flimsy
excuse. Yet what honest purpose lay behind this request? Did the now
standing maid wish to speak privately with him to voice a complaint or
make a plea? Nay. His eyes narrowed to a penetrating slant. The huskiness
in her voice and melting lavender of her eyes were a clear invitation to an
assignation his passion soared to meet—but it couldn't be! Likely she
sought, at most, a few furtive and unsatisfying kisses in the dark, while he

greatly feared 'twould be impossible to halt at so limited a taste of the feast he longed to consume. That she was too innocent to understand what she tempted was no excuse, certainly no excuse for the instant physical reaction of a man with experience enough to control the situation.

"Please, Will." Cassie bravely took one of the sword-calloused hands into her soft fingers to gently urge his rising.

Forewarned, as now, Will lied to himself as he rose stoically to his feet, surely he could manage the situation, convince her of the folly in wiles wrongly wielded and see their meeting to a safe conclusion. Toward this exercise in control, he firmly rejected the quiet inner voice mocking any possibility of him winning success by this strategy.

Looking into the cold of his grim face, Cassie was not encouraged. It seemed too clear he'd recognized her ploy. Yet once the battle had been enjoined, she would not so easily surrender brave hopes, and instead bravely turned to lead the way. With time so limited, she refused to feel shame or aught but relief that he saw through her thinly veiled attempt to win his company in the privacy of night—'twould surely ease her path. She hoped.

Inordinately aware of him stalking so close behind, she knew that, were she to suddenly halt, he'd come up against her—a thrilling possibility, but a temptation resisted with hope of more once a closed door lay between them and the world beyond.

Despite his vexation with her attempted manipulation of him, Will could not quell a consuming desire roused by the knowledge of her so near he had but to reach out a short distance to drag her into his arms where, 'twas plain, she wanted to be. The fact that she'd not fight but rather welcome him full well, made holding to his duty the harder, and it took as much willpower as he possessed to prevent the action. His salvation lay in reaching her chamber and having done with this confrontation in all possible haste.

Although the climb took no more than a few moments, it seemed endless to the pair ascending. Finally they arrived at the door both longed to reach—each regarding it as the symbol of a far different goal.

Destination achieved, Cassie's heart pounded under a strange mixture of hope, fear, and longing. In this emotional muddle, she led the way across the dark room to the shutter in question, half open to the chill mists of foggy night.

While Will gave his attention to the recalcitrant shutter, Cassie quickly took the next step in her battle plan. She'd no notion of precisely how to seduce a man, but she did know what it was about herself that seemed of most interest to Will. Goal eased by a plait already fallen from atop her head, she soon had the braiding undone. She ran her fingers through freed tresses before loosening laces once fastened tight at her throat.

Will suspiciously studied the shutter oddly blocked and found the obstruction—a splinter of wood carefully wedged into the hinge to prevent complete closure. It was easily dislodged. He turned and then froze in an earnest attempt to turn himself to ice. Black eyes drifted in slow appraisal over the enticing sight of her lush body, inadequately shielded. Will's firm mouth curled downward while he sought to exercise a measure of discipline over the ever faster rush of passion roused by seductive glimpses of sweet flesh too well remembered and emphasized by a thick tangle of silk-soft hair. Although Cassie's blush was so deep a hue 'twas plainly seen even in a room only dimly lit by cloudy night, she stood boldly before him.

Will was stunned but hid it behind an impassive mask while he held the errant piece of wood outstretched to her. "This you could easily have removed on your own. So, what was your true purpose for luring me here in the dead of night?"

Will's low voice was so emotionless it frightened Cassie, yet she drew a deep, reaffirming breath before unveiling the whole of her strategy, too likely hopeless now.

"Soon, too soon, you mean to send me where I've no wish to go, to return me to people who've no more care of me than I of them. Aye, 'tis a high price you will force me to pay for my wrong in coming too close to your forest. You intend to exile me from a life far more satisfying than any I will ever know again, send me from the one man I will hopelessly love for all my days."

Stunned, Will gazed into wide eyes aching with doomed love and brimming with a liquid turned silver by the hazy light of night. 'Twas assuredly not the first time a woman had lured him to her bedchamber under false pretexts; and, indeed, 'twas the purpose he'd suspected was Cassie's. But this was the first time a woman of good birth had offered him a fervent declaration of love.

On first recognizing in her words a love selflessly bestowed upon him, he'd known it for the gift he most hungered to possess yet had dreaded to hear, as even shared love could make no difference to cold facts as they were. He desperately wanted to sweep her into his arms and echo the precious words, but bowed to reality and began the arguments he'd come prepared to make.

"There can never be any relationship between us save captor and captive." Will's dark eyes were as emotionless as solid granite, but behind their barrier lay a pain he'd feel for the rest of his days. "You were born to a station in life far above my humble lot."

Cassie bravely stepped forward to lay her hands against his broad chest and looked up at him with love bared in her eyes. "I've my 'station in life' by virtue of birth, but have never been comfortable within its confines. In truth, I never knew contentment until I came here, and in the last few weeks have reveled in the life and company that's yours by virtue of your own choice. I regret more than words can say that I've been robbed of choice by the circumstances of my birth."

Will was amazed that anyone rued the good circumstances of noble birth with as much resentment as he had once rued the bastard lineage that was his. Such a possibility had never before occurred to him. Still, it made no difference to what must be. Though now he could almost believe she might truly admire the simple life he'd chosen, she must return to the life of a noblewoman while he remained in the forest.

"I know." Cassie spoke, voice choked with unshed tears. "When the ransom arrives, you must return me to Guy—"

"Nay, never to Guy, never would I see you delivered into that brutal man's hold." A harsh fury wove threads of steel through Will's words.

Cassie shrugged helplessly, feeling that whether to Guy or to Henri, it mattered little when the emotional pain she'd feel would be the same and fierce enough to overshadow any physical abuse.

"No matter, you will send me back to France. But if you must, first give me this one night." The pain in her voice hurt Will as deeply. Yet when his eyes narrowed against the blow, Cassie thought her chances were slipping away and abandoned all pretense. "I 'lured' you to my chamber, intending to seduce you into sharing with me all the secret joys I've no hope of finding with another." She wrapped her arms about his neck and pressed her lush form tight to his long, hard body.

Will damned the instant response of his own body and unclasped her hands to hold her away—not a fine idea, as it gave him a too clear view of the cleavage revealed by her loosened laces.

"Don't tempt me, little innocent. I am far too experienced a hunter to fall prey to your wiles." He only wished he spoke the truth, for in reality it took a monumental effort to curb his dangerous needs. "With the taking I would both defile you and lessen your value to the brother who pays ransom for your safe return." The words were cold, while hidden beneath burned a fire bright enough to give lie to his words.

Restrained by strong hands holding her a pace from him, Cassie was sadly amused. "The world will have no care for the truth. By the mere fact that I've been the captive of the bold Willikin of the Weald—the infamous English knight who despises all things French—'twill be assumed he stole my virtue as ruthlessly as he takes the lives of all male invaders."

Will bitterly acknowledged how unlikely were her countrymen to believe him a man of honor. Of a certainty they would believe he'd fully claimed the tempting French beauty who came too near.

"If I am to be branded your lover, then leastways give me the memory of its pleasure—'twill be my only recompense for all the cold years and vicious slurs I'll be called to endure."

Suddenly golden fires of blinding hunger burst in black eyes. Aye, she spoke the truth, and 'twas only fair they should enjoy the sin they'd be damned for.

As his grip slackened, Cassie saw a breach in his defenses and instantly advanced to once more twine her arms tightly about his neck. As if they'd a will of their own, his arms swallowed her in a passionate hold he'd lost any power to deny. Yet if this were to be their only experience of mutual love, then he meant to see it so memorable, so pleasurable, they could both live on its treasured memory for all the lonely days to come.

As his warm, ardent mouth descended, she sighed and closed her eyes, drinking in his strength and masculinity. He made her feel cherished and threatened all at once. When his tongue invaded her mouth, a sudden explosion of feeling rippled through her body and she stiffened, not in rejection, but in pleasure.

Will smiled through his own growing excitement, and his hands began an adventure, a slow searing path up her sides from the first gentle swell of her hips to the sensitive flesh beneath the arms wrapped about him and then down. He repeated the motion again and again, moving fractionally closer together until his palms imperceptibly brushed against the sides of her breasts.

His ever-returning light touches trailed fires of tender torment over the ripe hills and valleys of Cassie's trembling body. Her breath sounded odd, and caught in her throat to sigh out in little gasps as his hands slid around and under her ripe curves, holding their soft weight as he leaned a breath away to gaze down into passion-glazed eyes.

An enticing virgin and a love too sweet to longer forgo. He swept his Cassie up into his mighty arms and carried her to the simple straw pallet which in that moment was a goal of ultimate value. As he gently lowered her to the prickly mattress with its one lone pelt, the small voice of cool reason cautioning him to duty had no hope to win against the raging fires of desire.

Afraid he meant to leave her alone, and burning with unfulfilled passion as he had once before, Cassie held tight to his neck while her body stretched upward in wordless plea for the weight of his to provide anchor in this depthless sea of wanting.

Although drowning in his own fiery need, Will felt a flicker of loving amusement for this tender rabbit's untutored enticement of a wily wolf. Truly she had become a temptress, laying here with her delicious, yielding body promising heaven—even could it be naught but a temporary respite for the torment of loneliness to come. Slowly lowering himself to rest at her side and, leaning above her on one elbow, he brushed the fingers of his free hand down the soft curve of her cheeks, across passion-swollen, half-parted lips, and down the line of an elegant throat.

Heavy lashes fell while layer upon layer of burning sensations seared Cassie's flesh and steamed through her veins. She welcomed the whirl-wind of his fire as it gathered her into its vortex.

Will's hand tangled in loosened laces and gently tugged them wider. A masculine satisfaction widened his potent grin when he realized she wore no camise beneath. His fingertips smoothed tantalizingly across silky skin thus revealed, easing near his whole hand beneath the now gaping cloth, to claim the velvet softness of her bounty with his palm.

Cassie cried out, too lost in a haze of smoldering hunger to realize the sound might be interpreted by others as pain.

"Shhh, sweeting." Will's voice was low and rasping. "Elsewise, some-one may well come and bring an unsought end to our pleasures." Again he bent to her sweet mouth, kissing it as if he'd die trying to get enough of its berry-wine nectar.

Too lost in desire's haze to fully understand, still Cassie bit her lip to prevent a like sound's escape when a hand whose impatience was carefully restrained rubbed more firmly across aching flesh. After first shoving of-fending cloth aside, Will completely stripped it from her body. Only when he'd laid her luscious body bare to his burning gaze did Cassie surface enough to fear he'd find too generous curves repulsive.

"Never have I seen such perfection—as generous as your spirit." He lowered his dark head and brushed his mouth tenderly across the full bounty filling a large cupped hand to overflowing. A soft whimper slipped from her tight throat, and a small satisfied smile curled the tormenting lips of a man intoxicated by the sound.

Under this shocking pleasure, Cassie's fingers instinctively twined into black strands striving to bring the source of such delicious torment even nearer. Will held back, purposely driving her deeper into the fire's depths, teasing her senses mercilessly until she arched against his mouth, striving to achieve an unknown goal. Yielding at last, he settled his mouth over the tip of her breast. Unable to prevent it, another deep moan rose and escaped Cassie's tight throat. Overwhelmed by blazing sensations, her mind had ceased all rational thought. As his hand slid down her back and turned her hips full against his, she shifted restlessly against him, wanting to be closer, wanting something more.

With a deep growl of his own, Will pulled away and Cassie softly cried a protest of her loss. He divested himself of his clothing with all the speed unheeding of care or cost. Heavy lashes lifted and, far beyond embarrassment, Cassie's desire-glazed eyes watched with awe as the superbly masculine image of the nude man was revealed—powerful enough to steal her breath. In feverish need she lifted her arms, and Will surrendered to sweet temptation. He returned to pull her into the hungry cradle of his arms. Dark eyes closed, he savored the feel of her soft flesh melded to the hard contours of his body.

Cassie smoothed her hands over the strong muscles beneath the satin skin of his back. Clinging to him, she felt the heavy beat of his heart and twisted against him, reveling in the searing heat of their embrace and the fires blazing in her veins. Another harsh groan came from her knight's throat, and his hands slid palm flat down her slender back to cup the perfect curve of her derriere and pull her tighter. Shaking with a depth of desire previously unknown, she pressed even closer as he began to rhythmically rock her against him.

Aware that her deliciously trembling hunger was more temptation than he could withstand, and feeling the limits of his control quickly slipping from his hand, he was yet determined their one hour of passion not be a memory of pain. Going still for a long moment with eyes tightly closed, he fought for the control necessary.

Cassie saw his closed eyes and taut face and feared he meant to pull back even now. "Please, Will, please," she whispered, pleaded. "Don't leave me now." Recklessly she arched up, brushing her soft curves in a tantalizing caress across his chest, glorying in the rasp of its curls over the sensitive tips of her breasts. Her enticing, inciting motions drove Will beyond any hope for restraint, and he urged Cassie onto her back with trembling gentleness. Rising above her, resting on his forearms, he gazed down into eyes deep purple with her wanting of him as slowly he joined their bodies in the most intimate of embraces.

Cassie's moment of pain was overwhelmed by the building of a pleasure near too great to be borne. Lost in the firestorm's center, she was aware

only of the gentle abrasion of his skin against hers as his steady movements built to a rhythm that made the earth seem to shift beneath them.
She followed his hard, sharp movements with desperate abandon, striving
toward the goal he led her toward, a goal just beyond reach. His harsh
breathing slid into low velvet growls. But determined not to lay Cassie
bare to the scorn of others by revelation of their joining, when at length
an explosion threatened to rock their sphere, he laid his mouth over hers
to absorb the unmistakable sounds of their fulfillment.

In the afterglow, Will held Cassie's trembling form against his, smoothing the now tangled mass of her hair, pressing gentle kisses to the top of
her head until at last she drifted into dreams. He'd been a fool—again. So
oft he'd accused her of trying to make him one when, in truth, it was he
who'd done the deed. Even were Cassie's reputation—her value as virginal
mate to some great French lord—the only cost of their deed, 'twould not
excuse his dishonorable actions. Yet the joys of love shared might be worth
the price to them both. Unfortunately it was not their only wrong, nor
might they be the only ones to pay. 'Twas a lesson his own heritage taught
him full well!

How could he allow a child of his to be raised by another man? Or
damned to walk the narrow fault line of illegitimacy which he knew so
intimately—never belonging anywhere.

Aye, he'd fallen once, and that one instance alone might well demand a
terrible price of the woman he loved—and an innocent babe. The Holy
Scriptures said that the sins of the fathers would be visited upon their
children for generation after generation. And it was true—he was the
third in his line and paying still. He could only beseech God and every
saint whose name he could recall to see his wrong go unpunished at the
cost of a blameless child. To earn such merciful forgiveness he would
promise God on the Blessed Cross that he would never, never permit such
a sinful action again!

Chapter
❧ *16* ❧

DECORATED WITH GARLANDS of yew branches and swags of holly, Will's hall echoed with boisterous good cheer. Cassie had accomplished what she'd set out to perform—the delivery of twelve days of festive fare and entertainments worthy of the season. It had proved to be a task not so difficult as expected, what with men free of other duties offering their services to hunt for meats to fill spits and pots for the feasts—deer, wild boar, and sundry smaller game. Edna, too, had caught the spirit, enthusiastically lending help with the baking and creating special dishes from mundane items.

From her position at the lord's table, placed center front of the overflowing hall, Cassie surveyed the gathering grown rowdy with abundant ale. The crowded tables were an odd assortment either of the trestle variety brought from the men's cottages or makeshift affairs thrown together for the occasion. Yet neither their unusual appearance nor the traditional dishes made of untraditional ingredients lessened the participants' enjoyment one whit. Cassie had only two regrets: that this Feast of Twelfth Night marked the conclusion of an eventful fortnight, and that the meal's merriment had an edge of desperation—as if tensions set aside for a time had grown and loomed with the first light of an inescapable morrow.

Cassie, again garbed in the rose gown precious to her for the memories it held, glanced down to see Sarah's fragile fingers edging toward the slices of cheese and fruit on the trencher they shared.

"Go ahead, Sarah."

The child jerked her hand back as if she'd been caught stealing. Cassie's soft heart cried for the little waif plainly born to a home where food was scarce and severely rationed.

"Truly, here you may always eat as much as you like." Sarah's wide brown eyes studied the benefactor of such largesse as she hesitantly accepted the fat piece of cheese Cassie lifted and offered to her.

Cassie found the amount one so small could consume amazing, but the child had as well eat it all. More than the smallest nibble made Cassie feel ill. And, like her appetite, the season's warmth had deserted her days past. In the chill gray haze of dawn Will had turned to her a face of granite. That fateful morn following the night spent in his embrace and every moment since, did she dare venture too close, eyes of black ice froze her in place. During the dark night she had naively thought their pleasures fiery enough to permanently thaw the oft frigid wall betwixt them. But by the cold light of day it seemed clear her inexperience had merely fooled her into believing that a thing eagerly sought was so. The more likely truth was that her inexperience had disappointed Will, and he'd found her limited gifts a poor recompense for their cost to his honor. The soul-wrenching thought deepened lavender eyes to violet.

Her heart's desire Cassie had bared to Will, but he had said nothing at all of his. Because his love burned for another? Mayhap he felt he'd betrayed his Beata by the taking of another? Was it the marriage rite so recently performed that had cast him into this bitter gloom? Whatever the reasoning behind his withdrawal, the fact was that Will spoke to Cassie only when unavoidable, and he was never near, save when required at mealtimes—as now. And for this last night's feast he'd found a way to circumvent even that innocuous proximity.

Cassie glanced sideways to the bride and groom, who for their special evening took the lord's place at the center of his table. Beata was radiant in the gown of silvery green which Cassie had altered to fit her slight figure, while Vauderie looked handsome and bursting with pride for his hard-won wife. Their wedding had been a fitting denouement to a fortnight's celebration, a day whose joy had not been dampened by the abbot's departure immediately after the ceremony in order that he might be in his chapel for the holy day's last mass.

Will's handsome face was strangely impassive amidst a gathering wherein high spirits prevailed. Silently he acknowledged the marvel of this feast conjured up by his remarkable feminine hostage for the enjoyment of her captor and all his men. The urge was strong to quietly thank her for the meal, and not that alone, but for the warmth she'd given a cold camp of harsh warriors. Yet he dared not speak and risk even so seemingly harmless a contact between them for fear of weakening a willpower already proven disgustingly flimsy where this one tender damsel was concerned. Fortunately, he told himself, words between them were impossible.

Never under any circumstances would he have begrudged the new-wedded couple their place at head of his table, but it was an honor gladly given and more welcome for providing him excuse to claim, as nearest kin, a chair on the bride's right. Cassie, as the person in Kensham closest to the groom, sat on Vauderie's far side—two people distant. Such seating was best for the safeguarding of the pledge Will had made to God.

However, since the two people between himself and the tempting damsel were so absorbed in each other they had as well be on the moon, Will was all too aware of pain-shadowed violet eyes oft upon him, wordlessly pleading for explanation of his actions. Could she really be so naive she did not know what dangerous consequences they'd tempted with their passionate play? To prevent himself from responding to her silent call, he glared down at the remnants of the feast's final course laying on his trencher.

'Twas a wonder, Cassie thought, that 'neath golden flames in dark eyes neither did innocent bits of cheese melt nor did apple cores sizzle. In the next instant those dark eyes turned her way, filled with disgust—for her, himself, or them both? Where once she would immediately have looked away, she proudly met the penetrating gaze of the man magnificent this night in a red velvet tunic. She even added a wistful smile of such intensity it caught his breath.

In the first weeks of her captivity Cassie had decried the Weald for its ability to loose hasty words from her tongue, but now she blessed it for loosing the much braver spirit trapped so long inside. Her smile deepened with a wordless admission that the useless restraint had been of her own making, fabricated by the cowardly excuse that only a beautiful noblewoman such as the imaginary Lady Cassandra was entitled to either pride or courage. The realization had come too late and brought little comfort. What use had she for either characteristic in the bleak future awaiting?

Will blinked first. He'd once suspected the timid rabbit might mature into a dangerous creature, and she had—she'd been transformed into a worthy mate for a dangerous wolf. Clearly seeing this doomed truth only worsened his yearning for an elusive treasure that could never, would never be his to rightfully claim. He bitterly damned both his heritage and hers for the impenetrable barrier thus laid between them.

"Let us toast our lovebirds!" A slightly tipsy member of Will's guard stood unsteadily at a table in the midst of the room with a precariously uplifted goblet.

Chairs scraped and feet shuffled on the rush-bestrewn floor as the entire group rose, save for blushing bride and new husband. Humble crockery goblets and simple mugs bumped one against another in off-key harmony.

"And once more—" Harvey spoke before the first was complete. "To our lovely Lady Cassandra, who has provided this feast and more, much more for we of the Weald."

For the first time in several days warm pleasure brought a delicious rose tint to Cassie's pale cheeks. That this gruff old warrior who, on taking her captive, had initially found her a craven and useless being, now praised her for her efforts, made the whole complicated task worthwhile.

Cassie had risen for the first toast and was still standing, providing her misty lavender gaze an excellent view. Attention shifting from the one who proposed the toast to his son, she found Clyde beaming approval as he held his drink high in her honor. Beyond the table where Edna had joined her family for the toast, Cassie glimpsed Odo and his wife, the elderly couple who had been so generous, if misguided, in their efforts to help her. The elderly woman squinted in the direction her husband indicated, while wide grins laid deep wrinkles in their cheeks. Tears pricked at Cassie's eyelids, tears both of happiness for an acceptance never known afore and of sorrow for the shortness of time to be shared.

Will, too, stood with goblet upraised and waiting. This gratitude, least-ways, he owed Cassie, and 'twas surely safe to give in so public a demonstration. Forced by the power of a night-black gaze, she lifted to him eyes brimming with shimmering liquid. Will had noted Harvey's naming of her as "our Lady Cassandra," and as he gifted her with a stunning smile, he despairingly wished she truly were. Then, nodding in her honor, he sipped the fiery brew no more potent than she.

As Cassie took her seat again, she felt a hesitant tug on her sleeve and glanced down into large brown eyes full of curiosity.

"Are you truly a 'Lady'?" Sarah's awestruck question was spoke hardly above a whisper and yet 'twas enough to attract Beata's attention.

"That she is, my small friend." Leaning forward to look past both Vauderie and Cassie, Beata smiled gently at the timid waif. "But for a goodly time I've thought her a much more exalted being—Cassandra, Queen of the faeries who guard the Amethyst Pools of Elfland."

These mystical words caught Sarah's total attention. She fair fell from her chair striving to scoot nearer and listen as Beata recounted the nursery fable with all the relish of an experienced tale spinner but no hint of a pretty illusion believed.

As Beata concluded the story, she and Cassie exchanged indulgent

smiles for the joys of childhood past. Just beyond Beata, Cassie caught a
brief glimpse of Will's relief at this further sign of Beata's maturity. She
was near as pleased as he. Now Beata had returned from unnatural youth,
Cassie's prayers on the other woman's behalf would focus on pleas for
God's mercy. Cassie would beg Him to see that when—and if—memory
of the assault that had fueled Beata's retreat into the past came back, the
woman would feel no differently about the man into whose hands she'd
committed her life.

Beata sensed the source of Cassie's concern. But as her honeyed gaze
lifted to the man now hers, she was certain, despite the ominous gap in
her memory, that Vauderie was the most wonderful thing that had ever
happened to her. Surely his coming was worth the unknown cost.

Vauderie laid a gentle palm over the delicate fingers resting atop his
arm. Feeling he'd been awarded an undeserved gift, he made an inaudible
vow to be worthy of the unquestioning trust in her golden gaze. He meant
to cherish and hold her safe from either further physical harm or the
hurtful disdain of others in his noble world. Never did he delude himself
that this goal would be easily attained when both his uncle and brother
were sure to recognize the maid they'd sought to defile. Made spiteful by
their loss at Vauderie's hand, likely they'd whisper to his haughty peers of
her common background and boast of having taken her first—no matter
its untruth.

Growing ever more impatient with the limitations enforced by an injured leg, from his seat on Will's right Kenward watched in mute irritation as another performed his proud duty as loyal page at his lord's board.
For Clyde's part 'twas only at his mother's behest and despite his pride in
being a warrior grown that he collected platters emptied of all but bones.
These he delivered to the assortment of dogs anxiously awaiting outside.
'Twas the beasts' one compensation for being evicted from the house by
the sheer number of humans gathered within its walls.

Their way cleared, members of Will's guard lost no time in disassem-
bling every table, save the lord's, to make way for a last evening's entertainments. Under the pressure of rapidly dwindling hours devoted to good
cheer, ale had been more freely consumed than was wise with dawn and a
full day's labors so near. Few in the company were sober enough to join
any game, and chose instead to collapse on the floor with backs to the
walls while quaffing even more fiery liquid from the most recently opened
cask.

At the start of a round of blind man's buff, Will excused both couples
at his table from taking part. He refused, despite the vocal disappointment

of men too sotted to think clearly, to put either his too luscious Cassie or the new bride within reach of pawing hands.

Lacking the restraints of feminine participants, the game quickly descended from play to a half-hearted brawl. It was into this event's general pandemonium that a messenger arrived. The man, having yet to sample generously flowing ale, was light on his feet and easily evaded the random assaults of those in the hall's midst as he approached the lord's table.

"Sir William?" the newcomer hesitantly began, thrown off kilter by a gathering such as he had never seen here afore. Moreover, the leader he'd come seeking did not sit at the table's center where rightfully he belonged.

Will recognized his visitor, a young man who lived on the edge of the forest and lent vigorous aid to the cause whenever summoned. Thus it was that Bevis knew the secret path to Will's base. However, he would not arrive uncalled without serious need.

"A group of strangers approached my home this morn." The lanky man sounded aggrieved. At all times past when the enemy had approached, Willikin or one of his men had been there firstly.

Will frowned. Were the French prince and his cohorts already afoot? Or were these marauders members of De Faux's band? If by virtue of the period of allowed festivity harm had befallen one of his own, Will would never forgive himself. "Did they do violence to you or yours, Bevis?"

Hearing that his hero, the hero of all in the Weald and many more besides, knew him by name, erased any lingering grudge. Bevis grinned as he emphatically shook his head. "Nay, only did they give me a parchment and say as did I fail to see it reach your hand, they'd wreak a fierce retribution upon me such as I'd not wish to know."

Narrowed black eyes closely watched as work-roughened and none too clean hands dug into a pouch slung around Bevis's thin neck. Here, then, was the long expected response. 'Twas almost a relief to have days, weeks of tense waiting done. Yet Will found himself unaccountably reluctant to take the folded sheet in Bevis's outstretched hand. On this page, harmless of itself, assuredly lay the certain end to time in the company of the forbidden woman he loved and the end to a contentment only such sweet emotion could bring. Moreover, 'twould, beyond doubt, demand decisive actions, some scheme he had yet to devise which would allow the holding of his honor and earning the coins of ransom for his king while, too, saving Cassie from De Faux's cruel hold.

Face gone coldly emotionless, Will accepted the offered message. He earnestly hoped Cassie—patiently listening to more of Sarah's whispered words—hadn't noticed the document's distinctive seal: a griffin with snake gripped in its toils. Pray God reading this parchment would provide him inspiration for attaining all three of his difficult goals. He tucked the stiff vellum page into the folds of his crimson tunic with apparent indifference. In truth, beneath his mask of control apprehension battled anticipation for supremacy. He forced both emotions into abeyance. Read this fateful document and lay his plans he would—later and alone.

"Join us, Bevis, in our Twelfth Night revelries. Although I fear we've consumed the whole of the meal, there's ale aplenty—perhaps too plentiful, if the condition of my men is an honest indication." With a rueful grimace he nodded toward the roisterous group of men, too tipsy even to brawl longer, who'd fallen into a heap and begun singing bawdy songs in poor harmony.

"Moreover," Will added, "I've a task for you on the morrow." Bevis's arrival was propitious. Already had he ordered Harvey to depart at first light with a sizable contingent of men to stand guard along the Weald's furthermost boundaries. He'd intended to also dispatch someone to rally supporters to watch the forest's neighboring borders for sign of the French prince. Now that he'd the ransom response, he dare not further deplete his guard, and it was fortunate that Bevis was here and could be sent instead.

Bevis's initial surprise at Willikin's casual reaction to the parchment delivered with a threat was overwhelmed by the thrill of being invited to join his lord's celebration. Quickly he sought out a full mug and settled down amidst the line of befuddled drinkers against the wall.

A heavy hand descended on Cassie's shoulder. She looked up into Edna's solemn face.

"Of a certainty our sodden friends'll be where they lay till the dawning." She cast a glance heavy with disgust to the stretch of floor where resided both her husband and son. "Lucky we are that there's many a man in the Weald beyond these few, elsewise there'd be a great risk of defeat by any French force with good wits enough to attack."

Even from several chairs distant the look Will sent Edna was hard enough to demand her attention. But knowing him too well to mistake the gold glint of wry amusement in the depths of dark eyes, she glared at him with an equally strong dose of mock censure before turning back to Cassie.

"I come 'cause the wee one needs her sleep. Since I've no wish to spend the night on the hard floor amidst these drunken fools, I'm off to my home, and this night would be glad of her company."

Cassie quickly glanced down to find Sarah more than half asleep, dusky head pillowed on arms folded atop the table. As oft as not Sarah slept at Kenward's side by the huge fireplace in the hall, but tonight 'twould be impossible, and Edna's offer would greatly ease the confrontation Cassie was determined to bring about. Though she'd shielded the fact from perceptive eyes, she had seen the seal on the parchment so recently given Will. By the seeing she'd recognized the frighteningly narrowed limits to her hours in his company and was adamant, leastwise, to know why he refused her further burning memories to hoard against descending cold. That she expected no more of him she had surely made plain. So why did he deny her the comfort of his embrace during their rapidly shrinking time together?

"Thank you, Edna." Cassie's words were sincere and intended as gratitude for far more than the opportunity opened. "You've always the right answer to any need. Tonight the men gave me credit for their fortnight's enjoyments, but 'tis you whose knowledge, whose experience made it possible. I much appreciate all you've done these last twelve days—and before."

Gruff Edna sought to hide her broad grin, shrugging while arguing facts wrongly emphasized. "That's as may be, but I've been here for years and gave no thought to such celebrations. Nay, their gratitude is rightly yours. 'Tis you who'd the notion in the first instance, and in the next the resolve to make it a reality."

Embarrassed by her own uncharacteristic wordiness, Edna gently hustled Sarah from her chair and thence from the house. This first departure from the lords' table was excuse enough for the newly wedded pair to rise and escape to a chamber above.

Cassie was relieved that here in the simpler life of the Weald couples were not subjected to the ceremonial bedding observed at the marriages of those well-born. Horribly embarrassing and distasteful—that was what she'd always thought of the tradition whereby the new husband was escorted to the bridal chamber. There, ensconced in the nuptial bed, awaited a bride sometimes barely covered. The wedding party would then strip the groom and watch to be certain he climbed in beside her. The question of what was meant to follow when the chamber door closed the world out had once embarrassed and frightened Cassie. Now it evoked the image of Will as he'd looked divested of clothing, devastatingly masculine, dangerously predatory, and lowering his powerful form to her hungry flesh.

Across the two now empty chairs between them Will saw Cassie tilt her head to better hear footsteps moving down the corridor above, and next the closing of a door. The wistful cloudiness of lavender eyes went abruptly to amethyst glittering with memories he could see too clearly. Oh, how he longed to taste again the berry nectar of her lips, to feel the fiery brand of soft curves crushed against him. His body emphatically responded to the burning memories shared of flesh against flesh, wild abandon and exquisite pleasure. Knowing the depths of the secret satisfaction she embodied had only increased his anguished craving many times over.

Will shifted uncomfortably, striving with small hope for success to drive dangerous thoughts from his head. Even two seats distant her presence was too dangerous when he'd vowed never to fall to such dishonorable deeds again. His sharp motion had summoned her attention, and he grimaced at the love laid bare in eyes half shuttered and drowsy with heated memories. Damn! Had she no notion of the danger they had risked? To forestall further temptations he abruptly rose, shoving his chair back so roughly it wobbled and near tipped over.

Cassie instantly came to her feet and reached out to wrap her fingers about the strong forearm Will raised as if to ward off a foe.

"Why, Will?" She could not let him leave, mayhap preventing her from ever learning the answers she wanted so badly. "Why do you turn me away when only do I seek the comfort of your presence?" She stepped nearer and her voice dropped to an aching and whispered plea. "In my lack of skill did I do some wrong? Are my too abundant physical attributes repulsive or my inadequate responses too deep a disappointment? Or is it that I'm so poor a substitute for Beata?"

The hall's myriad flames of rushlight and fire glinted over Will's black hair as he shook it in frustration. How had he, an experienced ladycharmer, managed to so badly bungle the one moment of passion he'd ever share with the only woman he would ever love that she harbored such ridiculous fears?

Will glanced wildly about, only to discover, to his deeper disgust, that they were the focus of not only Kenward's curious eyes, but the attention of most still gathered in his hall. 'Twas no comfort that the latter were so besotted they were unlikely to remember much on the morrow or that words softly spoken while tuneless voices sang could never be understood even by Kenward.

"Come." The order was as short as his temper had become, yet Will gently laid her fingers atop his upheld forearm and folded his free hand atop them.

Cassie gladly accompanied Will to the outgoing portal where he plucked a cloak at random from those piled on one side. He twirled it about her shoulders before donning his own and leading her into the frigid night beyond sturdy planks.

Although Will shut the door behind them, he'd no intention of moving farther away from the relative safety of the many in his home. Only could he hope the winter night's bone-chilling air would serve to reinforce a restraint he might not elsewise find. Will refused to look down at a temptation too near—only recall how amidst a foggy night he'd once almost taken her on the glade's frozen ground.

Cassie feared the rejection he was plainly preparing to deliver, but while dreading the coming words, she bravely gazed up at the stunningly handsome man she loved, reveling in the warmth and power he exuded.

"Cassie." Will began his answer to hurt-filled questions she'd posed in the inappropriate setting of his hall. "I love Beata . . ."

Here it seemed was confirmation of the most painful possibility, and Cassie involuntarily shrank back from the blow.

"As a younger sister, I love Beata." Pained at this evidence of a further hurt to the tender damsel, Will immediately reached out and caught Cassie in his arms. Drawing her close, he sought to repair the blundered damage few of his acquaintances would have thought possible for a man with his renowned gift of charm. "A little sister," he repeated, cheek pillowed on the decorously entwined braids atop her head. "Just that and no more."

Cassie tilted her head back and gazed straight into the golden fires within his eyes while in a voice of rough velvet he told her more than she'd dared to dream could be true.

"You are to me all that any woman could be." A rueful smile tilted lips as he drank in the view of the sweet temptress wrapped in his hungry embrace. "And your only wrong was in proving yourself too perfect a partner in passion—so perfect I dare not trust myself to stand too close." Aye, he wordlessly acknowledged, and see how in upholding that aim a famous warrior had failed at the gentle hand of a tender damsel.

Cassie did not see his welcome response to her as the bar to their mutual joy that he obviously did but, wanting to lengthen her time in his arms by any means possible, she wisely held her counsel while he continued.

"Raised as you were to the virtuous life of a lady-born, you've failed to recognize that the wrong is in me—a wrong beyond our warring nations, a wrong extending back beyond even a single generation." With this bitter statement he released her and tried to step away.

"Nay, Will," Cassie argued, clinging to him with a strength he hadn't the will to break. "Knowing that I love you, it can be no surprise that I think you are all that any man could ever be." Ignoring the reference to his "tainted" bloodline, she purposefully paraphrased his declaration, but it failed to earn a like response of joy.

As Will looked down at her, cynicism curled his lip. "Oh, aye, many a well-born woman has found me adequately handsome and gallant and brave—for her bed. But not one of them would take me for husband, even had the men holding their reins agreed."

Although momentarily startled by his reference to previous bedmates, Cassie boldly scoffed at the right thinking of such women.

"Proves that most members of what you termed my 'station in life' are a witless lot."

Will laughed with a trace of honest humor, but he returned soon enough to the point he must make.

"Think about it, Cassie." He put his strong hands on her shoulders and pushed her a step away, while through the night gloom piercing black eyes delved into her soul, demanding and receiving serious attention. "If 'tis none of the aforementioned points, what is it which makes me so ineligible?"

Cassie's soft lips firmed into a stubborn line, she saw but refused to consider so useless a prohibition.

Will saw her obstinate reaction and emotionlessly stated the facts. "Though I am not illegitimate, my mother was and naught but one quarter of my blood is noble. 'Tis stain enough to ruin the whole for generations to come."

"I've no care for so trivial a matter when you are all of honor and bravery and justice and—" Cassie met his gaze full on and tenaciously objected to this wrong-headed reasoning.

Head thrown back, Will laughed freely but held up his hand, palm out, to halt her litany. "To you who have a wonderfully biased view . . ." The smile turned upon her was both tender and so powerful it threatened to melt her bones. A moment later the acid of unchanging reality burned away his fleeting delight. "But never to the brother who holds the keys to your future, and to your brother you go too soon." A bleak darkness drove the last golden gleam from his eyes.

"But that our time is limited," Cassie desperately argued, feeling the promise of even a moment's happiness slipping from her hands like cool spring water on a summer's day, "makes it only more important that we waste none now."

Will stood rigid and slowly, firmly shook his head in unyielding denial. "How can you fail to see that, by our pleasures too well claimed, 'tis more than possible I've planted my seed in you."

Cassie's eyes widened. She knew as well as most others how babies were got, but simply hadn't thought to equate their loving with such plain facts. Yet from the first glimmer of recognition, she more than welcomed a possibility that some small part of him might remain forever a part of her. Her eyes went dreamy but his lips firmed into a harsh line.

"Never would I willingly allow a child of mine be born to that cruel path nor raised by a man who would, at best, despise him. I've fervently prayed 'tis not a deed already done, and am determined to keep my distance from your too generous allure. If you love me as truly as you say, then take pity and do not tempt me to fail myself, and you, and an innocent babe."

He abruptly flung open the door, thrust her inside and shut it again with him on the outside—on the outside, as he had been for most of his life.

In the lord's chamber weaving flames from the hearth cast a flickering light. Vauderie helplessly watched as Beata, all womanly seduction, slowly loosed tawny strands from confining braids and lifted a bone comb to stroke repeatedly through the shining silk while he stood immobile like some awkward human dumbstruck by the magical appearance of a woodland sprite. She'd talked to Sarah of a faerie queen, of how she'd thought Cassie such a one. But, in truth, Beata was nearer to being a member of some ethereal elfin band.

Hair a glittering cape, Beata surreptitiously peeked at the unmoving man whose gaze never shifted from her while she leisurely untied the cord holding her pale green gown's neckline tight to her throat. She widened it with equal languor while blue flame sparked and burned in her new spouse's eyes. She urged the loosened cloth to fall in a shimmering pool about her feet, leaving her garbed only in a thin linen camise. It ended at mid-thigh and was so sheer it tantalizingly revealed as much as it hid.

When Beata's fragile arms reached out in invitation, Vauderie walked into them like one in a dream. By virtue of this beguiling woman's constant enticements, he had for weeks been in a sweet torment of her making. Now he'd the right to exact payment for her many delicious misdeeds. And a payment of joy it would be, joy for them both. He closed his arms about her fragile form and carefully pulled her close, fearful of crushing so dainty a being with his much greater size and strength.

No longer a child in any sense, Beata was not content to be embraced as one. Twining slender arms about Vauderie's neck, she rose on her toes, melding her tender curves to the taut contours of his body. She set out to tempt him beyond the limits of his control, secure for herself the full power and heat of the man she desired. She won, and in the winning they both triumphed.

Chapter

❦ 17 ❦

A DEJECTED CASSIE felt as if fire-forged weights of lead were attached to her feet and she was doomed to drag them behind as she slowly descended the stairs. A weak predawn struggled to lighten cloud-burdened skies from black to dull gray. Likely 'twas prelude to a day as bleak and dreary as her soul. Throughout the whole night Cassie had failed to find the path leading into the comforting realms of sleep. Rather, she had laid on her cold pallet endlessly analyzing every word Will had spoken. Although initially warmed by his assurances that she was all a woman could be and that she was "too perfect a partner in passion," soon had come the disheartening realization of what he had not said—that he returned her love, beyond a shared bed.

The hall was still and silent save for the rare crackle of a brave spark surviving in the fire fallen to coals and the rasping snores of a goodly number of guardsmen still lost to the world on whose return they'd be punished for gluttony and overindulgence in ale. That their company was greatly diminished proved Harvey had risen and hauled those required out on the commanded mission. Will was nowhere to be seen, and Cassie tamped down a disappointment able only to deepen her dispirited awareness of time seeming to move ever more quickly into the lost past. With little choice and much empathy for his feelings, she accepted Will's decision to disallow her the warmth of his embrace, yet she'd longed leastways to be permitted to share the same room. Now even that had been denied.

In the hush of early morn, floor rushes crackled under her every footstep with a loudness threatening the peace. Her trifling noise was revealed for the innocuous sound it was by comparison with the sudden shouts coming from the glade beyond the house's walls. Without thought she hastened to the door and stepped outside. The commotion was not one born of danger but one of a young man's thoughtless joy.

"I'm back, Cassie! I said I would be and I am!" Tom quickly swung down from his steed, a fine destrier recently and proudly acquired. With little care for the danger of ground turned to ice by snow frozen overnight, he rushed toward the lovely French damoiselle hovering in surprise at the frost-rimed top of the house's entry stairs.

"But why are you back, Tom?" Will's cold voice sliced through the chill air like an icicle falling from the roof's edge to cleave a soft snowdrift.

"Will!" Tom came to an abrupt halt and turned toward the overpowering knight, but the proud grin on his face grew only brighter. "I'm a knight now, and with Earl Garrick's charge I've come to join in your fight." He pulled a folded parchment from his tunic and eagerly extended it to Will.

Will was frowning. Earl Garrick's charge? Had his noble uncle sent the boy to him although the man knew he'd no wish to have Tom here? Will opened the missive and quickly read its contents, frown deepening.

"My uncle says you pleaded so long and so hard that he could no longer restrain you. 'Tis a far different thing than being sent by the charge of an earl, don't you think?"

Tom grinned sheepishly but was clearly unrepentant. "No matter. I'm here, and if you don't allow me to remain, I'll move on to join the king's forces elsewhere. Not every lord is so reluctant to accept new fighting men when they've all too few."

Now that Tom was a knight, his argument was irrefutable, and Will grudgingly knew himself trapped. Leastways here in the Weald he could look out for him. Aye, better the boy remain here rather than see him go haring off to who knew what greater danger with no true understanding of the grisly nature of the conflict he sought to join. Nay, only did Tom know of tourneys and jousts—bright games of war—and heroic stories spun by the minstrels. Such perfect fantasies were formed of fleeting rainbows and insubstantial morning mists, both easily dispersed and far, far from the reality of blood and pain against which he'd sought to shield him.

"You say you are a knight, but plainly you've yet to learn control for your impetuous ways. My camp lay in the last precious moments of a rest too soon gone when you arrived, yelling to wake the dead. I doubt you've endeared yourself to your new companions in arms, who've reason to resent any loud noises."

These words reminded Will of the additional problem Tom's coming would aggravate, that of his unending conflict with Clyde. Will had neither time nor patience to waste in dealing with petty squabbles amongst men who for their own survival must, of a certainty, work in harmony.

Tom bit his lip. He'd erred again! 'Twas his excitement at finally winning his goal that had overcome the good sense, the prudency, he'd promised Earl Garrick he would exercise.

"I crave your pardon, my lord." Tom formally apologized as, with an ingratiating smile, he swept a low bow, expecting to win forgiveness for this surely minor wrong.

"The point is moot." Will shrugged and nodded toward men flooding from the house, some irritable and others groggy but all with a sharp glare for this new arrival. "This is hardly the right moment to thrust your company upon those so rudely awakened, so best you come in to join our morning meal." Without taking his gaze from the shame-faced recipient of his further oblique rebuke, Will waved Tom toward the house and added, "Doubtless you have news of Tarrant to share." Will meant to keep the conversation as far from present complexities as possible until he'd the opportunity to talk privately with a bridegroom likely lingering abed with his bride.

As he moved to follow the younger man, Will saw Cassie watching him from before his home's again-closed door. 'Twas a position that seemed her natural setting, and for the very first time he had reason to hope that there she might always remain.

After thrusting Cassie into his house the night past, Will had retreated to the ghastly hovel wherein both Cassie and Vauderie had once been lodged. He'd spent the dark hours first reading the odd conditions stated on the parchment delivered by Bevis, then pondering the treacherous purposes too likely underlying the whole, and lastly devising a possible plan to meet problems raised—and win all his goals. But the whole hinged on Vauderie.

Inside the house Kenward, left in solitude, had worked himself up to stand on one foot and lean against the fireplace wall to prod coals to life. When he heard the door open, he turned expectantly. Plainly he, too, had heard his brother's unmistakable shout.

"Tom!" Kenward bravely tried to hobble forward and meet his brother, but would have fallen had Tom not rushed forward to catch him.

"Kenward, what have you done to yourself?" Tom asked, adding with a grin, "Been chasing pretty maids, have you?"

Kenward blushed and, though holding tight to his brother's shoulders, playfully jabbed him in the ribs. "I were out on an important quest and 'twas I who found the prize."

"Some prize be it what broke your leg," Tom cheerfully mocked.

While the brothers affectionately tussled, Cassie quietly slipped to the hearth to begin preparations for the simple morning meal. An intent waylaid by the sound of another.

"Aye," came a voice from atop the corner stairway. " 'Twas a valiant struggle, and to Kenward goes the credit for discovery of the prize." Blond hair sleep-ruffled, Vauderie descended to meet the curious scrutiny of a young man he'd not met before.

Tom carefully lowered his younger sibling to a place at the table and turned to fully meet the steady blue gaze of a man unknown and unexpected.

"This, Tom, is your uncle Vauderie." Will's black eyes gleamed with amusement for the blank expression his announcement summoned.

Bemused, Tom slowly shook his head as if to clear it of meaningless words. He'd an uncle by blood, his mother's brother Karl, and his foster uncle Will, but now that Beata's Johnny was gone, he'd no other.

Cassie watched this unique introduction unnoticed by the principal participants. Long concerned about the possible consequences of memory returning to Beata, she hadn't thought of the likely complications in explaining the marriage to any beyond the severely limited borders of the Weald. Now, of a sudden, she recognized a prospect far more threatening than Tom's confusion: the impossibility of Vauderie presenting Beata to his family as his wife, presenting her as his bride to the two men responsible for her attack!

"I'm honored to meet another of my bride's kinsmen." Vauderie took his cue from Will and serenely played along, extending his hand to the bewildered young man.

Without thought, Tom responded by taking the blond man's arm, but puzzlement clouded his expression as he met azure eyes. "Wife?" The word came out an annoying squeak too closely resembling the long outgrown embarrassing shifts in voice timbre.

"Beata and Vauderie were wed only yesterday." Will, fully aware of Kenward's bright amusement with an older brother caught unprepared, took pity on Tom, who nonetheless deserved this bit of foolery for arriving uninvited.

"But Beata is . . ." Tom's voice dwindled to silence as his hands made awkward gestures helplessly indicating her state when he'd left the Weald.

"She has no memory of any event between childhood and the attack, but her mind no longer lingers in that childhood." Vauderie was quick to assure the boy he'd not have believed him so low as to take advantage of a woman thus injured.

"He speaks the truth, Tom." Will added his reassurances to Vauderie's when he saw disbelief on the young man's face.

"But who are you? And how did you, surely a stranger to us all, come to claim my Aunt Beata?" Tom had implicit trust in Will's judgment but was still suspicious of arrangements too hastily made.

"He is the 'shining knight' who saved me from a dreadful danger, and I love him." Beata stood half hidden in the gloom at the top of the steps. Slowly she descended to stand a pace from a gaping Tom. "Welcome back. Did Meg return with you?"

"You remember me?" Tom asked, uncertain of his footing on the surely treacherous ground he trod. He quickly glanced to the side and found a strange expression on Kenward's face, as if his brother were restraining a grin with some difficulty.

Beata gently smiled and reached out to affectionately squeeze his hand. "Of course, you and Meg brought me here. Much I have forgotten, but I remember everything from the moment I awoke in the forest, safe at Vauderie's side. Moreover, as I've been told you and Kenward are Meg's sons, I know you are my nephews."

Tom saw in her steady and utterly lucid gaze that Will and the other man had spoken the truth. She was returned from unnatural youth. Mayhap 'twas a blessing that her memory had not been restored and she couldn't remember the bad. Yet he still wanted to know how Vauderie had entered the scene. However, for a change he exercised caution and recognized this was the wrong time to demand answers.

"Come to the table," Cassie gently called, breaking the strained silence and diverting attention. "Tom, you can share what news you have for Will while we eat."

The purpose behind Cassie's words was plain to all and welcomed by them. A thoughtful person, she always sought to ease the way for others. They promptly obeyed her summons.

The morning table lacked for a cloth cover as the house's full complement had been used at the previous night's feast and not a one had escaped unsoiled. Unconcerned by the lack of cloths temporarily sacrificed to a worthy cause, Cassie and Beata soon distributed the gruel, cheese, and bread of the meal before coming to sit with the others.

"Were your holidays merry ones?" Kenward asked of his brother, better able to bear the thought of his absence from Tarrant's festivities by his enjoyment of Kensham's, despite the limitations imposed by his broken limb.

"As always, our Christmas was most merry!" Tom laughed. "An occasion the more joyous for our celebration of Lady Nessa's return to full health."

"I was at Castle Dungeld naught but a few months gone by." Will joined the conversation with intent to keep its focus on distant matters. "And at that time Tiernan and his recently found mother planned to visit Tarrant for the holidays—were they there?"

"Aye, both Lady Sybil and Tiernan were a part of Tarrant's Yuletide, much to Amicia's joy—though it seems she finds the thought of her mother's retreat into an abbey's solitude painful. I don't know why when, by all accounts, they saw little enough of each other while sharing the same abode."

Will made no comment on this subject to one too straightforward to understand the myriad emotions bound to the decision. Asides, although Will had known Amicia for but a brief time, he was certain she understood Lady Sybil's choice. He much doubted Amicia would begrudge her mother this balm for past woes too deep, and only regretted the lost opportunities to draw closer.

"Oh," Tom added, swallowing the hunk of bread in his mouth almost without chewing, in his haste to impart a suddenly remembered bit more. "I've news of greater significance, too. This summer Amicia will provide another heir for Tarrant—leastwise if the babe's a boy. If not, doubtless Galen and she will see it so soon enough." He shrugged with a shy grin of awareness for the deed behind the fact.

With its limited dishes, the morning meal was never a long one, and no sooner had Tom imparted what news he had than Will was ready to begin laying the important plans that gave him promise for attaining his all-important goal. He rose to his feet, bumping the table in his haste and sloshing a little from the half-filled goblet of milk before Cassie.

"Vauderie, do me the honor of riding with me this morn."

As Tom half rose, intending to seek permission to join them, Will sent him a look from dark eyes cold enough to freeze him mid-motion. He fell back into his seat with a thump.

The two knights, so different in coloring but similar in size and power, strode firmly from the hall without a backward glance. By Will's insistence on privacy, Vauderie knew a serious matter had arisen. And doubtless the parchment delivered the past night, almost certainly a reply to Cassie's ransom demand, held the reason why his solitary company had been sought.

Both men made their way to the side of the house where their destriers were stabled. As they entered the lean-to structure's gloom, their steeds nickered in welcome, and Vauderie looked to Will with an unspoken query in blue eyes.

Smiling grimly, Will nodded a wordless answer. In continuing silence he led Nightfall out into a quiet glade emptied by men long since departed on commanded errands. Vauderie and his gray stallion followed. Will did not speak until they'd cantered far into the midst of densely-grown, black tree trunks where a chill breeze set white crystals of snow adrift.

"This concerns you and is the purpose behind our private ride."

Vauderie accepted the extended parchment, and a laconic smile crept across his face at sight of its familiar seal, the same pattern as was on the cloak Beata had returned to him and which he now wore. Both mighty destriers were reined into a slow gait, freeing Vauderie to carefully read and reread the document. At length, golden brows lowered in a heavy frown, he purposefully refolded the missive and returned it to the dark knight patiently waiting.

"You are a brilliant tactician, Will. No one of French blood could think it elsewise," Vauderie calmly stated while steadily meeting a penetrating black gaze. "Doubtless 'tis as plain to you as to me that Cassie's return has become naught but a ploy to get close to you."

"Aye." Will's voice was heavy with satire. "A rescue to be performed only if first it serves your uncle's purpose in seeing me dead."

"Dead." Vauderie emotionlessly agreed, gazing into the hazy shadows of fog-draped undergrowth. "Or captured and humiliated before all those who name Willikin of the Weald hero."

"Cassie warned me 'twas certain Guy would be determined to see me dead for the sake of vengeance." A wry smile did nothing to warm Will's cold face. "The prospect was no more alarming than the threat of the multitude of foes for whom the slaying of me has surely been the ultimate goal for a good many years."

"As you say, 'tis a dream shared by near all Frenchmen, but from that" —Vauderie gestured toward the parchment held tightly in Will's fist— "seems the goal has become an obsession with Guy—of a certainty to satisfy his vengeance, but also to further his ambitions and provide a feast for his ego. Cassie represents only an expendable step toward this goal."

Will tightened his grip, crushing the flimsy sheet representing her danger. "His threat to me alone I could face without qualm, but as it seems his intent is to involve Cassie in his scheme . . ." He did not finish the statement, but the pulse throbbing in his clenched jaw said it all. The thought of Guy de Faux's vile scheme infuriated Will, but he was a warrior with experience enough to know uncontrolled anger would do nothing to free her of the danger. Instead he concentrated on what good could be wrought with the smooth execution of his plan. Consciously he relaxed his hold.

"I wonder, then, if you've care for Cassie's well-being, why you waste time pondering any response to this at all. Surely 'twould be better to leave it unanswered."

"Methinks neither your prince nor my king's war leader—both of whom assuredly know of the well-born Frenchwoman I hold—are apt to leave go of it so simply."

Vauderie shook his head. Will had it aright. This confrontation could only have been avoided by never having sent news of his hostage in the first instance. Had it never been done, Cassie's disappearance would have been a negligible loss quickly forgotten as but another casualty of war— along with the father daft enough to bring her into a land of conflict.

Will could hardly fail to follow the line of Vauderie's thoughts. "I have regretted the ransom message sent since near the moment it left my hand. . . ." Dark eyes shifted to the side, unwilling to have another see the pain he could not hide.

Vauderie suppressed a grin, yet for his friend Cassie's sake he sought confirmation of a truth firm enough to give reality to her wistful dreams. "You thought the better of seeking recompense of your own and thought 'twould do more to advance your cause were she sent to be hostage of your king? Or did you simply mean to claim a higher ransom from hers?"

Will sharply glanced back to his blond companion and saw an odd gleam of amusement in blue eyes. With a grimace Will acknowledged he had as well state his desires openly. Forced to ask much of the Frenchman, 'twas only right the man know it all. And if his distaste was for the thought of a humble knight of bastard line claiming his friend, so be it.

"All I truly seek to win by this venture is to claim and hold Cassie ever near." Wary black eyes met blue for a long moment.

"For love of you she'd pay any price." Vauderie's statement was delivered with a brilliant smile. "Thus, I am relieved to hear 'tis your intent to give her her heart's desire."

Black eyes narrowed upon the blond knight. "You do not find me unworthy of a woman, nay, lady well-born?"

"Cassie was never comfortable in the pretentious way of life into which she was born, and I've no doubt she'll happily surrender it for the more forthright joys of your home. From the day of her birth her every action has been tightly controlled and little happiness has she known. If she is returned to those who exercise that control, she'll likely know even less in the years to come—whether they are spent with my uncle or another of their choosing."

Vauderie looked hard at his listener to be certain he would recognize his words for the offer of aid they were. "Cassie and I are friends, and I would do much to see her escape that prison of unhappiness and even more to free her of my uncle's hold—a danger the like of which I've already warned you."

"Aye, I know what manner of danger Guy represents to Cassie, and have sworn never to release her to him. But as I sent the ransom demand to the damsel's brother Henri, I am honor bound to return my hostage to him—if he pays the ransom. You've warned me of Guy's threat, but what of Henri? Will he pay the sum demanded—or even one 'negotiated'?"

Vauderie's answer was accompanied by a mirthless smile. "Never. He assuredly possesses the wealth, but he'll not 'waste' a single coin upon so negligible a return—unless my uncle asks it."

"Then if your uncle proposed risking Cassie's life, Henri would make no protest?"

"Henri is an ambitious man, not overly sharp-witted, and easily swayed by stronger men. While he has a greater wealth, my uncle Guy has the power and position Henri craves. Henri would give much to seal with him a firm alliance—his sister in marriage or her possible death." Vauderie's cold words lingered so long on biting air they seemed never to fade.

"Leastways, he would," Vauderie clarified, "be the reward of value enough to him, and Guy would see it so."

"I'll not give her back into the ruthless hands of either man." Will's fierce determination lit gold fires in his eyes. " 'Tis my intent to foil not only Guy's scheme, but to keep Cassie ever safe in the Weald—hopefully with me, but here with my people even if I am slain."

When Will paused, Vauderie waited patiently for him to carefully weigh the words he next spoke.

"Yet, after hours of pondering the matter I've been able to devise but one plan to accomplish these aims. A plan wherein you play a role, a crucial role which without the whole would fail."

Will watched Vauderie nod with slow deliberation, and feeling a pang of guilt, immediately cautioned him. "Vauderie, consider well. I've come to know that we each are knights who prize our honor. I would feel I'd tainted my honor if, by accepting your promise of aid, I forced you into actions which you then deemed a compromise of your own, deemed it even a sundering of your oath of fealty to your king."

Vauderie looked at him perplexed.

"By aiding me in foiling Guy," Will explained, "you prevent my death
—a deed which could not help but be a boon to your king's campaign."

"I've sworn no oath to further either Guy or Valnoir's greedy plans, and
their success in causing your downfall would assuredly advance their political aspirations far more than it would aid my king. Moreover, I've made a
deeper vow—a vow sworn before God to protect my wife, my Beata. The
wrong already done her by my family sundered what little tie ever lay
betwixt us."

Will admired his fellow knight's clear reasoning. He felt the same
deeper loyalty to Cassie. As committed to upholding his oath of fealty as
Will was, if it came to choice between Cassie's health and his king's cause
—he would see her live.

"First let's have clear agreement on what dangers we face," Will began.
"Knowing of the twin who is your exact duplicate, I think we both see the
basic scheme behind his arrangements with equal clarity."

Azure eyes met a steady black gaze and Vauderie nodded in recognition
of shared thoughts before adding more to the facts Will already knew.

"My uncle Guy does not trust me, never has. A distrust likely justified,
as I've no trust for him either. Moreover, 'tis certain he'd not consider
sending me back to you on a mission endangering my friend Cassie's life.
Yet despite his distrust of me, he's no reason to suspect you might have
learned of Valnoir's existence from either of the hostages he doubtless
believes are cruelly held."

The drifting mists ever trapped at the base of the dense forest hid their
destriers' hooves and billowed around their shoulders yet left a clear view
of their faces as they rode on in silence. After a few moments Will spoke
again of the suspected plot.

"So, we agree, by his plan, your uncle intends that you ride out to meet
him with one of my supporters to serve as hostage and ensure 'honest
dealings' . . ." The phrase quoting the ransom response brought a wry
twist of disgust to Will's firm mouth. "But 'twill be your twin brother who
returns with the promised 'negotiator' from amongst his men."

These arrangements of themselves were so odd they stank of treachery
—as surely Guy must know. Plainly, he had such confidence in his arrangements he had no care for all they revealed.

Vauderie rightly read the disgust in Will's expression. "You can see my
uncle's arrogance in this. He's made it abundantly clear that more is at
stake than Cassie's return, elsewise they would simply claim my return and
use the English hostage to demand a direct exchange."

"It could still happen thusly." By Will's tone of voice 'twas obvious he thought it most unlikely.

"It could." Vauderie nodded but his sneer proved he, too, doubted it so. "If the hostage exchange is the true result, you've my oath I'll see your man safely returned to you."

Will smiled warmly at this foe earnestly offering such aid, and was the more pleased by the gift he planned to give to the other. "So you and my man go out, but your brother and another return. However, be I not waiting at the forest edge, they'll have no choice but to allow my guardsmen to bring them to me—in a place where I await prepared to meet their threat."

"My uncle is a wily warrior and likely expects such an action. Thus he will choose his minions well." Vauderie sent a meaningful glance to Will. "His guard captain is a man uniquely qualified for the chore we assume Guy intends. Though Ailon Charveil is not as tall as either you or I, he is strong enough to stand against us both at one time and lay us low—even be we armed and he not."

Will looked skeptical.

"Truly." Gray daylight glowed on blond hair as he solemnly nodded. "I have seen the man in battle, and he is a battering ram of his own, and fiercely loyal to Guy. Indeed, to all De Faux."

"And is he intelligent enough to come as negotiator with your brother?"

"Nay." Vauderie laughed. "He lacks the slightest modicum of sophistication, but possesses an abundance of skill and training to meet any challenge in battle, to anticipate his foe's every move and even to devise an attack of his own. But wits to participate in any normal conversation?" Vauderie gave his head a small shake. "My uncle claims 'tis the reason Ailon is such an inexorable fighter—he doesn't know when he's been beat. 'Tis a trait which makes him all the more dangerous. And if 'tis he who arrives, you'll have confirmation that the sole purpose of the 'meeting' is to see you reach your mortal end."

"And I will recognize him by his size?" Will asked.

"His size alone should be enough but, too, he has the unique talent of using either hand with equal efficiency—deadly in any fight hand to hand."

"I accept the warning and the challenge with hope that, by being prepared to meet their treachery, I will end the confrontation with several additional hostages to bargain for the one I sent. And—" A broad smile flashed across Will's face. Here was the purpose of the whole. "—if it should seem Cassie died in a mock fray . . ."

Vauderie grinned. The English knight was a fine tactician indeed. As Will's foes had created the scheme with little intention of regaining Cassie and a willingness to sacrifice her for the attaining of their goal, they could hardly be surprised by her apparent death. Nor would they have reason to suspect it untrue.

"Yet," Will continued, mouth firming into a grim line, "if my lamentably fragile plan goes awry, they will see my days of guarding the Weald at an end and kill the hostage I send." He somberly looked at Vauderie. "And what price will you pay?"

"I've no reason to fear for myself in my uncle's hold. He may not trust me, but he would not see me dead. For, you see—" Vauderie cast the Englishman a cynical smile. "—so long as I am alive and healthy, by my very existence I provide the buffer betwixt he and Valnoir which holds my brother's avarice in check."

Will was startled not by the utter ruthlessness of the French family, but by the frank admission of it.

Vauderie was amused by Will's reaction. He knew the dark knight was, like himself, too cynical to be oft surprised. "I must explain the facts of my 'honorable' family. My brother and I are our uncle's only heirs—so long as another son is not born to him. Thus, my brother would do anything to prevent Cassie, or any other woman, from wedding Guy and giving him a son, unlikely as it may be.

"By these facts you see I am safe in my uncle's camp. And," he added with a conspiratorial smile, "I swear that if all goes as intended, during the night's dark hours, I will free the one you send to serve as hostage. One, I pray, who knows the way back to your camp from the forest border. Thus, together we'll return. I'm certain you understand I cannot, will not, leave without my sweet bride."

Will smiled. "You've my deepest gratitude for lending your aid to my plan. I wish 'twere based on more certain truths and fewer assumptions, but 'tis the best chance we have. If we come to success. I swear I'll see you and Beata free and safe away to France."

Vauderie's smile deepened. He willingly admitted both a liking and admiration for this English knight and spoke his thoughts aloud. "We are foes by birth but friends by choice. Moreover, as you gave me your foster sister in marriage, we are brothers of a sort."

A slow smile came to Will's lips as Vauderie continued.

"And as you gave me Beata for wife, how could I do else than see you claim your love or do my all to assure that the two of you have long lives in which to enjoy each other's company?"

"Once our fine feats are done," Will concluded the spoken pact. "We will remain loyal to our lords and have no further contact—until our lands find peace between them. Truce?"

Vauderie and Will bound their forearms, affirming a personal bond of greater depth than either shared with any other man.

IN THE HOUSE, while Beata and Sarah sat at the table laughing over the game of draughts being played by Kenward and Tom, Cassie fidgeted endlessly over the mending of a small rip in one of her homespun gowns. Having pricked her fingers over and over, the cloth was in danger of darkening under small drops of blood.

She was certain Will had taken Vauderie off on a ride to discuss the long-dreaded ransom response. Since Will had pushed her into the house the night past, she'd had no opportunity to speak with him. Now he and the bridegroom she was certain would rather have stayed with his bride had been gone the whole long day, returning not even for the noontide meal. Had danger befallen them? Had they gone out to meet Guy and Valnoir without word to any other? Without taking men to back them? Danger, hideous danger, had Cassie's pulses near threatening to explode.

Surrendering to a growing tension only worsened by the constant pricking, Cassie wove the needle safely into the coarse cloth. She set the mending aside as a hopeless task, rose to pace to the window and stared out through a crack in shutters closed against the cold. The scene was unmoving save for the slow drift of fog and the darker column of smoke rising from the cook house where Edna toiled over the men's daily rations.

The heavy door's sudden opening startled Cassie. Plainly the two knights had ridden through the forest behind the house and directly to the stable lean-to on the far side, thus she'd missed their approach. Their arrival was surprising enough, but when Will immediately turned to gift her with one of his devastating smiles, her eyes widened. In her amazement at his abrupt shift in attitude, she saw neither Beata rushing to welcome Vauderie's return nor the dawning comprehension on Tom's face.

Will's answering laugh was gentle. There was hope and he meant to secure it, to make it fact. Cassie had become his that fiery night in the chamber above and, God willing, soon he could proclaim it to the world. He gazed down into dazed lavender eyes and shook his head to postpone answers to questions unasked but doubtless forming.

Their meal that eve was far simpler than those in recent days, but just as warm as any the holiday season had produced, although shared only by the house's inhabitants. Cassie reveled in the golden gleam of dark eyes near constantly upon her, even though Will spoke to her only of mundane matters. Tom watched their byplay and fully acknowledged the truths it revealed. The flicker of jealousy thus roused was smothered by the appropriateness of their bond—how else but that his hero should claim his heroine?

Will was called from the house by one of his guardsmen, and hadn't returned by the time the new-wedded couple climbed the corner stairs to the chamber they shared. Cassie followed their steps to seek a cool darkness, the better in which to sort through thoughts and heated emotions tangled by the unpredictable responses of her beloved.

A knock on her chamber door destroyed that hope—a fact rousing no regret once she opened the portal to find Will filling its frame, dark eyes smoldering and white smile shaking her with its potency.

"Will . . ." She sighed, with no care for her response's betrayal of how vulnerable she was to him.

"I've come to explain my actions this eventide." He brushed a gentle finger down her cheek and she trembled. "Give answers to unasked questions."

Cassie took his hand and, backing away from the door, pulled him inside. He kicked it shut behind him as he swallowed her into his embrace, burying his face against the ebony tendrils again escaped to lay against her satin cheeks.

"Tell me honestly . . ." Hands gently curled about her shoulders, Will leaned back. Through the dimness of a room lit only by the lone taper she'd carried above, he looked down into solemn eyes. "Now is not the time for half truths or lies, as the path of the rest of our lives rests on your answer."

Cassie's heart pounded with an anticipation counterbalanced by apprehension of a great disappointment were her hopes unfounded.

"You've claimed an appreciation for life in the Weald and a desire to remain, but could you be satisfied with the quiet days and menial duties demanded of a mere knight's wife?"

The dream she had feared to give name seemed suddenly hers. Cassie felt joy bubbling up inside like the waters of a hot spring.

"I can be happy with nothing else," she instantly responded. "So long as that knight is the incredible Sir William of Kensham."

"Then, sweeting, on the morrow we wed." With no thought to keeping his presence in this chamber a secret, Will laughed unrestrained.

"Tomorrow, tonight, or never, so long as you keep me at your side." Cassie's words were fervent.

"Tomorrow it had better be, as after tonight the likelihood of your breeding my son will increase several fold." His mouth descended to stifle the delighted gasp of belated understanding. Beneath the warm crush of his lips it became a welcoming moan as she melted against his powerful body, twining her arms about his neck.

Cassie had no notion of what miracle had brought about this sweet fulfillment of every hope, every longing, nor would she question the deed, for fear of seeing it collapse into the insubstantial haze of a dream. Wrapped close and overwhelmed anew by his height and breadth, she whispered, "I love you, love you, as I'll love you forever."

Will swept the temptress now his into a possessive embrace, refusing to acknowledge any threat to their future. He would defeat them all, hold her safe to himself forever, or leastways safe from her brutal betrothed and mercenary brother. Even if the worst should happen and Guy laid him low, once they were wed, any child of their union would bear his name. Moreover, born here in the Weald, 'twould be raised amidst a proud people who would hold both mother and babe safe from intruders.

Reveling in the growing strength of the hold binding her to him, Cassie went hot all over. Under the heat of remembered pleasures, she lifted her mouth to boldly seek the caresses for which she'd longed. The first brush of his lips was so light it was torment, and she tangled her fingers into thick black strands, pulling his kiss nearer. He fit his mouth to hers with exquisite care and then deepened the kiss to a hungry ferocity that grew hotter each moment.

Feeling the tension in powerful muscles change and build, Cassie was driven to incite in Will a response as unmanageable as her own and writhed against his powerful form. As she sensuously twisted against him, Will's skin felt the contact like the lick of teasing flames. He stroked his hands down the curve of her back, pulling her even closer to the changing contours of his body and urging her deeper into his embrace. His breath turned harsh and uneven, and the sound of it quickened Cassie's pulse. With searing lips he trailed fire across her cheek and down the soft flesh of her throat, alternately nipping and soothing.

Cassie's hands roamed over his arms and back, fingers clenching while sparks of wild pleasure trembled through her as Will nibbled at the base of her throat. Holding her in the circle of one strong arm, his other hand moved around to her front. Slowly he stroked widespread fingers in welcome torment down her body, curving them teasingly over a breast all too soon abandoned, to brush down her sides to hips and thighs. Then, with the same exquisite slowness, his touch slid upward again until his palm hovered a whisper above her breast. Cassie's hand covered his and urged its return to aching flesh.

"Sweet, so sweet." The words were a deep and darkly textured growl as he gently cupped and squeezed its luscious weight until her labored breathing caught on a desperate cry of longing. He freed his fingers to pull loose the tie holding cloth tight to her throat and slowly, agonizingly, widened the opening. Then, with tantalizingly light brushes of slightly callused fingertips, he gradually exposed the perfect bounty of her petal-soft flesh to his burning gaze until at last he uncovered their tips, deep rose and hard. As he lightly brushed his thumbs over the center of the ache he'd roused, Cassie bit her lip to restrain another desperate moan, yet an aching sound escaped. Will rewarded her and himself by dipping his head to deliver a frustratingly brief kiss, a slight suction on a tip teased too long. The reaction was painfully sweet but able only to increase the cravings of them both as he leaned a whisper away to gaze down at the pale cream and tender rose of her perfection.

Biting berry-bright lips to hold back a plea for his torment's return, a slight blush warmed Cassie's cheeks while the scorching flames in hungry eyes examined her, seemingly intent on consuming her. However, what embarrassment she felt was easily overwhelmed by the wild excitement roused by Will's undeniable admiration of what she'd learned to view as an uncomplimentary contrast to willowy feminine perfection. She found pleasure in the fiery desire on his tense face, an expression that further melted her insides like candle flame to wax.

Will's hands trembled as he brushed the cloth completely from her shoulders to fall in a disdained puddle about her feet. Her breasts were ripe and full, and his heart was racing. He wanted to grab her, drag her down to the floor and crush her beneath his urgent desire. Yet he wanted even more to cherish her, to build erotic pleasures until together they burst into the incomparable paradise of passion replete. To see it so, he suddenly withdrew his arms and jerked the offensive cloth barrier between his flesh and hers up over his head and flung it carelessly aside.

Lost in the hungry fire he'd ignited, like molten ore Cassie mindlessly

flowed to her male lodestone. At the first tempting brush of her delicious
bounty surging against his aroused body, Will shuddered.

The shocking pleasure of her bare skin crushed to the heat of his broad
chest increased Cassie's feverish need. When with his great strength Will
lifted her until his hungry mouth could nuzzle soft, white mounds and
feast on their abundant sweetness, Cassie gave up the useless attempt to
restrain her small gasps and quiet cries. Burying her hands in his thick
hair, she urged his teasing mouth to a point he'd tormented too long.
Heavy lashes fell as the delicious suction he applied wrung an uncontrolla-
ble moan from her depths.

Will allowed Cassie to slowly slide down his powerful body, but overcome by blazing hungers, her legs were too weak to support her. A harsh
groan was torn from his lips as Will admitted his own unmanageable need.
He caught her up in his arms and carried his soft rabbit turned vixen to
the humble fur-layered pallet. There they fell into a fiery well of welcome
passion unbridled, and before dawn broke, Will—with Cassie's unrestrained cooperation—had done his best to see the predicted babe conceived.

For the first time since her arrival in the Weald, Cassie rode alone atop
a gentle steed. Heavy clouds rolled threateningly above and a low ground
fog had risen, yet the view from the height of her gray palfrey was clear
and her heart rejoiced. Smoothing the soft rose velvet of the same gown
she'd worn to entice him into her bed, surely appropriate for their wedding rites, she glanced around the edge of her hood to the black-cloaked
man at her side. In the intensity of his dark gaze she saw recognition of
the reasoning behind her choice, and she welcomed the golden flames in
their depths, lit by memories of the past night's fiery delights and hot
enough to warm her and defeat the day's cold.

The gloomy sky and biting chill of the air were no impediment to Beata
and Vauderie's enjoyment either. Vauderie knew the danger he and Will
would enter on the morrow, but during their previous day's ride they'd
chosen to tell no one of their plan until after dark had fallen this night.
Hopefully this would lessen others' fears and prevent even the remote
possibility of news spreading to unfriendly ears. For fear of sending Beata
back into unnatural childhood, they'd also chosen to share nothing with
Beata either now or later. But with the morrow's dawning, they'd perforce
to tell Cassie and see her prepared to meet and fulfill her part in their
plan's success.

While in the abbey, Vauderie meant to see candles lit and prayers offered in supplication for a right resolution to coming events. Soon Cassie would be Will's mate, and a better match there could never be, save for he and his Beata. A tender smile curved Vauderie's lips as he glanced again at the dainty figure riding close by his side.

By the magic of frost, the trees of the forest had become white sculptures. So caught in their beauty was Beata that she failed to sense the tension in Vauderie, although she felt the weight of his gaze and happily returned it with a loving smile.

Will picked up the pace as they neared their destination. Anxious to see leastwise this one goal attained, Cassie would be his and safe from Guy or any other man of his ilk. A lady born, she deserved to be wed in a fine cathedral with all the pomp and beauty it would bring. He couldn't give her such grand rites, a fact depressing enough that he was determined, leastwise, to prevent her simple wedding day from being tainted by fear for the morrow. But refusing to speak with her of the coming confrontation, he'd been unable to adequately explain his command that only the couple riding with them and the abbey inhabitants know of their marriage. Now he feared she might think him ashamed of the deed.

Were his people to know of this marriage, doubtless they'd await his return with a great and dangerously incapacitating celebration. He remembered too well Edna's laughing remonstrance at the Twelfth Night feast of how easily his men would be defeated were their enemies to fall upon them after a night of merry and drunken festivity. He couldn't explain to Cassie the necessity of seeing his lamentably few available men well rested and prepared on the following day without fully explaining the dangers to then be met. 'Twas a dreadful tangle but one on which Cassie, with her understanding and gentle spirit, had never questioned him. Further proof she was the perfect mate for him.

When at length they arrived at the abbey gates, they found a dark cowled figure waiting to greet them. With remarkable grace for one of his size, Will dismounted and turned to lift Cassie down as Vauderie performed the same courtesy for Beata.

"Sir William, welcome." The sonorous voice held little inflection.

"My messenger arrived?" Will's question was accompanied by a smile. Plainly it was so, but right manners required that he ask.

"Aye. All is in readiness. Follow." Obviously words were uncommon on the tongue of a monk who spoke as few as possible.

Will formally proffered his arm to the quietly watching woman soon to be wife. With a grin and a quick curtsy, Cassie laid her fingers atop the velvet-clad arm. That he'd taken as much care as she in choosing the garments worn for this auspicious occasion warmed her already loving heart. He walked beside her, a stunningly handsome figure in his crimson tunic, trimmed by black bands embroidered with golden thread and fine black wool chausses. Her heart fair stood still with the joy of knowing this powerful warrior had chosen her of all women to love and would soon pledge himself hers throughout eternity. She, too, refused to allow the bleak certainty of a coming confrontation to mar this joyous occasion.

At the end of a narrow covered pathway between stone gates and chapel, two heavy doors were spread wide. In their opening stood a sizable man, awaiting with a broad smile. When the approaching party drew near, Abbot Jerome stepped forward with a small ring of shiny holly leaves and red berries in his hands.

"Brother Anslem, knowing how difficult 'tis in winter to secure a bride's chaplet—even when the festivities have been months in the planning— created this for you." The portly man's gentle grin was a gift of itself, and Cassie blushed in pleasure. "He trimmed the thorny downward edges and, Lady Cassandra, if you'll lower your hood, I'll place it with great care."

Cassie obeyed, nudging cloth headwear to fall and reveal a bride's traditionally unbound hair. Will's eyes held a softness the abbot had never afore seen in them as the knight watched masses of midnight tresses, freed by the lowered hood, flow like a tumultuous black sea down some distance below the bride's waist.

As the abbot gently settled the ring of deep green and scarlet atop the damsel's head like a crown, ebony tendrils caught and curled about it as if in welcome. He gave the bride a gentle smile, pleased that Will had settled at last. Moreover, during the short time he'd spent in Kensham for the previous wedding, he'd come to know her as a woman who cared enough to work very hard on others' behalf, and he was certain the famous knight had chosen well. With a satisfied smile he turned to the groom.

"It pleases me that you've kept your oath, Will, to give me the charge of performing this ceremony." The shaven pate gleamed while the gray ruff about it glowed as he nodded emphatically to the dark knight and then immediately began the temporal vows which were traditionally exchanged at church door.

Will spoke the vows making her his with unwavering solemnity, and Cassie repeated hers with a smile so bright it far outshone the gray daylight.

Once these, to the abbot's mind, less important aspects were done, he motioned them to follow him into the sanctuary for the wedding mass and God's blessing upon their union.

As they stepped inside, a beautiful chorus of many voices began as a whisper and rose to a magnificent chant while the abbot led the bride and groom with their two friends to the simple wooden altar. Cassie was so overwhelmed by the great joy of a dream becoming reality, she hardly noticed that the small chapel, surely austere in the normal way of abbey life, was bedecked with greenery and a myriad of candles. Their light caught and glimmered on her holly chaplet, and once the cloak had been removed, glowed on the rose of her velvet gown.

The wedding mass was solemn but beautiful, for all that it was brief to allow a safe return journey in daylight. As together they knelt to receive the abbot's blessing, Cassie fervently prayed for a safe end to Will's meeting with Guy and a soon coming peace for the Weald and its people.

Once the ceremony was done and they'd returned to abbey gates, Cassie's happiness broke the restraints she'd forced upon it for fear some wicked sprite would rise and awaken her from a dream too precious to lose. No matter what happened now, Will belonged to her and she to him. Looking up, she saw a like satisfaction, tempered by the grimness of deeds to come and dangers to be met, in steady dark eyes. With slow deliberation Will pulled her close and lowered his mouth to hers for a devastating kiss, a mating of souls.

"Clyde." Cassie stood at the foot of the house's outgoing steps to resolutely call through the gloom of dusk.

The one summoned turned toward her reluctantly. He'd a feeling he knew her purpose, one to which he dare not yield. The unusual riding party had returned before his task was complete, a thing his lord had asked he prevent. Now it seemed he'd summoned the curiosity Willikin had wanted to avoid.

"Why are you polishing Vauderie's sword?" It had to have something to do with the odd deeds afoot. Vauderie had no need for a sword as captive, and as the weapon belonged to a captive, why would Will arrange that it be tended to?

"I got my orders and I do as my lord commands," Clyde answered. This truth was no secret, but he feared she'd ask more. She did.

"Who does your lord mean to wield it?" She took several steps nearer to the uncomfortable young man.

" 'Tis his choice."

"Aye." Cassie looked straight into his guarded eyes. "But do you know who his choice is?"

This direct a question Clyde could not answer, and shuffled uneasily.

"Clyde, you swore you'd lend me your aid wherever and whenever I asked it." She again moved forward and now stood a mere three paces from him. Although she sympathized with his discomfort, the goal of Will's safety was too great for her to allow the loss of any opportunity to know the nature of the threat, and by the knowing mayhap aid Will's cause. "Do you not mean to hold by your oath?"

Clyde shuffled once more and twisted his head as if the neck of his tunic had suddenly shrunk several sizes.

"Plainly, Clyde . . ." Cassie hoped that 'twould facilitate matters if she merely asked him to confirm her suspicions. "My husband means both he and Vauderie to go out together, armed. That, I think, can only mean my ransom time has come—aye?"

Well, Clyde rationalized, if he didn't speak it, he wouldn't verbally betray his lord. He slowly nodded.

"When?" Cassie tilted her head quizzically, and hair again braided fell over her shoulder.

This he could not answer with a simple nod and dare not answer at all.

Cassie returned to the only tactic that had worked so far. "We're going to play a game of questions, Clyde. I'll ask, and you need only nod or shake your head. All right?"

Clyde's eyes widened but he reluctantly nodded.

"Sometime within a sennight?"

Clyde nodded.

"Within three days time?"

Again Clyde nodded, albeit reluctantly.

"On the morrow?"

The widening of Clyde's eyes was answer enough, a fortunate thing as it took some little time for him to nod at all.

"But why is Vauderie going? And to what destination?" These mused questions she asked more of herself than of Clyde, nonetheless he answered.

"I don't know," Clyde earnestly responded, and when she looked at him with a suspicious narrowing of lavender eyes, he added, "I don't and that's God's own truth!"

"What do you know of God's truth, Clyde?" Tom scoffed from shadows aside the stairway.

"Plainly more than you." The two young men moved to face each other with but a scant distance separating them and bristling with an animosity never mellowed.

"Cease!" Cassie instantly stepped between the two protagonists, irritated that they should squander time on trivial disputes when a far more important matter was pending. Bringing her temper into line, she laid a palm on each chest and looked from one to the other as she made a plea.

"You both swear you are my friends, and if you truly are, you'll put aside your petty envies in deference to the greater woe looming too near us all. Will and Vauderie go out on the morrow to a meeting too likely meant to bring a deadly end and at the least will decide the path of my future."

The two thus chided looked uncomfortably at the muddy track laid in snow gone to slush on the well-worn path.

"I ask you, Tom, are you truly my friend?"

Tom's serious gaze met hers as he emphatically nodded.

"And you, Clyde. Were you sincere when you promised to lend me your aid?"

"I gave you my oath, and I'll never see it forsworn." Nondescript brown hair flew about his head as Clyde fervently reaffirmed his promise.

Cassie turned her gentle smile from one to the other, a soothing balm for their discord. "Then by your friendship for me pause to realize you both fight for the same cause, you are comrades in arms—not foes. Surely you've enough real enemies to battle that you need no more."

The two young men looked at each other through guarded eyes, uncomfortable with the truth she'd forced them to hear.

"Mayhap you will never be friends, but for the length of this conflict you must set aside your own disharmony and join your diverse talents to win the battles to come." The two shifted uneasily, and she saw a thawing in their attitude as she added, "For my sake if not for your own."

When Clyde held out his arm to the other, diffidence lifted his chin against possible rejection. A tight smile came to Tom's mouth as he joined his arm to the one outstretched, but the smile on Cassie's face was brilliant, and as if to bless the action, she laid her fingers atop the pact given and accepted.

"Now, Tom, your comment as you joined us seemed to indicate you've more knowledge than we." Cassie picked up the trail she'd begun with Clyde. "Do you know more of the morrow's plan?"

Tom sheepishly shrugged. "Nay. Although I came as knight to join the fray, I've been left in the safety of the house since my arrival and don't understand the purpose behind anything that's happened afore, let alone what's to come."

Cassie nodded absently. Plainly Will and Vauderie were holding their plans close and had meant none to know even about the meeting only hours hence.

"Likely," Clyde tentatively offered Tom. "I can tell you what's happened and why, but I did not lie when I swore I'd no knowledge of the morrow's strategy."

Cassie smiled her approval and left them to the truce reinforced by this sharing of facts. Retreating, she quietly opened the door and stepped into the house she could now rightfully claim as her home. Leaning back against the solid planks closed with care so as not to disturb the peaceful scene inside, she studied the gathered few—friends all. She was far too aware that this appearance of contentment was a precarious facade laid atop nebulous dangers unseen but assuredly threatening to permanently mar the whole.

At length she stepped forward to lay out the evening repast, prepared by Edna in their absence. While gathered about the table to partake of roast salt pork and other simple offerings, uncomfortable silence gave way to the even less comfortable sound of strained words on unimportant matters. All were relieved when the enforced gathering came to an end. While the knights remained at the table that Beata cleared, Cassie tidied away the meal's remnants.

Meaning to busy nervous hands with a laggardly pace in finishing her chore, when Beata was done, Cassie waved her toward the chairs and pelt still outstretched before the hearth. Kenward rested atop the latter with the small, quiet girl-child to whom Cassie was growing increasingly attached. Cassie intended to seek Will's agreement in keeping Sarah with them always and ensuring the child would never again go hungry.

As night aged, the fire dwindled while Sarah dozed trustingly against a reclining Kenward. Nearby Beata sat alone in one of the huge padded chairs. Unnoticed by the two knights sitting at the table's far end and talking in low voices of things they clearly wished not to share, Cassie moved to the vacant seat and joined Beata.

While the two women exchanged troubled glances and closely watched their husbands, they seldom spoke. The evening hours passed in a troubling hush which increased their strain. Eventually both women surrendered to the men's pointed distraction and, leaving Kenward and the child at his side deeply sleeping, rose to excuse themselves.

"Will . . ." Cassie gently called from a scant distance behind his broad back. "The day has been long, and I go to seek *our bed.*" She hoped the emphasis she gave to the "our bed" would entice him to accompany her above.

Black eyes were reassuringly intent as their glittering fire swept over her from head to toe. She felt as if he were taking possession of her without a physical move, and welcomed the reality they promised. Will clamped down the desire to fall prey to her wiles—best he continue and see plans laid well enough to ensure they'd have many more opportunities to delve into the fire and find the sweet paradise at its end.

"Sleep well."

Tingling from the intensity of that too brief visual bond, Cassie found Will's succinct wish depressing. 'Twas one hardly likely to be granted when plainly danger loomed. Soon he went out to face his foes, and she had hoped for one more memory to reinforce her courage for the facing of a possibly horrifying loss. Nonetheless, she recognized an irrefutable denial when she heard it, and would not seek to force more upon him when already he had given all and more than she'd ever thought could be hers.

As she climbed the stairs she heard Beata make a similar declaration of intent and receive a like response. She waited for the other woman in the gloom at stair top. Their ploys had been equally unsuccessful.

"What are they planning?" Beata whispered, eyes concern-darkened to near a flat brown.

Feeling at a loss herself, Cassie shrugged helplessly. "Would that I knew." In this moment likely it was best she did not, for she feared the unknown reality might be enough to stunt if not crush Beata's fragile recovery.

With nothing more to be said, they parted company to enter chambers on opposite sides of the corridor. As the night wore on toward the dawning, neither woman—both yet a bride—was comforted by the fact that her husband failed to come to her bed. Sometime before the frigid brightness of a winter dawn broke over the Weald's towering trees, weariness overcame both fears and worries with a dreamless sleep.

Once the women were safely abovestairs and enough time had elapsed that it could be assumed they were at rest, Will dispatched Sarah to Edna's care. He then quietly summoned Tom, Clyde, and several other members of his guard to a muted meeting in his hall. Here he and Vauderie laid out the plan for the morrow's surely dangerous deeds and the parts to be played by each.

Chapter

⇜ 19 ⇝

THE SUN, WINTER-WEAK but riding a clear sky, shone for the first time in many weeks as from shadows at forest edge Will gazed out across the glitter of a snow-covered field to dark figures waiting in the distance. The time so long expected had come. He was relieved that leastways 'twould soon be done, although still he rued the indefinite nature of a plan containing far too many variables for his liking—too many actions whose doing relied upon uncertain facts. But they'd no choice. They must work with what was known; and, hopefully, Vauderie knew his uncle well enough to have correctly anticipated his actions.

Some little distance from his supporters and concealed from unknowing eyes by dense-grown trees and snow banks, Will turned his attention to the small party of horsemen on the Weald's edge. While their steeds grew restive under their tension, they watched for the signal to begin their mummers' play. With a smile utterly failing to warm black-ice eyes, Will nodded toward the knight whose blond hair was hidden 'neath a chain mail coif and half helm.

Vauderie held thin leather reins tight in a gauntleted fist and spurred his destrier forward. Accompanied by Clyde he rode forth leaving Tom and two others in the shadowy fastness of the forest, to approach his erstwhile confederates, fully aware of the danger they represented, possibly even to himself.

To Will, a man of action forced to passively mark time while others performed necessary deeds, it seemed the pair's journey toward the gathered Frenchmen took far too long. At last, when their figures had become small, dark, and indistinguishable, the crowd moved to meet them. Even piercing black eyes could not distinguish one man from another as the two horsemen dismounted and were instantly surrounded. Long moments passed and Will began to think the French had taken Clyde merely to barter for Cassie's return—a possibility neither he nor Vauderie had believed likely. Disgust for having fallen to so obvious a ploy had firmed Will's strong jaw by the time a return party mounted the same steeds and set out toward the Weald.

Cold daylight glittered on the mail of the two men approaching. One was, as Vauderie had foretold, a hulking giant of a man. To any unwarned, the other would seem to be Vauderie. He wore an unvarying suit of chain mail and a cloak embroidered with the same insignia as on those of all De Fauxes. Only the garment's richness proclaimed it surely a belonging of either Guy or one of his nephews—but which could not of a certainty be known.

Once close enough to see the faces of the small group awaiting their coming, the azure eyes of the knight in the lead narrowed to scrutinize them all. Assuredly the famous knight of the Weald was not among their number, but he'd hardly expected it to be elsewise. He was surprised, however, that such an important task had been entrusted to a near beardless whelp, knight or no.

Shoving his coif back to reveal bright hair, the blond knight announced, "I've returned with the promised negotiator, but as a first step 'tis insisted you take him to Lady Cassandra so he may judge her health." He shrugged with fine nonchalance. "Uncle Guy has no trust in my word." Blue eyes measured the young English knight with unconcealed disdain for this stripling lad sent to do a man's work.

From his secret position, assuredly unseen by the two Frenchmen, Will allowed thick lashes to fall momentarily while he acknowledged the uncanny resemblance between the twins—even the timbre of voice was the same. Yet when Will looked again, he found on the blond knight's face an unfamiliar, brittle charm utterly negated by the calculating cold of the eyes above. Of truth, this man was as unlike Vauderie as night from day.

In obedience to Tom's wordless command, his two guardsmen companions blindfolded the arrivals, took the reins of their steeds, and immediately wheeled about to lead them into the ground haze held low by many trees. Soon their figures were indistinguishable amidst a multitude of dark trunks, like shadows chasing shadows. As they departed, behind bulwarks formed overnight of snow, hidden archers remained to guard against any Frenchman foolhardy enough to follow.

While Tom led his group on a circuitous route to Kensham, Will set out on the more direct path to reach his home firstly. He was accustomed to the tension ever present 'neath the approach of battle and could deal with it easily enough on his own behalf. However, the additional worry of Tom's full involvement and Beata's proximity to a danger returning increased his tension twofold, while the entanglement of Cassie in the same morass was more distressing than any experience he'd ever been called to survive. He forced calm upon himself with prayers that Cassie would be able both to pretend her old timidity convincingly enough to fool Valnoir, yet have courage enough to feign death amidst a fast-paced and possibly violent scheme. Too, he prayed that Edna would keep Beata safely occupied elsewhere until the scene to be enacted in his home was done.

"Lovely bunch of friends you got here," Clyde whispered to the blond knight as tightly wrapped in stout ropes as he. "If this is treating you like the lost compatriot you say you are, what are they like to do with me?" They laid side by side on the cold, damp ground in a tattered tent plainly used only for storage of supplies and not meant for human habitation.

Despite the discomfort of hands tied behind his back, Vauderie rolled to the side and looked at his young partner in this foray, self-mockery lifting one corner of his lips. "I foolishly thought 'twould do my uncle Guy more ill than good to see me thus. But now . . ." He gave his head a slight shake.

"Mayhap 'tis true your uncle would not see you so, were he alive." The unexpected voice earned the instant attention of both bound men, and their eyes lifted to the overly slender man ducking into the pitiful tent.

"He is dead?" Vauderie was surprised, an emotion that seldom plagued him—surprised by the news and surprised by the fact that Henri Gavre had ventured this close to the realm of the infamous Willikin. Henri was not noted for his courage. For his greed and ambition, yes, but never his courage. Asides, if Guy were dead and Valnoir in the Weald, who stood in even nominal command of the besieging force outside Dover Castle?

"Aye," Henri answered as he swaggered farther into the small enclosure, glorying in this rare opportunity to stand in power over a De Faux. "In a tiny village supporters of the infamous English knight came upon Guy and the band he led out in search of you. One of their arrows accomplished the deed—took weeks, but it did."

"So . . ." Vauderie mused aloud on the certain reason for his present predicament. "I am all that lays between my brother and the De Faux inheritance?"

"Seems so." Henri spread his hands wide in mock regret.

"And 'tis why I'm here and thus restrained." Vauderie stated it as fact, not question. "Plainly with promises to provide all you desire, he has purchased your cooperation in my killing." Barely visible in the cold gloom, one golden brow arched and his smile was more a sneer. "But how is it that I am yet alive? Have you come now to dispatch me to my mortal end?"

Henri was uncomfortable beneath the knight's cool disdain, and defensively answered, "I gave him my oath to keep you here, but I refused to do the deed."

Vauderie's short laugh held no mirth. "Am I to be grateful for this boon of death postponed when your selfish action merely provides you with a more potent weapon to wield above Valnoir's head?"

Henri's narrow face sharpened. He was pleased with his good fortune in events that had conspired to put such a valuable instrument in his hands. His satisfaction grew as Vauderie clearly defined the tactic and its application.

"Your continuing threat to reveal his slaying of blood kin should be worth a great deal—survive you long enough to exploit it."

Henri's face went white. That several stacked baskets tumbled to the ground as he fell back a step went unnoticed in his consternation. He'd not considered the likelihood that 'twould be better for Valnoir if none who knew survived to tell of his deed.

"You haven't weighed the matter wisely, Henri," Vauderie quietly admonished. It only proved the man as dull-witted as Vauderie had always thought him, but it provided an opportunity to play upon Henri's natural cowardice. "No matter, I'll give you the opportunity to atone for your wrong. I am the De Faux heir; and, as my uncle is dead, I have already inherited it all. Therefore, I can provide you with as much as Valnoir." Vauderie's eyes narrowed on the now cowering man as he added, "More, if you consider that I would allow you to live long enough to enjoy it."

In an attitude of forbearing calm Will was seated at the center of his bare table when a scuffling at the door heralded expected visitors. So apparently unruffled was he that 'twould seem he'd been long awaiting this advent. In truth he'd arrived only short moments before.

Rather than looking toward the opening door with its glimpse of dwindling day, Will glanced to the side. Kenward lay before the fire with Sarah sitting next to him. That Cassie had failed in seeing these innocent youngsters moved to a place of safety did not bode well. Now 'twas too late, and he could only pray the danger threatening him would not extend to them.

As the two newcomers were escorted into his hall and freed of blindfolds, Will's attention was held by the sight of Sarah's eyes, wide and fear-filled, yet burning with an uncommon hostility.

A self-important Frenchman stood ignored before the infamous Willikin. His gaze followed the insulting host's, and he blinked against the startling animosity in the eyes of a child only faintly familiar. He shrugged. What danger could a tiny maid be? The sound of light footfalls caught his attention, and he glanced back over his shoulder. What a hapless figure the homespun-garbed Lady Cassandra made as she studied the floor and sidled nervously around the group near blocking the door. Quickly she scurried to the fireplace and awkwardly busied herself with the caldron bubbling above low-burning flames. He found more than a touch of cruel satisfaction in recognition of the ill fortune that had befallen this lady who'd thought to become Guy's countess. Looked as if she'd been reduced to the menial role of the wretched English knight's servant—servant in his hall and servant in his bed?

Will's dark face revealed no emotion, but he was amused by his past unfounded fear about Cassie's ability to fool the French knight. He should know by now that she could do anything she willed herself to perform.

"Lady Cassandra, meet your betrothed's aide-de-camp, Ailon Charveil." With this introduction, Will rose and moved to stand within a few steps of her.

"I am honored to meet you, Monsieur Charveil," Cassie replied in a whisper-soft and trembling voice. Neither did she move nor lift her gaze from the path of crushed rushes laid on the floor during her earlier impatient pacing away of strained hours spent waiting for this scene to commence.

"As you see," Will began, casually waving toward Cassie while looking directly at Charveil and turning an insulting shoulder to Valnoir, "Lady Cassandra is in fine health. Thus, there is nothing to negotiate. I affixed the price for her ransom on the basis of seeing her remain so, and I have. There is no justification for quibbling now. Either your lord pays my price or his betrothed remains with me—possibly under less honorable conditions."

It was the blond knight who laughed a harsh response. "What reason have we to accept as truth your claim to have treated her honorably heretofore?"

Will's smile was cold. "You've my sworn word and need nothing further."

"We've no reason to trust an Englishman." Valnoir strode irritably forward to stand a mere handsbreadth from Will, and in his inconsiderate disdain for all others, very nearly stepped on Kenward. "Just see how willing to break a sworn fealty and desert their king they've proven to be."

"Ah," Will spoke, eyes narrowed to glittering slits. "But how unfortunate for you that I have never done either—elsewise you'd have free access to the Weald, and we would not be here now. But why do I argue the point with you when 'tis Monsieur Charveil who has come to speak for the count." Will turned his back on the arrogant man trapped and fuming in the role he'd chosen for himself, one that left him unable to reveal his position of power.

Charveil sensed the imminent conflict and moved to stand as close to Will in front as Valnoir stood at the dark knight's back. A commotion at the entryway disrupted the clash of strong personalities.

"Beata, no—" Edna's voice was near a wail, and the attention of all shifted to the open door from whence a dainty figure rushed toward a broad back topped by thick blond hair. The agitated woman, puffing along in her wake, was a victim of her own girth and unable to overtake her escaped charge.

"Vauderie, you're back!" Tawny hair tangled in the flight flew about Beata's cheeks as she came to an abrupt halt a scant three paces from the blond knight who had turned to face her.

Cassie's breath stopped in her throat, and in the flash of a single moment her gaze flew from a grim Will to golden eyes darkened to a well of pain and bitter memory.

"It's you! You!" The first was a faint gasp, but the second a cry of anguish. Without rational thought to the impossibility of securing any minor victory by hurtling her small self against the imposing, mail-clad knight, Beata's clenched fists lifted. She was intent on exacting from him some portion of the pain and misery he'd wreaked upon her.

With the swift reflexes of a knight trained to deflect danger, a hidden dagger flashed in Valnoir's hands. Taking a step back, lending sufficient space to raise his blade, he was prepared to sink it into the dainty woman. Will instantly moved to intervene, but Ailon Charveil wrapped huge, powerful hands about the English knight's neck and jerked him away from Valnoir with a deadly intent of his own.

A small blur too near the ground for either man to note launched itself against the back of the French knight's knees. As he fell backward the blade slipped from his hand to be lost in rushes scattered beneath the impact of his sizable form. Kenward, on the floor at near the same place, immediately pulled his own dagger free and laid its sharp point tight against the fallen assailant's throat.

Fearful that Valnoir might throw Kenward off and retrieve his dangerous weapon to finish a foul chore, Cassie scrambled to recover it firstly.

Even as she did so, she fervently thanked God for the inspiration to assign these two youngsters to surreptitiously guard the hall.

Yelling for help, the two guardsmen who had accompanied these vile visitors into the hall leaped forward the instant trouble began. But knowing where their primary allegiance lay, they were fighting to release the massive Frenchman's grip on their lord.

Once freed of crushing hands, while his struggling opponent was restrained by a man on each side, Will's one powerful blow laid Charveil senseless on the floor. He whirled to find an injured boy holding two gleaming knives to Valnoir's vulnerable throat while Cassie sat on the man's legs and Sarah sat on hands pulled above his blond head.

After commanding a newly arrived Tom to fetch rope and aid his cohorts in binding the unconscious man, Will moved to secure Valnoir's arms behind his back. He used the same length of coarse cloth that earlier had been wrapped about the man's eyes. 'Twas a temporary restraint to be replaced with stout cords as soon as they arrived, but enough to relieve the trembling child called upon to exercise an amazing courage.

Once the initial shock of horror drained from Beata, she'd crumpled into a sobbing heap on the floor. With Edna's help Cassie lifted the devastated woman and half carried her up the stairs to the private warmth and security of the lord's chamber.

Once Valnoir had been tightly bound and rolled over, blue eyes of vicious poison glared into Will's emotionless face. "You dare not kill us," he spat out. "Elsewise you risk the life of the hostage you sent."

"The life of my man, but what of your brother's life?" Will's eyes were the flat, daunting black of an impenetrable wall. He meant to know whether or not he'd truly sent not only his young supporter, Clyde, but his French friend into a deadly trap. "Do you mean also to take Vauderie's life, ensuring that your uncle's title and lands come to you alone?"

Even bound uncomfortably, Valnoir managed a disdainful shrug. "What matter to you the health of a foe you surely would have no compunction in killing yourself?"

Valnoir was not sure how the English knight had come by this much information on the De Faux line of inheritance, but it could matter little. Even as the thought came to him, he remembered thinking much the same thing about the wee girl-child who'd brought him low. A frown darkened his brow but he would say no more. He'd no intention of revealing how his uncle had promised to see it all his and then disobligingly died before assuring it a fact.

After watching the two new hostages being hoisted up and carried off to their respective cells—one to the tiny hovel used amazingly oft for such purposes, and the other to the locked cold house—Kenward turned to young Sarah. She still quaked with delayed reaction to the danger so recently past, and in an effort to distract her from unhappy thoughts, Tom winked.

"We make a fine team, you and I."

Although Sarah gave Kenward a brave smile, it was clear she was too overwrought to be cheered by inappropriately light chatter. Tilting his head toward the door through which their French foes had been roughly removed, to the little maid he said, "As Cassie warned might be, he's the one what attacked your home?"

Hair wildly disordered in the recent fray brushed Sarah's pale cheeks as she solemnly nodded.

"Aye, but now our Willikin's got him and the wretch'll pay the price for his wicked deeds—with that wee bit of help from us."

Sarah wordlessly accepted this well-intentioned comfort—the best that could be had when 'twas impossible to restore her family and home. She leaned forward and laid her head against his narrow chest while silent tears began to flow.

Abovestairs Cassie sat beside an anguished Beata. Gazing into unwavering golden eyes staring blindly ahead, Cassie saw a determination whose source she feared to know. Plainly Beata now remembered all she'd once forgot—but what of Vauderie? For the horror at Forest Edge Farm did Beata lay upon Vauderie a share of blame equal to that of Valnoir and Guy? Did she want to be permanently rid of her new spouse? Or would the shocking scene just past drive her back into childhood to escape the whole skein of life's broken and tangled threads?

Cassie was ashamed to admit she lacked the courage to speak. Indeed, she doubted she could cross the expanding ocean of silence between them. Wordless time stretched fathomless and dark while the two women sat unmoving on the edge of the chamber's huge draped bed.

"Did that evil fiend do ill to Vauderie?" Beata's unexpected verbal bridge across the chasm of silence startled Cassie. "Did he steal Vauderie from me so that he might take my love's place and furtively enter Will's camp unrecognized for the worm he is?"

Cassie was amazed by the fragile damsel's clear and calm assessment of the situation, but in it found reassurance. Beata's concern for Vauderie made it plain the returned memory made no difference in her feelings for him.

"You've your memory back?" To prevent any possible missteps Cassie asked what seemed certain.

With the lengthy time of their immobile quiet at an end, Beata stared at the toes of slippers she steadily tapped against the bottom rail of the high bed as she nodded.

"And you do not blame Vauderie for any measure of the woe that befell you at Forest Edge Farm?" Worried, Cassie held her breath as she waited for the answer.

Beata smiled sadly. "How could I blame the man who spirited me safely away? How could I blame the man I love?" She reached out and took Cassie's hand to demand her full attention. "I loved my Johnny, but by knowing Vauderie, I now realize the love I had for Johnny was warm affection for a friend rather than passion for a lover—a fact which does not lessen my care of Johnny nor make the loss easier to bear. I will mourn Johnny's end always." Eyes deep pools of brown anguish went a glittering gold as she added, " 'Tis a pain which makes it even more important that I do all in my power to see Vauderie escape such dangers." Squeezing Cassie's hands, she spoke with an intensity unwavering. "I've answered your questions, now you answer mine. Where is Vauderie?"

As Beata plainly possessed sufficient courage to face the truth, and had already paid far more than its price, Cassie deemed it more cruel to keep her in the dark than to tell her the whole—no matter that Will would likely disapprove. Thus, Cassie told Beata all she knew of the day's plan. Its results were surely obvious enough without words.

"A plan shattered by my meddlesome interference." Beata saw that fact clearly enough. "Will should have trusted me with the truth. Even had he not told me of the expected substitution but merely asked me to stay away, I would have."

Doubtless Beata's earnest statement was sincere, yet it won from Cassie only incredulously raised brows. "Under the possibility that Vauderie was in danger, you would have stayed away? Stayed away while there existed even the slightest chance you might be able to warn or shield him?"

Beata's gaze dropped to her feet. "Nay," she sheepishly admitted. "I daresay I'd have been unequal to that depth of restraint."

Cassie had no desire to gloat over the accuracy of a suspicion born of her own inability to do elsewise where Will's safety was at risk.

Anxious to return their talk to the important issues at hand, Beata asked, "What does Will mean to do now?"

"I don't know, but intend to find out—I've a suggestion which may well provide him with valuable information for a revised plan." Exchanging a conspiratorial smile with Beata, Cassie rose and slipped downstairs.

A frowning Will again sat at the table, and Cassie joined him there to burrow her hand into his. Will welcomed her comforting presence and turned upon her a smile whose potency was undiminished by their present dilemma. Ebony silk, for once wrapped in demure coils atop her head, came to rest on his broad shoulder while she drew on his strength and shared the warmth of her support. Long, quiet moments passed before Cassie felt his tension easing and, in an offhand manner, spoke soothingly.

"Our visitors are 'resting comfortably' in the same hovel where both of your previous hostages were once held?"

An unsuspecting Will merely shook his head. Without opening eyes closed in pure enjoyment of her nearness, he absently explained, "Charveil is there, but I choose not to give the two of them any opportunity to scheme together. Thus, Valnoir is 'resting' in the cold house—which at this time of year is little colder than the structure containing his cohort."

"Then allow me, in homespun as I am, to go to Charveil with scraps from this abode's last meal—not to Valnoir, who hates me merely for existing. Already Charveil thinks me reduced to a timid servant and likely will tell me what information he has of the purpose and future intent of his fellow warriors. It might be enough to see you—us—triumph over them all."

Will didn't like the notion of Cassie within reach of the fearsome man. Firelight glinted on dark hair as he emphatically shook his head. Cassie was not so easily dissuaded, and continued presenting persuasive arguments on each of the fine possibilities opened by her plan. In the end he agreed—with certain safeguards. He with Tom and likely more would stand just beyond the flimsy walls, listening to every word and waiting only for the merest hint of trouble.

Agreement secured, Cassie lost no time hustling about the fireplace gathering up a loaf of dark rye bread, a wedge of cheese, and a full mug of ale. With these items loaded atop a sturdy wooden platter, and heart pounding under a strange mixture of dread and hope, Cassie set off to perform her small part in the greater scheme of the whole.

The glade was shrouded in night gloom when she paused at the hovel's door. She shifted the tray in her hand to rest on one hip while pulling the badly warped door open, not daring to have any of her companions do the deed for her in fear it might reveal their presence.

Ailon sat rigidly atop piled straw, a massive and formidable figure. So

formidable Cassie found little difficulty in feigning timidity as she carefully navigated frozen puddles to safely lay the tray at his side.

"I am not allowed to loose your hands for you to eat, but I may feed
you," she softly announced, peeking at him from beneath thick lashes.

Ailon glared. "You could release me if you chose."

"Nay, here there are many men," she lied with convincing alarm.
"They would kill me for the deed." She pulled a hunk from the loaf of
heavy bread and laid it against his compressed lips.

Yielding to her urgings, certain he would need all his strength in the
hours ahead, Ailon abruptly opened his mouth to take in the whole of the
sizable chunk, near biting her unsuspecting fingers with the ferocity of his
greedy action. Cassie took a quick step back, strangling the gasp in her
throat for fear Will would burst in if he heard it.

"What happened to Valnoir?" Ailon asked, mouth disgustingly full.

"He's being held elsewhere—I don't know his location, as they refuse
even to let me take him food." The tone she affected seemed to prove her
appropriately affronted. "Likely they deem it wiser not to house the two of
you too closely together."

"Aye, if one wins free, the other would as well." Ailon recognized the
rationale as one not uncommonly used, but 'twould do the English knight
no good. He muttered, "No matter, 'tis I who come to do the deed."

"What deed?" Cassie's heart thumped erratically, but she held her
voice to a simple curiosity.

"See that bastard Willikin destroyed, I will. A task of crucial import
and one I soon will see finished."

Cassie shivered, and Ailon was uncertain whether from cold or distaste
for the violence of which he spoke.

"But you've no weapons." She spoke with a doubtful hesitation.

"My hands are all I need." His menacing grin revealed an apparent
oversupply of yellow and crooked teeth. "They're more lethal than any
sword." He said it with such pride it struck terror in Cassie.

"But you are helplessly bound, and what of me?" She made the last
three words sound a forlorn wail.

Ailon shrugged. "Release me and I'll take you along on my escape."
What he didn't say, but which leering eyes and lecherous smile made
clear, was that he'd return her to neither De Faux nor Gavre. Rather he
would keep the temptingly rounded and appropriately submissive damsel
for himself.

"To Guy or to Henri?" Cassie asked with assumed guilelessness.

"Guy is dead," Ailon emotionlessly stated. "As for your brother, he sent us here to see Willikin a corpse, not to save you—he won't part with the gold to see it done."

Cassie had never truly fooled herself that Henri would do else without Guy's impetus. Yet it hurt to hear how little regard he had for her so cruelly stated. She firmed her spirit with the acknowledgment that now she could sever all ties with her family and past without guilt. Distracted by such thoughts, she missed the moment Ailon flexed bulging muscles and burst the restraints he'd been steadily striving to weaken since deposited in this poor excuse for a prison cell. When he lunged toward Cassie with a lewd intent too plain to miss, she dodged his outstretched arms and screamed.

With sword menacingly bared, Will leaped into the small hovel. Cassie instinctively fell against his broad form, seeking a protection he gave by wrapping his free arm about her. From the safety of his embrace she watched Charveil. Backed against the wall, his small eyes gleamed with the same dangerous desperation as any wild beast cornered. She shivered again, and Will reassuringly hugged her tighter to his side. Then, peering over Will's sturdy shoulder, violet eyes found Tom filling the door, blade held proudly across his chest.

"So, Guy is dead?" Will's cold expression froze even the scowling beast trapped. With the repeated fact, a horrifying thought struck Cassie. That Guy was dead meant only Vauderie stood between Valnoir and the De Faux inheritance. It meant Vauderie and Clyde were in deadly danger!

Resenting the other's natural dominance, Ailon responded, "Aye, Guy is dead—felled by an arrow shot as we rode from a burning Offcum."

Will looked at his captive with suspicion. Was it true? Had the retribution he'd sworn to take been done before he'd the chance to see it so? Had Guy fallen by the hand of another? "We found no body of a well-fed and richly dressed lord."

"He didn't die immediately—took days and days, but die he did, and die unmourned."

"As you will be?" Will instantly answered, certain Charveil was no better beloved, although he was surprised to hear this coming from a man Vauderie had termed "fiercely loyal to De Faux."

"Mayhap—but not for some years to come, as it only reinforces the truth that the life of your fellow will be called forfeit be I and Vauderie not safely returned."

"Not Vauderie but Valnoir," Will calmly stated, baiting the loutish bear he preferred to have know he was not so easily gulled.

"Who is Valnoir?" Ailon boldly sought to face his captor down and then immediately shifted the focus of his attack. "Where did you hear the name? Some piece of gossip forced from a tender captive—or in the heat of your whore's passion?"

Will's fierce temper flared and the golden flames in his eyes threatened to sear the transgressor.

"*Lady* Cassandra is no whore, but rather my wife!" Instantly regretting the words he'd allowed his anger to speak, Will tossed instructions over his shoulder to guardsmen lost in deep shadows.

"Fetch cords, cords too stout for him to break. Then bind him over and over and over so he has no hope of winning free again."

Footsteps quickly pounded away as men departed on their commanded errand. Ailon knew that this was likely his one remaining chance of escape. Willikin had one arm wrapped about his whore wife and was as ill-prepared as could be hoped. The other who lingered in the door was a small obstruction of little consequence. Launching himself against Will, shoulder striking the vulnerable abdomen 'neath vicious sword, Ailon sent both the dark knight and his woman roughly to the ice-crusted puddles below. In the next instant the French knight disarmed the inexperienced boy dressed like a knight and left him in a humiliated heap on one side of the outgoing door as he disappeared into the dark of the night forest.

Chapter
❦ 20 ❧

EVEN WITH WILL'S strong arm about her and sitting cuddled next to him in the large padded chair drawn up to the hall's great fireplace, Cassie shivered. Too close loomed the bitter cold of a menace, free and surely lurking near with unrelenting intent to fulfill his lethal mission. Will had posted men to guard the perimeter of the house while ordering that bright torches be placed about the cold house where laid Valnoir and tripling the guard there. 'Twas not enough to relieve Cassie's strain nor, apparently, Will's. He had been sitting here brooding and gazing sightlessly into leaping flames for what seemed an interminable time.

Glancing sidelong to where Beata sat alone and lost in the second vast chair, Cassie saw the other woman's tension, like a spun thread drawn too tight on the spindle. Leastwise, for the moment Cassie had Will at her side and safe while the condition and fate of Beata's beloved was uncertain. Shamed by the incredible selfishness of her view, Cassie immediately sought to ease Beata's wounded spirit by seeking hope of some plan to cure the whole.

"What more can we do, Will?" Violet eyes stroked comfort over the powerful man plainly as concerned as they.

Before Will could answer, Beata spoke, disconsolate at thought of Vauderie's possible danger. "I ruined your original plan and would do any task in penance, any task to see Vauderie safely returned to me."

"We knew when we set out this morn that our plan had many dangerous variables. Yet we felt compelled to try. Your action was but one of the unforeseeable possibilities, and you can no more be blamed than we who set the plan in motion. There is no penance for you to pay when 'twas neither a plan of your making nor a deed against which you'd been forewarned." Will sought to comfort Beata, though he felt like a liar when beneath gentle words he knew 'twas likely her husband and the young man who'd accompanied him were dead already. Still, if he could prevent it, he'd not have her blame herself for Vauderie's end when she'd far too much honest woe to face.

"As for what 'we' can do . . ." Will grimly smiled into Cassie's concerned face. "You two can go above and seek your rest to meet whatever awaits us on the morrow." When Cassie immediately tangled her fingers into Will's to ensure his company on the upward journey, with a mournful grimace he rejected her ploy. "I need time alone to ponder the strategy and preparations for what is yet to come."

Once again Will rued the lack of adequate men to meet the loosed menace. Having sent a fair number to the far side of the Weald to watch for the prince, and others to guard against any potential invasion launched by the Frenchman camped in the fields, he had precious few left to call upon. Tom was now retired to ensure his freshness for his turn as guard at the cold house, and no more than a score more remained in Kensham. Yet he held Valnoir, and though possibly not as dangerous, he was assuredly more valuable than Charveil. 'Twas why Will had ordered torches be placed about the cold house, hopefully thus preventing Charveil from using night gloom to win his cohort's release. Moreover Will had stationed not swordsmen alone, but archers as well, to guard the remaining hostage who provided some dim hope of an exchange for Clyde and Vauderie—did they live.

Cassie did not want to leave Will while danger walked so near but realized her presence was more hindrance than help. Giving him a brave smile, she rose to lead the way upstairs. She had to step over Kenward, sleeping on the pelt stretched between the chair she left and the one from which Beata was rising. Small, courageous Sarah, extreme tension soothed by the fire's warmth, slept curled next to the boy.

Beata trailed behind as the two women silently climbed the steps. When they reached the upper level, however, Cassie waited for her companion to join her in the narrow corridor between two chambers, and after wordlessly motioning Beata to enter the lord's chamber, she followed. Cassie was certain the other woman was as filled with anxiety as she, and hoped their burden would be more easily borne for being shared.

Cassie attempted no trite words of comfort, as she was certain any would merely trivialize undeniable perils. Thus she simply helped Beata stretch out on the huge bed, relieved she needn't lay in that dark cavern which seemed ice cold and overwhelmingly large, leastwise not without Will to fill it with his size and heat. But after settling in a padded chair near the fire she, too, felt a cold unjustified within the hearth's ring of warmth. Toward the flames she leaned as if by absorbing their fiery strength she might secure her love's protection against all manner of risks and hazards.

"Make one sound and I'll see you both dead."

Cassie sat bolt upright and Beata twisted violently about to gape at the huge man leaning back against a closed door with a smile of cruel satisfaction twisting his lips and flame light fiercely gleaming on two daggers held one in each hand.

"You've my gratitude for easing my task by shutting yourselves in the same chamber," he continued, foul smile broadening. "Though I'd have succeeded just the same, it would've taken twice as long, and 'tis always best to waste no moment."

"How did you get in?" Cassie managed to gasp around the lump of alarm lodged in her throat.

Ailon shrugged his disdain. "This house was not built for defense, elsewise no window would there be above a roof reaching down near to the ground."

"But there were guards," Cassie immediately responded. Of a sudden she realized that, in addition to daggers held, he'd a sheathed broadsword strapped to his waist and a mace attached to his belt—an arsenal of weapons not rightfully his.

"There *were* . . ." He shrugged, snickering at the thought of the two effortlessly laid low and relieved of their arms. "Enough of purposeless questions. You'll not waylay me so easily. Get up and come to me or I will prove the folly of a laggardly pace by slaying one of you before the other's eyes. Now which one of you will it be?" To reinforce his threat and urge them into obedience, sharp daggers steadily moved from side to side. Their well-honed blades caught and reflected violent red flames.

"Now!" The repeated command was a growl. To further frighten them, he dexterously flipped the daggers and caught them again with wickedly gleaming points directed straight toward the heart of each.

Beata scooted to his side, but Cassie proudly rose and calmly approached with disdain darkening her eyes to glittering amethyst.

"Not the shy creature you would've had me believe, hmm?" As Cassie stepped within arms' distance, he tossed one dagger to join the other in his right hand and reached out to wrap her ebony braid about his left hand and tug her closer.

Despite the pain, Cassie held back against the force he exerted, compressing her lips to stifle a moan of pain.

Without an instant's hesitation Beata threw her full weight against the man, seeking to knock the daggers from his hold. Both women screamed

so loudly the walls reverberated with the sound. In moments came the
thunder of booted feet ascending wooden steps two at a time. Yet when
the door flew open before Will's fury, Ailon had one woman entrapped in
each of his mighty arms with a sharp blade pressed tightly enough against
the throat of each so that trickles of blood appeared.

Will's face was an ice-hard mask but he spoke not a word, only met his
vicious foe's glare full on.

"Welcome, Sir Willikin of the Weald." Ailon spat the title out with a
venomous sarcasm. "Your arrival is a little too precipitous, but such un-
wonted haste cannot alter the festive occasion I've planned. As you see,
I've adequate feminine company, but I'll allow you to play host and grant
my every whim."

Still Will said nothing.

"Fret not. No harm will come to tender feminine flesh—so long as you
are generous with your hospitality. Leastways no more than already in-
flicted." With an evil grin he moved the tip of the dagger at Cassie's
throat and smeared crimson drops down to the point where her gown's
laces interfered. "And so long as neither they nor you make further foolish
attempts to ruin my entertainments."

Will seemed carved of granite, as enduring and unmoving as Hadrian's
Wall. By the weapons in Charveil's possession and the fact that the man
could only have gained entry through the same window from which Cassie
had escaped, Will knew the two guards he'd posted at the stable wall were
almost certainly dead. He would mourn their loss when this danger had
been met and overcome. For now he dare only acknowledge the blow it
was to his seriously depleted forces. 'Twas fortunate the man had no idea
how limited Will's garrison truly was at the moment, elsewise he might've
found no purpose in seeing any of them survive. Unaware of this fact,
Charveil plainly meant to use them to win freedom for himself and his
lord.

"From the opened door of the chamber across from this one I listened
to your talk a short time past and know both women are of value to you. I
promise to leave them to your mercies as long as you return my lord to me
and lend us safe conduct to our fellows."

Still no response from the English knight, and its lack began to make
Ailon uncomfortable. But he reassured himself 'twas no matter. He had
the women, and that lent him power over the other man, a power that
taking the English knight alone would've failed to provide. A single hostage, even be he as important as Willikin, could not protect Ailon both

back and front while the knight's surely staunch supporters would assuredly be near enough to put an arrow in any area of vulnerability.

"Lead our procession down the stairs and no trickery or I swear at least one of your women will die before you can do me harm."

Black eyes narrowed, but Will impassively turned. Descending the stairs, he was conscious of the hulking creature behind dragging two helpless damsels down steep, narrow steps.

Will cursed himself a fool for not having put guards in the same room with Cassie and Beata or having kept them near to himself. 'Twas amazing that once Charveil won free, he'd come not for Will but after the unarmed women. It seemed to prove Charveil had sharper wits than Vauderie had given the man credit for possessing. Apparently Charveil recognized that his foe would be difficult to kill or even disarm in combat one to one. But on learning his foe's affection for these females, he'd recognized a more valuable weapon. For their sake the infamous knight of the Weald would do whatever was demanded. Until, Will fiercely told himself, only until he found the way to defeat Charveil and find the way he would.

He'd no question what demands Charveil would make—the freeing of Valnoir and a "safe" return provided to their fellows. As if Will was so witless as to believe they would then free either himself or the women.

Cassie resolutely kept her eyes firmly upon the broad back descending ahead and her attention far from the prick of the dagger against her throat as, crushed against the unyielding wall of her foe, she stumbled down one step after another. Upon reaching the bottom step, she let her gaze shift to the pair of horrified youngsters before the dwindling fire. Sarah's brown eyes seemed to have widened enough to swallow the whole room into their apprehensive depths, while Kenward wildly besought his dagger.

"Warn your young protector of the dangers in threatening my intent," Ailon growled to Will.

Will glanced to Kenward with enough icy warning in his eyes to freeze the lad's hands mid-motion.

Ailon sneered his victory as he nodded toward a discarded pile of twine earlier used to bundle small pieces of kindling. "Use those cords to bind the two securely." The twine appeared flimsy, but he was fairly sure 'twas strong enough to hold these children.

With his back to the intruder, Will gave the youngsters a reassuring if grim smile as he knelt at their sides to do as he was bid. "Don't worry for us," he soundlessly mouthed before rising to again turn a cold face upon Charveil.

Ailon nodded, brow raised in mockery of the great knight brought so low as to restrain his own supporters. "Now we go to release Valnoir. First open the door, stand in its frame and order the guardsmen waiting without to lay their weapons down—all of their weapons—and leave them behind as they lead the way to where you hold my leader, or know the death of these women will lay upon your head."

Will had yet to speak a single word but he turned to do as bid. From the doorway he spoke to the two guards standing just outside.

"Norman, Darwyn, put your weapons on the ground and precede me to the cold house. Make no threatening move now or later lest Cassie and Beata pay the price with their lives."

The two men, shocked by these unthinkable words coming from their lord, nonetheless obeyed without hesitation. He'd never command such a thing but that it be necessary. Following Will's direction, they led their lord through the dense shadows of night toward the bright ring of torch-light ringing the cold house while a monstrous foe and two endangered women followed.

"Instruct the guardsmen here to pile their weapons to one side of the stairway and step back to the torch on the far side. Warn them, too, of the consequences of any threatening action—an end to all three of you."

When the nine guardsmen about the half-buried structure had complied with the order Will relayed and stood armed with naught but the pointed barbs of their glares, Ailon had another demand to make of his knightly hostage.

"Fetch my lord Valnoir and safely escort him to join in our leavetaking." Ailon was wallowing in the joy of his new ability to command a famous knight, and made no attempt to restrain his taunting sneer of victory.

As Will descended the narrow stairway, Cassie's heart cried out for his distress. 'Twas a discomfort shared and turned to pain by virtue of the fact that merely by being here she'd laid him in this danger. 'Twas all her doing. Had she not run in the first instance, her father wouldn't have brought her to this land. The anguish contained in the thought of never having known Will's love was nothing compared to that dwelling within the idea of his death or even defeat because of her. Marriage with Guy would have been all of wickedness and cruelty, but she would gladly have paid the price to save Will from even a wound to his pride.

Unlocking the door with a key pulled from a small pouch hidden behind his wide leather belt, Will stepped into the featureless dark of the cold house. He moved forward with the assurance of familiarity and bent to release a startled Valnoir. Without aid of sharp blade to sunder the cords 'twas a lengthy process, during which Valnoir recognized the near certain facts behind this event. When they reached the top of the frost-laden stairway leading out, a gloating Valnoir was carrying the surely useful cords untied.

With a sword lifted from amongst those dropped to the white-layered earth and gleaming 'neath torchlight, Valnoir motioned all eleven of the disarmed guardsmen down into the cold house's dank depths. Once they were crowded inside, Valnoir locked the door with the key Will surrendered and, once done, tucked the key 'neath his own leather belt. Gathering up weapons unwillingly abandoned, the blond knight tossed all save one chosen sword and one dagger into a deep drift of snow, then spread more white crystals atop to cover their hiding place. Mayhap Willikin's men would break the door down from the inside or others would come to release them. But Valnoir believed his actions would gain them precious time to first get as far away as possible.

In the ring of torchlight Cassie looked across a wide expanse of beefy chest to see Beata's gaze trained upon Valnoir with a depth of animosity she would once have thought impossible for the gentle woman to feel. Plainly, with her beloved endangered by this man who had already robbed her of one husband and physically injured her, all lesser emotions were eclipsed. Cassie understood. She felt much the same. Whatever feat was required to see these two wicked foes routed in their threat to Will, she would willingly, anxiously perform.

At swordpoint Valnoir forced Will to stretch out on the snow and lay unresisting, while Valnoir bound Will's hands behind his back and his ankles tightly together, Ailon told his leader of the stable whose roof he'd ascended to enter the house. Having no time to waste in searching for the steeds that had carried them into the Weald, Valnoir fetched the two destriers housed within.

Ailon settled Cassie just in front of the saddle atop Tom's steed and mounted the well-trained beast before Valnoir put Beata up behind his cohort and fastened the two women's bound hands to the saddle. Then, after laying Will facedown on Nightfall, Valnoir climbed into the saddle behind the enemy he enjoyed humiliating. He had no notion of how fortunate he'd been in laying the famous knight across the mighty black horse, who would not elsewise have accepted any other upon his back.

Valnoir was certain Will was a fine enough tactician not to have left the edges of the Weald unguarded. Yet although the two Frenchmen concluded that 'twas unwise to approach the forest edge before dawn when enemies could be seen, they moved a goodly distance into the forests' night gloom before dismounting.

Will was tossed to the ground 'neath one tree while the two women were tied together and left below another. None of those taken from Will's hall wore cloaks to protect them from either winter-chilled ground or the thick layer of snow quickly icing over.

The two Frenchmen agreed to take turns guarding their prisoners. Valnoir, who had dozed during his hours of imprisonment, took the first watch and was irritated when Will's thick lashes descended to lay unmoving on his cheeks as if the man hadn't the slightest concern for his predicament. In truth, though Will's eyes were closed, every muscle was tense. Mentally alert, he sought a way free of this coil.

Vauderie had said all Frenchmen knew him for a "brilliant tactician." And he had known better than to risk a plan where any variable was uncertain. 'Twas too late now to rue past mistakes. He must devise a new and certain method to rescue them all. It seemed an overwhelming task, but he was the one man responsible for holding the French at bay with naught but the proud, common men of the Weald. He could do it. Moreover, with the men assigned to guard forest edge, he felt certain he would do it!

Tom threw up his arm, wincing against the pink light of a clear day's dawning as he stumbled from the cottage where he'd plainly overslept. How was it that he'd not been awakened to take his turn at guard? First thinking it a possible insult, he peered through squinting lashes at Will's house—and the chimney from which no smoke arose. That ominous fact chilled his heart far more than the cold of day met without cloak.

Through the muttering of others newly awakened crashed a horrifying likelihood. Tom dashed over snow-covered and dangerously uneven ground. Precariously he weaved across the glade to slide down the path toward a strangely still house.

At the pounding sound of approaching feet, Kenward resumed yelling with a voice left raw and hoarse from earlier hours of doing the same. When the door smashed open, he near cried with relief. Help had arrived at long last.

"What happened?" Tom tersely demanded, dropping to his knees beside his brother to loosen the cords binding him to the girl-child.

"The big Frenchman held daggers to Cassie's and Beata's throats and forced Will to tie us up. Next I heard him order our uncle to lead him to where the other captive was held."

Tom's frown was fierce. This disaster could be laid at his door. 'Twas his fault, born of his wrong in failing to halt the escaping hostage in the first instance. Nay, worse than that, he'd allowed the Frenchman to overpower him and claim his sword. Had he prevented that, none of this would have befallen them. What sorry excuse for a fine and courageous knight had he proven to be.

"What are we going to do?" Kenward prodded his older brother, hopeful of magical deeds to see this ill undone.

"Olly and Stephen are dead." The flat announcement came from a guardsman who stood in the doorway Tom had left open in his haste to reach the bound pair.

Surprised, Tom looked to the man, who appeared no less than a decade older than himself. Merely by virtue of his knighthood, he realized, this man and likely the others who survived expected him to take command. With Will and even Harvey gone, they'd no one else. Pulling the tattered edges of his self-confidence together, Tom squared his shoulders and silently swore that with renewed courage he'd redeem his lost honor.

"I'll lead our remaining complement of men in a successful attempt to rescue our own." Tom prayed seasoned warriors would lend him sufficient faith to follow his lead on this crucial quest.

By the time the night guardsmen were released from the cold house and the two dead men laid out on its floor, Tom had fully recognized his foolishness in thinking war a bright game. With a new maturity, he mounted one of the dead men's steeds and motioned a force of depressingly meager proportions to follow the trail departing destriers had left in the snow.

"You fool!" Valnoir snarled, bared sword tip jabbing Will's back as he glared over a broad shoulder at the open stretch of white fields unmarred by the dark shapes of a French encampment. "You led us to a false end— in hopes your men would overtake us from behind to rescue you before we'd joined our supporters?" The bitterness in his voice revealed an alarm that such might well become truth.

Had Valnoir been able to see the face of the man who stood before him, in dark eyes he'd have seen proof that this barren sight was as unwelcome to Will as to he.

How could it be? That the French force was gone, Will cared little, but what had happened to the archers he'd left behind these snow barricades to guard the Weald's outer edges? He'd willingly directed his French

captors to this right point of departure with the confident belief that he'd
be accompanying them into an unexpected trap.

Still atop the steed from which Charveil had dismounted to join the
two men standing amidst the line of trees marking the forest's border,
both Cassie and Beata saw the icy mask drop into place over Will's face
and knew he'd not expected this scene. Beata gasped and Cassie's breath
froze when Valnoir shoved Will, hands still bound behind his back, to the
ground. Sword lifted in both hands, Valnoir obviously meant to drive it
down through the infamous knight's heart. Will rolled to the side just as
the wicked blade descended. Before Valnoir could again lift the blade and
advance against his foe, an unexpected voice distracted them both.

"You've not been misdirected, brother mine." Vauderie's voice was
heavy with satire. " 'Our' supporters have decided to return to from
whence they came and where they're honestly needed. They go to rejoin
the besieging force encamped about Oxford Castle."

"But on whose behalf have you appeared? To fight with your fellow
Frenchmen or play traitor for the English?" Valnoir caustically questioned, whirling to measure with a narrowed gaze the unloved twin standing but two paces behind. "You, too, think to fool me? After all these
many years, you ought know me better. Henri is a coward, and though
doubtless anxious to retreat into the relative safety of the many about the
castle, he is also far too ambitious to depart without seeing me restored to
safe hands."

Vauderie's answering laughter contained no humor. "The power Henri
seeks is not yours to give, but rather, by our uncle's death, 'tis mine."

Valnoir's eyes spit blue venom but he said no word.

"And . . ." Vauderie shrugged in mock carelessness. "I have promised
more than you offered, thereby winning his allegiance for myself."

Overcome by fury, Valnoir rushed toward his brother with sword upraised. "I meant to see you dead, and it had as well be done now when 'tis
plain you are a traitor."

Vauderie swung his own blade to meet the attack with a ferocity which
sent Valnoir's weapon flying harmlessly into an abandoned snow barrier.
Valnoir lowered his head and lunged into his brother. The two fell into a
fierce hand-to-hand struggle.

Ailon held a dagger in each hand. Yet from the edge of their fight's
close heat watching an ever-shifting pattern of two clad in matching mail
and cloaks, he could not distinguish one twin from the other, leaving him
able only to stand helplessly by. So intent on their conflict was Ailon that
he failed to see a young man kneel behind Will and sunder the bonds

about the famous knight's wrists. Only when the unarmed Willikin leaped to his feet did Ailon realize their hostage had been freed. Instantly he charged forward with a deadly blade in each hand. Will caught each of his foe's wrists in a mighty grip.

Once he'd freed Will, without pausing long enough to see Charveil's attack, Clyde moved to a massive destrier and used the dagger Vauderie had supplied to free Beata of her bonds and help her dismount. Thus, the way was cleared for the freeing of Cassie—a goal unmet when the sight of his unarmed lord assaulted demanded his immediate attention.

Clyde rushed to the perimeter of the area where Will and his huge foe struggled. In frustration he watched while their constantly changing positions made it impossible for him to intervene. But he was certain the moment would come, and he meant to be at the ready.

Cassie, too, helplessly watched. Bound by tight cords that fastened wrists tied behind to the saddle, 'twas impossible for her even to fall free of the massive destrier.

Unnoticed by others too involved in Will's near hopeless struggle, Beata retrieved the sword knocked from Valnoir's hand. The weapon, horribly heavy, would in the norm likely be impossible for her to heft. Yet as she was filled with a desperate determination, 'twas a weight hardly noticed. Amidst chill air, steam seemed to rise from the pair locked in mortal conflict while golden eyes narrowed on the unguarded back of her enemy. With a fierceness unusual upon her fragile face, and an unswerving intent, Beata used the full weight of her slight body to steadily drive the sword into Valnoir.

When his brother's mouth fell open and blue eyes widened in dazed shock, Vauderie fell a pace back. Valnoir crumpled facedown in the snow while a slow crimson tide welled from the blade planted in his back. Vauderie gave the sight but a moment's attention. He turned instead to catch the tender damsel now trembling in reaction.

"You saved my life, sweeting," Vauderie whispered raggedly into her ear, rocking her gently in his comforting embrace.

"I did it for you," Beata said, silver tears welling in eyes gone to brown velvet. "But I did it for me as well—to free us both of the past."

Gazing down into her solemn expression, Vauderie realized her memory had returned. Yet she laid in perfect trust within his embrace. A sense of incredible relief washed over him. She loved him enough to forgive him the manner of their meeting.

So involved were they in their own struggle's denouement that they missed the conclusion of their companion's battle.

Cassie held her breath and fervently prayed for divine intervention in the lethal scene being played out before eyes she couldn't close. Will held Charveil's wrists clamped in his mighty hands, restraining the descent of glittering blades. Finally Will knocked the daggers from his opponents hands, and Cassie drank in a deep breath only to have it stolen by Charveil's words.

"Now I've got you!" The cry was one of triumph as powerful fingers wrapped Will's throat in a crushing hold.

The pair fell to the ground and rolled wildly, squashing bare bushes and laying wide ruts in deep snow. At length Charveil had Will trapped against the unyielding wall of a broad oak's trunk. Cassie gasped as the huge man rose up to lend his whole weight to the strangling vise he had about her beloved's throat. Only the strength of Will's extended and surely tiring arms prevented an immediate end.

Massive back at last steady before him, Clyde slashed down again and again with his dagger until the seemingly impervious man collapsed across Will.

"I couldn't be certain of striking the wretch until the pair of you held firm for more than a moment," Clyde anxiously apologized to the lord who'd suffered much while he stood safely aside. He wanted the man to know he'd not held back in cowardice, but in fear of harming the one he meant to aid.

Will had recognized the young man's quandary and would never have thought to accuse him of cowardice. Indeed, he was fortunate Clyde had not truly taken the safer course of allowing the battle to be resolved by its two main protagonists.

Exhausted by the long battle, Will lay immobile while Clyde pulled the pressing weight from his chest. By the time he was relieved of the unwanted burden, he'd recovered breath enough to speak.

" 'Twas a brave and noble deed you did for me, Clyde. You saved my life, and for the deed I mean to see you knighted for valor on the field of battle—though a small battle it was."

Clyde's eyes widened with disbelief. Had he, merely by doing his duty, won what for so long he'd dreamed of possessing? He deemed the action and himself unworthy of the reward and ruefully argued.

"Only did I do that which is demanded of all men—the upholding of duty to my lord."

" 'Tis only that which is demanded of a knight, and a thing which too few of those routinely knighted seem willing to perform," Will calmly stated. "You deserve the title, and I believe that, at my request, Lord William Marshall will add you to the list of those so honored."

The mere notion of being knighted was enough to thrill Clyde, but that the Lord Protector of England might be willing to do the deed left him speechless. A fine thing, as Will had rolled to his feet, retrieved one of Charveil's daggers, and departed to approach the woman yet bound to a destrier.

"I've the feeling," Will said with a grin as he halted a short distance from Cassie, "that I owe our foes gratitude leastwise for the boon of seeing you safely restrained on the outskirts of danger." Laughter gleamed in his eyes.

Cassie had watched the conflict while both heartbeat and breath had seemed to freeze with fear. Now, so relieved was she that the magnificent man stood before her alive and all of a piece, Cassie could do little more than gaze at him with the glow of love pouring from lavender eyes.

Impatient to hold her near, Will sliced through the tight cords of her fetters and kissed the bruises they'd left on her wrists.

Cassie laid her hands on broad shoulders and leaned down, leaving Will, even in the unlikely event that he wished it, no choice but to catch her as she fell from the massive destrier's wide back. She molded herself to a strength she'd feared forever lost to her and buried the tears of released tension against the soft wool covering his chest. Only then did she realize he'd met a mail-clad foe without like protection.

A deep tremor shook Cassie, and Will realized anew what a small, soft creature she was, for all her fierce courage. "The danger is past, sweeting. Now and forever we belong to one another." He brushed kisses across the top of glossy black tresses until she turned her tear-stained face up to him and offered him the heady berry wine of her mouth.

"Pray pardon our interruption," Vauderie wryly said. "But what would you have us do with this carrion?"

Will looked over Cassie to see his French friend motioning toward Charveil's mortal remains while Clyde hovered at his back.

"Leave them for now. Later my men will see them treated the same as are all foreign trespassers caught in our Weald." Will chose not to describe the common practice of hanging their bodies from trees in warning to others thinking to dare the same wrong. Asides, they'd more important matters to discuss. "How did you win safely free? Moreover, what truly happened to the French once camped on that field?" Dapples of cold sunlight falling through bare branches gleamed on Will's black hair as he nodded toward the pristine whiteness of the empty field.

" 'Twas just as I told Valnoir. Henri preferred my terms to his and, after freeing me and Clyde—for the purpose of bartering for Cassie . . . and another poor hostage—he decided to slip away."

Both men glanced to the fragile woman Vauderie had lifted atop an imperviously waiting steed.

"Oddly enough," Vauderie continued, "as Clyde and I returned to the forest, your archers made a unanimous decision to chase and harry their retreating foes." From Vauderie's grin it was plain he found it neither surprising nor distressing. "We had traveled but a short distance into the forest's cover when we came upon your happy little band."

Will growled in mock disgust with the term.

"Certain we'd find an appropriate moment to intervene, we followed." Vauderie concluded his explanation with a shrug, as if 'twere a simple matter requiring no special choice or deed.

Will recognized the honest friendship Vauderie's action demonstrated. Before coming forward, he could as easily have allowed Valnoir to kill the man who was assuredly one of the French invasion's greatest enemies. But Vauderie had not delayed, and with the power of a black gaze melded to blue, Will wordlessly acknowledged the precious gift in a friendship of such strength.

"Praise God and all the saints!" a voice earnestly called from a distance down the unmistakable path they'd left in the snow.

All on the ground turned toward the mounted party approaching. Tom was so relieved to see Will alive and free, he gave even Clyde a brilliant smile.

"You came after us?" Will was surprised, yet pleased by this proof of his nephew's ability to organize and lead a rescue attempt. He'd not thought Tom steady enough to perform such a feat.

Tom slowly nodded, bursting with pride, but a pride tempered by his first glimpse of the harsh face of war.

"And just in time, too," Will added, then grinned at the confusion his words put on the younger man's face. "You and the men you lead will have the honor of disposing of our wretched foes' remains in a manner befitting their wrong."

Although Tom had rather return to Kensham with those he'd come to rescue, he was no longer anxious to force others to grant his wishes, and chose to accept Will's command as an honor. While those afoot set about mounting destriers, Tom and his group climbed down from their steeds to begin the required task.

Mounted, Will held his arm down to Cassie. She clasped it and reveled in the strength that pulled her up to sit across the destrier. Settling into her husband's welcome embrace, she relaxed against the powerful wall of his broad chest in delicious contentment. Strange how when earlier this day she'd sat before a man atop a massive destrier, her stomach had churned with disgust. Now, but few hours later, with Will's strong arms wrapped about her, she melted. Doubtless, she thought, Beata must feel much the same, cradled as she was in Vauderie's arms.

Neither couple found it surprising that Clyde took one look at the two mounted pairs and begged permission to lend his aid to Tom's duties. Thus the two couples rode alone through the utter stillness of the winter forest. While Cassie drank in its peace, hers for always—as was its lord— the two men discussed the additional plan they'd laid and which could be the more successfully completed by all that had passed this morn. Neither man said it, but both recognized what a blessing both Guy's and Valnoir's deaths had been for their plan.

"Then on the morrow I and the poor hostage I've saved from the fearsome Willikin's hold will depart for Winchester," Vauderie agreed with a grin gently mocking his "fearsome" friend.

Will laughed at his friend's foolery. "Aye, and a wicked fact able to explain why she arrives in France, possessing precious little save the clothes on her back."

"Once safe in France, I will mournfully pass the news of Lady Cassandra Gavre's death even as I happily introduce my precious lady-bride." Vauderie gazed down into the brown velvet seduction of Beata's eyes and wished their companions instantly a very great distance away.

Eyes closed and lost in a haze of happy dreams come true, Cassie was pleased by the thought of her friend's new life. Beata was far more suited to the life of a lady than ever she had been. And with Vauderie's company, doubtless Beata would find a happiness in it that Cassie never had.

Glancing toward her gentle friend, Cassie found Beata enticing Vauderie to a limited sampling of sweet pleasures. Sensing Will's attention upon her, she looked up to find he'd noted the other couple's dilemma and longed to partake of the same feast. Cassie willingly tumbled into the depths of dark eyes where slumbered a hunger she was more than anxious to satisfy—or leastways for now to provide tempting tastes. Beata had the right of it when faced by the question of how best to pass long rides which, with familiarity, the steeds could accomplish unguided.

Snuggling closer to Will, Cassie allowed heavy lashes to fall, the better to savor the feel of his big, hard body. Will welcomed this sweet invasion of the senses and wrapped his arms tighter about her to turn her more fully against him. When she crushed soft breasts into his broad chest, tingles of pleasure trembled through her body. One powerful arm instantly pressed her nearer still, and as Will looked down, a slow, sensuous smile tugged his lips. He saw no shame in a little light loving with his bride, and lowered his mouth to rub tormentingly back and forth across the smooth, soft curve of her luscious lips. She felt the brief tantalizing brush with an ache that threatened to moan up from her depths but which he stifled with a devastating kiss.

'Twas a lead Vauderie lost no time in following. For a time massive steeds moved at a leisurely pace unnoticed by their passionately preoccupied riders. At length desires reached dangerous depths, and without need for spoken word, the two knights—who each had discreetly ignored the other—now silently acknowledged their folly in dallying with willing brides while the place and time were so purely wrong. Powerful mounts were urged to leap forward and race toward the longed-for privacy at journey's end.

But when, at long last, their small party reached Will's house, it was to find that as they dallied in tormentingly limited pleasures, those they'd left behind had somehow passed them to arrive firstly. Moreover, the wonderful news they'd carried had spread with the speed of windblown wildfire through a forest.

With a frustration barely contained, both knights lifted their ladies down. Yet smiles were forced to curve stiff lips, clearly passion-swollen, as they entered and met the joyous welcome of so many of the Weald's own that the hall was packed near too tight for any to breathe.

In the hall that night there was a feast far merrier than any earlier gathering, despite its hasty arrangements. 'Twas a celebration both of victory over their French foes and of their lord's marriage to the lady they'd coveted for the Weald's own.

Yet once the meal was done, the toasts made and met, Will led *his* lady into the lord's chamber for the first time, and there in the dark cavern of his draped bed they renewed their commitment one to the other with sweet fire and deep love.

Epilogue

October of 1217

WILL PEEKED CAREFULLY around the bedchamber door. His wife sat dozing in the padded chair drawn near to a fire built for protection against the growing chill of another autumn. It had been near a year since first she'd entered his life, and what changes had been wrought—wonderful changes —one of which he'd come to share with her.

Cassie felt the welcome weight of a black gaze, and with a brilliant smile looked back over her shoulder at the magnificent man towering in the doorway.

"Shhh," she cautioned. "Little Will has only just drifted into sleep, and I had rather not wake him again so soon." She looked down with loving tenderness at the babe curled in her arms—so tiny and so precious.

"Edna says as how we are most fortunate he sleeps the night through with less than four weeks' experience." Will had come to stand behind the chair and gaze at the delightful sight of mother and son—his son, and already threatening to be his duplicate, equally dark and ever willfully demanding Cassie's attention.

"Aye, and to think how once you prayed he'd not be conceived." Cassie wickedly reminded Will yet again of the wish he'd spoken after their first night together.

"Might have been that night or might have been the night afore we wed when I certainly did my best to see it so."

Cassie grinned up at him and laid her cheek against his hand. "Sarah will always be our beloved daughter, but I hope to give her many siblings to keep her company."

"She's awfully impatient to have little Will grow enough to join her games now that Kenward has begun serious study for knighthood and has less time to devote to her."

"But knowing how important that goal is to him, Sarah understands."

Lavender eyes, misty with love, narrowed quizzically upon the dark man. "Why are you here at this time of the morn?"

"Clyde just arrived with a message from the Lord Marshall."

Cassie lifted her head and gave him her full attention. To Harvey and Edna's great pride, Clyde, attended by Will and Tom, had been knighted by the Lord Marshall in a fine ceremony. Since then, the new knight had been assigned the duty of riding near-constant messages between Will and the war's leader. That momentous events were under way was proven by the frequency of his trips and Cassie was anxious for news. "What does it say?"

"The peace was sealed on September twelfth." A slow smile came to Will's lips.

"Our Will's birthday?" Cassie gasped. "Truly, he is a child of peace."

Will nodded his dark head and gold gleamed in his eyes as he looked from Cassie to the child—so priceless a treasure Will could hardly believe his good fortune.

"And I've more to tell." He shrugged as if 'twere of small account, but Cassie knew him too well to be easily misled. Anxious to share this further news, he wasted no more time in pulling a folded parchment out from behind his wide leather belt.

Cassie saw the distinctive seal—a griffin with a snake in its toils—and grinned. At last they'd know how things stood with Beata and Vauderie. "What does it say?" She urged him to share with her its contents.

"They are comfortably settled in the castle of De Faux, and Beata is well accepted by the people, who, of course, believe she was once my hostage, my well-born hostage."

Cassie nodded with a warm smile. Though Beata was so sweet and generous of nature it seemed no one could do else than love her, Cassie had yet worried—thankfully needlessly.

"And, at the new year, the house of De Faux will have a new heir," Will added, his gaze going to his own and then back to the wonderful woman who had given him the child.

"Then they are as happy as we are." When Cassie let her cheek again rest on Will's hand, he came down to sit on his heels and nuzzle her soft cheek. "No one could be as happy as I, but I'm glad they're content."

Cassie gazed into the warmth of the fire and her smile grew. Aye, content. That was the word. Well content with the gift of a life far different than the one laid out for her only a year gone by. It was remarkable that while Beata, of humble origins, had found her happiness in a lifestyle Cassie disliked, Cassie had found her contentment and joy in a simple life more destined to Beata. They'd reversed roles and both were happier for it—not solely due to the manner of daily life, but more likely because of the partners who shared it with them.

Turning her head slightly, Cassie met Will's lips with her own in a kiss of tenderness which quickly grew to passion.

" 'Tis too soon, sweeting." Will reluctantly pulled back. With his unmanageable hunger deepened by weeks without more than tantalizing tastes of Cassie's pleasures, 'twas difficult to pull back now, but much more of this and he wouldn't be able to pull back at all.

"Edna says 'tis not necessarily so," Cassie whispered, eyes darkening to the familiar but too long restrained violet of her desire.

"But 'tis midmorn," Will argued, with little wish to be believed, as the nearing promise of smoldering pleasures and delicious satisfaction robbed him of steady breathing and sent searing blood rushing through his veins.

"And that makes loving wrong?" Cassie's brows rose in mocking question when many a time in the past they'd broken that rule, if a rule it be.

"Nay." Golden flames stroked Cassie. "And so long as the babe gives us the blessing of his sleep, I think we may once again prove it so."

Will gently lifted his son from Cassie's arms and settled him in the small cradle on one side of the hearth. Impatient for the joining he craved, Will turned to the timid rabbit become temptress and groaned.

Cassie stood before Will, divested of her clothing. She was as anxious for a return to shared pleasures and physical blending of souls as he, and meant to prove it so.

The unexpected sight of this luscious bounty forbidden him too long near robbed Will of strength, and with a hunger almost tangible, he swept Cassie into his arms to claim her again his—now and evermore.

—